W9-COM-733

The Wrong Hill
to Die On

Books by Donis Casey

The Alafair Tucker Mysteries
The Old Buzzard Had It Coming
Hornswoggled
The Drop Edge of Yonder
The Sky Took Him
Crying Blood
The Wrong Hill to Die On

The Wrong Hill to Die On

An Alafair Tucker Mystery

Donis Casey

Poisoned Pen Press

Copyright © 2012 by Donis Casey

First Edition 2012

10 9 8 7 6 5 4 3 2 1

Library of Congress Catalog Card Number: 2012910471

ISBN: 9781464200441   Hardcover
       9781464200465   Trade Paperback

Poisoned Pen Press
6962 E. First Ave., Ste. 103
Scottsdale, AZ 85251
www.poisonedpenpress.com
info@poisonedpenpress.com

Printed in the United States of America

Acknowledgments

As always, thanks to my friends at Poisoned Pen Press for their help and patience with this difficult book. Many thanks also to my manuscript readers and critics, Rebecca Burke and Don Koozer. And to Denisa Nickell Hanania, thank you for a great title.

I must especially mention how tremendously useful newspapers were as I went about researching and writing this book. Nothing is better for getting a sense of daily life and for what is on the minds of people during the time period one is writing about than reading the news reports of the day. Much of my period information came from the *Arizona Republican* newspaper from December 1915 through the end of March 1916. Since 2012 is the State of Arizona's Centennial year, several articles conveniently appeared on the early history of the Phoenix area, including Tempe and Guadalupe specifically, in the twenty-first century incarnation of the *Republican*, the *Arizona Republic* newspaper. Honorable mention goes to *Republic* columnist Clay Thompson for his entertaining and enlightening articles on the more colorful and arcane aspects of Arizona history. I particularly want to acknowledge Jay Mark of the Tempe Historical Society for his guidance. Any deviation from historical fact is strictly my own doing.

It was from the *Republican* and the *Muskogee* (Oklahoma) *Phoenix* newspapers that I learned the local reactions to Pancho Villa's raid on Columbus, about the epic rains and floods throughout the western U.S. during the winter of 1915–1916 which washed out roads, tracks, and bridges from the Mississippi to the Pacific, many of the particulars of the Hollywood crew's visit to Tempe, and the name of the Franciscan friar at Our Lady of Guadalupe church in the village of Guadalupe.

The Main Characters

The Tuckers
    Alafair: a concerned mother of ten
    Shaw: her husband, just as concerned
    Blanche: their daughter, age 10

The Kemps
    Elizabeth: Alafair's youngest sister
    Webster: her husband, a lawyer
    Chase: their son, age 6

The Stewarts
    Cindy: Elizabeth's neighbor and best friend
    Geoff: her husband, Webster Kemp's law partner

The Carrizals
    Esmeralda: Elizabeth's neighbor, a talented *curandera*
    Alejandro: her husband, an importer
    Matt: their son, a restaurateur
    Juana: their daughter
    Elena: their daughter
    Artie: their son

The Arrudas
    Bernie: handyman, mariachi player, actor, flirt
    Tony: his brother, a cook
    Jorge: another brother
    Natividad: Bernie's daughter

The Law
Mr. Nettles: Tempe town constable
Joe Dillon: U.S. Marshal

The Motion Picture Cast and Crew
Hobart Bosworth: *Tambor the Yaqui*
Dorothy Clark: *Lucia, Tambor's daughter*
Yona Landowska: *Ysobel, a rancher's sympathetic wife*
Lloyd B. Carleton: the director
Chris Martin: the camera operator
Miss Weston: Mr. Carleton's assistant

The Doctor
Benjamin B. Moeur: busiest doctor in Tempe, Arizona

The Clergy
Fr. Lucius, OFM

The Critters
Nina and Chica: two happy goats
Six unhappy doves
One disrespectful dog

Waiting Back in Boynton
Alafair and Shaw's other children:
Martha, age 24, and her betrothed, Streeter McCoy
Mary, age 23, and her betrothed, Kurt Luckenbach
Alice, age 21, and her husband, Walter Kelley
Phoebe, age 21 (Alice's twin), her husband, John Lee Day,
     and their daughter, Zeltha
Gee Dub, age 19
Ruth, age 17
Charlie, age 15
Sophronia (Fronie), age 9
Grace, age 3

The Man in the Ditch

He was as handsome a man as Alafair Tucker had ever seen. His unblemished skin was the color of caramel, his thick hair black as a raven's wing, carefully pomaded and combed straight back from his face. His wide eyes were black as well, eyelashes as long and thick as a girl's. His lips were parted just enough for Alafair to see the tips of his teeth. Having seen him for the first time just the day before, she knew the dazzling effect those strong, white teeth and full lips had on his smile. He was a charmer all right.

It was so sad that he was dead.

Alafair Tucker looked down at the body in the ditch and thought that there is no end of troubles and life is but a vale of tears. The end of this poor man's life was one more disaster on top of an entire season of disasters—murder and illness, rumors of war, invasion and rapine, and rain and floods worthy of the Bible. She had been glad to see the back of 1915, but thus far 1916 was not shaping up to be any better.

The dead man's earthly remains were half submerged in one of the ubiquitous irrigation ditches that crisscrossed the town of Tempe, Arizona, in a relentless, and Alafair suspected, ultimately futile endeavor to keep the desert at bay.

Perhaps he had drowned. How ironic that would be.

The irrigation canals probably made sense in a place where it seldom rained. But Alafair's thought when she had first seen the crisscross of open, water-filled ditches running through the neighborhoods rife with playing children was that here was a tragedy waiting to happen. Not a year passed without news of at least one child drowning in some convenient body of water.

The occasional adult as well. She could imagine the last moments of the dead man's life. Stumbling down an unfamiliar street in the dark. Did he trip on a stone or walk straight into the canal in the blackness of the night? Was he knocked out or simply too stunned by the fall to lift his head out of the water?

The only problem with that proposition was that he was face-up in a ditch that contained not more than six inches of water. He looked thoughtful, staring at nothing, as though he had been pondering his mortality as he died. He was dressed in a black *charro* outfit; short jacket, flared trousers studded with silver *conchos* down the outer seam of each leg, and a gaudy red scarf tied in a bow around his neck. The black *sombrero* with the elaborate white embroidery around the brim which he had been wearing the night before was nowhere to be seen. Had he fallen into the ditch, perhaps too drunk to save himself? He hadn't been drunk when last she saw him playing with the band late yesterday evening, singing Mexican love songs, his black eyes flashing with self-confidence as he winked at the ladies. Alafair did not know if Mexicans were any more prone to drunkenness than others, but the ones she had met since she had been here seemed like sensible people and not any more given to overindulgence than anyone else.

Had she seen him leave the party? Who had he been talking to? Shaw might know better than she, since she had spent much of the evening in the house with the women and he had been out in the back yard with the men.

Alafair had met so many people at the get-together that she could not keep everyone straight in her mind. What was the name of the man who had said such awful things about Mexicans, how they all ought to be run off back south of the border?

She bent over and put her hand on the side of the dead man's neck, though she already knew that he was dead. No pulse. His skin was cold, but then it was a chilly morning. It was hard to tell how long he had been there. She touched his hand. Stiff. It has been a while.

She straightened, wrapped her coat around herself more tightly and heaved a sigh. She had not wanted to come to this godforsaken town to begin with, this weird, rainless, cloudless, place surrounded by skeletal humps of mountains, filled with hard prickly vegetation and so far from home.

It was only fifteen yards from the ditch to the front door of the house, yet no one inside had heard anything during the night. Alafair walked back up the bare dirt path through the honeysuckle arbor over the gate and opened the screen door far enough to stick her head inside.

"Elizabeth," she said, "would you come here a minute? Don't disturb the children."

Alafair, her husband Shaw, and Elizabeth stood shoulder to shoulder. Or as close as they could come considering that Alafair was six inches shorter than her youngest sister and close to a foot less lofty than Shaw. They watched in silence as the constable looked over the body in the ditch. Several of the neighbors had become aware of the situation, and those who had not already made their way over were beginning to gather in groups in their front yards. Alafair could see her ten-year-old daughter Blanche watching the action from behind the screen door of the house along with her six-year-old nephew Chase Kemp. The children were under strict orders to stay inside but neither looked very happy about it. Especially Chase. Alafair could see that Blanche had a death grip on the boy's collar.

The dead man was small and young, but fully grown. Still, the fact that his life was a bit further along than a child's did not make it less of a tragedy that it had ended before it should have.

The constable looked up at Elizabeth. "You know him, Miz Kemp?"

Elizabeth caught her bottom lip between her teeth. "Everybody in the neighborhood knows him, Mr. Nettles. This is Bernie Arruda. He does odd jobs and handiwork for half the families on this street. Him and his brothers Tony and Jorge played music for us at the open house here last night. Bernie and his brothers have a nice little Mexican *mariachi* combo and for a dollar and eats they will play all night if you want them to."

"Y'all had an open house last night?"

"Yes, sir. My sister and her husband here and their girl just got in from Oklahoma a few days ago for a visit. We had us an open house and a pot luck for them to meet the neighbors yesterday evening."

Nettles' gaze shifted and slid across Alafair to Shaw. "Yes, I read in the *Daily News* about your adventure getting here, Mr. Tucker. Quite a trip."

Shaw Tucker was a tall man with a thick mustache and black hair which was currently in need of a comb. He scrubbed the back of his head with his palm, which made his hair stick up in the back even more than it already did. "Quite a trip it was, Constable. Looks like we are not done with excitement, either."

The corner of Nettles' eyelids crinkled. "Looks like not."

Do You Know This Man?

Shaw ran the back of a finger over his mustache as he regarded the earthly remains of handyman and part-time musician Bernie Arruda. "Do you reckon he drowned?"

Nettles did not look up. "Could be."

"But how?" Alafair wondered. "His head is not under the water and he isn't even wet in the front."

"The water level in these irrigation ditches can change almost hour to hour. There could have been a lot more water in it last night. And if you are not yet familiar with the climate around these parts, ma'am, I guarantee you that it don't take long to dry out once you're out of the water." Still crouched next to the body, Nettles pivoted on one foot so that he was facing a thin, dignified man with a white mustache who was standing a few paces behind the women. "How about you, Mr. Carrizal? Do you know this man?"

Carrizal gave a tight nod but said nothing.

Nettles stood up. Perhaps Carrizal would be more forthcoming without an audience. "You folks go on home now." He pitched his voice to be heard at the back reaches of the still-growing crowd of neighbors. "Y'all seen all there is to see. I'll come around and talk to everybody later."

The crowd reluctantly began to disperse amidst much murmuring before Nettles squatted back down. "Not you, Mr. Tucker, ladies." He spoke in a normal voice as Alafair and

Elizabeth turned to go. Shaw crossed his arms over his chest and shifted his weight to one foot, resigned to doing his duty. But the constable noted that neither woman seemed unhappy to be recalled. A nosy duo. "I have a couple more questions. Mr. Carrizal, stay where you are. I don't know this fellow. What did y'all say his name is, sir?"

Carrizal did not look happy at all. "Bernal Arruda. He worked in my son's restaurant. Everyone called him Bernie."

"Where does he live, do you know?"

"He rented a room behind the restaurant, but I do not think he lived there permanent. I only know him to see him. Our paths have crossed only a few times at the restaurant or around here while he was rebuilding someone's fence or painting a house. I assume he has family over in the barrio. My son Matt would know more."

Nettles nodded. "I'll go talk with him directly. Ladies, can one of you bring me an old blanket or some such so we can cover this fellow decently until Doc Moeur shows up?" He looked at Alafair when he made the request, which she thought logical. She was a visitor here and unfamiliar with local goings-on.

Elizabeth relieved Alafair of any anxiety she may have had over deciding which of her sister's bed linens to ruin. "There is a pile of old blankets and quilts on a shelf in the garden shed, Alafair."

As she left, Alafair heard Nettles question his witnesses. "Did him and his brothers all leave at the same time last night?"

She lifted the bar on the garden shed and entered the small, dim space. The early morning sun filtered in through the gaps in the bare plank walls and painted pale gold stripes of light on the dirt floor. Alafair drew in a breath of the earthy fragrance of soil and burlap, wood and seed, and was immediately sorry that she had. The lovely acrid aroma only made her long all the more for her own garden shed, and home.

The tattered bedclothes, so faded, torn, and stained that they were beyond any other use, were piled on a shelf to the right of the door just as Alafair knew they would be. She kept her own garden rags in a similar location, as had her mother and grandmother before her. She riffled through the stack and pulled out the largest, least soiled, and most intact blanket remnant she could find, then tucked it under her arm before stepping back outside. She supposed she ought to hurry for the sake of the poor dead fellow's dignity, but she could not manage it. She could see that the crowd of neighbors had dispersed back into their own yards. Nettles was still squatting down beside the ditch and looking up at Elizabeth and old Mr. Carrizal, who were standing with their backs to Alafair, an arm's length apart like good neighbors. Shaw had stepped back to stand behind them. Alafair could not see the body of the recently departed over the lip of the ditch.

She had started down the bare dirt path toward the front of the house when a movement by the back door caught her eye and she looked over to see Blanche eagerly gesturing at her. She altered her path to intercept her daughter and draw her back behind the corner of the house, out of sight of the people in the front.

Chase Kemp

"What's happening, Ma?" Blanche demanded, before Alafair had a chance to shoo her indoors. Alafair smiled in spite of herself. It was good to see her darling girl so engaged and full of life after a long, alarming winter of illness.

"Looks like some poor Mexican fellow may have had too much to drink last night and fell in the ditch and drowned, honey."

"Did somebody kill him?"

Blanche's question took Alafair aback. "No, nobody is suggesting that, sugar. It was just an accident. Now go back inside and check on Chase. That boy is too troublesome to be left on his own."

Chase Kemp was a cute, funny-faced boy with buck teeth and knobby limbs, long-legged and skinny. He had big dark eyes, long lashes, and even features. With Elizabeth for a mother how could he not be good to look at?

Otherwise he was an unattractive little child. He had a shifty look about him, and a shifty manner as well. He was irritatingly busy as a gnat, too, either underfoot clamoring for attention or sneaking about looking for something to get into.

Chase could not stay still to save his life, nor did it seem to Alafair that he was inclined to listen to anything his mother said to him. Alafair knew for a fact that he lied, and for no good reason that she could see. Just to see if he could get away with it, apparently. Not that he was a bad child. Just over-energetic and not properly saddle-broke. Nothing a bit of proper discipline would not fix, as well she knew, since she had had plenty of opportunity in the past few days to give him his due share of it. Alafair lived in a world where no one would hesitate to correct any child who needed it. Besides, Elizabeth seemed grateful for the assistance.

Elizabeth did not have much of a handle on Chase. To tell the truth she did not seem that interested in making him behave. As long as he did not kill himself or someone else, that was good enough for his mother.

"Chase is putting his shoes on." Blanche was more interested in the action outside than in babysitting.

Alafair seized the girl's shoulder and firmly turned her back toward the house. "Chase is six," she pointed out. "Go on and help him, now. I'll be in directly and let you know what's happening."

Blanche did not argue, but the return of her resentful pout as she headed for the back door was so familiar and dear that a lump came to Alafair's throat.

Doctor Moeur

When Dr. Moeur arrived on the scene, Mr. Nettles stood back and turned the proceedings over to the medical professional. Dr. Moeur was a big, balding man whose gruff, offhand manner did not bother Alafair a bit, since it was more than offset by the warmth and kindness in his pale blue eyes. Moeur had spent fifteen minutes doing nothing but standing over the body and looking. He did not move nor did he touch anything, but his sharp gaze moved unceasingly back and forth over the body, the ditch, the surroundings. He still had not touched the corpse when he finally cast a glance at the two patient stretcher-bearers standing in the road next to the delivery-truck-turned-ambulance.

"Okay, boys, you can pick him up."

The onlookers maintained a reverent hush as the men covered the late Bernie Arruda with a sheet and carefully lifted his body out of the mud and water, then loaded him onto the stretcher and into the back of the delivery truck. The neighbors watched the removal of the body but Alafair watched Dr. Moeur, who was still examining the place where the body had lain as carefully as he had studied the body itself.

As unobtrusively as she could she took a step or two nearer to him. "Did he drown, do you think, Doctor?"

Dr. Moeur's looked up. "Perhaps. At first glance I would say no. I will know more when I get a chance to examine him back at my office." He turned to face her and extended his hand. "I'm

Ben Moeur. We met briefly last night at Elizabeth's pot luck, though I spent most of the evening in the back yard. I talked quite a bit with your husband, however, and I read in the *Daily News* all about your trip out here. It sounded to me like your journey to Tempe was more of an odyssey."

Alafair did not know what that was but she took his meaning and smiled. "I surely remember you and your mighty pleasant wife Honor, Dr. Moeur. Yes, the trip was an adventure I could have done without. It is nice to finally get to see Elizabeth again, though."

Moeur nodded. "Indeed it must be. It's too bad that your visit has to be marred by this unfortunate incident."

"A sad end to a young life," she agreed.

Moeur placed his derby back on his head. "I'm afraid I must take my leave, Mrs. Tucker, but it was lovely to see you again. I hope we shall see more of one another before you leave Tempe."

"Doctor…" She extended a hand to delay him. "One reason my husband and I made this long journey was because my daughter is ailing. She got to coughing this last winter during all the rain and never did stop. Our doctor in Boynton said a trip to a dry place might help her out."

"So Mr. Tucker told me."

"You must see this sort of thing all the time, Doctor. When next you get an opportunity, would you be so good as to have a look at her and tell us if there is anything else we can do?"

"I'll be glad to, Mrs. Tucker. I'll come by this afternoon if that suits."

"Yes, sir, thank you. That suits just fine."

A Bad Winter

Blanche was the eighth of Alafair's ten children, a beautiful, delicate girl whose black-fringed eyes were the most startling gold-flecked green. *Blanche* was an inspired name for her as well, perfectly suited to her milky white, rose-tinged complexion that contrasted so fetchingly with her dark hair. She was the only one of Alafair's sturdy brood, though, whose constitution was not as strong as her will. Since she was a baby, Blanche seemed to come down with whatever was going around and take longer to get over it than any of the others.

And this had been a bad, cold, wet winter, with so much rain that Alafair and Shaw had jokingly talked about building their own ark. It had not turned out to be such a joke. The heavens opened up in December and stayed open through January, and nearly every river and stream from the Mississippi to the Pacific shore had broken its banks. The flood damage all over the western United States was without precedent. Millions of dollars of damage in Southern California alone, dozens of people drowned in Arkansas, and in some places between the two hardly a road, railroad track, or bridge left in place.

Alafair had never seen anything like it. She had lived through torrential rains and overflowing creeks before, but this had been relentless. Day after day of one downpour after another.

But their problem had not been loss to flooding, though it had been a daily fight to prevent it. The worst problem had been that everyone in the family had come down with the grippe, one after another and sometimes two or three at once. Alafair had spent her entire winter nursing feverish, coughing, cranky youngsters. The older girls had only come down with the sniffles. Charlie had developed a bad cold but Gee Dub had not gotten sick at all. The younger girls, Ruth, Sophronia, and Grace, had been wildly ill for a couple of days then suddenly well and impatient to leap out of bed and be on with it. But all had gotten through their illnesses and returned to ruddy health. Except Blanche.

Her cough would not go away and no amount of slippery elm bark, hot lemon tea, boiled rice, chicken soup, horseradish, ginger, hot oatmeal or mustard poultices, turpentine wraps or pennyroyal tea would shift it. Her raging fever abated, but then every day around sundown her temperature would rise enough that Alafair could see the red stain of it across her cheekbones. Alafair had spent each evening since the turning of the year feeding her listless girl a remedy of beaten egg white, lemon juice and honey, spoonful by spoonful, and bathing her limbs with a damp cloth until she fell asleep.

When winter wore on and Blanche did not improve, Alafair grew alarmed. Was it the white sickness? *Tuberculosis.* She could not say the proper word aloud when she finally raised her concerns to Shaw.

Doctor Addison's Diagnosis

"I don't think it's tuberculosis, Alafair." That had been Dr. Addison's diagnosis after Alafair had finally called him out to the farm. But her relief that her baby was not suffering from a deadly, incurable disease had been short-lived. "Bronchitis most likely. Her little lungs are inflamed. She needs to dry out. Pneumonia is a real risk in her weakened state. The best thing for her would be to go somewhere sunny and dry for a spell. Rest and breathe some clean air. Colorado is good for that sort or thing."

Alafair's hair had stood on end at the suggestion she send Blanche so far away to recuperate among strangers. She could not. She would not. She would take Blanche to her sister in Arizona and stay with her as long as she could. Elizabeth was a stranger to Blanche but at least she was blood kin.

What a horrible choice to have to make. Take your sick child a thousand miles away and abandon her in order to heal her, or keep her close and endanger her life.

Alafair seriously doubted she would be able leave the girl once they arrived in Arizona. But she needed to be home. She had never been away from her three-year-old, Grace. Her second-eldest, Mary, was getting married in May. Mary's fiancé had bought a parcel of land just to the south of the Tucker farm and was building a house that required quilts and linens, curtains and rugs. The two married daughters, twins Alice and Phoebe, were both expecting. Ruth was about to celebrate her seventeenth birthday. She would be going away to Muskogee to study music in just a few months and needed new clothes. They all needed their mother. All of them. But for the moment Blanche needed her the most.

All Alafair could think of was the Bible story of the lost sheep. *What man of you, having an hundred sheep, if he lose one of them doth not leave the ninety and nine in the wilderness, and go after that which is lost, until he find it?* "What else can I do?" she asked Shaw. "I have to take her away. I have got to save my girl."

Go, Shaw said, *and I'll make the journey with you.*

Go, I'll take care of things here, said Martha, their eldest at twenty-five, engaged to be married but for the moment still living at home and perfectly capable of running a tight ship.

Quite a Trip

The journey to Arizona had been a nightmare. An endless train trip with a sick little girl. All along the route floods had washed out bridges and portions of track. They had had to change trains twice as often as planned and ended up going through strange, out-of-the-way, backwater towns that neither Shaw nor Alafair nor anyone else who did not live in them had ever heard of. The trip they had expected to take ran from their home town of Boynton to Oklahoma City, then a change of trains and straight west through Amarillo, Albuquerque, and Flagstaff. One more change in Flagstaff to carry them due south through Prescott and Phoenix and then right in to Tempe.

But that was not how it had worked out. They did manage to get to Amarillo after a couple of delays and a very odd detour through Elk City, Oklahoma. But after that the journey took so many strange twists and turns that Shaw had begun to wonder if they would ever get where they were going, or if they were going to end up stranded in some collection of shacks with an unpronounceable name somewhere in New Mexico, sitting on their luggage beside the tracks during a dust storm while Blanche coughed her lungs out.

The tracks just west of Amarillo had been damaged by floods. They would either have to wait in Amarillo for days until the route was opened again or catch a train south to El Paso, then west to Deming, New Mexico, and south again to someplace called Columbus, where they could pick up the train into Tucson and northbound to Tempe.

When Blanche first became so ill early in the winter, Alafair had in turn become so single-minded, so wholly concentrated on her sick child, that she had little attention left for anything else. When they had decided that there was nothing left for them but to take Blanche to Arizona for the dry air, Alafair's first suggestion was that she alone would take Blanche to Elizabeth. No one was more competent or able to handle herself than Alafair, but Shaw had been unable to stomach the thought of his wife and little girl on their own so far from home. When he told Alafair he wanted to come with her, he could see the relief plain in her face.

She had abdicated all responsibility for the trip to him. He took care of everything while she cared for Blanche. When they were detoured because of washouts or stranded in strange towns he found accommodations and meals, arranged new routes, handled their luggage, updated the family by wire. When Blanche had a setback in Columbus, New Mexico, Shaw found a doctor and a comfortable room in the hotel so they could rest overnight. He held Blanche in his lap so that Alafair could eat, dress, and sleep. Otherwise she never took her hands off the child.

As they neared Arizona, it did occur to Shaw that he had not thought about his farm once during the trip. That was odd, since the farm had been his entire existence for over twenty years. But then he had left it in many very good hands, and at the moment he was infinitely more needed on this journey. He did not think much about the farm again.

When they finally, finally arrived in Tempe late in the afternoon of March 6, it was 79 degrees, blindingly sunny, and blessedly dry.

Elizabeth

Elizabeth was Alafair's youngest sibling, only six years older than Alafair's eldest daughter Martha. Alafair had honed a lot of her mothering skill on Elizabeth, though she expected that Elizabeth barely remembered a time when Alafair lived at home with her parents.

Alafair and Shaw had moved from the Arkansas hills to the Indian Territory when Elizabeth was eight. In fact, though they wrote to one another regularly, the two sisters had seen little of each other since then.

But family was family. So when her eldest sister had wired asking if she and Blanche could stay with her a while, Elizabeth Kemp would never have thought of saying no.

The evening that they had arrived on the train at the Tempe railroad station was the first time Alafair had seen Elizabeth and Webster Kemp since they had left Arkansas for the Arizona Territory nine years earlier.

Webster himself had picked them up in his Hupmobile and driven them the few blocks to the house. They had arrived just after the sun had just sunk below the horizon and the sky was still the color of new buttermilk.

The Kemp house was a long, eye-catching two-story affair built half way up of round gray river rock topped by light gray wood frame. The pitched shingle roof sported frame dormer extensions jutting out on either side. A deep, roofed porch surrounded by a low rock wall stretched across the front of the house.

Shaw leaned toward her as the auto rolled to a stop. "Yonder is Elizabeth."

Alafair's heart picked up a beat when she caught sight of the woman standing at the gate next to the road. Elizabeth had changed. The last time Alafair had seen her, Elizabeth had been a lanky twenty-one-year-old newlywed fresh and eager for the adventure of starting a new life in the untamed West.

She was not a teenager any longer. Tall, willowy, and graceful, she had their mother's features—the high cheekbones and large, dark, almond-shaped eyes. At first Alafair thought her sister had cut off the long hair she had always been so proud of, but on closer inspection she could see that only the top and sides were shorter, parted on the left, covering her ears and sweeping forward to cup her cheeks like wings. The bulk of her softly curling, dark hair was twisted into a loose pile at the back of her crown.

Alafair was out of the car almost before it came to a stop. Before she quite knew how she got there, she and Elizabeth were standing with their hands clasped, drinking in the sight of one another.

"Oh, my, my!" That was all Alafair could manage to say. "Oh, my, my!"

The White Lady

Elizabeth greeted them with many hugs and exclamations of delight before leading them through the honeysuckle-draped trellis that arched over the front gate. But not before giving her husband Webster an imperious order to fetch the luggage out of the car.

Webster was a pleasant man with pleasant features, dark blue eyes and brown hair neatly trimmed and parted on the side. He was average-sized for a man, well dressed and solid, with a square face and a ready if somewhat self-satisfied smile. He had always been friendly and easy to talk to, though without substance, Alafair thought. Lots of surface but not much depth. Was that a good quality for a lawyer? He was successful, so at least it was not a hindrance. When he and Elizabeth were first married, Alafair had told Shaw that Webster reminded her of a steer standing in a field ruminating on the nature of the universe, smug and well content with his lot in life.

Webster complied with Elizabeth's order with his familiar good humor, and Alafair suppressed a smile. It had not taken her long to ascertain who was the engine on this particular marriage train.

As they walked up the path toward the house, Alafair took a deep breath. The air was perfumed with a scent so sweet and heavy that it almost had a texture. *This must be what heaven smells like.* Not the honeysuckle. Wrong time of year. "Law! What is that flower I'm smelling?"

"My neighbor has an orange tree." Elizabeth said. "That's it yonder. It's coming into bloom a little early this year after the rainy winter."

It was quickly becoming too dark to see clearly. Elizabeth pointed at a row of small trees with rounded tops and glossy dark green leaves at the far edge of her deep back yard, just on the other side of the fence on the neighbor's property. Did they have white trunks? Alafair's bleary eyes felt as though they were full of grit. She squeezed her eyes shut and rubbed them briskly before squinting once more into the gathering gloom at the tree. Yes, white trunks. As she peered she became aware of a second white figure at the fence, and it slowly dawned on her that what she had at first thought was another tree, smaller than the others, was in fact a human figure standing quietly at the fence. A woman in a light-colored dress. There was something white on her head as well. Whatever it was, it reflected the fading light and created a ghostly silver halo around her head. There even seemed to be a sparkle to it. Or perhaps that was an effect of Alafair having just rubbed her eyes. A trick of the gloaming and her tired eyes.

She opened her mouth to ask Elizabeth if what she was seeing was actually there, but before she could speak her sister said, "I'm betting y'all are about to fall over. Have you had anything to eat? I have a big pot of soup and some sandwiches just made."

"I could eat a bite," Shaw said at the same time that Blanche whined, "I'm tired, Ma."

"Come on then, let me show you where y'all will be sleeping. You can settle your luggage back there, Shaw, before you eat. Then you can stretch out for a rest, Blanche, honey. My boy Chase is already in bed or I would introduce you to your cousin before you go to sleep. Are you sure you don't want a little something to gnaw on?" Elizabeth chatted away as they continued toward the house. Before they moved out of sight of the back fence the spectral white woman began walking away and Alafair caught sight of two dark figures trotting along beside her. Had they been there all along? At first she thought they were two good-sized dogs, but the shadow of small pointed horns and the sound of hollow bells in the still evening air told her they were two little goats. A cheerful bleat confirmed her realization.

As Alafair followed her sister into the house her spirits lifted. Coming as it did at the end of such an exhausting journey, the vision of the white woman and her companions seemed like a good omen. For the first time she felt a stirring of anticipation and a feeling that there might be something pleasant about this trip after all.

A Sharp Exchange

Elizabeth ushered them into her large parlor while Webster unloaded the Hupmobile. For an instant Alafair felt as though she had been shown into the lobby of a tastefully decorated hotel. Much of the first floor consisted of one large open space under a beamed ceiling. A curtained alcove to one side led to the stairwell. Three of the parlor walls were painted a pale forest green above oak plank wainscoting. The fourth wall was exposed river rock and sported a stone fireplace topped by a carved wooden mantlepiece. The fireplace opening had been fitted with a cast iron wood-burning stove with an open wire grate. Alafair was glad to see that the fire was lit. The warm afternoon had quickly given way to a sharp chill once the sun had set.

Elizabeth had used furniture, potted plants, and colorful scatter rugs to create four distinct seating areas in the parlor. Two large wingback armchairs stood side by side in front of the fireplace with an octagonal occasional table between them. One corner of the room near the front door was fitted with wooden bookshelves and a built-in window seat strewn with embroidered pillows. In the back, a rocker, a love seat, and a small wooden writing desk with a slat-back chair created a perfect nook for reading, letter-writing, or intimate conversation over a cup of tea.

The central area of the room contained two long upholstered couches facing one another over a low tea table. Two slatted oak chairs with wide wooden arms and fat padded seat and back cushions had been placed at one end of the open rectangle between the couches.

The style of the furnishings was like nothing Alafair had ever seen before; spare and simple, a lot of natural, rough-hewn wood, muted, jewel-like colors, mostly green and earthy browns set off by eye-catching accents in red and golden yellow with spots of amethyst and turquoise. The room was illuminated by gas lights in stained glass sconces on the walls. The kerosene lamps sitting on the tables were familiar in shape but with amber art glass chimneys instead of the plain affairs Alafair used at home.

The room was inviting and functional, a place Alafair would have liked to linger had she not been desperate for a meal, a wash, and a good long sleep.

Elizabeth led them through the parlor into the small kitchen at the back of the house and sat them down in the center of the room at a square wooden table just big enough for four people. Blanche crawled up into Shaw's lap in order to leave room for Webster. *How does she feed company?* Alafair wondered.

The table had already been set so Elizabeth busily began turning food out onto serving plates.

"I have coffee if y'all want it, or milk or tea. I whipped up a pan of cornbread and there is a pot of potato soup simmering here on the stove. I made some ham sandwiches, too." She put the platter on the table. "Yonder is a jar of piccalilli and here is a fresh bowl of *pico de gallo*. Try that if you've never had it before. It's good with a sandwich."

Webster appeared in the kitchen door with his arms full of luggage. "Where do you want me to put these cases, honey?"

A look came over Elizabeth's face that gave Alafair pause. "Where do you think, Web? I have been getting the veranda room ready all week." She did not actually add, "you dolt," but the epithet was implied in her tone.

Alafair and Shaw cast one another a glance, but Web did not seem to notice his wife's pique. His reply was chipper. "Oh, sure enough, then." He walked through the kitchen and out the back door carrying the Tuckers' three little carpet bags. Elizabeth's gaze bored a hole in his back as he passed.

She turned back to her guests, her demeanor perfectly pleasant. "I think y'all will be comfortable out there. It's airy and has lots of space to stretch out. It's one of my favorite rooms in the house. We built it onto the back veranda so we would have a good place for guests, but most of the time I am the only one who uses it. I call it my reading room."

Web returned to the kitchen after depositing their luggage and Elizabeth served him with no trace of her earlier ill humor. The Tuckers were so exhausted that much of the dinner conversation was monosyllabic small talk. By the time they finished their supper Blanche was asleep in Shaw's arms and Alafair was about to nod off into her soup bowl, so Elizabeth immediately showed them to their quarters.

They had to go out the back door to reach the veranda room, which was built onto the back of the main house and had its own entrance. The room was longer than it was wide, boasting many windows and several large sheepskin and cow skin rugs to soften the flagstone floor. The beds were set up on opposite sides of the room—a large double for the grown-ups and a single tucked into a corner for Blanche. Elizabeth lit a couple of oil lamps and left them to unpack while she went back into the kitchen to fill a pitcher with hot water for their evening ablutions. Alafair was glad to see that the veranda room was not fitted for gas. Gaslights made a very pleasant glow but Alafair did not trust them not to go out in the middle of the night and smother her in her sleep.

Blanche never woke, even as Alafair undressed her and put her into her long flannel nightgown before tucking her up into the big bed.

Shaw and Alafair sat down side by side on the small bed to await Elizabeth's return with the water. For a long moment the only sound in the dim room was their breathing.

At length Alafair turned her head to give Shaw a puzzled frown. "What was that sharp exchange between Elizabeth and Web?"

His mouth quirked. He was aware that the incident had been eating on his wife for the last hour. "It looked to me like the ill feelings were all on her side. Sometimes married folks get annoyed with one another, honey. It don't necessarily mean anything."

"We haven't seen those two together in dog's years, Shaw. Who knows how they're rubbing along after all this time? But if this is not a peaceful house I surely do not aim to leave Blanche here."

Shaw lifted one shoulder in half a shrug. "We will have a few days to judge. But if we don't think this is a good set-up for Blanche, we'll derive some other plan, sugar. Don't worry about it right now."

He had lifted an arm and draped it over her shoulder. Alafair did not reply but she did smile and lean into his side, feeling relieved.

Dr. Moeur Concurs

The gorgeous weather turned out to be as salubrious as Dr. Addison had suggested. It had been the right decision to come; for now, a mere five days after their arrival in Tempe, Blanche seemed to be improved beyond all expectation.

Alafair had begun to entertain the hope that when she and Shaw made the trip home in a couple of weeks, they would not have to leave their daughter with Elizabeth to recuperate for months in this faraway place. That had been the original plan, and if it was going to save Blanche's health and even her life, Alafair had been willing to do it. Even if the very thought of abandoning her ill baby to someone the child did not know distressed Alafair no end.

But Blanche loved her Aunt Elizabeth and Uncle Webster and her little cousin. And Alafair was glad of the chance to reacquaint herself with Elizabeth and Webster, even if her young nephew was a bit ill-behaved for her taste. And Blanche loved Arizona. The weird beauty of the place appealed to her, as did the piercing blue of the sky and the soft, mild air.

Even so, Alafair and Shaw anxiously awaited Dr. Moeur's verdict as he finished his examination. They sat behind Blanche in straight-backed chairs in Elizabeth's kitchen, shoulder to shoulder in parental solidarity. Dr. Moeur removed the stethoscope from his ears and hung it around his neck before giving Blanche a reassuring smile. The little girl's expression was tentative if friendly enough, one shapely eyebrow cocked in suspicion as this stranger prodded her.

"Now that was not so bad, was it, honey?" Moeur fished a piece of hard candy out of his pocket and handed it to Blanche.

"No, sir." Her mouth quirked up in one corner as she took the candy. She was aware she was being bought off, but she was willing to go along with it.

"You run along now and let me talk to your mama and daddy."

Blanche threw her parents a glance over her shoulder as she popped the peppermint into her mouth, and Alafair nodded at her.

Moeur waited until Blanche was safely out of the room before offering his diagnosis. "I think your doctor back home was right. It doesn't look like tuberculosis to me but more like a persistent case of bronchitis brought on by the damp. Otherwise she appears to be a healthy enough little girl. Bringing her out here was a good idea. Is that rattling cough new, Mrs. Tucker?"

"Yes, sir, just since we got here. All winter it has been a dry cough that distressed her, but now she says it don't hurt her chest to cough."

"That's good. Seems her lung congestion is breaking up. You just keep up with those hot poultices and herb teas. I've found hot chicken broth to be effective against chest congestion but I'm sure you have some good medicinals in your own arsenal. You may wish to consult Elizabeth's neighbor, Mrs. Carrizal. She is a *curandera* of some note around here."

He turned his gaze toward Shaw. "I have learned over the years that mothers tend to know what helps their children even better than we doctors do."

He unstrung the stethoscope from around his neck and placed it in the bag at his feet. "So I'll just tell you what you already know, Mrs. Tucker. Keep her warm and dry, see that she gets a lot a rest and drinks lots of liquids. I'll drop back by in a couple of days to see how she's doing."

Unnatural Death

After Dr. Moeur took his leave, Alafair tucked Blanche in for a nap and sat next to the bed until she dropped off. When Alafair finally left the bedroom, she found the doctor still standing on the front porch, deep in conversation with Shaw and Elizabeth. She did not have to ask what they were talking about.

She stepped out onto the porch to join them. "Doctor, what did you discover about that poor fellow who got found dead in the ditch yonder?"

"Well, ma'am, as I was telling your folks here, it seems he did not drown after all. Nor was it alcohol poisoning, which is what I expected. He had not been drinking at all, as far as I could tell on cursory inspection. Somebody struck him twice in the back of the head with a blunt instrument. The first blow probably stunned him and maybe knocked him out, but he would have recovered from that one with nothing more than a bad headache. He didn't survive the second blow. It caved in the back of his head. He had been dead some hours before he was found."

"Mercy!"

"Mercy, indeed. If those of you in the house didn't hear anything, his assailant must have taken him by surprise. Come up on him from behind and delivered a blow with a heavy object before Arruda could react or defend himself. Since this is now a killing rather than an accident, I'm sure someone from the sheriff's office will be around soon to see if any of you have remembered anything new since you talked to Constable Nettles."

Unlikely Killers

Shaw took his leave and went back into the house, but Alafair remained on the porch and watched Elizabeth escort the doctor back to his Franklin automobile parked on the street in front of the house. Alafair could not hear what they were saying as they stood and talked for a few moments. But like two old friends their conversation was pleasant and full of smiles. Moeur tipped his hat and slid into the front seat. Elizabeth's fringed shawl had slipped down on one side and she absently drew it back up over her shoulder. She gave a languid wave as Moeur drove away.

Elizabeth turned and picked her way across the grassy yard like an ibis, tall and slender, lifting and placing each long leg with every careful step, mindful of her leather pumps and white stockings.

She reached the porch and looked up at Alafair with a hint of a smile. "Doctor Moeur told me on the sly that Constable Nettles thinks Bernie was more than likely done in by somebody at the party."

Alafair's eyebrows peaked. "Does Dr. Moeur think so too?"

Elizabeth shrugged. "He knows everybody who was there as well as I do and probably better. They are all my friends and neighbors, and it's hard to credit that there is a murderer among them. Of course, we did hear some high words on the subject of Francisco Villa's raid into Columbus, New Mexico, and generally on the revolution going on down in Old Mexico. I have heard a lot of talk around town on that subject of late. To hear folks go on you'd think every one of the Mexicans who are coming across the border to get away from the fighting are murderers and criminals who are taking our jobs and money and the food right out of our children's mouths!" Her ironic laugh indicated what she thought of that idea. "And after the battle in Columbus, some are downright hysterical."

"There were some folks here last night who no one knew," Alafair pointed out.

"Well, yes, a few. The Pipers brought their cousin who is visiting from Provo, and I reckon we are not well acquainted with either Jorge or Tony Arruda. But the Arrudas likely didn't kill their own brother and Miss Piper seemed an unlikely killer."

Alafair stepped down off the porch to stand next to Elizabeth in the yard. She threaded her arm through her sister's and they began strolling back toward the canal ditch. "I have in mind the moving picture actors who came to the party, Elizabeth. They were certainly complete strangers to all but each other."

Aside from Villa's raid, all the talk around town was about the Hollywood moving picture that was being shot right here in Tempe, starring the famous leading man Hobart Bosworth and a cast of glamorous actors and actresses. The cast and crew were currently staying downtown in the same hotel building that housed the telephone exchange and newspaper, next door to Web's law office.

In Elizabeth's opinion the motion picture was the most exciting thing that had ever occurred or was ever likely to occur in Tempe, Arizona, and over the past few days she had taken every opportunity to tell Alafair about it. Elizabeth and her friends had spent several happy afternoons watching the filming at various locations around town. Webster often frequented the hotel restaurant and had become acquainted with some of the crew members, so Elizabeth had cajoled him into extending a blanket party invitation to the entire company.

To Alafair's mind the motion-picture folks had been pleasant enough, and Blanche was especially enchanted by the dark-eyed young actress Dorothy Clark. But aside from being better dressed than most, they had not seemed to be any different from ordinary people. Certainly not any more inclined to violence.

Elizabeth was appalled at the very idea that a member of the repertory could have been involved in mischief. "Sister, you cannot seriously entertain the notion that the three refined individuals who graced the premises that night would have it in them to kill someone."

"I'm sure you're right. But I do believe I heard that Bernie and at least one of his brothers had small acting parts in that motion picture."

"Oh, I knew Bernie was in the picture! That had slipped my mind." Elizabeth clapped one slender hand to her cheek. "One day when my friend Cindy and me went out to watch the shooting over by the buttes, he had a pretty good part playing a Mexican soldier." Her hand dropped and the doubtful expression returned to her face. "Still, what possible reason would any of the movie actors have to do away with Bernie?"

Alafair looked thoughtfully at the canal water, just a slow trickle at the bottom of the ditch today. "Do you know the Arruda boys very well, Elizabeth?"

"No. I don't know the older two at all but to see them on the street. I knew Bernie from his handyman business. Too bad he had to cross over Jordan right in front of my house." Elizabeth sounded more amused than upset.

"You're not surprised that Bernie was murdered," Alafair said. It was not a question.

Elizabeth shook her head. "He was the sassiest flirt this side of the Pecos. I fear it was just a matter of time 'til some aggrieved husband did him in."

Alafair was surprised that her sister had voiced aloud what she had been thinking. She had formed an opinion of the murdered man at the open house, but how accurate could that be considering she had spent less than ten minutes in his company? She was not acquainted with the particulars of his life.

Of course she had formed an impression nonetheless. She always got a sense of a person within moments of meeting him. Sometimes longer acquaintance proved her right and sometimes entirely wrong. Usually right, though. Often enough that she had quite a bit of faith in her intuition.

Her intuition had told her that this Bernie Arruda was a piece of work.

He thought he was irresistible to women. She had known plenty like him in her life, including some in her own family. The difference between Bernie and most other ladies' men was that he really was extraordinary: handsome, charming, and attentive. He could sing, too, his true tenor voice full of feeling as his fingers caressed the strings of his small guitar.

If only he had not been so aware of his gifts. Considering the fact that he was giving their wives heart-flutters, the men seemed to like Bernie as well as the women did. He would have been hard not to like, she admitted to herself, the way he made everyone he spoke to feel as though he or she was the most interesting person he had ever met. And if you were female, the most desirable.

The one thing she particularly remembered about Bernie was that when he looked over the women at the party—any woman from twelve to eighty, including middle-aged matrons like herself—his dark eyes smoldered with a sexual intensity that embarrassed Alafair. Well, obviously not everyone was enamored with Bernie, considering that someone had taken a notion to cave in the back of his skull. Still… "Harsh retribution for a few ill-chosen words."

"You know how men are, Alafair." Elizabeth stepped back over the ditch and they walked together toward the house. "Some will take exception when another man eyes his wife. Some will take double exception when a brown man eyes his wife."

"What do you aim to tell the sheriff when he comes by, Elizabeth?"

"There is not much I really know for a fact. I expect I'll cogitate for a spell about who all was at the house last night and what happened. Maybe you can help me. Perhaps we can remember something to tell the sheriff that will light a fire under him."

"Oh, honey, I can't be getting involved in this business. I'm here to see to Blanche, and besides we aren't going to be in Arizona very long. Even if we were, I don't know any of the folks around here, so there is nothing I could say about any of them."

"I don't expect to solve the crime, Alafair. I only wish I could come up with something for the law to go on and not just let it go with, 'you know how Mexicans are.'"

Alafair's gaze shifted as she considered all the people she had met at the open house. "Well, Elizabeth, I heard some saber-rattling language, but if anyone I met the other night is a murderer or a criminal, I am going to be mighty surprised."

Elizabeth's neighbors were just like Alafair's neighbors in and around Boynton. The men had gathered in the back yard and sat under the trees drinking sweet tea, loudly talking politics and laughing so much that Alafair had wondered if there was something other than tea in their glasses.

The women had congregated in the house, milling around the kitchen and parlor. Mrs. Carrizal had made a deliciously creamy hot drink flavored with cinnamon, vanilla, and chocolate that no one could get enough of. They discussed their kids and joked about their husbands and men in general, just like home.

Alafair had enjoyed the gathering very much, which had been something of a surprise, considering how hard Elizabeth had had to work to convince her it would be a good idea in the first place.

Tired

Alafair and Blanche and Shaw were so tired when they arrived that they had spent their first full day in Tempe piled together napping on the bed in the back bedroom where Elizabeth had ensconced them. Blanche slept the entire day and the adults rose only long enough to dress in the morning, wash, and eat enough to keep from starving. But on the second day Shaw had spent an hour or two downtown visiting Webster's law office, and Blanche was feeling lively enough to take an interest in the exotic new surroundings and her exotic new relatives.

Blanche's relatives were just as taken with her. Chase Kemp would have spent hours chattering away at his cousin and bringing her bugs and sticks and puzzles and pictures he had drawn, had Alafair not banned him from the bedroom most of the time.

Blanche and her aunt Elizabeth had taken to one another immediately. Alafair was amazed at how much the two were alike in looks and temperament. Both were tall, slender, and fragile-looking, with the same elegant cheekbones and creamy skin. They were both blessed with a languid, knowing gaze and large, almond-shaped eyes, though Elizabeth's were dark brown and not green. Both had oceans of sable brown hair that fell in graceful waves and stayed perfectly in place at any time of day. How had it come about, Alafair wondered, that her own long, dark, springy hair always looked like she had just been caught in a windstorm? Was she not of the same blood as her sister and her own daughter? Little wonder that Blanche adored Elizabeth. *They are kindred souls*, Alafair realized. Considering how restless and volatile, how stubborn and full of schemes Elizabeth had been as a child, that realization made her vaguely anxious.

By the third day, Blanche was ready to explore. But as happy as Alafair was to see Blanche feeling so much better, she refused to let her do more than get out of bed to take meals and use the chamber pot. Blanche expressed her unhappiness at the arrangement. But aside from an hour or so spent playing with her cousin or reading to her aunt, she slept much of the day in spite of her protestations.

Alafair did not leave her side. While Blanche slept she had amused herself by exploring the large, light-filled and airy veranda bedroom.

Two large, six-paned, double casement windows took up almost the entire width of the outside wall. The rest of the room contained the beds and a wardrobe, a couple of comfortable chairs, a tall bookshelf, and a long, narrow, wooden table along the back wall that was piled with the detritus from Elizabeth's various crafts and enthusiasms.

During the long afternoons that Alafair kept watch over Blanche's healing sleep, she whiled away a few of the hours by becoming acquainted with the evidence of her sister's eclectic pastimes. Boxes of fabric scraps for quilting and rug-making, spools of ribbon, a box of feathers, a rack of preserved flowers and reeds were scattered across the long table at the back of the room. Did she make hats? Alafair kept forgetting to ask. Elizabeth had carefully labeled a dozen or so rock fragments and pasted them to a large piece of cardboard. Envelopes full of newspaper clippings and a tall stack of magazines were piled on one corner: *Ladies Home Journal, National Geographic, The Nation, McClures',* a couple of dime novels, a theosophical treatise, mathematics and chemistry textbooks, the *Radical Review, Photoplay* and *Motion Picture Story Magazine.* Several books by one Dane Coolidge sat on a bookshelf under the window. When she picked one up to flip through it, Alafair discovered it had been signed by Mr. Coolidge himself. The bottom bookshelf was lined with law textbooks and tomes of Arizona and United States statutes. Amazing. Was there anything Elizabeth did not take an interest in?

Eventually Alafair abandoned her snooping and leaned over the bed to check on Blanche. She was sound asleep and looked so innocent and peaceful that Alafair could not help but brush the child's cheek with her lips. She tiptoed out of the room and through the quiet house to find Elizabeth sitting at the kitchen table with one foot propped on the rung of the chair next to her, cradling a mug of something creamy in one hand and reading a book.

Persuasion

Elizabeth looked up and smiled. "Well, greetings, stranger! Nice to see you out and about this afternoon. How is Blanche doing today?"

Alafair pulled out the chair on the opposite side of the table and sat down. "She's napping right now. She is better every single day, Elizabeth. As soon as we got out of Oklahoma she started to perk up, but just since she has been here, I swear it's like she took some magic elixir. I am afraid I'm not going to be able to force her to stay in bed much longer."

"Might be good for her to stretch her legs and get a bit of exercise."

"I know it. It's just that she has been sick so long that it's hard for me to credit that she's finally on the mend. I declare, Elizabeth, the air out here is a miracle, so clear and dry and perfect. I never knew there was a place in these United States where you could go about in your shirtsleeves and leave the windows open in February."

Elizabeth cocked an eyebrow. "You've come at the best time of the year. You would change your mind if you visited in July. And besides, it's March now, sister."

"Oh, yes, I had forgot. I kindly have lost track of time."

"Well, I am glad the sweet thing is feeling better. I'll tell you, Alafair, that is one beautiful girl you've got there. She's going to make all the boys cry when she grows up. You had better warn Shaw to keep an eye on her."

Alafair laughed, flattered. "Thank you, we think all our young'uns are good-looking. But she's not quite eleven years old yet. She has got a way to go before we'll need to lock her away from the fellows."

"You sound like a mama, all right. Our mama is the same way—can't quite see that the children are more grown up than she thinks they are. Mark my words about that pretty girl." She closed her book. "Did you read the article about y'all's trip that came out in the paper this morning?"

Alafair nodded, glad of the change of topic. "I did." Kemp and Stewart, Attorneys-at-Law, was located next door to the local newspaper. When Shaw had returned to the house after his visit downtown yesterday afternoon, he told Alafair a reporter friend of Web's had asked permission to write an article about their prodigious trip from Boynton, Oklahoma, to Tempe, Arizona. Shaw had obliged him with an interview and the article had appeared in the *Tempe Daily News* that very morning.

"Well, I don't know if you've been hearing all the comings and goings through this house today but I think every person we know in town has telephoned or dropped by to say hello. Everybody wants to meet y'all. Of course I gave them all a glass of tea and sent them on their way, since I figured Blanche didn't need to be bothered. But since Blanche is doing well and you must be getting bored by now, I am wondering if you and Shaw would object to us having an open house tomorrow evening?"

Alafair looked skeptical. "An open house?"

Elizabeth spoke over her before she could demur. "You'll not have to do a thing, Alafair. I would not dream of letting you lift a finger. You and Shaw can just sit on the porch like the king and queen of Cathay and talk to folks or not as suits you. I'll ask my friend Cindy to help me with the arrangements. She's married to Web's law partner, Geoff Stewart. They live right next door. She lost a baby recently, and she has been moping."

"Oh, I am sorry to hear that." Alafair's voice was full of sympathy. "How old was the baby when it died?"

"No, sister, it was an early miscarriage and not her first. They've been trying for a baby for years with no luck. It's gotten so that Geoff spends all his time working and Cindy fills her days with charity work amongst the poor Mexicans over in the Barrio. I've been looking for some way to cheer her up, and something like this may help. My neighbors, Mr. and Miz Carrizal, will help us set up the tables and the like. We'll have folks bring pot luck. Maybe the Arruda brothers can play some music for us. Why, I'll have Web invite some of the moving picture people who are staying at the hotel. Maybe one or two of them would like to come by and get some home cooking. That would be something! Cindy would love it. Oh, Alafair, I would love for you to get to meet the main actor, Mr. Bosworth. He's ever so handsome and charming…"

Alafair had been going to refuse outright until she saw how excited Elizabeth was. She looked so happy and hopeful at the prospect that Alafair could not make herself say no. It was not really for them that Elizabeth wanted to invite the local movers and shakers to her house. What could she do but be gracious about it? Besides, anything that may put a bit of pink in Blanche's cheeks was worth considering.

Elizabeth rattled on. "You must make the acquaintance of Mr. and Miz Carrizal. They are just the kindest people. They would do anything for you and act like you were doing them a favor to let them. Miz Carrizal loves Chase, too. He runs over there whenever he can and she feeds him Mexican eats and sets him to doing chores for her, even as little as he is. I don't know how she does it. He would just as soon eat a bug as listen to anything I have to say, much less turn a hand."

Children know where they are wanted, Alafair thought.

Elizabeth went on. "Mr. Carrizal is just as fine a person as his wife. He watches over me and Cindy, too. He's the one who arranged for Bernie Arruda to come and fix things around our houses and yards when they've broke, like my gate latch and when one of the shelves in the kitchen came loose. Things like that would just stay broke if we had to rely on our husbands to fix them. Web is so busy with that law practice that he's not home enough to notice what state the house is in. Of course his head is so empty of any thought but business that he doesn't notice when he is home, either. "

This was the first time that Elizabeth had actually said anything to confirm Alafair's suspicion that all was not well in the Kemp marriage.

"When you meet them you'll love the Carrizals, too. Maybe she'll bring some tamales! What do you say, Alafair? Oh, please say yes."

"Well, I'll ask Shaw about it, honey, but I reckon it will be all right. As long as Blanche holds up, though. If she tires out or gets to coughing, don't be disappointed if her and me disappear back into the bedroom."

"Oh, no, Alafair, I understand. But it will be good for Blanche. You will see. And for Cindy and for you and Shaw, too. This will make everybody feel so much better."

Villa's Raid

Alafair had intended to broach the subject of the proposed open house to Shaw as soon as he got in from downtown, but when he returned in time for dinner with Webster in tow, they were full of their own news.

Web could hardly contain himself, hovering over the women as they set the table under the ramada in the back yard. It was too pretty a day to eat indoors. "Bill over to the *Daily News* just got a wire from the A.P. that said Pancho Villa just attacked and burned Columbus, New Mexico, this morning with fifteen hundred men. Said at least sixteen Americans were killed before the Mexicans were driven back across the border."

The women stood agape at the news for a moment before Alafair said, "Columbus? Why, that's where we were stranded overnight on our way here, wasn't it, Shaw? Where the doctor was so good to come and help Blanche?"

"That's the place," he confirmed. "Looks like we missed the invasion by the skin of our teeth."

Alafair was distressed. "Oh, mercy! Folks were so nice to us there. I hope that good doctor and the wonderful lady at the hotel are all right."

"Bill told us that the troopers of the Thirteenth U.S. Cavalry pursued the Villa band back into Mexico," Web hastened to reassure her, "and at last report they were engaged in a battle some fifteen miles south of the border. Our fellows will whip them good, sure enough!"

Shaw took a biscuit from the serving plate in Alafair's hand before she could set it on the table. No matter what exciting news he bore, it was still dinner time, after all. "The wire report said that quite a number of the raiders were killed. Sounds like Villa's gamble has cost him more than it gained."

Elizabeth looked worried. "Do you suppose we're in any danger here?"

"Oh, I doubt it, honey," Web said. "We're a hundred and seventy-five miles from the border and three hundred fifty miles from Columbus. Still, Cap Irish has called out the Home Guard just to be safe. They're gathering right now over to the Normal School, on the quad in front of Old Main."

"Cap Irish is not a man to go off half-cocked," Elizabeth noted. "There must be some cause for concern."

"Villa and his bunch have been drifting around the border area for weeks but they never made any real move to come across until now," Web said. "I thought he told an American reporter that he wanted to take his army to Washington to let Wilson know he didn't have anything to do with that massacre of Americans at Santa Ysabel last January."

Shaw looked skeptical. "Personally, I was always of a mind to take that piece of news with a grain of salt. The idea that Villa would think he could get an army all the way to Washington City for a pow-wow with the president is about as hair-brained as you can get. I can't credit it. I never had the impression Villa was stupid."

"What should we do?" Elizabeth wondered. "Is there some help we can offer to the poor folks in Columbus?"

"Nothing we can do right now," Shaw said. "The news is still coming in, and things may change. I'll tell you one thing, though, I sure heard a lot of wild palaver on the street when the news broke. There's some folks act like they want to round up every Mexican-blood man, woman, and child in town and clap them into jail, then blow the country of Mexico off the map for good measure."

Alafair made a disgusted noise. "That's always the way of it. Like as not the hotheads will blow off steam and calm down directly."

Elizabeth was not as sanguine. "I hope you're right, sister. I'd hate to be a Mexican here in Arizona right about now." Her demeanor changed in a blink and she flashed a smile. "Still, it doesn't sound to me like anything that'll put a crimp in our little get-together tomorrow."

"What get-together is this?" Shaw wondered.

It was Alafair who answered. "Oh, Elizabeth has a notion to invite the whole town to a pot luck here at the house tomorrow evening. She thinks that write-up about us in the paper this morning has made all her friends want to meet us."

Shaw's raised an eyebrow. "Blanche would enjoy that, I imagine."

"I know she'd enjoy it," Alafair admitted. "But is she well enough yet? I don't know if Blanche is up to meeting a bunch of new people all at once."

"Why, it'd be good for her," Elizabeth's words rushed over themselves, so afraid was she that Alafair may be having a change of heart. "Don't you think so, Shaw? Don't you think a lovely evening with games and food and music would be just the thing?"

Shaw smiled. He knew Elizabeth was trying to recruit him to help her convince Alafair. His children did the same thing when their mother was less than persuaded about the wisdom of their schemes. "I think it's up to Alafair."

Alafair was just as amused at Elizabeth's alarm. "Don't fret yourself, Elizabeth. I won't spoil your fun."

Mrs. Carrizal

At her mother's insistence, Blanche had spent the day of the open house in bed. Not that she acquiesced graciously, but Alafair was a confirmed believer in preventive resting. Alafair sat by her side and read to her or helped her with her school work, and generally cajoled her into staying put. But by early afternoon Blanche was feeling well and rested and eager to get up and put on a pretty frock. Alafair could hear people talking and laughing in the back yard and she looked out the window to see Shaw and Web moving long wooden tables out of the storage shed. They were handing them off to an older man, a young man, and a boy of about twelve who were setting up the tables under the vine covered ramada in the center of the yard.

Time to meet the neighbors.

Blanche and Alafair dressed and primped and critiqued each other's outfits, then went out the back door to discover two lively, black-haired young women hanging bunting on the veranda. One was standing on a step stool and the other stood below her handing up long strands of colored crêpe paper, but both turned and flashed enormous smiles when they heard Alafair and Blanche emerge. "Hello, hello! Welcome!" Both women rushed to greet them as though they were long lost kin.

"Oh, Miz Tucker and sweet Blanche," the girl from the step stool exclaimed, "we have heard so much about you from our dear Elizabeth!"

"Everyone is just *perishing* to meet you," the crêpe paper girl assured them. "It's so wonderful to hear that you're feeling better, sweetheart! I'm Juana Carrizal and this is my sister, Elena. We came early to help Elizabeth get ready for the open house."

Elena clapped her hands, squashing bunting between them. "We just *love* Elizabeth! Our papa and our brothers Matt and Artie are helping Mr. Tucker and Web set up the buffet tables in the back yard, and Mama is in the kitchen with Elizabeth. Mama is *eager* to make your acquaintance. Blanche, maybe you would like to help us decorate after you say hello."

Blanche was grinning ear to ear when she looked up at her mother for permission, and Alafair was fairly infected with the Carrizal girls' good humor herself when she said, "If you're feeling up to it after we meet Miz Carrizal, I don't know why you can't help, sugar."

Juana and Elena dashed back to their task as Alafair ushered Blanche into the kitchen. Elizabeth was standing at the cabinet with her back to the door, cutting a sheet cake into tiny squares and chatting happily to a woman at the table who was arranging something on a platter.

The woman looked up. She was dressed in a maroon skirt and ivory blouse today, and her moonlit halo had turned into a crown of silver curls piled on top of her head, but Alafair recognized her at once. She stopped in her tracks and drew a sharp breath. "You are the White Lady!" she blurted, and immediately clapped her hand over her mouth.

Elizabeth turned, her eyebrows half-way up to her hairline, and laughed. "Miz Carrizal," she said to the lady, "this is my sister Alafair and her girl Blanche. Alafair, this is my back-door neighbor, Miz Carrizal."

Alafair could feel her cheeks burning. "Please excuse my bad manners, Miz Carrizal. It is just that I saw you that first evening we arrived. You were far off and it was just getting dark and you were standing in your back yard with your goats. You were wearing a white dress, and what with the moon on your hair and my bleary eyes I thought you looked like an angel! I never did get the chance to mention what I saw to Elizabeth and ever since then I've been wondering if I dreamed it all up. I am so glad to make your acquaintance!"

"You didn't dream it, Alafair. Miz Carrizal is an angel all right." Elizabeth did not sound like she was teasing.

Mrs. Carrizal was a small, refined woman in her early fifties with large dark eyes that radiated warmth. Perhaps it was due to her preconception of what the White Lady must be like, but Alafair was instantly impressed with the older woman. Her kind manner and knowing expression reminded Alafair of Shaw's mother, Grandma Sally, though Mrs. Carrizal was younger and not quite as sharp-edged.

"Now, Elizabeth." Mrs. Carrizal's voice carried a trace of amusement as she chastised Elizabeth for her hyperbole. Her lips curved into a smile and she extended her hand to Alafair. "Yes, Miz Tucker, I saw you that evening as well. I apologize for not coming over right then to meet your family, but Elizabeth had told us the situation. I hear that you have had a wonderful few days of rest. I hope you are all much improved. I cannot tell you how glad we all are that you are here." She looked down at Blanche.

Blanche began to raise her arm for a handshake but Mrs. Carrizal was having none of it. She enveloped the girl in a hug. "So glad you are here," she repeated. "You will be fine now, sweetheart, yes, I can tell. Soon all will be well."

Alafair's heart bounded at the woman's prediction, and she unconsciously placed her hand on her chest. She felt the burn of sudden tears. Mrs. Carrizal's words were delivered with such conviction that against all reason Alafair believed her. Perhaps she was an angel, after all.

Arrivals

Elizabeth had arranged her long, low, front porch like a pleasant outdoor parlor for the party. From her seat beside the front door Alafair had been able to get a good long look at all the guests as they arrived and before they were brought over and introduced to her and Shaw and Blanche. The three of them began the evening in chairs on the porch with Elizabeth and her friend and neighbor Cindy Stewart, while Web stood by the front gate and directed foot and automobile traffic. Chase flitted back and forth, generally making a pest of himself. Blanche sat in her mother's lap greeting the guests, sweet and shy. Mrs. Carrizal and her daughters were in charge of the kitchen, while Mr. Carrizal was in the back yard with his sons.

Alafair had first met Cindy early in the afternoon, shortly after the Carrizals had arrived. She had popped through the back door all in a flutter, carrying a little white cake as delicate as she was. "Elena told me you were all in here!"

When first she laid eyes on Cindy Stewart, Alafair had taken her for a child. But on closer inspection Alafair judged her to be in her late twenties or early thirties. She thought Cindy favored that Mary Pickford actress, small and neat-figured with a wide-eyed expression, her hair arranged in loose golden ringlets and fraught with ribbons. Alafair thought her very pretty, even if she did not consider it entirely proper for a married woman to wear her hair down.

Elizabeth had introduced them. "Alafair, Shaw, this is my dearest friend Cindy Stewart. Her husband Geoff is Webster's law partner. Since we never see either of them, Cindy and me simply do everything together. Cindy, this is my sister and her husband and their daughter Blanche."

Cindy had taken Alafair's hand, breathless. "Oh, Mr. and Miz Tucker, dearest Blanche," she had said, "Elizabeth has told me *so* much about you."

The first to arrive after the Carrizals and Cindy were Elizabeth's near neighbors, emerging one family at a time from their houses up and down the block and walking to the Kemp house. Children ran ahead of parents and grandparents carrying jugs and pans and casserole dishes. The entertainment arrived in a donkey-drawn cart, three small brown men in fancy black embroidered outfits and showy *sombreros*. They pulled up in front of the house and waited until Webster walked to the road and directed them to park around back. They were not introduced. Guests from further afield drove up in buggies and automobiles, so many that parked vehicles eventually lined the entire street up and down both sides.

Elizabeth took care of introductions as people made their way onto the porch to meet the visitors. Alafair was amazed at the number of people who showed up. When did Elizabeth manage to invite them all? There were so many that it was not long before Alafair lost track of who was who. She glanced at Shaw, who looked as befuddled as she felt. Were the Tuckers and their long train trip so interesting or were Elizabeth and Web that popular? Or was the entire town so eager to get together and discuss the raid on New Mexico? Or were the Tempeans just that starved for entertainment?

Soon the house and property were teeming with laughing, chattering people and the cheerful sound of *mariachi* music drifted over the crowd. Chase disappeared into a gang of children who came running around the side of the house. Then the beautiful music and the incredible smells coming from the back yard enticed Blanche to explore and Alafair let her go.

Elizabeth had just suggested that all who were coming had done so and it was time to mingle, when Cindy interrupted her.

"There is Geoff."

Something in Cindy's tone struck Alafair as odd and she followed Cindy's gaze with interest. There were so many people in the yard that she could not tell which one to look at.

Elizabeth leaned over the arm of her chair to murmur in Alafair's ear. "Geoff is Cindy's husband and Web's partner."

"I remember. Which one is he, now?"

Elizabeth pointed. "Yonder. The one talking to Web."

Geoff Stewart was about the same size as Web, fair-haired with a choleric red complexion. Unlike the other casually dressed guests he was wearing a business suit.

Cindy stood up, wringing her hands. "I guess he came here direct from the office." Her voice had once more taken on a breathless quality. "He is talking something over with Web. Do you think I ought to interrupt them?"

Elizabeth sounded impatient when she answered. "I think you ought to leave him be and go have a good time. Geoff can take care of himself without you waiting on him."

Cindy nodded, distracted. "Yes, I had better go see if he wants anything." She hurried down the steps and followed in her husband's wake as he and Web moved toward the back yard. If Geoff saw her he did not acknowledge her.

Elizabeth puffed. "I swear, you would think she is his servant rather than his wife."

Before Alafair could comment, one of the Carrizal girls came to fetch them into the house to join the party.

Geoff Stewart

Shaw had met Mr. Carrizal and his elder son Matt Carrizal for the first time that afternoon when he had helped them set up the chairs and tables in the back yard. Mr. Carrizal was a slight man with a fair complexion, very dark eyes, grey hair, and a thin white mustache, but he had presence enough to make up for any lack of bulk. Shaw guessed that the son, Matt, was in his mid-twenties, a head taller than his father, dark of eye and hair, with a thoughtful way about him. Shaw approved of the way he treated his father with respect and affection. Not to mention that Matt's laconic good humor reminded Shaw of his own eldest son, Gee Dub. He caught himself sizing the young man up as potential son-in-law and almost laughed aloud at his own folly. The father of eight daughters tended to do that even if he did not have a specific daughter in mind.

The three of them stood by the side of the house and chatted about homely things for a while, getting to know one another better. They had been too busy with arrangements earlier in the day to do more than plot and plan, lift and carry.

Carrizal told Shaw that he was an importer of goods from Mexico. Furniture, art, pottery and the like, which he sold to shops and stores around southern Arizona and even as far abroad as New Mexico and California. Yes, his business often necessitated travel down to Mexico, sometimes as far as Mexico City and Guadalajara. No, he did not go down there nearly as often these days, not much farther than Juarez or Nogales, not since all the civil unrest. A man could be kidnapped right off the train and held for ransom. Too bad, too. Mexico is such a beautiful country.

They were laughing and comparing family wedding and father-of-the-bride stories when Web approached with Geoff Stewart in tow.

The greetings were cordial but the merriment level dropped a couple of notches. Shaw had already met his brother-in-law's partner earlier in the week, the first time he had accompanied Webster to work. They had conversed over a luncheon or two but Shaw did not really have much of an opinion of the man. Not that he disliked him. He just could not make heads or tails of him.

Geoff Stewart was pleasant enough but he played it close to the vest. A very cold fish. That was Shaw's early impression, anyway. Odd pairing, Geoff and Webster. One man's personality was unknowable and the other's was nonexistent.

Shaw did not think he would hire the firm of Stewart and Kemp for legal services. It was not because he maintained a poor opinion of lawyers. Shaw knew plenty of good honest lawyers, including his own, Abner Meriwether, back in Boynton. But you should be able to tell if a man has your best interest at heart, and with either Stewart or Kemp how could you ever know? Shaw could only hope that his opinion of one man or the other would improve on better acquaintance.

The men did not get much past the hellos before Cindy padded up behind her husband and stood shifting from foot to foot. Since she obviously could not decide how to go about drawing Geoff's attention, Shaw took it upon himself to do it for her.

"Geoff, yonder young lady looks to have something to say to you."

Geoff's eyebrows lifted and he turned to see who Shaw was nodding at. When their eyes met Geoff seemed to inflate at the same time Cindy deflated. "What do you want, Cindy?"

"Can I get you anything, Geoff? Can I fill a plate for you?"

Geoff took a step forward, not to draw her aside or keep their conversation private, but in order to loom over her. "I'll take care of myself. Go back inside. I will talk to you later." His tone held no threat but his stance was another matter.

Shaw cast a questioning glance at Mr. Carrizal, but the older man was not looking at him. Matt's thunderous expression had caused Carrizal to place a restraining hand on his son's arm.

Rather than take her husband's offhand dismissal badly, Cindy looked hopeful and returned a tremulous smile. She melted away and Geoff turned back to his companions. "Shall we repair to the buffet?"

Web and Geoff moved away, unaware of Matt's aura of disapproval. Shaw hung back with the Carrizals, but neither of them had any comment about the incident. They walked together toward the table in silence.

The Motion Picture

After most of the guests had already arrived and Elizabeth and Alafair were just about to adjourn to the buffet table, a beautifully turned-out woman, an equally well dressed teenaged girl, and a natty young man drove up in an open roadster. The light was fading and for a moment Elizabeth peered across the yard, trying to place the passengers in the car.

She jerked up straight and made a little noise of recognition, suddenly alight with joy. "Oh, look! It's dear Dorothy Clark—the young one, there! She plays an Indian maiden in the moving picture! I recognize that man as the fellow who runs the camera. Chris, I think his name is. And the other woman…" She hesitated, trying to dredge up the name. "She's in the picture, too. I told you some of the film people would come!" She had floated down the steps to greet the new arrivals.

Alafair's lip twitched. "I reckon we're honored."

Elizabeth missed the irony. "Oh, we are!"

The reason Elizabeth was hosting such a large gathering may have been to introduce her visiting relatives to her friends, but at least among the female guests the stars of the party were young Dorothy Clark and Miss Yona Landowska. The Tuckers' seven-day journey, their layover in Columbus and the Villa raid, previously topics of intense interest, were all forgotten as the assembled ladies plied the actresses with questions about Hollywood, California, and what it was like to act before a camera and know that people all over the country would see your face right up there on the screen.

Alafair had not minded at all that she was no longer the center of attention, and the actresses had not minded at all that they were, which worked out well for everyone. Alafair had not known much about the film, this momentous event that added such glitter to everyone's life by its very proximity, or how it came to be made in Tempe. Women whose names she could not remember were eager to tell her all about it.

"It's called *The Yaqui*, Miz Tucker, and it stars Hobart Bosworth."

"What is a 'Yaqui'?" Alafair had wondered.

Honor Moeur, the doctor's wife, answered. "It's the name of an Indian tribe, Miz Tucker. They are from Mexico, but a few years ago a bunch of them got run off their land by the government. Many of them were even forced into slavery on some of the big *rancheros*. A group of them who left Mexico to get away from the persecution now live in a little town called Guadalupe, a bit southwest of Tempe, here."

Alafair shook her head. An Indian nation she had never heard of, and she had been around Indians all her life. "Is that what the picture is about, them getting booted out of Mexico?"

The actress Miss Landowska answered. "In a way. It's about how badly they were treated by the Mexican government. The story is about a Yaqui chief named Tambor who is separated from his wife and daughter when they are sold as slaves and sent far away. Tambor hunts for them and joins his family in their bondage. But before he can free them, his daughter—that's Dorothy, here—dies and his wife kills herself."

Cindy Stewart had not been able to keep quiet for another moment. "Tambor kills the white slave owner responsible for stealing his family and leads a Yaqui rebellion against the despot General Martinez. It is all so very heroic and tragic."

Alafair had struggled to retain a polite expression. But she had not managed to maintain any real interest in the subject and did not remember if she had been told how the story ended.

The Revolution

The actresses took their leave as the sun settled on the horizon, pleading an early start in the morning. Miss Landowska took the wheel with Dorothy beside her as they drove away, leaving Chris Martin, the camera operator and sometime chauffeur, to walk back to the hotel on his own later. After their stars were gone, the rest of the women left the house to join the men under the trees in the back yard. Alafair and Elizabeth sat down together next to Shaw under the ramada.

Alafair knew Webster Kemp, of course, and the Carrizals. Ben Moeur was there, and a fellow named Fred Irish whom everyone called "Cap." Then there was Mr. Woolf, Somebody Spangler, Chris Martin the cameraman, and a man called Estrada who told Alafair he was the town truant officer. A father and son by the name of Gillander sat side by side in a two-seat lawn swing situated just to Alafair's right.

Once the ladies were settled, the men resumed their conversation about Pancho Villa, loudly proffering their opinions as though they might make a difference in the course of the Mexican Revolution. Alafair observed that Gillander the father had stern opinions about Mexican nationals living in the United States, but the son—Levi, it was—was much more sympathetic to their plight. There was a lot of bantering as well as speculation about what, if any, effect this endless revolution was going to have on the border region. Two or three of the men had Spanish names like Estrada and Carrizal, but none of the Anglos behaved as though they were particularly aware of that fact. Neither did Estrada or Carrizal. The three Arruda brothers stood directly behind the arguing men, playing their guitars and keeping their own counsel.

Mr. Carrizal himself resurrected the topic. "I hear the Mexican government protested that after Villa's raid, Colonel Slocum crossed the border into sovereign Mexican territory in pursuit of the bandits."

Web Kemp snorted. "It said in the paper this morning that Washington stands squarely behind Col. Slocum in sending his troops into Mexico after Villa. After all, he had to go after them now while the trail is hot."

Shaw was a visitor in Arizona and did not feel qualified to offer an opinion about how the border dwellers should deal with the situation. But that did not mean he was not interested. "How big is this batch of invaders, anyway? Today the *Daily News* says two or three hundred, but yesterday it reported there were over a thousand."

"Villa's men are probably deserting him." Mr. Carrizal sounded like someone who knew what he was talking about. "I have heard from friends in Chihuahua that for the past couple of years one revolutionary army or the other has been grabbing fighting-age men and boys up off the street or out of the fields whenever they come across them, then making them join up whether they believe in the cause of that particular faction or not. I do not imagine Villa's army is made up of very many happy soldiers."

Web Kemp laughed. "Villa is carrying sixty mule-loads of looted gold with him. I reckon that would keep at least of few of his men interested in his cause."

Cap Irish was a tall, athletic man with white hair and spectacles who taught science and physical education at the Normal School. He was also the Captain of the Tempe Home Guard, so the men paid attention when he said, "What worries me is that I have heard the Germans would like nothing better than for us to get involved in a war with Mexico. That would keep the United States busy while they go about their fiendish business in Europe. All these Mexican revolutionary factions have German army advisors, you know. There is speculation that the Huns are supplying them all with weapons as well as 'advising.'"

An Unpleasant Turn

It was Gillander Senior who gave the conversation a particularly unpleasant turn. "The Germans are recruiting Mexicans to spy on us, too."

The discourse stopped for an instant before someone said, "Where did you hear that?"

Gillander was short but square and robust, a sour man with an old fashioned full beard and long hair slicked back from his forehead. The beard and hair had gone snowy white, but he had the pale, almost transparent complexion of a former redhead. *Master of all he owns and righteous in his convictions*, Alafair thought, judging from the ramrod-straight posture and hard attitude.

He continued. "It just makes sense, don't it? Mexicans got no love for us, and droves of them have come across the border into the U.S. in the past couple of years...."

Young Levi Gillander, a pale, rather sad-looking version of his father, attempted to head him off. "Most of the poor people who are coming over are good honest folks, Father, who are trying to get away from the violence down there."

Old Gillander was not happy about being corrected by his own son. "You do not know whereof you speak, Levi." His tone was dismissive, and Levi's face flushed red. The father continued, unaware of or unconcerned about his effect. "How better to hide a spy than in plain sight? Besides, even the honest ones are so poor that it would be easy for the Germans to bribe at least a few to send them information on our opinions and readiness to defend ourselves." Gillander raised his voice to be heard over the outburst of comment. "We need to be keeping a special eye on Mexicans who live mixed in with us. The Mexicans in the *barrio*, at least they're all together in their own place where we can keep an eye on them. These folks who live amongst us are more dangerous. It would be easy for one of them to spy on us and slip the information to anyone who meant to do us harm. Somebody had to have informed Villa of the unready condition of the troops at Columbus. Villa, he means to hurt us Americans for cutting him loose from our support like we done."

Matt Carrizal gave no indication that he felt personally maligned by Gillander Senior's comments. "Even if Villa does manage a few border skirmishes, I don't think we here in Tempe have anything to worry about. They could not possibly get very far into the country, not with General Pershing on the lookout, and we are a long way from the border."

"Besides," Cap Irish offered, "the Normal School Cadet Corps has just received a shipment of eighty Springfield rifles, and tomorrow I am going to start drills and training on campus west of Old Main."

"I'm pleased to hear it, but it ain't enough." The elder Gillander was determined to press his cause. "Ranchers all along the border have armed in case of an uprising of the Mexicans who live around them."

Ben Moeur was having none of it. "That is ridiculous, Duncan…"

Gillander interrupted. "There will be an uprising here in the States, mark my words. Mexico wants the land they lost in the war in '48. They have been making plans to get it back ever since we took it fair and square."

Levi Gillander was clearly embarrassed by his father's harsh views. "This kind of talk is no good, Father. It is true that lots of Mexican folks have moved up here in recent years to get away from the revolution. But many…most, I think…of our Mexican-blood neighbors were born right here in Arizona and have lived here all their lives, which is more than I can say for the rest of us." He looked squarely at Matt Carrizal.

An incoherent murmur arose. Elizabeth leaned toward Alafair and whispered in her ear. "Let's get out of here, sister. All this hot air is giving me a headache."

Webster Kemp chose this moment to speak up. "As for the Mexican folks who live amongst us, I think we ought to look at it the other way around, Mr. Gillander." He twisted in his chair so that he was facing the musicians. "Tony and Bernie and this other guy here can spy on the folks in Mexican town for us. What do you say, *amigos*. Want to make a buck?"

The music paused momentarily when the Arruda brothers realized they were being addressed. The older two managed a wan laugh and stepped back into the shadow of the overhanging eucalyptus tree, unwilling to be lured into a political minefield. The youngest, smallest, best looking one—Alafair had not known his name at that point—swelled like a rooster ready to defend himself. One of his brothers put a discreet hand on his shoulder, a warning not to make things worse. The young man took the hint and deflated before flashing a grin that had no humor behind it.

Web's comment was greeted by dead silence from the guests. *Poor clumsy Web.* Alafair could not help but feel sorry for him when she realized the effect of his words. He had just been trying to lighten the mood, after all. Alafair shot a glance at Elizabeth, who was sitting with her head down and her eyes closed. Humiliated? Exasperated beyond endurance?

If nothing else, Alafair had admired the way Webster made amends after he realized how unfortunate his joke was. He stood and drew the Arrudas to the far corner of the yard in order to make a quiet apology out of earshot before he returned to his guests. The musicians resumed their places under the eucalyptus and played on as if nothing had happened.

The conversation turned to a less incendiary topic, though Alafair could tell from where she sat that the elder Gillander had not softened his stance. "Damn foreigners," he murmured under his breath, as he leaned down to sheathe the small knife he had drawn out of his boot at the first sign of trouble.

Thirst for Justice

And now, on the day after the party, Dr. Moeur drove away from Elizabeth's house after pronouncing Blanche Tucker much improved. He had also pronounced Bernie Arruda murdered.

"You go on inside, Alafair," Elizabeth said. "I'm going to run next door to Cindy's and tell her what Doc Moeur had to say and warn her that the law may be by directly to talk to us."

Alafair watched her sister head briskly across the yard and disappear around the back of her neighbor's house before she went indoors and found Shaw standing by the mantel.

He looked up at her as she came toward him. "Is the doctor gone?"

"Just left. Elizabeth went next door to tell Cindy what he said."

"Now, which one is Cindy?"

"You remember. Geoff Stewart's wife."

"Oh, yes. The one who looks like a schoolgirl who is about to succumb to the vapors."

Alafair tried not to smile at his apt description. "That's her. You know, Elizabeth has a notion in her head about this killing. She thinks the law will not be much bothered to find out what really happened. She thinks we ought to…well, I can't say exactly what she is proposing."

Shaw listened with one eyebrow raised as Alafair repeated what Elizabeth had said to her about assisting the sheriff and hoping for justice. When she finished he regarded her in silence for a second before he responded. "And what did you say?"

His wary tone affronted her. "What do you expect? I said I could not be getting involved in any such business."

His mustache twitched but he knew better than to grin. "Don't get your back up, sugar. You have been known to get yourself into tight corners."

"Well, this does not have anything to do with me or mine."

Shaw draped an arm over her shoulders. "I believe I've heard those words before. Sounds like more than one of the Gunn girls has inherited a thirst for justice hitched to a wayward curiosity. Be careful not to let Elizabeth lead you down the garden path."

She sniffed. "I can't be bothered with anything but Blanche."

"Good, then." He felt much less satisfied than he sounded. He was fond enough of Elizabeth, or had been when she was a perky, mouthy, little girl. She looked a good deal like a taller, more angular Alafair, which predisposed him to like her. The two women had the same "I can see right through you but I like you anyway" expression in their dark eyes.

She was like Alafair in other ways, he thought, though the personality traits they shared appeared to have skewed off in different directions. Where Alafair was decisive, Elizabeth seemed willful. Alafair's life revolved around her family. To his observation, Elizabeth's world revolved around herself. Well, maybe she was just young. Though he did not remember Alafair being like that when she was Elizabeth's age.

Perhaps he could not be sure what Elizabeth would do, but he did know that Alafair would never stand by and let her sister get into trouble if there was some way she could prevent it.

His train of thought was interrupted by the creak of the front door as Elizabeth returned.

"You weren't gone long," Alafair observed. "Was Cindy any more surprised than you were to hear that Bernie's death was due to murder?"

Elizabeth looked troubled. "Poor Cindy. She nigh to burst into tears. That girl is so tender. Ever since she lost the baby I swear she wears her heart on her sleeve. And that inconsiderate Geoff is spending the night in town again. I did not want to leave her on her own so I cajoled her into coming over here to spend the night. She's packing right now."

Sunday Morning

The family rose early and walked to the Congregational Church, just two blocks north and two blocks east to the corner of Sixth and Myrtle. There were churches galore in Tempe. One on every corner, it seemed, denominations of every ilk, including a Baptist Church, which is what their father would have insisted on for Sunday worship (though Tempe's was not quite the proper kind of Baptist). The denomination that Alafair and Shaw preferred, First Christian, was only a block from Elizabeth's front door. Alafair knew for a fact that Webster had been raised as Freewill Baptist, as Elizabeth had, which is why their father had favored him for his youngest daughter. However, Alafair expected that Elizabeth herself was the reason the Kemps had joined such a 'high' church. Elizabeth had more than likely attended every church in town until she found one that suited her, and Webster in his good-natured if vague way went along.

The Congregational Church was a handsome, tree-shaded brick building on a large lot. It had a large congregation, and judging from their dress and the number of autos in the lot, the parishioners were mostly well-to-do. Webster seemed to know everyone, and Alafair wondered if she had been wrong about who had instigated the Kemps' conversion to Congregationalism. Going to church with the cream of Tempe society could only be good for Webster's business.

As she listened to to the sermon, Alafair understood why Elizabeth and Webster favored this particular brand of Protestantism, bearing as it did little resemblance to the guilt-inducing hell-fire-and-damnation religion of their childhood. It did occur to her that perhaps Elizabeth and Web had converted from pure religious conviction, and she felt a bit guilty that she did not believe it for a minute.

Geoff Stewart was still nowhere to be seen, and Cindy had not accompanied them, but stayed abed in Elizabeth's upstairs guest room. Alafair asked after them and was told that the Stewarts were Methodists, as though that explained their lack of religious zeal.

After a leisurely walk home, Elizabeth and Alafair prepared a substantial meal of leftovers from the pot luck, and dinner was already on the table when Cindy Stewart finally joined them. Her soprano sing-song call wafted into the kitchen from the parlor. "Elizabeth?"

"In here, Cindy," Elizabeth called back.

Today Cindy was clad in a drop-waist aqua blue dress that matched her eyes. It was another beautiful March day, so they ate at the long table under the back yard ramada. The young woman looked pale and so fragile that a stiff breeze might blow her away. As the day progressed, Alafair's early opinion of Cindy as a flighty girl without much depth modified. Cindy Stewart was a sad woman. Her loss—and maybe more than her loss—was weighing on her under all that forced good humor. Elizabeth did not fuss over her and she did not have much to say, but Alafair was glad to see that Chase's antics seemed to cheer her. By the end of the meal she was looking brighter.

While Web excused himself and retired to his study and his beloved law books, the rest of the family remained in the back yard with their coffee and dessert. They sat under the ramada and watched the children play, accompanied by the raucous bleat of little goats and the pleasant calming murmur coming from Mrs. Carrizal's dovecotes.

The afternoon was bright and snappy, the air so clean it felt like you could see clear to forever. "Gracious, Elizabeth," Alafair exclaimed, "Do you never have bad weather?"

"Not at this time of year," Elizabeth admitted. "We enjoy the cool days while we can."

Las Cabras

They were just finishing their pie when a light breeze arose and Alafair was once more overwhelmed by the sweet scent of citrus blossoms, heavy as a blanket. She closed her eyes and took a deep breath in spite of herself. "I swan," she murmured.

Blanche knew without asking what had caught her mother's attention. "That's the orange tree in Artie Carrizal's back yard, Ma. He showed it to me the other night." She grabbed Alafair's hand and tugged her toward the back fence. "Come on and have a look."

Chase danced around in front of his new hero Shaw. "Come on, Uncle, come on Aunt! Come see *las cabras!*"

"The goats," Elizabeth translated. "He can't get enough of those goats."

"Well, let's go then!" Shaw swung the boy up onto his shoulder and seized Blanche's hand and the family trooped to the fence at the back of Elizabeth's deep yard. Several exotic fruit trees were planted in a small copse that spanned both sides of the fence.

On the Kemp side of the property the tree trunks had been whitewashed. On the Carrizal side each tree was encased its own chicken wire enclosure. The goats would destroy them otherwise. Alafair admired the rounded shape of the pretty little tree. It was covered with glossy, dark green leaves and tight, pea-like flower buds interspersed with tiny, star-shaped flowers at the ends of the branches.

Cindy trailed her fingers through the small white blossoms, little bouquets that were hardly visible from a distance. "You would think that as big as that odor is the flowers would be as showy as hydrangea."

Elizabeth pointed. "Look yonder, Alafair. There are a couple of oranges that did not get picked last month. They ripen around Christmas and New Year. Why, I don't believe Christmas is coming unless the orange trees put on their decorations."

"Well, I declare! I never have seen an orange on the branch. Look at that, Blanche!"

Blanche had already been distracted by her father and cousin who were petting the two curious little goats whose noses were stuck through the wire fence in hopes of a treat.

Elizabeth made an exasperated noise. "Those goats started out as young Artie Carrizal's Cooperative Extension project. But then he got attached to them and his papa allowed as he could keep them. Miz Carrizal likes them for their milk, and she makes a lot of cheese, too. Chase loves them, but I think they're a menace. They should not be out of their pen. They'll eat the bark right off the trees and everything else they come across."

"Once one of them got into my yard and ate up half my beautiful bougainvillea, thorns or no thorns, before I knew what was what," Cindy said. "They are smart little imps. They figured out how to lift the gate latch a long time ago. Artie ought to fix it up with a lock or tie it with a rope or something. They would probably teach themselves how to untie a rope, though."

Alafair knew a thing or two about goats. "Or just eat it, most likely."

Chase was buzzing around their knees, running from adult to adult grabbing skirts and trousers, trying for attention. He jerked up a handful of grass and waved it about before tossing it over the fence. The goats ignored it in favor of Blanche's less frantic blandishments but Chase did not seem to notice. "This one is called Chica and this one is Nina. I like her the best. Sometimes I can't tell which one is which. Artie lets me feed them. He gives them food right from his dinner after he's done with it."

Shaw put his hand on the boy's crown to stop him from spinning like a top. "Slow down there, partner. We can't understand a word you're saying! Aunt Elizabeth, how about if I take Blanche and Chase and go on up to Miz Carrizal's house and tell her that the goats are out? Maybe she'll let the young'uns help her put these fugitives back in their pen."

Blanche seized her mother's skirt. "Oh, yes, Ma," she breathed. "Please let us go visit Miz Carrizal."

Alafair looked down at her, amused. She was quite aware that there was someone besides Mrs. Carrizal Blanche wished to visit.

Artie

Blanche had been very much taken with Artie Carrizal when she met him for the first time at the pot luck. He was a tall, handsome, black-eyed boy, a couple of years older than Blanche. He had been dressed up for the party in a light-colored suit of knickerbockers and a belted, pinch-back jacket. Mrs. Carrizal had turned in her chair and beckoned across Elizabeth's parlor for Artie to come and meet Blanche, and the boy had ambled over and put a hand on his mother's shoulder. He looked at Alafair with a straightforward, friendly gaze. Alafair would have known who he was without an introduction. He was a perfect image of Mr. Carrizal, minus forty years.

"This is my son Arturo," Mrs. Carrizal said. "Arturo, this is Miz Kemp's sister Miz Tucker and her daughter Blanche, come to visit all the way from Oklahoma."

Arturo put his hand on his chest in a courtly gesture. "Pleased to meet you, Miz Tucker."

"Hello, Arturo," Alafair said. "Glad to meet you, too."

His gaze shifted from Alafair's face to Blanche's and he smiled. "Howdy, Blanche. Call me Artie. Everybody else does but my ma."

His mother was unchastened. "Arturo, Miz Tucker was just telling me that Blanche has never seen an orange tree before. Why do you not take Blanche out back and show her ours? This is the perfect time for it. It is in bloom right now and there are still a few oranges left after the harvest."

Most boys of his age might obey sulkily if their mothers told them to entertain a strange little girl, but Artie seemed to think this was a capital idea. He held out a hand. "Okay! Come on, Blanche. How about a fig tree? You ever seen a fig tree?"

Alafair could feel the electric jolt that went through Blanche's body when Arturo took her hand. Had the two children been five years older she would have been alarmed, but as it was Blanche's reaction amused her and made her happy. Artie's touch had infused Blanche with more energy than Alafair had seen in the girl in months. She hopped down off her mother's lap, still clutching her new friend's hand. "All right, Mama?" She asked the question without taking her eyes off Artie's face.

Alafair noticed the sudden pink tinge on Blanche's cheekbones. She did not attribute it to the return of her fever. "That is a fine idea, honey. Go on. Just don't get too tired and be sure and come back inside if you get to coughing again."

Blanche made an obedient sound and the children were gone out the front screen door. Alafair looked at Mrs. Carrizal. "I declare! That is the perkiest I have seen that child in an age," Alafair said. "Thank you."

Mrs. Carrizal had been watching the children as they dashed out of the room, but when Alafair spoke to her her attention shifted to the younger woman. "Sometimes one gets in the habit of sickness, I think, and only needs something or someone to take her mind to another place for awhile."

Interrogation

If it would give her an opportunity to see Artie again, Blanche was only too eager to let Chase drag her away to the Carrizal's to report the goats' escape. Alafair watched with a smile as the children left and Shaw followed.

Elizabeth was relieved to see them go. "I declare that boy wears me to a frazzle, Alafair! Blanche is mighty patient with him."

"She has had plenty of practice dealing with overexcited little ones, what with all the brothers and sisters she has. It's not good for Chase to be an only child, Elizabeth. He needs a brother or sister of his own to calm him down. You got any plans in that area?" Alafair did not feel the need to be tactful or discreet. Elizabeth was her sister after all, and who else but kin was going to come right out and say to you what you need to hear?

Unused to such straightforward talk, Cindy gasped. But Elizabeth was a Gunn and made of sterner stuff. She bit her lip to forestall a guffaw. "Well, you don't beat around the bush, do you, sister? The answer is no, I have no plans. I've got my hands full with that one." She hesitated, then added, "Truth is I haven't been exposed lately, so I don't expect to get the condition any time soon."

Elizabeth's forthright comment did not surprise Alafair overmuch. It had not taken Alafair five minutes after her arrival to see that there was something disagreeable going on between her sister and her brother-in-law.

Before Alafair could pursue Elizabeth's comment, a rangy man in a suit and Stetson came around the corner of the house and the women turned to face him.

He removed his hat as he strode across the yard toward them. "Is one of you ladies Miz Webster Kemp? I am Marshal Joe Dillon. I want to talk to y'all about the death of Bernie Arruda."

The clean, crisp, sunny day was too beautiful for anyone to undertake unpleasant business indoors. They situated themselves around the table under the grapevine-covered ramada, the marshal at the head with Shaw and Webster next to him on his left, Elizabeth and Cindy on his right, and Alafair at the opposite end of the table. By hasty agreement the children were still with Mrs. Carrizal. Cindy Stewart hunched down in her chair beside Elizabeth, looking perfectly miserable. She had tried to excuse herself, but the marshal had told her that since he was going to interrogate her anyway she might as well stay and save him a special trip to her house.

Alafair was surprised that he was not questioning them one at a time, but he did not seem to be concerned that they might influence one another's recollection of events. They had already filled him in on who the Tuckers were and why they were visiting, though he already knew much of their story from the newspaper.

"How did you come to find the body, Miz Tucker?" This was his first direct question about the murder.

Alafair closed her eyes before she answered, conjuring a memory she would rather not revisit.

Alafair had arisen that morning to a cool, pink, cloudless dawn, feeling more rested and content than she had in months. She left Shaw getting dressed and Blanche still asleep and made her way out onto the veranda and through the back door into the kitchen. She found Elizabeth frying eggs at her little gas stove and Web and Chase sitting at the table, each with a big goblet of milk before him and a look of anticipation on his face.

"Morning, all," she said.

Chase catapulted out of his chair and flung himself at her, wrapping his arms around her knees with a cheery greeting. Alafair attributed his impulsive hug more to an excess of energy than to an excess of affection and patted him on the head, amused. "Well, good morning, sugar-pie."

"Chase, sit down," Elizabeth ordered. "How did y'all sleep, Alafair?"

She could not help but smile. "Like a bunch of logs. I will tell you I had my doubts about spending an evening with a passel of strangers after Blanche being sick for so long and all. But I have to admit you were right, Elizabeth. We admired your neighbors all to pieces and I think it did us good. Web, I can't thank y'all enough for what you have done for us."

Elizabeth did not give Webster time to respond. "I'm so pleased to hear it, sister! I knew it would perk you up."

"You sure were right about that. Now, what can I do to help with breakfast?"

Elizabeth turned back to her frying pan. "Well, I'm low on fresh eggs and I haven't been out to the hen house this morning."

Alafair accepted the egg basket Elizabeth held out to her. "It would be my pleasure," she said.

Elizabeth's little chicken coop was tucked up behind a screen of shrubbery at the far side of the yard, behind the garage. She only had a handful of hens and no rooster, which Alafair thought was odd. But with only three people to feed she supposed it was less trouble for Elizabeth to simply buy more chicks if one of her hens stopped laying. She opened the gate to the small fenced chicken yard and slipped into the coop, where she robbed the indignant hens of half-a-dozen eggs before slipping out again.

She walked a few steps back toward the house and stopped to take in a deep breath. The air was cool and scented by citrus blossoms and the pleasant acrid odor of burning wood. The dawn was so pretty, so bracing and quiet, that she was loath to go back inside.

In order to make her excursion last another couple of minutes she walked around to the front of the house to get a better look at the blush of light on the eastern horizon.

She went up to the fence that surrounded the yard and looked up and down the street to see if anyone else in the neighborhood was stirring. She did not see any neighbors.

But there was something in the ditch.

Alafair opened her eyes and looked at Dillon. "I came outside to gather some eggs for breakfast." She nodded toward Elizabeth's chicken yard just visible at the far side of the property. "I had slept good, which has not been usual lately, and it was such a fair dawn that morning that I walked around to the front of the house to get a better look to the east."

"You went out the front gate to the street?"

"Not right away. I just went up to the fence and looked up and down the street to see if anyone was stirring. That is when I saw something in the ditch. The light was still shadowy so I could not tell what it was. But the size and shape of it gave me the shivers. So I went around and out the gate to get a better look."

The marshal looked up from his notes. "Later, you can show me right where you were standing when first you saw the body. Did you recognize him?"

"Well, I didn't remember his name but I recognized right off that he was one of the lads who had played music at the party last night."

"Did you touch him?"

"I felt his neck for a pulse, but nothing else. Then I fetched Shaw and Web and Elizabeth to see."

Elizabeth continued the tale. "We pondered the sad sight for a spell. Then I went back in the house and wrapped some bacon in a tortilla for Web to take with him to work, and he drove his Hupmobile to the constable's office to report the tragedy."

"Which I did," Web added.

"What did y'all do until Nettles arrived?"

"Nothing," Elizabeth told him. "Me and Alafair made breakfast for the children while Shaw stood watch over the body to make sure nothing got disturbed before the law got there."

Dillon looked at Shaw, but Shaw anticipated his question. "I didn't touch anything, either, Marshal. Just stood there and jawed with Mr. Carrizal when he showed up directly."

This interested Dillon. "Carrizal? His house faces out on the next street. How did he know to come over?"

"Chase run over there and told them as soon as he could escape," Elizabeth said. "But I corralled the little hyena before he could get out front to see the body."

Web leaned back in his chair. "Have you interviewed Geoff Stewart yet, Marshal?"

"Not yet. I expect to directly."

"Have you spoken to the poor dead man's family?" Alafair had her own notions about the proper order of investigation.

"First thing, Miz Tucker."

"Now as best I remember, Bernie left the shindig a little before his brothers did," Shaw said. "One of the others packed up Bernie's guitar and they took it with them when they finally went home. What did the brothers say happened after they left? Do they know where Bernie went?"

Dillon flipped his notebook closed and flashed a tobacco-stained grin at the curious faces around the table. "Now, who is questioning who, folks? Don't y'all worry about it. Everybody in town will know what we find out soon enough."

If he expected the Kemps or the Tuckers to look abashed he was disappointed. He cast a speculative glance at the one person who had had nothing to say. "When did you go home, Miz Stewart?"

Cindy shrank even further when Dillon looked at her, but answered readily enough. "Later than most. Maybe eight o'clock. I stayed for a bit afterwards to help Elizabeth and Miz Carrizal clean up."

"See anything odd when you left?"

"No, sir. I left out the back and went into my house through the back door, so I didn't pass by the street at all. But everything seemed normal as far as I could tell."

"When did you first hear that a body had been found?"

"A little after dawn. I heard the commotion in the street and looked out the front door to see what was going on. I was still in my dressing gown so did not care to go outside. I called to young Ellen Piper from across the street and asked her what was happening and she told me that Bernie Arruda had drowned in the canal."

"What did you do then?"

She blinked at him. Though her face was ashen she was composed when she answered. "I felt so awful. He was a nice man. He repaired my front fence just last month."

"When did you learn he had been killed and not drowned?"

"Elizabeth told me yesterday after Doctor Moeur left. I was shocked, of course. I do not know of anyone who could do such a thing."

"Did your husband stay late to the party, too?"

Cindy's eyes shifted away from the marshal's face and back again. "No, he left an hour or so earlier than me."

Elizabeth jumped in. "Lots of people left out the front way after he did, and I can promise you that no one saw a body in the canal."

Dillon cast her a glance but continued questioning Cindy. "So was Mr. Stewart asleep when you finally made your way home?"

Cindy bit her lip and flushed, but said nothing. There was an instant of silence before all four of the others leaned forward and propped their elbows on the table. "Where was your husband, Miz Stewart?" Dillon's tone was neutral.

For a moment Cindy looked as though she was going to cry. "Well…after he left the party, he went back to his office to catch up on some work."

High Feelings

The marshal laced his fingers together. "When did your husband finally get home that night, Miz Stewart?"

Cindy looked away again, an embarrassed expression on her face, and did not answer. Dillon asked, "He didn't come home? He ain't home now?"

"He has a big filing deadline coming up directly. He often spends the night at his office, Marshal. That's where he is right now." Cindy's expression was earnest. "He has a cot in the back. It is way easier on him than making his way back here on foot in the wee hours of morning."

The marshal's eyes narrowed.

Web spoke up in Cindy's defense. "Both me and Geoff do that sometimes—stay over to catch up work. There is a cot and a washstand in a little room behind the offices."

Dillon did not comment. He turned back to Elizabeth. "I hear Matt Carrizal and Bernie got into a scrape."

Elizabeth drew back as if she had been slapped. "What? I was not aware of any such of a thing."

"Me, neither." Cindy and Alafair spoke at once.

"There were some high feelings expressed that night about the situation on the border, Marshal," Shaw said. He hesitated, oddly unwilling to mention Matt's reaction to the way Geoff Stewart had treated his wife. "But I didn't see Matt Carrizal get tangled up in any 'scrape.'"

Dillon looked skeptical as he listened to the recounting of events. "Nobody drew a knife?"

There was an instant of silence as everyone at the table digested his question.

He has spoken to someone who has made out Matt Carrizal to be at fault, Alafair thought. She was unwilling to let that impression stand. "That was Mr. Gillander," she offered. Both Cindy and Elizabeth gasped as Alafair continued. "Somebody made a joke that one of the Arruda boys took poorly, and I reckon the old man thought there might be an altercation. He reached for a boot knife. But he didn't even get it all the way drawn before the whole business blew over."

"Who made this joke?"

Alafair glanced at Elizabeth and said nothing.

"Who made this joke?" Dillon repeated.

"It was me," Web admitted. His face was red with embarrassment

"If you were better acquainted with my husband, Marshal, you would not take any ill meaning from his poorly timed jest." Elizabeth's tone was more exasperated than reluctant.

Uncivil Words

Dillon gave them all an introspective once-over. "And nobody remembers seeing Matt Carrizal take Arruda aside and exchange uncivil words right before he left?"

"Who said he did such a thing?" Elizabeth demanded, but Dillon did not spare her a look.

Shaw straightened. "Matt Carrizal and the Arrudas did converse for a spell. I didn't hear what was said but it all looked right civil to me. If you mean what I think you mean, somebody other than Matt Carrizal exchanged heated words with Arruda, and as far as scrapes go, it was not much of a one."

"Tell me about it, Mr. Tucker." Dillon was cool.

Shaw hesitated. "Well, I hate to say, but it was Geoff Stewart. He came late, as you know, so most folks were already here when he showed up. He seemed tired-like to me and not in the best mood, I figured from working late. But he did stop to talk a spell with Levi Gillander. I couldn't hear what they were talking about but whatever it was like to put Stewart out, and he didn't have much to say to anybody after that. He stayed maybe another half-hour before he decided he would leave. He passed right in front of the band on his way out, and I saw him exchange a word with one of the boys. I didn't know one from the other so maybe it was Bernie he spoke to and maybe not, but from the way they were carrying on, the talk they were having was not a pleasant one. Didn't last but a minute before Stewart stomped off. I thought he went home, 'cause he headed across toward his own back door. Nobody came to blows that I saw, though. Is that the scrape you are talking about?" Shaw was gazing narrowly at the marshal as though still not convinced this was the incident in question.

Dillon's answer was a question. "That's all you saw?"

As far as Alafair was concerned this put a whole new spin on the situation. "From what I'm hearing, you had best be looking at Mr. Gillander rather than Geoff. He sounds like a rabble-rouser. He was going on like ninety about how everybody of Mexican blood who lives in Arizona is going to revolt and they're spies and all. More than likely it is that comment that put Bernie out of sorts rather than Webster's poor joke or Geoff's tempersome remarks."

"Alafair!" Elizabeth sounded shocked.

Dillon was scratching away in his notebook. "I don't know this Gillander. What is his first name?"

Elizabeth cast a worried glance toward Cindy before she said, "Duncan."

"How do y'all know him, Miz Kemp? Is he one of your neighbors?"

This time it was Cindy who answered. "He is my father, Marshal."

Alafair nearly fell out of her seat, but the marshal was not fazed. "Are you of the opinion that your father has a particular problem with Mexicans, Miz Stewart?"

"Now, wait just a blamed minute, Marshal." Elizabeth's tone was sharp. "I have known Mr. Gillander for years. I admit that Webster has been known to speak before he thinks, though he never means ill. Mr. Gillander is a blowhard, and Geoff has a big mouth—forgive me, Cindy, but it's true—but that don't mean any of them is a killer. "

"I'm not calling anybody a killer." Dillon's tone was mild. "Miz Kemp, I'll require that you relate to me when each of your guests left, to the best of your ability. Let's start with Mr. Gillander."

Elizabeth's expression was mutinous. But she answered the question. "He left just about dark like most folks did. My Carrizal neighbors and Cindy's brother Levi stayed on for an hour or so to help Shaw and Web tote chairs and tables back into the storage shed and clean up the yard."

Dillon nodded and wrote, then handed Elizabeth his notebook. "Now, Miz Kemp, take a minute and write down a list of everybody you can remember who was here that night." He turned to Cindy. "While she is doing that, do you mind if I have a peek inside your house, Miz Stewart?"

Cindy looked as though she was going to faint. Her mouth worked but no words came out.

Elizabeth took Cindy's hand. "Wait, Cindy. Geoff is a lawyer, Marshal. I do not expect he would much appreciate you rummaging through his house without his permission, especially if you do not have a warrant."

"I know Geoff well enough to second my wife's opinion," Web added. "I expect a warrant is necessary in any event, Marshal."

Alafair and Shaw followed the exchange, heads swiveling as though they were at a tennis match.

"Miz Stewart's permission is all I need."

Cindy's words finally burst forth. "Oh, I cannot, Marshal, not without Geoff says it's all right. You will have to ask Geoff."

Dillon's glare suggested that he would happily throttle both Elizabeth and Webster, but he maintained his professional civility. "All right, then, I will be back later with a warrant. While I'm at it, Miz Kemp, I will have the judge issue a search warrant for your house as well."

Elizabeth did not look up from the list she was making. "Be my guest. I have nothing to hide."

Web had been listening with calm interest, his hands folded comfortably over his stomach. "Marshal, I have a question. I've been wondering why a marshal is investigating this murder and not a sheriff's deputy. Is there some reason the federal government should be involved in a local case?"

Dillon's reply was mild. "I'm just helping out. Sheriff Adams has had his hands full lately." Without further elaboration, he stood and put his hat on. "I will wish y'all a good day."

"Hang on, Marshal." Dillon paused when Shaw spoke. "Can you tell us at least if Dr. Moeur has given his opinion on what sort of instrument was used to do murder?"

"I can tell you the doc thinks that it was something broad and smooth. Not uneven like a rock, nor narrow, like a fireplace poker or cane."

Shaw nodded. "Metal, does he think, or wood? Maybe a brick?"

The marshal's cheek twitched, whether in amusement or annoyance was hard to tell. "I reckon that's all I aim to tell you right now."

After Dillon's broad back disappeared around the corner of the house, Elizabeth gave Shaw a curious look. "You have an idea what he may be looking for, murder-weapon-wise?"

"Sounds like Bernie's head was stove in by something like a club." Shaw leaned back in his chair, a thoughtful expression on his face. "Or a baseball bat."

"Oh, mercy," Alafair groaned. "There were bats galore abroad that night."

Baseball

Someone had brought out a baseball bat as the evening progressed, which prompted a neighbor to produce a baseball. A rock, a burlap bag, a palm leaf served as bases one, two and three, while squarely in the middle of Willow Street a newspaper held down by a handful of pebbles served as home base. Elizabeth found a couple more bats in her storage shed and Cindy sent Artie Carrizal to her house to retrieve Geoff's bat and glove from a bedroom closet. A few more balls of various sizes and conditions eventually appeared. Team makeup was fluid. Groups of players coalesced, dissolved, reformed. At one point there were nine people in the outfield and two shortstops, but no one seemed to mind. At first, most of the players were boys, but that did not last long. Cap Irish joined in as catcher almost immediately, followed shortly by several other men, then a number of girls. Blanche begged to be allowed to play, but Alafair's refusal was adamant, so Blanche ended up as the equipment manager and sometime umpire for the evening.

A few women took their turns at bat, including Alafair, who hit a double when her ball got lost for a time in a honeysuckle hedge in right field. She was put out at third, but Shaw managed a home run during one of his at-bats. He scooped up Chase on third as he went around and carried him across home base under his arm for a score of two.

Alafair was mildly concerned that runners had to leap a narrow irrigation ditch to get from second to third, but even the smallest players were unhindered by the jump. In fact, it seemed to add an extra degree of interest to the game.

Levi Gillander had a particularly colorful style at home plate which involved three taps on the base, several hip rotations leading to an aggressive crouch, followed by a couple of whiffs and a high choke on the bat.

Artie Carrizal had been the pitcher for the evening. He had a good arm, Alafair thought, able to deliver a scorcher across the plate for a grown-up, or toss a softy to a six-year-old that seemed to float in the air until the youngster figured out how to lay his bat on it.

The game went on until it was too dark to see the ball, and families began to take their leave. Levi Gillander, Matt Carrizal, and several of the children went around to pick up balls, bats, and bases and either return them to their owners or stow them in the Kemps' shed to be claimed later. Web and Shaw went to the front of the house to bid farewell to the guests and see that everyone got to their vehicles. Artie Carrizal and his father began gathering up chairs and tables while Elizabeth and Cindy were having a quiet word with the musicians as they packed up their instruments. Alafair saw Web, Matt, and two or three other people hand one of the players coins or small envelopes. The evening's gratuity, she expected. Alafair and the Carrizal women began to help clear the leftovers and bedraggled decorations from the makeshift buffet under the grape arbor, and eventually Elizabeth joined them. As they walked past on their way to their horse-drawn cart, Alafair noticed that there were only two Arruda brothers now instead of three. It had not meant much to her at the time.

She Has Her Rights

"I could bite my tongue off, Cindy! If I had known Mr. Gillander was your daddy, I would have never opened my big mouth." Alafair gripped Cindy's hands in her own as she apologized. "My aim was to get the marshal to consider that there are others besides Geoff who bear looking at."

"Oh, it's all right, Miz Tucker. How could you know? Elizabeth is right. Father is a blowhard and always getting himself into trouble with his injudicious remarks. Even so, Geoff is going to kill me when he finds out the marshal is getting a warrant to search the house."

"It's not your fault, Cindy," Web told her. "Dillon will end up getting warrants to search the houses of nigh to everybody who was here that night anyway."

"Now, you look just about done in," Elizabeth interjected. "Why don't you go home and have a lie-down? I'll come over later and see how you're doing."

Web stood and offered Cindy his arm. "I'll escort you."

Cindy was relieved to be dismissed. Elizabeth, Alafair, and Shaw watched in silence until she and Web crossed through the back gate. The second they were out of earshot Alafair rounded on her sister. "Why did you tell her not to let Dillon search her house?"

Elizabeth crossed her arms and settled back in her seat. "I was trying to save her some trouble, sister. I know Geoff. If she had allowed Dillon to poke through the house without him knowing about it beforehand there would have been the devil to pay. Besides, I don't like to see Dillon taking advantage of her like that. She has her rights, even if she is too innocent to know it."

"Now he's likely suspicious that she is hiding something," Shaw observed.

"I doubt it." Elizabeth shook her head. "Now he likely thinks Cindy is weak as dishwater and I'm a big old interferer. And you know what? If he had hunted though her house without a warrant and found something that incriminated Geoff, he would not have been able to use it as evidence in a court of law anyway. This way anything he finds is fair game for the prosecution. Dillon knows it, too. You notice how he was interested in Matt Carrizal, who may have a Spanish name but is the most unlikely person in the world to kill somebody. Dillon just don't want a prominent white lawyer to be the killer."

Shaw was surprised. "You think Geoff did it."

A rueful smile passed over Elizabeth's face. "No, I don't, really. More's the pity."

"You really do not care for Geoff Stewart." Alafair stated the obvious.

Elizabeth neither confirmed or denied. "We had better fetch the children back and get this food cleared away before we draw flies."

The Search

Early the next morning, Dillon showed up at Elizabeth's door with a search warrant and three deputies.

Shaw had gone into town, but Cindy had returned to Elizabeth's house not long after sunup, dressed in a voluminous smock, rumpled and floury after making cookies to bring for a morning snack. Artie Carrizal was there, as well, having obtained his mother's permission to skip school this once and spend the day with his ailing new friend. When Dillon's crew showed up, Elizabeth and Alafair calmly ushered Cindy and the children onto the front porch. The females sat sipping tea while the boys pressed their noses against the outside of the windows, watching enthralled as the lawmen methodically opened every drawer and cabinet and poked into every corner of the house.

After the men finished with the house they moved on to the yard and the outbuildings. As one of the deputies walked toward the hen house, Elizabeth called to him. "While you're searching the nest boxes, Mister, be a dear and gather today's eggs for me, would you?"

The fellow tipped his hat, amused at her brass, before he disappeared around the corner. Artie and Chase trotted after the deputy, barely acknowledging Alafair's warning to stay out of the searchers' way. Blanche followed the boys at a more demure pace.

Cindy was hardly as sanguine about the turn of events as her friend. "Aren't you afraid that they will find something incriminating, Elizabeth? If Dillon takes a notion, he could make something out of nothing and you'd be in a world of trouble."

Elizabeth pooh-poohed the idea. "There is nothing to find, Cindy, as Dillon well knows."

Alafair wondered at Elizabeth's untroubled demeanor. "I hope you're right."

Elizabeth's eyes crinkled mischievously, which made Alafair's widen with amazement. Elizabeth was enjoying herself!

As the thought crossed her mind, a deputy walked across the yard with a baseball bat in either hand, and Cindy emitted a squeak of dismay. "Oh, Elizabeth!"

Elizabeth shared an exasperated glance with Alafair. "Cindy, for goodness sake. Those are the bats we always keep in the shed. Everybody in town owns bats. Before they're through hunting for the murder weapon, they'll confiscate a dozen bats and clubs and chair legs from every house and shed they search."

"I expect they'll look at them all for traces of blood or hair," Alafair explained.

"What if one of those bats is the one? What if the killer stashed it in your shed!"

Elizabeth laughed. "Ooh. What if Web did it? Wouldn't that be something?"

"Now, Elizabeth," Alafair scolded, "there's no need to be so flip. A life has ended, after all."

Elizabeth sat back in her chair. "You are right, sister. I regret teasing you so, Cindy, but your imagination is overwrought. They will not find the murder weapon, not here, probably not anywhere. Dillon has been dithering about, threatening all and sundry with search warrants. Unless the killer is stupid beyond human understanding, he got rid of the weapon long ago."

Elizabeth's logic seemed to calm Cindy, and she even smiled. Dillon came back into the front yard trailing the children a few yards behind him, and stopped at the foot of the porch.

"I assume you have what you came for," Elizabeth said.

Dillon took a folded paper out of his coat pocket. "Here's a receipt for everything we confiscated for testing, Miz Kemp.

I'll let you know when and if you can reclaim your property." Elizabeth leaned forward and reached across the porch wall to take the list out of the marshal's hand. Dillon withdrew a second paper and turned to Cindy. "And now, Miz Stewart, we are ready to move on to your property."

Seated on either side of her, Alafair and Elizabeth each grabbed one of Cindy's arms to keep her from falling out of her chair. Her reaction seemed to give Dillon some satisfaction.

"We'll just stay right here, Marshal." Elizabeth's tone was brittle. "You let us know when you're done so we can clean up the mess."

Dillon turned on his heel and was just walking through the front gate when Elizabeth said, "I'd like to smack that smirk right off his face."

"What shall I do?" Cindy managed. Her voice shook.

"You shall do nothing," Elizabeth informed her. "You have nothing to feel guilty about."

They were distracted by the appearance of Dillon's deputy coming around the side of the house holding his hat in both hands. "Here you go, Miz Kemp." He held the hat out so the women could see the half-dozen eggs cradled in the crown of his fedora.

"Well, now," Alafair said. "I reckon we should bake a cake."

The house was in surprisingly good shape, Alafair thought, considering that several men had been rearranging things. Alafair and Elizabeth, with the help of the children, cleaned and mopped and put furniture and clothing back in order. Since she was already flour-dusted, Cindy set to baking a cake and preparing dinner, a task labor-intensive enough to keep her mind occupied while Dillon's troops pawed through her belongings.

Elizabeth looked surprised when a deputy finally knocked on her door. The searchers had spent less time at the Stewart house than they had at the Kemps'. "Here's the inventory of what they took, Cindy." She waved the paper at her. "It isn't a long list. He told me to let you know that the warrants are good for several days more, and they might be back. He did ask me if I knew when was the last time y'all burned your trash. I said I didn't rightly know and he should ask you, but he said he'd rather put it to Geoff."

Cindy blinked. "Burned our trash? Why would he…? Geoff usually takes care of that. Not since before the open house, I think."

Elizabeth put her cup down. "No, it was the day after, Cindy. I didn't notice till the afternoon because of all the hubbub with finding Bernie's body and all, but your incinerator was still smoking when I went out to feed the hens after dinner. The wind carried the smoke over and it stung my eyes."

"I never noticed! Geoff must have done it before he left to go back to the office. Do you expect they found something in the ashes?"

"I wouldn't worry about it, honey," Elizabeth soothed. "They likely came up with something they can't identify and want Geoff to tell them what it is. He'll clear it all up when they talk to him."

Esmeralda

Mrs. Carrizal sat in a bright yellow cane-bottomed kitchen chair with a carved back and legs, holding a dozing Chase in her lap. This was the first time Alafair had been inside the Carrizal house. She was almost as impressed by the decor as she was by the decorator. *This is more like it,* Alafair thought. The large, homey kitchen was filled with light and color. In fact all that Alafair had seen of the house was rife with eye-popping color, from the walls to the painted wood furniture to the upholstery, rugs, and cushions. The surfaces were covered with weird succulents and blooming cactuses and the walls were covered with family portraits and religious icons, including a crucifix that Alafair could barely keep her eyes off of. Elizabeth had told her that the Carrizals were Catholic, and apparently it was true. She felt strangely excited to be sitting inside the home of an actual Roman Catholic.

Mrs. Carrizal had sat them down with steaming mugs of milky tea and a plate of sugary donut-like pastries she called *buñuelos* and listened in silence as Elizabeth related Dillon's interview.

"He'll probably be around to talk to y'all before long, Miz Carrizal." Elizabeth paused long enough to dip her pastry into her tea and take a bite. "I declare, I never had occasion to meet the marshal before, but I must say I did not much cotton to him. He asked us all sorts of questions about Matt and Bernie and how they got along. I expect he has already figured out in his head what must have happened and he is going to bend and twist the facts around to make them fit his theory."

Alafair felt she had to add a note of caution. "Now, Elizabeth, to be fair he has just started asking around. He's likely to hear all kinds of tales about what went on the other night. I'm sure he'll pick out the wheat from the chaff."

"I hope you're right."

Mrs. Carrizal smiled and shifted the sleeping boy in her lap. It crossed Alafair's mind that this was the quietest and most content she had ever seen Chase Kemp. "Alejandro and I have been expecting that the marshal would want to speak to us. There is no reason to worry about us. There is no reason to worry about Matt, either," Mrs. Carrizal added. "He is a friendly young man, as anyone will tell you, and it is no surprise that he spoke to the musicians. After all, all the Arrudas have worked in Matt's restaurant at one time or another. This is more than likely why Dillon is interested. Besides, none of us will have any trouble explaining where we were during the night when the poor Arruda boy was killed."

Elizabeth sighed. "I hope so. I do fear that Dillon may have his suspicions up about Geoff Stewart and Mr. Gillander, too!"

Oh, dear!" Mrs. Carrizal's eyes widened. "Such a worry for Cindy. That poor child does not need more grief. I will make a point of visiting her this evening."

"Excellent notion," Elizabeth approved. "Take some of these *buñuelos* with you, Miz Carrizal. These would cheer up anybody."

Alafair had not noticed it earlier, but today she was detecting a slight lilt when Mrs. Carrizal spoke. A bit of a Mexican accent? Alafair was not familiar enough to know.

"How long have you lived in Arizona, Miz Carrizal?" She thought that was as discreet a way to ask about the woman's background as any.

Mrs. Carrizal surprised her. "Oh, I was born right here in Arizona. My papa Elian Ruvio owned a cattle ranch outside of Tubac. The King of Spain granted parts of that land to the first

Elian Ruvio in 1701. My nephew owns it now." She smiled. "It was part of the United States by the time I was born. Alejandro grew up in Tucson. His father was quite a successful business-man down there."

Blanche, who had been playing with the goats behind the house, wandered into the kitchen and helped herself to a sweet bun before climbing into her mother's lap. At nearly eleven years old and long limbed, Blanche was almost too big to be sitting on anyone's lap, so Alafair absently adjusted the girl on her knee as she spoke to Mrs. Carrizal. "What did you say your husband's name is? Alejandro? How beautiful that is! May I know your Christian name, Miz Carrizal?"

"I am called Esmeralda. In English, it means 'emerald'."

"Oh, that is just lovely. Mexican names are way prettier than our English names."

"Your name is 'Alafair', yes? That is quite as lovely as any Mexican name. What does it mean?"

Alafair shot a glance at Elizabeth, who seemed as interested in hearing the answer as Mrs. Carrizal was. "I must admit that I don't know. I was named after my great-grandmother Alafair Napier. She lived a good long life and died when I was eight. To me she seemed like a big, laughing woman who ordered everybody around. She had a snow white braid down her back. That made a big impression on me."

Mrs. Carrizal shifted the napping Chase on her lap so she could lean forward and take Blanche's hand. "'Blanche' is a wonderful thing to be called, *carita*. We have the same name in Spanish, but we say *Blanca.*"

A delighted smile turned up the corners of Blanche's mouth. "I like that!"

"And you have such beautiful green eyes! Perhaps your mama should have called you 'Esmeralda' as well." An odd expression came over Mrs. Carrizal's face as she looked into Blanche's eyes. "How have you been feeling, honey?"

Something in her tone caused Alafair to catch her breath, but Blanche rather expected adults to make incongruent shifts in topic when they spoke to her and she answered readily. "Way much better since I been here, ma'am. I don't hardly cough much at all any more, nor does it hurt so much when I do."

Mrs. Carrizal looked up at Alafair, her black eyes pools of concern. "Did Doctor Moeur have a look at her?"

"He did. He said the same thing as our doctor back home, that her lungs got inflamed over the wet winter and a spell of drying out would do her good."

Mrs. Carrizal nodded absently. "Doctor Moeur is very good with problems of the chest. Some inflammation of the lungs, yes. But something more, I think."

"What makes you think so?" Alafair was alarmed.

The older woman made a pass with two fingers in front of her face. "Something in the eyes."

She looked back down at Blanche, who had sunk back against her mother's shoulder and was gazing at her with her familiar wary expression. Mrs. Carrizal's smile returned. "I am sorry, Blanche. I should not talk about you as though you are not here. Tell me, did it happen a while back that you were in some dirty water? Perhaps you went swimming in a pond last summer, or fell into the river?"

Blanche's eyebrows knit. How would Mrs. Carrizal know to ask her such a thing?

Bathtub Boating

For Blanche the winter of 1915 and 1916 had already been like no other in her short life. To begin with she had never seen so much rain. Christmas had almost been ruined by it. At first it was kind of fun running around the house inspecting for drips. And when you found one you got to put one of Mama's old pots or a worn dishpan under it. It got so it was hard to sleep, what with the sound of all that plinking and plopping and clinking. Her next-to-youngest sister Sophronia said it did not bother her so much because it was kind of like music. But then Fronie was odd that way.

All the gullies had run deep and swift for days on end, and it had been lots of fun to take the old rusty tin bathtub out of the storage shed and a couple of sawed-off brooms and go boating. Of course there was that time that she decided to stand up in the tub and row like one of those fellows in Italy whose picture she had seen in her geography book. She supposed she got to rocking too much because she fell over into the muddy water. It was cold, too, and she was so shocked that she took a big gasp and gulped that dirty stuff before she knew what was what. She was a pretty good swimmer but that had got her all discombobulated. She hadn't known which way was up and flailed around for a spell until her brother Charlie grabbed her by the collar, hauled her out on the bank, and pounded on her back until she had spewed out about a gallon of ick. They had contemplated not telling

Mama, but Blanche had looked too much like a drowned rat to walk into the house saucy as you please and pretend nothing had happened. Mama had just laughed, but then she had made Blanche take a warm bath and go right to bed with some hot flannel-wrapped bricks at her feet.

The coughing had started pretty soon after that.

Curandera

"I don't remember that!" Alafair was incredulous. She briefly closed her eyes and rubbed her forehead as she tried to recollect the incident Blanche had just related. She supposed it was no wonder that particular event was lost among all the other hundreds of mishaps and mischiefs a mother of ten dealt with every day. She could not count the number of times over the past winter each and every one of the children had come into the house soaked to the skin. Or how many days in a row her screened back porch had been webbed with lines of dripping clothing. How many hundreds of gallons of water she had heated for hot baths, soups, teas, water bottles, throat balms, steam pots?

And that old washtub boat! Every year since Martha was old enough to drag a tub along by herself some child or another went boating in whatever likely body of water was handy. The older ones had taught the skill to the younger ones, just as she had taught her younger siblings and her older cousins had taught her.

She opened her eyes and looked at Mrs. Carrizal, but it was Elizabeth who asked the question. "Do you think there was something in the ditchwater that got into Blanche's lungs, Miz Cee?"

Blanche's eyes widened. "Ma?"

Alafair gave Elizabeth a withering glance before wrapping an arm around Blanche's middle. "Sugar, there is no reason for you to be scared. We can fix whatever ails you. Why don't you take Chase back outside while we study on this. I will tell you all about it later and not keep any secrets from you. Would that be all right?"

Chase heard his name spoken and was awake instantly. He hopped down from Mrs. Carrizal's lap and hurled himself toward the back door. "Come on, Blanche!" His imperious summons hung in the air as the door slammed behind him.

Blanche looked Alafair in the eye. "Promise? I'm not a baby anymore."

"I know you're not. I promise."

Blanche had never had reason to doubt her mother's promises. She stood and smoothed her skirt with dignity before following Chase outdoors.

Elizabeth spoke first. "I am sorry I was thoughtless with my remark, Alafair. I would not scare that child for the world."

"Don't fret about it, Elizabeth. Now, Miz Carrizal?" Alafair let the question hang.

Mrs. Carrizal bit her bottom lip as she considered how to explain her diagnosis. "I think Dr. Moeur and your doctor at home were right. The cold and damp Blanche endured made it hard for her to get better. But do you know how sometimes after a long period of wet weather mold will grow in places that cannot dry out…" The look on Alafair's face gave her pause. "I will say to you what you said to Blanche, sweetheart. Do not worry. I have seen this before, and there are many things that can be done."

Elizabeth gave Alafair's arm a shake. "Listen to Miz Carrizal, sister. I have had many occasions over these past years to take advantage of her skills, and I swear, no doctor knows more of the healing arts."

Alafair did not quite know how to feel as she listened to Mrs. Carrizal's diagnosis. Terrified? Hopeful? Doctor Moeur himself had told her that Mrs. Carrizal was a talented *curandera*. A vision of the white lady she had seen that first night in Tempe arose unbidden in Alafair's mind. *Nothing happens by chance,* she thought, and was flooded with gratitude that she had been led to come here.

"I will come over tonight with a healing tea that I will brew for the child," Mrs. Carrizal said, "if that is convenient, Elizabeth. With the help of our Blessed Lady, I believe we can drive the evil out of Blanche's lungs once and for all."

Out of the Ashes

After she and Elizabeth left Mrs. Carrizal's house, it took Alafair a few minutes to locate Blanche in order to tell her everything that was said in her absence. Chase was still playing with the goats in their pen, and he told them that Blanche had said she was going to wait for her mother in her bedroom.

"I expect she's anxious," Alafair said to Elizabeth, as they walked back toward the Kemps' house.

Elizabeth colored. "I apologize once again, sister. Blanche seems older to me than she is, I reckon. Yet I didn't consider my words when I speculated on Miz Carrizal's meaning."

Alafair came within a hair's breadth of telling Elizabeth she agreed with that assessment, but stopped herself before the words left her mouth. Her sister realized her error, and it was not going to help anything to make her feel worse than she did. Instead Alafair said, "Children are aware of a lot more than we give them credit for," and let it go at that. "I'll go in and tell her about how Miz Carrizal is going to make her a curing tea. Truth is that I am feeling right good about Blanche's prospects after hearing what Miz Carrizal had to say. Blanche is already so improved as to be almost well. And now I hold out hope for a total cure."

Elizabeth looked relieved. "She is likely to feel a heap better after you tell her that."

Alafair paused when she noticed Artie Carrizal in a corner of the yard. He was alone, engaged with his own thoughts, languidly swinging back and forth on the inner tube that Web had suspended from a eucalyptus limb. He looked their way when they passed through the gate into the Kemp property, then disentangled himself and came over when Alafair beckoned.

"Yes, ma'am?"

Alafair put a hand on the boy's shoulder. "Son, were you watching the deputies when they searched through Mr. Stewart's outbuildings and property?"

"Yes, ma'am. Me and Blanche watched them from over by the gate. Was that wrong?"

"No, y'all didn't do wrong to watch the deputies search. I want to ask if you saw them find anything that caused a stir. Anything in the back yard incinerator in particular?"

"Yes, ma'am, the fellow who was raking out the ashes come up with something and called over Mr. Dillon to look at it. They put it in a cloth bag and took it away."

"Could you tell what it was?" Elizabeth asked.

Artie held his hands about a foot apart. "It was a hunk of wood, yea big. It was mostly burned and black, but it had a turned knob on the end. It looked to me like the grip end of a baseball bat."

Alafair and Elizabeth locked eyes, shocked, but in order not to alarm the boy, neither said anything. Even after Alafair thanked Artie and sent him on his way, the women were silent. This revelation demanded thought.

Beautiful Girl

Alafair and Elizabeth parted on the veranda. The north-facing bedroom that the Tuckers shared was already beginning to grow dim in the afternoon light, so it took an instant for Alafair to see Blanche lying on the double bed. She was curled up on her side, facing her mother, asleep. Alafair crossed the room and put her hand on Blanche's forehead. Her cheeks had a rosy flush but her skin felt cool. No fever. Sleep had smoothed all anxiety from her features. In the shadowed room, her hair seemed to be no more than a cloud of darkness falling in waves down her back and over her shoulder. Long, black eyelashes and arches of black brows stood out against her creamy skin.

Suddenly Alafair perceived with crystal clarity what her sister had meant when she said Blanche was destined to make all the boys cry. Her darling little girl was beautiful. But rather than give her pleasure, the realization caused her a stab of fear. All of her children were attractive, but her third daughter Alice, tall and witty with pale blue eyes and hair the color of ripe wheat, was generally acknowledged to be stunning. Alice knew it, too, and had always used her looks as well as her intellect to get what she wanted. She had gotten herself a handsome, successful husband who, Alafair suspected, was going to break her heart.

Since the day Alice had married, Alafair lived in fear of her downfall. She had no desire to live in fear for Blanche as well. Not for her health or for her happiness. Not her darling Blanche.

No, Alafair had to admit that of all her beloved children, any one of whom she would die for a thousand times, it could be that Blanche was her favorite, her sweet, pouty, work-brittle little girl who was always so eager for affection and ready with hugs.

She stood over the sleeping child for some minutes, considering whether to wake her. She decided not to disturb her healing sleep just yet. She could fulfill her promise later.

Observations on a Killing

Alafair found Elizabeth on the front porch, sitting in a rocker with her hands clasped in her lap, staring thoughtfully into middle space. "You look rapt," Alafair observed.

Only Elizabeth's dark, almond-shaped eyes shifted to look at her. "I still am worrying over that burned bat. Shall I go over and tell Cindy what Artie saw? Do you think it looks bad for Geoff?"

Alafair shrugged. "I don't know. Why would Geoff want to kill Bernie? But then why would he want to burn a bat if not to get rid of it?"

"Maybe it wasn't Geoff who fired the incinerator," Elizabeth speculated.

"Who else?"

One of Elizabeth's shapely brows lifted. "Bernie's killer, of course. You can't see into the Stewarts' back yard from ours unless you're standing right at the gate, so anybody could have gone over there and done it without our knowing about it, I reckon. Or maybe the bat was under the other trash and Geoff didn't see it if he's the one who set the trash alight. That is most likely what he'll tell the marshal."

"I'm guessing that the marshal is at the law office right now putting the thumbscrews to him, though."

Elizabeth abruptly stopped rocking and turned to face Alafair. "No, he isn't. Dillon will ask Geoff what he knows about it and Geoff will say he knows nothing, and the marshal will take his word for it. I will bet you fifty dollars that Dillon don't expend his energy on trying to find out who killed Bernie. He's way more interested in finding out if Bernie was a follower of one particular revolutionary faction or another. He's wondering if there is a nest of spies in Tempe and somehow Bernie's murder has something to do with Villa's invasion."

Elizabeth's unexpected rant rendered Alafair speechless for a moment. It was her sister's passion that surprised her and not Elizabeth's cynical assessment of the situation. She did not imagine that justice was any more colorblind in Arizona than it was in Oklahoma.

"Do you care so much about Bernie Arruda?"

"Not particularly. But I do not care what a man's station is in life, he deserves justice."

Had Elizabeth become a social activist in the past decade? Rather than populist outrage, though, Elizabeth's shining eyes and high color smacked more of excitement and intrigue.

She caught her bottom lip between her teeth. "I wonder what Bernie's brothers had to say about last night?"

Her sister's overt eagerness to see justice done gave Alafair a bad feeling. "Elizabeth, in my experience no good comes from getting yourself involved in such things…"

She was interrupted by a piercing whistle from the street and Elizabeth stood up, happy to be spared a lecture. "Yonder comes Shaw, Alafair. He's back earlier than I expected."

Shaw had just turned the corner and was walking toward them from the end of the tree-shaded avenue. When he saw the women look his way he waved at them. Something white was in his hand.

Alafair's eyes widened in happy anticipation, her warning forgotten. "Oh, maybe he has a letter from home!"

All the News

They had been keeping the family in Oklahoma informed of their progress by telegram. But since they had arrived in Tempe they had received only one less-than-satisfactory telegram in return, and that was from their daughter Martha's intended, Streeter McCoy, acknowledging their messages. The lack of word was no surprise. The farther from home they got, the more expensive it became to send a telegram. Why, the ten-word message Shaw had sent off after they finally arrived in Tempe cost sixty-five cents. This was not an extravagance they could indulge in on a daily basis. And at a rate of over five dollars for three minutes, telephoning from Arizona all the way to eastern Oklahoma was out of the question.

Shaw met the women at the front gate, grinning from ear to ear. "Letter from Martha," he said.

Alafair snatched it. "Well, hallelujah! I thought you looked to be in a good mood." He looked good altogether, she thought, dressed for a trip into town in his three-piece suit, black cowboy hat and best boots, and the white shirt she had made for him with the crisply starched, attached collar.

"Let's go inside and get comfortable," Elizabeth suggested. "We've learned a few things today that'll pop your eyes, Shaw."

After they had settled on the couches, Alafair and Elizabeth between them brought Shaw up to date on Mrs. Carrizal's diagnosis and offer of a treatment, and on the discovery of the bat fragment. He was properly impressed on both counts.

"Well, that is interesting about what the deputies found. It explains why Dillon was so hot to talk to Geoff when he came by the office a while ago. Geoff wasn't there, and I never did quite find out where he got off to, but Web and the marshal closeted themselves up for quite a spell. Web said he'll be home shortly, Elizabeth, so I expect he'll tell y'all what was said."

Shaw was amused at Alafair's hungry look as she watched him. "I had me quite an afternoon, too. The California folks are shooting their flicker right on the main street today, Elizabeth. Before I came back to the house, I talked to Chris Martin, the cameraman who was at the party the other night. I'll tell y'all about that in a bit. But first I want to read this letter before Alafair busts."

Martha's letter was dated March 6, 1916, the very day that Shaw, Alafair, and Blanche had arrived in Tempe. The letter was so fat it barely fit in the envelope, and it had required so many stamps that there was barely room for the address on the front. Martha explained its prodigious size by noting that she had been writing since the day her parents left Boynton, and that each of the other children had also added a note. Everyone was doing well, though three-year-old Grace thought her eldest sister was way meaner than Mama. The twins Alice and Phoebe, both married and pregnant, were feeling fine and would write soon.

Sophronia misses Blanche and got an A on her spelling test. G.W. comes home from the Agricultural and Mechanical College every Friday night and leaves early Monday morning. Betwixt him and Kurt and Charlie and the Welch brothers the farm is running like a clock, Daddy. Mary is happy as a little red heifer as always, what with finishing up her last year of teaching and making plans for her and Kurt's wedding. Ruth has been spending more and more time at her music teacher's house. She says she is getting ready for when she goes to study at the Conservatory next year, but I think she is tired of helping me plant the vegetable garden. Grandma and Grandpapa come by every day to bring us something from the garden and make sure we have not burned the house down. Grandma will be sending a letter. The post scriptum squiggle is from your granddaughter Zeltha.

Martha finished with: *We all miss you more than I can say. I am managing all right. We have not had any big crisis and things are going well, but I will say I do not believe that after I marry Streeter I will be having any ten children myself, Dear Parents.*

Your Loving Daughter and Sister, Martha Tucker

Shaw lowered the pages to his lap and looked up at Alafair and Elizabeth sitting on the couch opposite him, intending to comment. He hesitated when he saw Alafair wiping her eyes with the white linen handkerchief she kept tucked in her sleeve.

She gave him a wan smile. "Law, I hate to be away from the children! I wonder if she got the letter I sent the day after we got here?"

"She mailed this to us right about the same time, so I'm guessing she is reading yours aloud to the kids around the kitchen table right about now. Sounds like they are getting along fine without us." His tone was teasing. He was unwilling to let her know that he was missing his family as much as she was.

Alafair emitted a rueful chuckle. "I noticed, and I ought to be happier about that than I am, oughtn't I? Mercy me, this letter cost a fortune to mail! Hand it here, Shaw. I intend to read it from front to back and top to bottom and write back right after supper. First I want to tell you more about what Miz Carrizal said to Blanche and me this afternoon."

But Elizabeth had other things on her mind. "Before y'all get off onto other subjects, tell us about the playacting you saw in town, Shaw."

He smoothed back a hank of black hair from his forehead with the flat of his hand. "Oh, yes, I like to forget. It was a lot of excitement, let me tell you. You couldn't hardly go anywhere downtown without tripping over film folks. You would have thought you were in the middle of a war! I have never seen the like of it. There must have been a hundred men dressed up in Army uniforms both Mexican and American, running back and forth and pretending to shoot one another, raising dust fit to choke a camel to death. They were acting like Mill Avenue was the border between Mexico and the United States and they were having a skirmish right in the middle of the street. Every once in a while they would have to stop and wait for some passer-by to get out of the picture!" The memory tickled him and he laughed. "That's where I saw the camera operator we met the other night, Chris Martin. Chris told me that the marshal came up early this morning and talked to some of the crew. Seems he was asking if any of them could tell him something about Bernie Arruda."

As anxious as Alafair was to read the rest of her letter, this piece of information interested her. "Do you suppose that Dillon thinks there is something suspicious about Bernie's motion picture career?"

"I figure the marshal is just trying to find out everything he can about the murdered man, honey," Shaw said. "He'll try to put Arruda's life together like a jigsaw puzzle and see if he can get a picture that shows who might have wanted to kill him."

Elizabeth perked up. "You know, the director Mr. Carleton hired a lot of local people here to work on that project. Did Chris tell you what any of the crew said to the marshal?"

"He told me that the marshal didn't ask him anything personally, but the director did look surprised to hear that Bernie was dead. And that head actor Mr. Bosworth was downright flabbergasted."

"I'm surprised they even knew who Bernie was, as many people as are working on that flicker," Elizabeth said.

"Well, Chris sure knew him when he saw him at the open house," Shaw told her.

Chris Martin

The cameraman had arrived at the open house that afternoon in a fancy open touring car, along with the actresses Dorothy Clark and Yona Landowska. After the women were shown into the house, he had introduced himself to Shaw and Webster and the three men walked together toward the back yard where the guests were gathering. Martin was a chipper young fellow, Shaw thought, with an almost incomprehensible accent from somewhere back on the East Coast. He was dressed in an open-necked blue shirt and khaki trousers held up by dark blue braces that matched his flat linen cap. "I figured it'd be exciting to come out here and shoot a Western 'cause I done it once before down in Tijuana on a Paramount picture, and did we have fun! But this director keeps a tight rein on the crew, I gotta tell you. Anyway…" As they rounded the corner, Martin stopped in his tracks and pointed at the three musicians under the mulberry tree. "Hey, it's the general! Hey, General, you a singer as well as an actor?"

The good-looking musician with the small guitar flashed a grin and acknowledged Martin with a wave of his black and silver *sombrero*.

Martin elbowed Shaw in the side. "That's Bernie. He's one of the extras who've been hired to play Mexican army soldiers. We call him the General 'cause he likes to charge right out ahead of the rest of the army like he was the general. He loves the camera, yessiree, always dyin' or killin' somebody in a real gruesome way so he'll stick out. The director likes him, believe it or not. Always givin' him a little extra to do. Hey, look at all the grub!"

Martin charged ahead toward the buffet, leaving Shaw and Web to follow in his wake.

"Reckon he's hungry, yessiree." Shaw's tone was ironic.

Outnumbered

"Shaw, did Chris tell you whether they stopped the filming this morning after the marshal told them Bernie was dead?"

"No, they didn't, Elizabeth. After the law left the war started right back up again. Chris was het up about the fact that on Wednesday they are going to start working on the most exciting scene in the picture. Said they were going to go out to an old abandoned schoolhouse east of town and blow it up."

Elizabeth straightened. "Oh, yes, I knew about that! Alafair, remember when Miss Landowska told us that the company had brought hundreds of pounds of explosives with them on the train from Hollywood? She said that they had gotten permission to blow up the old rural school that has been standing empty for years way out east of town."

"Of course I remember," Alafair said. Her voice was so flat that Shaw smiled at her lack of enthusiasm.

Elizabeth did not notice. She grasped Alafair's wrist. "Seven hundred pounds of explosives! Oh, Alafair, we must go and see that! It's just a short ride out there to the Rural School. It should be quite exciting."

Alafair almost laughed, but Elizabeth was so sincere that she refrained. "Blanche is doing so much better that I thank Jesus for it every day, but I do not want to do anything that might cause her to have a setback. If you want to go, Elizabeth, don't hesitate on our account, but I think…"

"Don't say no, Alafair." In search of an ally, Elizabeth turned toward Shaw. "Miz Carrizal's medicines should have her hale and healthy by then. And if Wednesday is as pretty a day as today, and it will be, the clean, warm, dry country air will do Blanche a world of good. And she could use a bit of exercise. She would love to see it, you know she would. And so would y'all! It's so much fun to see the filming, all the handsome actors and beautiful actresses. Why, it's just like a fairy tale!"

Alafair looked at her husband. Her heart sank when she saw the expression on his face. He always was eager as a boy to indulge in a little harmless dirt, noise, and general mayhem.

"How about if I telephone Dr. Moeur's office tomorrow and get his opinion on the matter, darlin'?" he suggested. "If he says it may be too much for Blanche, we'll forgo the pleasure and Elizabeth can go without us."

"Mama?"

Alafair turned in her chair to see Blanche standing in the door, her bare feet splayed, her hair tousled from her nap.

"Have you been eavesdropping on us, you little pitcher?"

Blanche pattered across the floor and flung an arm across her mother's shoulder. "Please, Ma, I want to go see them make the flicker. I'll take it real easy."

Elizabeth could see victory on the horizon. "Come on, Alafair, she will likely never have such an opportunity again!"

"Please, Ma…" Blanche tried not to whine, but it was difficult. She felt better now. So much better that she wanted to talk back when her mama made her rest so much. Sometimes she would pretend to doze until her mama left the room. Then she would get up and play with her doll or stare with longing out the bedroom window at the beautiful sunny backyard with all the intriguing things to look at. She was in Arizona! She didn't even know anyone who had been so far away from home except for Georgie Welsh's brother who had come up to visit her from Florida.

And now there was a possibility she might get to see real live movie actors play in a real live moving picture! It was almost worth a season of feeling bad to be able to have all these new experiences. When she finally got home she would be the center of attention for years! She gazed at her mother with such longing that Alafair bit her lip.

"I'll tell you what, sugar. Daddy will ask the doctor if you're well enough to be outside and on your feet for half a day. If Dr. Moeur says yes, then I reckon it will be all right…" She held up a warning finger when it looked as though Blanche might dance around the room. "…for a little while. *If* he says yes. And if me or Daddy thinks you're tired and say it's time to go, we go and you don't argue."

Blanche was so happy that she gasped in a breath and would have cheered if it had not made her want to cough. She suppressed the urge with a heroic effort and gave a solemn nod, afraid to make a single noise that could possibly give her mother second thoughts.

Elizabeth was as encouraged by Alafair's conditional agreement as Blanche was. "Why, you're looking so pert that I know the doctor will say yes, sugar. We'll have a grand time."

Mrs. Carrizal showed up at Elizabeth's back door shortly after supper carrying a large stoppered glass jar containing a peat-colored concoction. "Here is the tea I promised for Blanche. Give her about a half a cup every few hours tonight and tomorrow. Heat it beforehand, but do not use a metal pan. Elizabeth has an *olla*, a clay pot, I think."

As Alafair received her instructions, Blanche stood at her side with her arm around her mother's waist and a dubious look on her face. Mrs. Carrizal paused and her eyes crinkled with amusement at Blanche's expression. "It does not taste as bad as it looks, *querida*. You may sweeten it with a little honey if you wish. It should not make you feel bad, but tonight it will make you cough up what is making you sick. Then you will feel very much better in the morning." She turned back to Alafair. "I also brought some eucalyptus leaves. Boil them in water and let her breathe the steam."

Blanche found the tea to her liking, much to Alafair's relief, and drank her doses down with no more than token resistance. She began a loose, rattling cough almost at once, and before bedtime she had easily coughed up a quarter-cup of greenish mucus. Since no discomfort was involved, the ten-year-old and her little cousin found the whole procedure pleasantly disgusting. Blanche slept in loose-limbed abandon that night, so deeply unconscious that Alafair, who spent the night with one eye open, got up several times to check on her.

When the sun rose, Blanche awoke refreshed and happy and breathing easily. Alafair was tired, but also breathing easily for the first time in weeks.

Cindy's House

They had their breakfast in the parlor the next morning. Elizabeth served up bowls of grits with butter and syrup, a platter full of link sausages, thick pieces of toast, pots of strawberry jam, coffee for the adults and warm, sweetened milk in mugs for the children, all dishes that could be comfortably eaten around the tea table between the couches.

Alafair thought the informal breakfast a wonderful way to start another fine sunny day. Elizabeth had thrown open the curtains, and Blanche took advantage of the bright morning sun by sitting on a cushion on the floor before the tea table, still in her nightgown, basking in a shaft of light and soaking up warmth like a lizard.

Web took his leave and Chase disappeared, leaving Elizabeth and the Tuckers sipping their drinks in high content.

"I think I'll go over and ask Cindy if she wants to come with us to see the school get exploded tomorrow." Elizabeth said. "Is that all right with y'all? Going out to see the actors always cheers her up considerable." Before anyone had time to respond, Elizabeth was interrupted by a crash from upstairs. A look of exasperation crossed her face and she stood up. "Good grief! That boy."

Blanche giggled at the sound of her aunt's voice bellowing "Chaaase!" as she disappeared up the stairs.

"Has Chase been particularly troublesome lately?" Shaw asked.

"No more so than usual," Alafair answered. "I declare, I hope she doesn't find that boy drowned in the canal one of these days." In her opinion six years old was too young for any child to be free-range. Especially a boy as headstrong as Chase Kemp.

Shaw gave her a wry smile. "She don't have the mothering experience you do, Alafair. He'll bust a lip or step on a bee one of these days and they'll both learn. Maybe you can give her the benefit of your wisdom while we're here."

Alafair's answering smile was just as wry. "Unless she's changed right down to her backbone over the past nine years she would rather poke herself with a nail than pay a lick of attention to me, Shaw." She leaned forward and whispered into Blanche's ear. "Now, don't you go repeating this to your aunt, honey. We don't care to hurt her feelings."

Blanche puffed. After a lifetime of keeping the secrets of more siblings than anyone had a right to have, she knew how to keep her mouth shut. "Yes, Ma, I'm not stupid."

A couple of months ago her sass might have earned her a reprimand, but now Alafair simply squeezed her knee. Better sass than lethargy.

Elizabeth came down the staircase hauling her squirming son by one arm. Though her color was high she seemed more amused than angry at the boy. "This little rascal tried to climb up into the top of his daddy's closet and brought hat boxes, papers, valises and all down on top of him. It's a wonder he didn't get himself squashed!"

Shaw leaned forward in his chair and drew the boy toward him. "Come here, pard, and tell your old Uncle Shaw all about it." Chase had been twisting like an eel in an attempt get away from his mother, but he eagerly clambered up Shaw's leg and into his lap. Alafair was glad to see that Shaw seemed to want make the boy his project. She knew that he felt sorry for the child. He had a lot of empathy for naughty boys.

"Oh, good!" Satisfied to have her son taken care of and off her hands, Elizabeth turned her attention to Alafair. "Sister, why don't you come with me over to Cindy's? If we gang up on her, perhaps she'll be more willing to come with us to the movie shoot! Besides, I would like for you to see how nice Cindy has done up her house. "

Blanche was all for it. "I want to go see Miz Stewart's house, Ma!"

"Blanche, you're barefoot and your hair looks like you've been in a high wind! And we don't want to leave your daddy and Chase here on their own."

Shaw had been listening to the women's conversation with one ear as Chase prattled on about goats. "Pshaw, Alafair, if after all the daddying I've done I can't watch after a young fellow for half an hour I should be switched and run out of town."

Alafair shrugged. "All right then. Elizabeth, if you can wait five minutes for Blanche to throw on some shoes we'll go with you to visit your neighbor for a spell."

Cindy's House

They entered the Stewart house through the back door into the kitchen. Alafair's immediate thought was that the kitchen was miniscule. How could a woman be expected to cook a proper meal in a broom closet? Her second observation was that Cindy had piped-in water and a shiny new white enamel gas stove. Not much use to have all the modern appliances in your kitchen if you did not keep it clean, though. Alafair wrinkled her nose at the sight of a stack of crusty dishes sitting next to the built-in sink.

Elizabeth did not seem to notice. "Cindy, it's Elizabeth!" she called. "I've brought company, so get decent!"

"Elizabeth?" Cindy's girlish voice drifted in from somewhere in the front of the house. Alafair took Blanche's hand and followed Elizabeth into the parlor just in time to meet Cindy coming out of her bedroom. Alafair was shocked to see that she was still in her dressing gown, a fluffy, mauve affair with écru lace trim. Her golden hair lay loose about her shoulders in charming disarray. She had been weeping. Her pale pink complexion was mottled, and her blue eyes shone with feverish intensity. "Oh, dear. You should have warned me you were going to pay a visit, Elizabeth!" She shot Alafair an embarrassed glance. "I apologize for the state of my house, Miz Tucker. And myself. I promise that I am usually in better order at this time of day."

Alafair opened her mouth to say something soothing but Elizabeth gave a dismissive wave and launched straight away into her purpose for coming.

"Cindy, Shaw told us he talked to Chris Martin yesterday and found out that the moving picture people are going to blow up the old Rural School tomorrow. We aim to go out and watch the fun. Come with us, won't you? It should be real exciting."

"I can't think about that right now, Elizabeth. I just feel so bad about poor Bernie Arruda getting killed like that practically on my doorstep." She hesitated, then continued. "And about those men pawing through my house. And Geoff having to be away from home for so long and all. Besides, I promised to deliver some used clothing to the mission in the barrio."

Elizabeth's expression was part empathy and part impatience. "You can do that anytime. I will not take no for an answer, Cindy. You've been about as gloomy as a wet day for weeks. Why, the other night at the pot luck was the first time I've seen you smile and act normal in a long time. I know you're still feeling frail because of your loss, and that's why all these unfortunate occurrences have upset you so. I know it's awful. Bernie was a scoundrel, but he was a likable one and he didn't deserve to get murdered. But it won't do him or you a bit of good to sit around and weep. The marshal's men are come and gone and no harm done, and Geoff will be done with his deposition directly. So dry your tears and get dressed. We'll take our minds off it and soldier on the best we can. I brought my sister and niece over to see all the lovely things you have."

She turned to Alafair. "Cindy brought wagonloads of family heirlooms with her from Iowa—her grandma's china from France, all this beautiful upholstered furniture, lace and velvet comforters. Just look at those hand-tatted lace curtains in the window there. Blanche, Miz Stewart here has the prettiest collection of china dolls you ever did see on a shelf in her bedroom. Maybe she'll let you have a look at them if you promise not to touch."

Blanche's expression was eager. "May I, Ma?"

"That's up to Miz Stewart, honey."

Elizabeth's brusque and unsympathetic manner had given Alafair pause, but she obviously knew how best to handle her fragile friend. Cindy had grown visibly more cheerful as Elizabeth enumerated the treasures in her house. "I would love for you to see my dolls, sweetheart! Why don't you ladies have a seat? Blanche can come with me and look at the dolls while I dress. Elizabeth, would you play hostess? There is lemonade in a pitcher in the icebox. I'll be back in a jiffy."

Blanche followed Cindy into the bedroom and Alafair sat down on the tufted divan. "I believe I'll forgo the lemonade, Elizabeth. I'm fine."

Elizabeth's smile was ironic. "Cindy's kitchen does not usually look like she's been feeding field hands." Alafair's expression of chagrin at being so transparent made Elizabeth laugh. She sat down and leaned in confidentially. "I thought Cindy seemed cheered considerable after being out among folks the other evening, but I reckon such close death has given her a setback."

Alafair agreed. She had experienced her fair share of suffering. "That's natural. The only cure for the grief of losing a child is enough time, I expect. Even after you're able to crawl out of the worst of it, for a long while any little thing can set you off."

"She surely is taken with Blanche," Elizabeth observed. "Maybe they can help each other get better. Sure enough, Alafair, I think going to see the action tomorrow will do both of them a world of good. Cindy has been mighty interested in the movie company. The two of us have been able to go downtown a couple of times to watch them film, and after both times she has been like her old self. At least until something reminds her of her misery." A sour look came over her face. "Usually Geoff."

Elizabeth would have said more, but Blanche skipped back into the room with Cindy on her heels. "Mama, come look at Miz Stewart's beautiful doll collection. She's got one with red hair and freckles that looks like Fronie!"

Alafair took the girl's hand. "Just in one minute, sugar. Don't get too excited, now. Your cheeks are all red. Sit down for a spell and Miz Stewart will take us back there directly."

Cindy's ringlets were now caught up with a pale blue ribbon and cascaded from her crown to the nape of her neck like a golden waterfall. She was dressed in a more utilitarian frock this morning than she had been on the evening of the party, though it was still nothing that Alafair would wear to do housework. The one-piece, light and dark blue checked gabardine dress sported a high collar of white piqué that stood straight up over a blue sateen bow at the neck. Two rows of ivory buttons marched in a straight line from the top of each shoulder and down the front of her dress. The hemline of her softly pleated skirt stopped three or four inches above her ankles, revealing ivory stockings and a pair of low-heeled beige leather pumps. A wide belt that matched the bow tie encircled Cindy's waist. Alafair eyed the slim figure, trying not to feel envious. She had been that slender once, before twelve pregnancies.

"What say we make plans for tomorrow, Cindy?" Elizabeth was not giving her friend a chance to decline her invitation. "I figure we can gather over at my house for breakfast then get on the road before the sun comes up. We can be out to the Rural School in Web's roadster in half an hour, easy."

"Will Web be coming?" Alafair asked, surprised.

Elizabeth glanced at Cindy before she answered. "I am sure neither Web nor Geoff could care in the slightest."

"Shaw has only driven an automobile a dozen times, to my knowledge. I don't know if he'll want to take on Web's Ford and all us females for that long a trip."

"I am perfectly capable of driving Web's Ford." Elizabeth did not seem offended, but she was quite emphatic.

Alafair did not know whether to laugh at herself or apologize for her gaffe, so all she said was, "Of course you are."

"I would like to go with you, Elizabeth," Cindy said. "If Geoff has no objections, that is."

Elizabeth puffed. "Why should he care? He won't even be here."

"Still, I should telephone Geoff's clerk and have him ask when it is convenient." Her ears pinkened. "I'd go down there, but he doesn't like for me to interrupt him at the office. I expect it will be all right, as long as I am here to give him his supper if he decides to come home tomorrow night."

The Photograph

Alafair could tell by Elizabeth's expression that she was about to say something incendiary. It seemed like a good time for a change of topic. "I'm looking forward to seeing how these actor people do their work. Why, even I have heard of Hobart Bosworth."

The atmosphere in the room changed instantly. Elizabeth was energized. "I expect! He's been in a bunch of pictures and is right famous. He used to live right here in Tempe. That was before me and Web moved out here. "

Blanche was enchanted. "Have y'all got to meet any of the other movie actors beside Dorothy and Miss Landowska, Aunt Elizabeth?"

"Oh, yes!" Cindy answered for her. "Several of them. Me and Elizabeth have even talked to the director, Mr. Carleton, and to Mr. Bosworth himself. He is just a charming man. One evening last week, he hosted the whole town at the Goodwin Opera House for a special showing of the first motion picture he was ever in. It was called *Fatherhood*. Did you ever see it?"

"I never did." Alafair did not mention that she had never seen any motion picture.

"That was the best fun!" Elizabeth clapped her hands. "Over a thousand people showed up. They had to show the flicker twice and still they could hardly get everyone into the theater. And then Mr. Bosworth and all the actors got together in front of the Opera House with everybody who came, and we all had our photograph took."

Cindy jumped up. "I have a copy of that photograph. Oh, wait until you see this." A moment later she returned to the parlor with a large framed photograph in her hand and squeezed herself onto the divan between Alafair and Blanche.

The photograph was taken from above and at some distance. Alafair guessed that the photographer had been standing on the roof of a building across the street so he could encompass the entire crowd. "My word, that is more folks than I've ever seen all together in one place. Did everybody in the whole town show up?"

Elizabeth stood to peer over Alafair's shoulder. "Just about. See, there are the actors right in the front. That's Hobart Bosworth." She pointed. "You recognize Dorothy Clark and Miss Landowska. And next to her is Goldie Caldwell. She plays the Yaqui's wife. Jack Curtis there is the villain Martinez, but in real life he is a very nice man."

Elizabeth enumerated the rest of the cast, but Alafair was too caught by Bosworth's image to pay much attention to the others. He looked vaguely familiar to her, but she probably had seen his image on a poster in front of the O&B Theater on Main Street in Boynton. He was a tall man, dressed like a rich industrialist in a three-piece suit and a striped tie, with a crisp white handkerchief peeking out of his breast pocket. It was hard to make out individual faces, but she could see that Bosworth sported a tousled head-full of very blond hair. "This man plays an Indian chief?"

"When you see him in his costume you will hardly believe he is the same man, Alafair," Elizabeth assured her.

"Where are you, Miz Stewart?"

Cindy's finger tapped a place just to the left of and behind the actors at the front the mob. "There we are, Blanche, dear, me and your aunt. We were standing right behind Goldie."

"I see you!"

Blanche had good eyes or a good imagination, for all Alafair could make out was two white ovals topped by big hats. "Is Bernie Arruda in this picture?"

Elizabeth gave Cindy a furtive glance before she answered. "All the Mexicans are in the back row, see? It's hard to make out who is who. I never have tried to find him before." She leaned down and peered closely at the picture in Cindy's hand before she indicated a dark man with a big grin. "That may be him there, or one of the other Arrudas. They favor one another."

"Look, there's Honor Moeur! I recognize that bonnet with the white peonies on it." Cindy pointed out the doctor's wife with such enthusiasm that Alafair suspected she was more interested in getting off the topic of Bernie Arruda than in identifying her friends.

"That must be Doc Moeur beside her, then," Elizabeth said. "See how the light reflects off his bald head?"

They spent another few minutes picking people out of the crowd, but most were strangers to Alafair. She studied the indistinct, smiling faces gazing upwards at the camera, and wondered which of them was a murderer.

A Morning Drive

They arose before dawn to a chilly morning. Alafair dressed Blanche in her warmest woolen dress and stockings. From their veranda bedroom, the Tuckers entered the house through the kitchen to find Elizabeth in her usual place at the stove, scrambling eggs with chiles and cheese and toasting tortillas in a skillet. Within seconds she had whipped up plates for them and sent them into the parlor, where they found Web, Chase, and Cindy seated on the sofas around the long, low tea table, eating their eggs and tortillas and sipping from mugs of hot coffee.

After breakfast was done, Elizabeth wrestled Chase into his coat and the two of them left out the back for the Carrizals, where Chase would spend the day while the rest of the family made their trek to the movie set on the eastern edge of town.

As soon as she returned, Web left for work and everyone else bundled up for a drive. Alafair was swallowed up in one of Elizabeth's travel dusters, and the sleeves of Web's duster were six inches too short for Shaw's long arms. But they gamely donned the borrowed coats after Elizabeth told them it could be a dusty trip over unpaved roads to the Rural School.

Elizabeth climbed into the driver's seat of Web's Hupmobile with Cindy beside her in the front, while Alafair and Shaw squeezed into the narrow back seat with Blanche wedged between them. Blanche was bundled up like a bear cub in a coat and hat and covered with a blanket. Much to her chagrin, her mother made her cover her mouth and nose with a scarf, making her feel like a bandit. Her cough was all but gone after a day of drinking Mrs. Carrizals' healing tea and breathing eucalyptus-infused steam, but Alafair was taking no chances with her fragile lungs.

The sun was just rising when they set out. The passengers sank back into the Hupmobile's plush leather seats as Elizabeth pulled away from the house.

Tempe was about the same size as the Tuckers' home town of Boynton, some eighteen hundred souls. All the homes in Elizabeth's neighborhood were on very large fenced lots, and most boasted chicken yards, big truck gardens, small orchards, rabbit hutches, dove cotes, and pig sties, maybe a cow or two and some sheep and goats. The place was more like a collection of small farmsteads than an urban neighborhood.

There was a lot of water around, considering they were in the desert. Many of the streets had irrigation channels like the one in which Bernie Arruda had met his maker; large, open ditches half full of turgid water running down either side and a fair-sized ditch leading into every yard. One channel that Webster had called the "Willow Ditch" could have been mistaken for a small creek, except for the fact that it ran straight and true down the side of the road for which it was named.

Every time Alafair looked to the east toward the sunrise the single streak of cloud that hovered over the horizon had changed to some brilliant new shade; orange to gold, salmon to pink. Colors she had never seen, fading just before the sun came up to a shade of delicate pearl that reminded her of the inside of the abalone shell one of the kids had given her a few years before.

The sky had taken on its clear winter blue by the time Elizabeth turned the automobile south onto the main thoroughfare, Mill Avenue, named for a large adobe flour mill at its end, next to the broad Salt River which made up the northern boundary of the town. Alafair commented to Shaw on how wide Mill Avenue was and what a spacious feeling the town had. All the streets in town were unpaved, but Mill was lined with concrete sidewalks shaded by ash trees, and many of the red brick buildings sported balconies and second floors with deep overhanging roofs. The soft morning light gave the town such an air of elegance and refinement that Alafair wondered aloud how on earth anyone had decided to build a such lovely town here in the middle of the desert.

Cindy turned and hung an arm over the back of her seat. "Back in '70, old Mr. Hayden started a ferry crossing over the river for travelers heading south toward Tucson."

Alafair was surprised. "It's a much older town than Boynton, then."

Shaw laughed. "Plenty old. It's a year older than me!"

Elizabeth turned east off of Mill onto Eighth Street and drove them past the Tempe Normal School campus, eight red brick buildings surrounding a pleasant green quad with a fountain in the middle. By the time they turned south again onto Canal Street, the campus had given way to clusters of houses, then farms and fields of winter wheat glimpsed through a corridor of mature ash and sycamore trees lining the road. The country outside of town was beautiful, but strange. Directly behind them them to the north a conical butte poked out of the flat landscape, and in the distance rose a strangely pink-tinted humpback mountain. Far to the east, a range of mountains lined the horizon, so tall that the four distinct points of the tallest peaks were still snow-covered.

"Those are the Superstition Mountains," Elizabeth told them. "They say there is a lost gold mine somewhere in those hills."

Lush cotton fields and pleasant farms were situated next to desert so barren it was frightening. Blanche excitedly pointed out a stand of two or three giant cactuses that looked like silent creatures with raised arms. "They look like they're calling down a blessing from heaven, Mama!"

Let it be a blessing and not a curse, Alafair prayed. To be stranded alone in the middle of such country with no mode of transportation would be a death sentence.

Blanche slipped her hand into Alafair's. "It's nice here, isn't it, Ma?"

Alafair took a deep breath. "It is, honey."

Rural School

It was not a long drive once they turned onto Canal, perhaps three miles. They could see the abandoned school rising up out of the land like a mushroom. It was a one-room affair, but good-sized, with a bonnet roof that shaded the low porch on all four sides. There was a covered well a few yards from the front of the building, and two outhouses in the back—one for the boys and one for the girls.

"It looks like a nice building," Shaw said. "Why are they letting somebody blow it up?"

"There will be a new school here, I understand," Elizabeth told him, as they turned up the drive from the road. "Mostly farmers' kids go to school out here, but the town is growing out this direction. I reckon they think eventually they'll need a bigger place."

A young man directed them to a sunny area of bare dirt where several autos were already parked. The horse-drawn vehicles were being sent to a tree-lined spot nearer the school. "I reckon they figure the automobiles don't need shade like the horses do," Elizabeth speculated, as she pulled in next to a Ford and killed the engine.

Quite a number of spectators had made the trek all the way out from town to see the performance. Alafair thought there were close to fifty people milling around the designated viewing area on the other side of the drive from the school. She took Blanche's hand and they walked toward the activity, leaving Shaw, Elizabeth, and Cindy to haul the canvas folding chairs out of the Hupmobile's boot. A woman with long blond braids who was dressed in riding trousers, a blousing white shirt, and a floppy straw hat herded them into the spectator's corral, where Alafair and Blanche made their way to the front to hold a place for their chairs. Alafair hadn't been able to tell from the road, but they were on a slight rise that gave the gallery an excellent view of the action.

Two large cameras were set up on tripods near the school-house, but if it hadn't been for that, Alafair would have thought she was watching a tribe of Indians standing around and chatting pleasantly with armed Mexican soldiers.

Blanche was so excited she was practically hopping from foot to foot. "Hey, Mama, hey, Mama, look, there's Chris who was at the party! Where's Dorothy? Do you see Dorothy?"

All Alafair could see of Chris Martin was his back as he peered through his camera lens, made a tiny adjustment, peered through the lens again. She noted with amusement that he had turned his cap around backwards so the bill would not impede his view. She scanned the crowd of actors, but didn't recognize either of the women who had come to Elizabeth's gathering. "I'm guessing she's one of the Indian girls, sugar. I doubt if she looks the same today as she did the other night."

Shaw, Elizabeth, and Cindy elbowed their way through the spectators, folding chairs held high to keep from braining any innocent bystanders. They spent a couple of minutes setting themselves up along the edge of the drive, next to the dozen or so other civilians who had had the foresight to bring their own chairs.

Blanche crawled up in her father's lap and Elizabeth leaned over in her chair to give Alafair's shoulder a nudge. "There's the director yonder, Mr. Carleton. "

Alafair looked in the direction Elizabeth had pointed and saw a middle-sized man in boots, jhodpurs, and a broad-brimmed hat stalking up and down the line in front of the abandoned schoolhouse, his pleasant face furrowed with concentration as he studied the shot. He lifted his hat and ran his fingers across his scalp, momentarily exposing a shock of greying hair and clear blue eyes behind a pair of rimless spectacles.

Hobart Bosworth

A very tall, good-looking man dressed in nothing more than a loincloth and moccasins broke away from his castmates and walked across the drive toward them. Everyone began to murmur, and Elizabeth and Cindy stood up as he neared. "It's Mr. Bosworth," Elizabeth said over her shoulder, though Alafair had already gathered that from the whispers around her.

He bore little resemblance to the image she had seen in Cindy's photograph. His skin was darkened with makeup and his blond hair covered by a rather obvious black, shoulder-length wig, a beaded headband low on his forehead. He was working the crowd, greeting the spectators, shaking hands, speaking to the women and children. His smile was broad and white, his incongruous blue eyes sparkling with what looked like real pleasure. Alafair and Shaw exchanged a glance. No wonder Elizabeth was enamored.

"Mrs. Kemp, Mrs. Stewart!" the actor exclaimed as he neared. "I do declare that you two ladies have been the most faithful followers of our little enterprise. I've missed you the past few days!"

Cindy blushed becomingly before she smiled and ducked her head, but Elizabeth wasn't in the least star-struck and answered like she had known the man all her life. Alafair smiled at her brass. Some things never changed. "We have missed you, as well, Mr. Bosworth. Sir, this is my sister, Alafair Tucker, her husband Shaw Tucker, and their daughter Blanche, come to visit us all the way from Oklahoma."

Bosworth looked into Alafair's eyes as though no one else was around when he took her hand in greeting, and followed up with a hearty handshake for Shaw. He turned his full attention to Blanche, who had pushed herself in front of her father. "I am honored to meet you, Miss Blanche. What a beautiful little girl you are!" He looked up at Shaw. "Now, here's one who could have a career in the cinema when she gets a little older."

"I'm afraid she'd have to step over my dead body," Shaw joked.

"Oh, Daddy!" Blanche was exasperated. "It'd be fun to be in the flickers."

Alafair could not let this pass without some teasing. "Why, honey, your grandfolks would fall over dead from shock to see you flaunting yourself in front of a camera for the whole world to see."

The remark served to galvanize Blanche's resolve. "When would Grandma and Grandpapa ever see a moving picture? I could be in every picture from now to forever and they'd never know about it. Mr. Bosworth, is it true that a person can make a lot of money from acting in a picture show?"

Bosworth winked one very un-Indian blue eye at Alafair before he answered. "Some can, dear girl, if they are lucky enough to get a lot of parts, but it's a hard business."

"See, Ma, if I got a lot of parts, I could buy y'all a house and an automobile and some clothes."

Shaw laughed. "Then you'd be too high-falutin' to keep company with your plain old folks."

"I don't care about the money," Elizabeth interjected. "Why, I would adore to act in motion pictures just for the adventure!"

Bosworth turned to look at her, a spark of admiration in his gaze. "Well, Mrs. Kemp, you would change your tune about the excitement of the moving picture business if you did it for a living as I do. I spend much of my day letting people get me up in ridiculous outfits. Then I stand around for hours in the hot sun while my beloved yet temperamental director decides the exact spot to place his camera. After which I get to spend fifteen minutes making a monkey out of myself while the camera man films it for all the world to see."

Elizabeth puffed. "Sounds like exhilaration itself compared to the drudgery of my life, Mr. Bosworth."

"Yes, indeed," Cindy breathed.

"Well, ladies, if you're so keen, why don't you sign on as extras? The very last shot of this picture is coming up at the end of the week, and it calls for several townswomen such as yourselves to engage in a bit of running and screaming."

Both Alafair and Shaw chuckled at the very idea, but Elizabeth exclaimed, "Why, we'd love to!"

Cindy paled at the thought. "Oh, no, I couldn't. My husband would never let me do such a thing."

Elizabeth would not be deterred by her friend's faint-heartedness. "Unless you tell him. By the time Geoff finds out, it'll be too late, and you will have had some fun and made a dollar!"

Bosworth was taking the conversation in a spirit of fun. "That is exactly right, Mrs. Stewart. What possible harm could it do? Why, you might even find yourself a new career!"

The director was waving impatiently at Bosworth, who waved back. "Well, it was nice to meet you good people. I hope you enjoy the action. It should be most entertaining."

He turned to go, but Elizabeth held out a hand. "Mr. Bosworth, is Bernie Arruda's death going to cause any difficulties for your picture?"

Bosworth hesitated and gave her an odd look. "No, he was only a bit player. But he had quite the personality, and I was sorry to hear that he died. Why do you ask? Did you know him?"

Elizabeth waved in Alfair's general direction. "It was my sister here who discovered his body that morning in front of my house."

The actor's eyebrow's knit. "Oh, my goodness, how distressing. He was a nice young man, so proud to be in our motion picture, especially since he was actually a Yaqui, one of the very people whose story we are telling here. He and his brothers helped us a bit with costume details, and Bernie scouted some locations for us. It was he who found this abandoned school. I certainly hope whoever killed him is brought to justice."

"I didn't know Bernie was a Yaqui himself!"

"Yes, I figured that was why he portrayed his Mexican army officer character as so cruel. Bernie had some ability, the poor fellow. He could have had a career as a character actor out in California."

An assistant director was calling Bosworth's name by now, and he cast an amused look over his shoulder. "And now I really must be going. Every moment of delay costs money, you know." He turned back to Elizabeth and Cindy. "And, ladies, if you change your mind about appearing in our little play, report to the casting director as soon as you may. Tell her I sent you. Blanche, darling, you look me up in about ten years if you decide to pursue a film career. Mr. and Mrs. Tucker, so glad to meet you. And don't worry for a moment. There is nothing in any of my films that I wouldn't be proud for a ten-year-old to see."

They watched for a moment as the actor walked away, until Alafair broke the silence. "Bernie was a real-life Yaqui?"

"Sounds like he was more involved in this film endeavor than we realized," Elizabeth noted.

"Mr. Bosworth remembered our names," Cindy said with a sigh.

A Hard Rain

The spectators watched enrapt as the film crew shot a scene in which several "Yaqui" women and children were herded into the abandoned schoolhouse by sinister-looking Mexican soldiers. They did three or four takes, moving the two cameras around for different angles, and there was a lot of emoting and swooning from the actors which looked less than realistic, Alafair thought. Even so, she did find herself feeling anxious about the fate of the captive Yaquis. Fortunately, Mr. Bosworth's character, Tambor, the hero, managed to foil the evil soldiers and free the captives just in time.

Carleton finally decided he had enough footage to work with and dismissed his extras for the day. Then for the next hour, there was a great deal of inexplicable scurrying about on the set, yelling, and other mysterious activities that Alafair could make neither heads nor tails of. The spectators talked, strolled around, broke out snacks and drinks, and seemed not in the least bored. Alafair, Shaw, and Blanche took the opportunity to walk a little way out into the countryside and admire all the little prickly plants and creatures.

When everyone had reclaimed their places and shooting finally resumed, the director sent two crew members into the schoolhouse to make sure it was clear before he turned toward the spectators and shouted at them through a megaphone.

"Ladies and gentlemen, we are about to blow this school-house to kingdom come. For the last hour, my explosives expert has been placing seven hundred pounds of dynamite at crucial points within the building, and when I give the signal to blow it up, the blast will be epic. It will also be very dangerous and extremely loud, so please follow Miss Weston up the rise to the safe area behind the rope at the top of the little hill. You should be able to see everything. I'll give you plenty of warning before Mr. Johnson sets off the dynamite, and I will suggest you cover your ears when I give the signal. Keep your children on a tight rein. I don't want any accidents. Now, we only have one chance to get this shot, so I'm going to insist that everyone cooperate, or we will remove you from the set."

It did not take a second warning to convince Alafair and her party to pick up their chairs and follow the pigtailed Miss Weston a few yards up the rise to the safe zone. Alafair did not want to stay at all since she hated loud noises, but she was overruled. Shaw tried to contain it, but she could see the spark of boyish eagerness at the prospect of blowing things up. So she resigned herself. There was no possibility that she would leave Blanche with a bunch of people who had temporarily taken leave of their senses.

She wanted to stand behind the press of watchers, but Blanche slithered through the crowd like an eel to the front of the crowd and pressed against the rope. Shaw would have lifted her up onto his shoulders if Alafair had not objected. He ended up holding Blanche in his arms while Alafair pressed up next to his side with one arm around his back and the other clutching Blanche in a death grip.

The actors, still in costume, were sitting in canvas chairs under a canopy off to the left of the spectators, chatting calmly amongst themselves. Below, they could see Carleton wave a white flag. The assistant director, a tall youth in a tweed cap and shaded spectacles, turned and faced the onlookers. "When Mr. Carleton lifts the red flag, ladies and gentlemen, that will be the signal to cover your ears."

It took another ten minutes of unexplained activity on the set, ten minutes of unpleasant anticipation that Alafair did not appreciate, before Carleton lifted a small triangular red flag over his head. The explosives man, Mr. Johnson, came out of the schoolhouse door, walking backwards and rolling out a length of wire. Some yards from the building he dropped to his knees and attached the wire to a small box with a plunger.

"Stick your fingers in your ears, gals," Shaw said to the women around him. "Clean up to your elbows, if you can manage."

Down went the flag and the explosives expert depressed the plunger.

The schoolhouse disintegrated before their eyes, suddenly nothing but dust and shards of board flying straight up into the air. Alafair felt the shock before the sound of the blast reached them. Even with her hands pressed tight over her ears the noise was unlike anything she had ever heard, and she had fired many a shotgun in her time. The unrecognizable remains of the little wood schoolhouse seemed to float motionless in the air for a second, then begin to fall in a noisy rattle like hail. Or like shrapnel.

They were being pelted with debris. Seven hundred pounds of dynamite was apparently overdoing it. The crowd scattered like chickens, arms and hands over ducked heads. Alafair grabbed the back of Shaw's coat and felt herself jerked into a run. Shaw was already halfway down the backside of the rise carrying Blanche squashed up against his chest, pressing her face into his waistcoat with one hand. *If this is even a little bit what war is like,* Alafair thought in awe, *how can anyone make himself fight after the first cannon is fired or bomb is dropped?*

If the schoolhouse shards had rained on the spectators at such a distance, what had happened to the movie crew, she wondered as she ran? But she did not take the time to turn and look.

Everyone was yelling. Her eyes were squeezed shut, but she recognized Blanche's high-pitched squeal and Shaw's baritone yelp. They sounded more excited than alarmed. Alafair did not know whether or not she herself was hollering. It was too noisy to tell.

Ouch! It felt just like hail pounding her arms and shoulders, big hail, or even stones. She cracked open an eye as she ran to check on Blanche, clutched in Shaw's arms, but the child was completely shielded by her father's hunched body.

It took Alafair a moment to realize that what was falling from the sky was more than bits of vaporized schoolhouse the size of nickels and dimes.

It *was* nickels and dimes.

Money was raining down on them from heaven, and the squealing she was hearing had more to do with delight than pain and fear.

By the time they reached the bottom of the rise, the storm of money was over, and the ground around them was covered with scattered bits of silver and copper. Multicolored scraps of paper were floating gently to the ground. Alafair bent over and scooped up a couple of coins—a penny, and something she did not recognize. The silver coin was about the size of a quarter, but instead of Lady Liberty, the front was stamped with the image of an eagle clutching a snake in its talons and the inscription *"Daily Newsa Mexicana."*

Many in the crowd of spectators had run straight for their buggies and autos and headed for home when the blast went off. Some were standing at the side of the road in a daze, rubbing their bumped and bruised arms and heads. Those who had managed in time to realize what was falling from the sky were now scrambling around on the ground like a flock of hungry birds, laughing in awe and relief and stuffing their pockets. She spotted Elizabeth and Cindy among the mob, scooping up coins in high good humor.

An Honest Bunch

Shaw patted Blanche down before he gave Alafair the once over. "Everybody all right?"

Alafair was glad to see that Blanche looked stunned and excited rather than stunned and terrified. "I declare, Shaw! I never seen anything like that in all my born days! Looks like everyone here is in one piece. I hope the actors and filmers didn't get hurt!"

Still holding Blanche in his arms, Shaw managed to wipe his dusty face with one hand. "I'm guessing they miscalculated how much dynamite to use on that little wooden building. I hope that director got a good shot, because there sure ain't nothing left to try again."

Blanche was squirming. "Put me down, Daddy, I'm all right. My ears are ringing. Wasn't that something?"

Alafair barked out an ironic laugh. "That was something all right, though I'm not prepared to say what. Law, I think motion pictures must be a dangerous business to be in!"

Elizabeth, red-cheeked and heaving, dashed up and took her arm. "Y'all uninjured? Us, too. Cindy went back to the chairs for a sit-down. She needs to get her breath. Come on, sister, Shaw, let's us make sure that all the actors and them didn't get hurt by the blast."

Alafair had no desire for Blanche to see if someone in the crew had been horribly injured. But before she was able to forbid her from going back up the hill, Blanche thrust her hand into Elizabeth's and the two adventure-seekers were gone. Shaw and Alafair followed hot on their heels.

When they topped the rise, they could see a haze of dust hanging in the air over the shallow crater where the schoolhouse used to be. The crew and actors seemed to be uninjured and in good spirits. Some were checking themselves and their friends for bumps and lacerations, but others were picking up money and carrying it to the director, who was gathering it together in a big burlap feed sack. Everyone was covered from head to toe in white dust, perfect camouflage against the pale desert. Small, spear-like shards of board lay all around the shooting area. It was a wonder no one had been impaled.

Some of the actors, including Bosworth himself, were checking the welfare of the remaining spectators. "Is everyone in your party all right?" he called, when he saw the Tuckers' little group coming down the rise toward him.

"Looks like everyone made it through unscathed," Shaw called back.

"We would like everyone to come down and wait under that tree." Bosworth pointed toward a stringy eucalyptus overhanging the boys' privy. "Mr. Carleton wants to speak to you before you leave, please."

Shaw waved his hat in acknowledgment and Bosworth moved on.

One thing you could say about Director Lloyd Carleton and his company—they were an honest enough bunch. Carleton sent a couple of assistants through the small group of civilians and actors to offer first aid, a drink of water, a damp cloth, and ask that they return any money they had picked up. Carleton was addressing the group of dusty listeners through his megaphone.

"I have no idea what foolish person decided it would be a good idea to stash his life savings in an old school building in the middle of the desert, but I do think the right thing to do would be to turn this loot over to the law and let them try and determine how it got there and to whom it belongs."

He paused, expecting comment, but got none from the dazed spectators. He continued. "I have sent Mr. Martin back to town to fetch the marshal. I hope he will come quickly and you won't be inconvenienced long. In the meantime, if you will be so good as to turn any coins or paper you have just found over to Miss Weston or young Nick, we will see that it gets to the proper authorities. You're more than welcome to stay and watch us deliver it into the marshal's hand. If you would like to petition the marshal for the eventual return of your found bounty, we will be glad to give you a receipt that I shall sign personally."

Alafair leaned in to murmur in Shaw's ear. "He puts paid to the idea that moving picture folks are naturally immoral, don't he?"

His hazel eyes crinkled. "It does go to show you can't believe everything you hear, darlin'."

Questions

Alafair was resigned to spending the rest of the day in enforced idleness, chatting with actors and movie fanatics under the eucalyptus tree, but the marshal did not keep them waiting long at all. Chris Martin had torn out in the company's roadster the moment he received his assignment from Carleton, raising a cloud of dust that limned his route almost all the way back into Tempe. He apparently found the marshal the moment he got into town, for he was back within an hour. Alafair was amazed. He had to have driven a good thirty miles an hour both ways.

Martin's auto came to a halt in a cloud of dust. Joe Dillon unfolded his lanky self from the passenger's seat and cast a narrow gaze over the knot of actors and spectators sitting under the eucalyptus on canvas chairs, rocks, empty crates, each other's laps, or wandering the area and trailing after playing children. He paused momentarily when his eyes lit upon Elizabeth's party, then continued his inspection with no change of expression.

Bosworth and Carleton both came up to meet him, and the three men stood with their heads together for some minutes. When they broke from their huddle, Carleton called for his megaphone.

"Mr. Dillon has asked that if anyone has any information about this explosion of treasure, please come forward. Otherwise, those of you who are unaffiliated with our enterprise and only drove out from town to pass a pleasant morning can leave your names and where you can be located in case the marshal needs to contact you later. Kindly form a line over there and allow Miss

Weston to take your information, after which you can leave. If after our adventure here at the Rural School, you would like to watch the filming of more scenes of *The Yaqui,* shooting will resume after dark tonight near the Double Buttes in Tempe."

As they stood in line waiting to give their particulars to the ubiquitous Miss Weston, Alafair kept an anxious eye on Blanche, who with a dark-haired girl about her own age was wandering around the lot scouring the ground for stray coins that may have been missed. Alafair was concerned about the effect of the dust and debris on the girl's fragile lungs, but Blanche seemed to be none the worse for wear. In fact over the past day or two, she had been entirely her charming, manipulative self. Alafair shook her head in amazement. She resolved not to leave Tempe without Mrs. Carrizal's recipe for healing tea and a bag-full of eucalyptus leaves for making vapor pots.

They had made their way to the head of the line by the time Alafair turned her attention to the matter at hand. Elizabeth and Cindy had already moved on and Shaw was giving their information to Miss Weston. Marshal Dillon stood beside the woman's chair with his hands clasped behind him, silently giving everyone the once-over from under the wide, downturned brim of his Stetson. Alafair realized to her discomfort that she was the object of the marshal's interested observation. She blinked at him and his lips curved upward in a smile that was far too sardonic for her taste.

"Miz Tucker," he said. "We meet again."

"So we do, Marshal."

They gazed at one another for a moment, both unwilling to be the first to look away.

Alafair decided she might as well use the stare-down to good advantage. "How do you suppose the money got into the schoolhouse, Marshal?"

Dillon was willing to speculate. "I'm guessing that somebody was using the abandoned building as a cache for his savings. Or his ill-gotten swag."

"How much money do you reckon was there?"

The marshal shrugged. "There's no way to tell, now. Most folks around here are honest enough, and I reckon most of the money they picked up got turned in when Carleton asked for it. But I'm sure a lot of those coins ended up in pockets and handbags. Carleton's man is still counting it, but he thinks they retrieved around two hundred dollars worth of U.S. and Mexican currency."

Shaw finished his business with Miss Weston, tipped his hat to Dillon, and took Alafair by the arm.

"How are you going to find out whose money it is, Marshal?" Alafair asked over her shoulder as they moved out of the way of the next person in line.

"Well, somebody will have to be able to prove that it's his before we turn it over, and I don't rightly see how that can be done. Even so, we'll keep it in the City Hall safe for a spell, just to be fair. Then I suspect that the money will end up going to the town for improvements."

They retrieved Blanche and joined Elizabeth and Cindy, who had already walked back to the Hupmobile and were buttoning up their dusters. Elizabeth was still red-cheeked with exhilaration as she handed the Tuckers their protective wear from the back seat. "I told you this would be an adventure, didn't I?"

Matt Carrizal's Restaurant

The trip back to Tempe was rife with speculative chatter. Elizabeth drove along at an easy pace that raised little dust and allowed her passengers to enjoy the sparkling winter day and the company. Cindy was laughing and bright-eyed, her unhappy situation momentarily forgotten. Blanche's elbows were perched on the back of the front seat so she would not miss a word of what her aunt and Cindy were talking about. Alafair had little to say. Shaw recognized her absorbed silence. She was not thinking things over. No, her silence was deeper than that. She was quieting that active mind and letting things think themselves over. It was a rare and rather odd talent she had which her husband accepted without trying to understand.

"My goodness, look at the time!" Elizabeth exclaimed. "It's near to two o'clock. Y'all must be about to faint from hunger. Say, would you enjoy to have dinner at Matt Carrizal's restaurant? He has the nicest little place on the corner of Fifth and Ash."

Cindy clapped her hands. "Oh, let's! I haven't had dinner at Matty's restaurant in I don't know how long."

In the few days they had been in Arizona, Shaw had developed a taste for Sonoran-style cooking, so he agreed enthusiastically and at once. Alafair was more interested in seeing how Matt Carrizal made a living.

The route back into town was nearly the reverse of the way they had driven out. Elizabeth turned west off of Canal Street onto Eighth, then north again when they reached Mill Avenue.

Then a left turn onto Fifth Street and only one block to the corner of Fifth and Ash. Carrizal's Restaurant was located in a free-standing adobe building with a pitched shingle roof. It looked like a converted cottage with a large, multipaned picture window in front and practically an entire garden of herbs and flowers in big clay pots all along the front. A hand-painted sign directed them to a graded area for customers to park their conveyances, horse-drawn and otherwise, in a vacant lot half-way down the block.

The interior of the restaurant was just as homey and inviting as the exterior. Some ten tables were scattered around a large dining room, all covered in cheerful lemon-colored cloths with vases of little red petunias in the center. Alafair looked around with approval. The place was clean and bright and welcoming, like sitting down to eat at a neighbor's home. Still, she wished she could inspect the kitchen.

Matt Carrizal himself greeted them at the door. The dining room was empty at this late hour, so he pulled together two tables for them next to the sunny picture window.

"I am so honored you have decided to grace my humble establishment!"

Elizabeth gave him an insouciant wink. "Why, Matt, I couldn't let my kinfolks spend any time in Tempe without treating them to your delicious fare."

Cindy agreed. "Matty serves the best Mexican food in Tempe." She placed a hand on Matt's arm and turned to address Shaw and Alafair across the table. "Did you meet Matt at the pot luck the other night? Matty and I have known one another ever so long, since we were teens, really. We had a poetry class together at the Normal School. Then when I married, I discovered that Geoff's house is neighbor to Matty's parents'. Can you imagine?"

Matt reddened as she gushed. Embarrassed at how she was fussing over him, surely, but Alafair noted how the pupils of his dark eyes widened as he gazed at her.

He emitted a laugh. "As you can see, Cindy and I are good enough friends that I allow her to call me Matty." His tone was teasing.

Elizabeth was too hungry for banter. "Well, Matt, we've been out and about all day and I dare say there's no one at this table who couldn't eat a horse. What do you have cooking this afternoon?"

"Leave it to me, Elizabeth. I'll serve you up a feast."

He served them himself, though judging by the way he was dressed, in a dazzlingly white shirt, sharply creased twill dress trousers and matching waistcoat, he usually acted the host and left the waitressing duties to the apron-clad young woman with dark hair who handed the dishes out of the kitchen into his hands. He brought out dish after dish, starting with a steamy, meatball-filled soup he called *albondigas*. The Tuckers had already had their first taste of tamales and enchiladas at Elizabeth's open house and attacked the main course with gusto. Matt supplemented the meal with a piled-high platter of corn tortillas fresh off the grill, and a delicious green dish he called *nopal*.

"This tastes like green beans," Alafair observed.

"It's fried-up prickly-pear cactus pads," Elizabeth told them gleefully.

The food was delicious, but foreign, and Alafair worried that in the way of children, Blanche would refuse to eat it. At first she did appear to be skeptical, but gamely tried each dish and decided she liked it. Not for the first time Alafair was glad that none of her kids were picky eaters. They ended with dishes of sweet, custardy *flan* smothered in a creamy caramel sauce. When the last dishes were taken away, there was a long contented silence as everyone contemplated the feast they had just enjoyed.

Matt came out of the kitchen and stood sleek and satisfied as his guests plied him with compliments.

An Upsetting Matter

Elizabeth placed her yellow-and-white checked cotton napkin on the table. "Sit down with us for a spell, why don't you, Matt? Tell us what you had to say to Marshal Joe Dillon when he came by to talk to you about poor Bernie Arruda."

Her change of topic cast a chill over the merriment. Alafair cast a quick look at Cindy, who sagged back into her chair, still too weak to hold on to her good humor in the face of an upsetting matter. Elizabeth obviously cared for Cindy, but Alafair thought her sister was not as sensitive to her friend's fragility as she ought to be. Not everyone was as emotionally tough as Elizabeth Kemp.

Matt sat down readily enough, not as much upset as willing to trade information about the untimely death of his late employee. "Yes, Mama told me what you said about Mr. Dillon's visit with y'all. I cannot think of who might have killed Bernie, can you? When Dillon came here early on the morning after Bernie died, I told him that Bernie worked for me sometimes. He did repairs and clean-up around the restaurant, sometimes played his guitar and sang in the evenings. He even waited tables once in a while. Dillon asked me about my relationship with Bernie, of course, but I didn't have much to tell him. I know his brother Tony much better. He is my head cook. In fact, he's in the kitchen right now."

"He made this delicious meal?" Shaw asked.

Matt smiled. "He did. Tony is the one who first told me Bernie was dead, that next morning when he came in for the breakfast shift. It is sad. The brothers were close. Dillon showed up right after to talk to me."

"Did he ask if you and Bernie had a fight that evening at the open house?" Elizabeth asked.

Matt rared back, surprised. "No, he did not. Did someone say so?"

Elizabeth shrugged. "All I know is that when he came by to question us, he asked if we'd seen you and Bernie get into a fight."

"A 'scrape,' is what he said," Shaw corrected.

Matt's laugh was incredulous. "Not hardly. I did have a few words with all three Arrudas that night, but it was all quite cordial."

"What did you talk about?" Elizabeth's forthright questioning may have been impolitic, but it was to the point. Alafair placed her elbows on the table and leaned forward, interested in spite of herself.

For the first time, Matt's gaze slid away before he answered. If she had not been looking right at him, Alafair would not have seen it. "The usual folderol, mostly about the restaurant," he said. "I spent more time talking to Tony than Bernie or Jorge that night."

"Well, Dillon had his nose atwitch about something you and Bernie may have said to one another that night," Elizabeth said. "Could you tell what Dillon had on his mind when he questioned you?"

"Not that! He must have got that idea from somebody he talked to between when he talked to me and then y'all. He did ask me if I thought Bernie was a *Villista*. I reckon that with all this worry about Pancho Villa's roving army coming across the border Dillon thought he had better make sure Bernie had not been an advance scout or something of the like."

"And what did you tell him?" Shaw wondered.

Matt laughed. "I told him not hardly. Bernie hated Diaz, Huerta, and Villa, the whole bunch of them, after his family was displaced by the war. But of course Dillon doesn't know one revolutionary faction from another."

"Well, he asked us a bunch of questions about you when he was by my house, though I think we put him onto another scent. You'd best be on the lookout for another visit from the marshal, though, Matt. Just in case." Elizabeth tapped a finger on the table as she delivered her warning.

Cindy spoke for the first time since the subject of Bernie Arruda had been raised. "I do not like that marshal." Her voice trembled.

Matt looked at Cindy across the table, his entire mien softening. "Mr. Dillon has a tough job, Cindy." His tone was soothing. "He has to be tough to do it. I can put up with a hard line of questioning if that is what it takes to discover who did this cruel murder."

Elizabeth looked amused at Matt's gentle handling, but Alafair and Shaw cast one another a glance.

Cindy sniffed. "I suppose you're right, Matty. He had our houses searched, though, and I cannot stand the thought of those men pawing my things. Web thinks he'll search the homes of everyone at the party, so be warned."

Matt's eyebrows knit. "He searched your house?"

Cindy leaned across the table and covered his hand with her own. "There was nothing for him to find. Still, I didn't like it one bit."

Elizabeth made a disdainful noise. "Oh, pooh, Cindy. He doesn't really think any of us conked Bernie. He just wanted to give me a hard time for my lip."

Money

Cindy seemed comforted by Elizabeth's certainty and eager to change the subject. "Oh, Matty, we've had the most wonderful adventure today. We spent the morning out at the old Rural School, watching them make the motion picture."

Matt grinned at her enthusiasm. "Did you really? I've seen the shooting once or twice since they have been here. It is interesting. I think that by now most of the actors and workers have had a meal or two here, as well."

Blanche spoke up. "Did you meet Dorothy Clark?"

"Is she the young one? Yes, she has been here with her mother and some of the others three or four times. She is a very pleasant young lady."

"Why, Matt," Elizabeth teased, "such luster and glory! You should place a big sign right outdoors. 'Famous Actors Ate Here!' You could charge extra for folks to sit in the same chair Hobart Bosworth sat in."

Cindy giggled. "Oh, Elizabeth, you are awful."

Matt was willing to go along with the joke. "That's not a bad idea! So tell me, I heard there were going to be fireworks on the set today. Was it exhilarating?"

"Thrilling!" Cindy exclaimed.

"Loud," Alafair said.

"Eye-popping," Shaw agreed, "and more than the film people bargained for, I'll allow. The explosives man planted a hair too much dynamite and blew that building into toothpicks, and somebody's cache of money sky high."

Matt's eyes widened. "Money," he repeated.

Elizabeth held out a slender arm and pushed up her sleeve to reveal a small round bruise. "You would not have believed the evidence of your own eyes, Matt. Coins and bills of every ilk came tumbling down among the shards of wood like a golden rain from heaven. Some poor wretch picked the worst place in the world to hide his poker winnings."

Elizabeth, Cindy, and Blanche enthusiastically finished the story, too wrapped up in their tale to notice that Matt had not blinked or twitched a muscle since the word money was uttered. When they finished, Alafair observed that Matt's olive complexion had paled a couple of shades.

Tony Arruda

Shaw walked with Elizabeth to retrieve the automobile, leaving Alafair, Blanche, and Cindy sitting content on a bench in front of the eatery. Blanche was eager to restore her new friend's good humor with talk of the motion picture, so Alafair left the two to their pleasant reminiscence and took the opportunity to walk a little way up the sidewalk for a better look at the neighborhood. She got as far as the corner of the little adobe house when she glanced down the alley and caught sight of the screen door at the back of the restaurant fly open and a man with the stub of a cigarette in his mouth step outside. He was pulling on a twill jacket over his white bibbed apron, walking like a man with a destination in mind. He was small, smaller than Alafair, and she was no more than middle height for a woman. His complexion was the dark red-brown of polished mahogany. Without his rakish black and silver *charro* outfit, Alafair would not have known him on the street, but after Matt's assertion that he was at that moment working in the kitchen, she expected this was Tony Arruda, Bernie's brother.

She cast a quick look over her shoulder to see Cindy and Blanche still sitting on the bench with their heads together. Shaw and Elizabeth had not yet turned off the street into the restaurant parking lot. She had a few minutes.

"Excuse me, mister!" She started down the alley, and the man stopped and turned his head to look at her.

As she walked toward him his eyebrows knit, plainly wondering what on earth this strange Anglo woman could possibly have to say to him.

As she neared, Alafair could see that he bore a disturbing resemblance to the dead man. "Excuse me for bothering you, sir, but are you Tony Arruda?"

He blinked at her. "Yes, *Señora*. How can I help you?"

"My name is Miz Shaw Tucker. I am sister to Miz Webster Kemp, at whose house you and your brothers played music the other night. I am the one who found your brother's body the next morning, and I wanted to take this opportunity to say that I'm very sorry for your loss."

The expression on Tony's face grew more skeptical as she talked, as though he seriously doubted her sincerity. "Thank you, *Señora*."

"I understand Mr. Dillon delivered the horrible news to your family."

"Yes."

"Do you have any idea who may have murdered your poor brother?"

He shook his head. Alafair could tell that he was anxious to get on with his errand and was not inclined to discuss the matter with her, but he did offer her a soft answer as an acknowledgment of her expression of concern. "Bernie knew many people, *Señora*, and had his hand in many pots. He was a man with much emotion, laughed easy and fought easy, too." No more speculation than that.

Alafair came at it another way. "I understand he enjoyed his acting job in the motion picture."

"He did."

"Was Bernie married?"

"His wife died in Mexico, *Señora*, but he has a daughter here. She lives with our mother."

"Oh, I'm so sorry. Where do they live?"

"In Guadalupe." He crushed the cigarette under his heel then looked back up at her, his manner still deferential but a spark of defiance lit his black eyes. "Why do you wish to know?"

Alafair approved of the lift of his chin. "Would it be all right if I made a call of condolence to them?"

Tony smiled for first time. "You are kind, *Señora*, but it is not necessary."

"Has the marshal released you brother's body?"

"He has."

"When is the funeral?"

"Tomorrow."

"Alafair?" She turned at the sound of her name. Shaw was leveling a curious stare at her from the head of the alley. "You ready to get on back?"

"Coming," she called, and turned back to Tony. "I am sorry, Mr. Arruda. Please express my condolences to your family."

By the time she reached Shaw, Tony had disappeared around the back of the building. Shaw took her arm and ushered her toward the Hupmobile, which was waiting in front of the restaurant with all hands on board. "That was Tony Arruda, Bernie's brother," she said, anticipating his question. "I was just telling him I was sorry for his loss."

Shaw knew Alafair better than that. "Did he have any idea about who did his brother in?"

"If he did he wasn't going to tell me about it." They climbed into the back seat next to Blanche. "Elizabeth," Alafair said, as they took off, "where did you say this town of Guadalupe is?"

Unrequited

They stopped long enough to retrieve Chase from Mrs. Carrizal's tender care and to drop Cindy off at her front door. They walked into Elizabeth's house feeling tired and grubby after their adventure. Alafair hauled Blanche into the veranda bedroom and washed her down, made her drink a cup of healing tea, and lie down for a nap.

She found Shaw and Elizabeth in the parlor. They had draped themselves comfortably across the divans, and Shaw withdrew one long leg so she could sit down next to him. Chase was nowhere to be seen. *Elizabeth has probably sent him outside to wander the neighborhood like a stray dog,* Alafair thought, and wished they had left him with Mrs. Carrizal until supper. For a few minutes the three of them sat in silence, sipping mugs of sweet tea.

It was Shaw who broke the spell with a laconic question. "So, Elizabeth, how long has Matt Carrizal been in love with Cindy?"

Alafair sputtered a laugh. Trust him to read her mind.

Elizabeth, on the other hand, was stunned. Her mouth dropped open. "Why, Shaw Tucker, where did you get such an idea?"

It was Alafair who answered. "Oh, come, Elizabeth, you'd have to be blind as a post hole not to recognize that moon-struck look. I have four daughters who are spoken for, and I've seen that look in the eyes of each of my sons-in-law."

Elizabeth slowly leaned forward and placed her goblet on the tea table, giving herself time to consider. "Well, I'll be switched.

That is something that never occurred to me. Of course, I don't get the chance to see the two of them together very often." She sat back. "I'll tell you this, though. If Matt has tender feelings for Cindy, she don't return the sentiment. Not in the same way, at least. Cindy and I have been friends for a long time, and she has never hinted that her eye has wandered. Of course, I met her after she married Geoff and moved in next door. Until today I had no idea that Matt and Cindy knew one another before that. She was crazy about Geoff when I first knew her, and she still would be if he'd give her the slightest reason. As it is, now she's just crazy because of him."

Neither Alafair nor Shaw spoke, so Elizabeth shifted in her chair and continued. "I declare, if what you suspect is true, I wish Cindy had known that Matt fancies her before she fell for Geoff! But then Matt is too good. Cindy don't think a man loves her unless he runs roughshod over her. That's the example she learned from the way her daddy treats her mama. Geoff already owned that house when they married. All he needed was the right kind of wife to keep it for him and produce an heir. She'd have been much better off with Matt, but there would have been no possibility—her daddy would never allow her to involve herself with a Mexican-blood man, no matter how respected and successful. Those Gillanders are a proud bunch, cross-ways to all but their own kind."

It was Shaw's turn to laugh. "Doc Moeur said almost the same thing to me about the Gillanders on the night of the party!"

An Inordinately Proud Bunch

The Moeurs had been among the last guests to leave that night. Shaw had walked Dr. Moeur to his Franklin roadster parked in front of the house and the two men had gazed up at the star-filled sky and talked while they waited for Mrs. Moeur to say her farewell to the hostess.

"How'd you get out here to Arizona, Doc?" Shaw had told his own story so many times over the course of the evening that he was eager to hear someone else's tale for a change.

Moeur was willing. "Well, after I got done with my medical studies and married Honor, I was looking for someplace to set up practice. My brother Bill was already here, and he said I ought to come out because Arizona was wide open and full of promise. So out we come. We ended up here in Tempe almost twenty years ago, now." Moeur paused to light an enormous stogie. "I was born in Tennessee, myself. But I went to school in Arkansas to study doctoring."

"Where at in Arkansas?"

"Fayetteville."

Shaw was as delighted as if he had accidentally met a heretofore unknown relative. "Why, that's our old stomping ground! My daddy's family has lived around Mountain Home for as long as any living soul can remember, and my mama's folks ran off from the Trail of Tears and hid back up there in the hills near to a hundred years ago."

"Well, I'll be. It is a small world, isn't it?"

"It is that. Do y'all like living out here?"

"I love it," Moeur said, amid plumes of smoke. "Bill was right about Arizona being full of promise. You wouldn't believe the growth around here since we joined the Union." He paused. "You know, I worked as hard for statehood as anybody. I even helped write up our state constitution. But as much progress as has been made in the last four years, I have to say there are some things I liked better about being a territory."

Shaw gave a sage nod. "I know just what you mean. We moved out to Oklahoma from Arkansas in '93, right after the bank panic. It was still the Indian Territory then. We got statehood in '07, which it's nice to be able to vote for President and all, but now there are a lot more rules and regulations than there used to be. And some of the carpetbaggers and speculators who have moved in lately..." He let the comment hang and took the opportunity to broach another topic. "What'd you think about Gillander's hubbledebub?"

Moeur chewed his cigar for a moment while he considered his reply. "Oh, old Duncan is harmless. They're an inordinately proud bunch, those Gillanders. Sort of think God created a special place in the universe just for them. Scotchmen, you know."

Shaw thought of Alafair's Gunn relatives and smiled. "I know."

"What worries me, though, is that there are a lot of folks around here that agree with him. Too many believe that all the Mexican immigrants are just coming across in order to take what we have."

Shaw caught the doctor's tone. "But you don't."

"Like Levi said, there is a terrible lot of violence and unrest down there right now. I'd want to get my family out of that situation, too." Moeur had sighed and flicked a column of ash into the ditch.

Anything is Possible

"Matt seems like a fine man to me, Elizabeth," Shaw said. "I'd be proud to have him for one of my girls. Do you know him well?"

Elizabeth shrugged. "I know him through his folks. I reckon any son of Mr. and Miz Carrizal is a person worth knowing. Why? What are you thinking?" The fact that Shaw and Alafair had so quickly noticed something about her friend Cindy that she had not gathered after years of acquaintance had shaken her.

Alafair answered as though it was she who had posed the question in the first place. "Well, nothing to speak of, really. It just seemed to me that Matt was awful distrait when he heard about the cache of money that got blown up."

Elizabeth's expression said this was going too far. "Now, if you are suggesting that Matt Carrizal is connected with that money or anything else distasteful, you are seeing things that aren't there, sister. If you threw a rock into a crowd, whoever you hit would be as likely to be the culprit at Matt."

"All right, honey, you know him way better than I do. I'm just thinking aloud."

Elizabeth looked stubborn. "Don't think such thoughts aloud when Joe Dillon is around. You know he's fishing around for some reason to latch onto Matt."

"You're right. I'll keep my speculation to myself." Alafair's tone was soothing, and Elizabeth seemed satisfied.

The conversation moved on, and Alafair had little to say until Elizabeth picked up the tea glasses and took them back into the kitchen. When she was out of the room, Alafair leaned close and spoke to Shaw just loud enough to be heard. "That money was put there by Bernie Arruda."

He turned his head to look at her. "What makes you say that?" She often pulled these conclusions out of thin air, which both amused and annoyed him. She was often right, which amused and annoyed him even more.

"Mr. Bosworth said it was Bernie who found the schoolhouse location for the motion picture..."

Shaw interrupted her. "Then he would have known they were going to dynamite the building. Why would he hide his money there?"

This little detail did not bother her. "He meant to fetch the money away before the explosion. But he didn't get the chance before he got killed. Also, Tony Arruda tore out of Matt's restaurant in a hurry after we left. I figure Matt told him what happened out at the film set and he was off to tell someone else. I meant to ask him about the money when I saw him in the alley, but he made his escape before I could finagle it out of him."

"So somehow Matt is involved and Tony, too? Now that's convoluted thinking, Alafair. If Bernie's murderer intended to steal his money, he must have killed Bernie before he found out where it was. Not a very good plan."

"Or maybe the murderer did know where the money was, but not that Mr. Carleton aimed to destroy the building today."

"Where do you reckon our Yaqui handyman got himself a bag of money and what do you figure he aimed to do with it?"

"I don't know. Could be he's been saving it for a long time. Elizabeth said he was a lover. Maybe he expected to run off with somebody. Or maybe it had to do with the revolution. Does it matter?"

Shaw was not going to let her get off that easily. "Or more likely, the stash isn't Bernie's, the killer didn't know anything about the money, and Bernie got done in for some different reason altogether."

Alafair smiled. "Anything is possible."

"Anything is possible inside your head, honey," he teased.

An Afternoon Drive

Since Webster had decided to take the day off on Thursday, the family enjoyed a lovely homestyle dinner late in the morning consisting of fried chicken, biscuits and gravy, Elizabeth's own canned green beans, and a spring salad of baby lettuce, green onions, and radishes fresh from the garden, dressed with hot bacon and its drippings. They ate outdoors, taking advantage of yet another warm, dry, sunny, March day.

The Carrizals were taking the air in their own back yard, and it was not long before Artie Carrizal joined Blanche and Chase in a rousing game of kick-the-can on the Kemp side of the fence.

"This would be a nice afternoon to take a drive, don't you think?" Alafair posed the suggestion innocently enough, but Shaw gave her a suspicious look along his shoulder. He had no reason to suspect her motives, since Alafair had not bothered to tell him that Bernie Arruda's funeral was today. It was just that Alafair seldom did anything innocently enough.

Elizabeth jumped at the idea, always up for any activity that took her away from the house.

"I'd just as soon stay home," Web said, and Alafair looked over at him, startled. *Oh, yes, Web!* She had forgotten him, and he was sitting right next to her.

He was still talking. "I like to read my paper of an afternoon. But y'all go on ahead if you've a mind."

Elizabeth bit her lip. "I expect Blanche would rather stay here and play with Artie, if I'm any judge of girls."

Shaw came to the rescue. "I'll stay here with Web and keep an eye on the young'uns. I reckon I've had enough of gallivanting about for a day or two."

Now it was Alafair's turn to give Shaw a considering look. She quickly dismissed the thought that he might be on to her and seized her chance. "Good, then! Elizabeth and me will meander around a while, just us two sisters. She can show me some of the countryside."

They bundled up in their travel dusters, hats, and scarves, and lowered the Hupmobile's top, all the better for sightseeing. Elizabeth had barely pulled the vehicle out of the garage shed and turned onto Willow Street when Alafair spilled the beans.

"Yesterday, when you and Shaw were off fetching the auto after we had dinner at Matt's place, I had a word with Tony Arruda out in the alley. He told me that the family is holding Bernie's funeral today out in Guadalupe."

Elizabeth gave her a shocked glance, but when she spoke her voice was bubbling with laughter. "Why, Alafair, you are full of surprises! Can you be suggesting that we make a call upon the bereaved and incidentally see if we can glean any information that could help solve the mystery of Bernie's murder?"

Elizabeth had encompassed her entire less-than-savory purpose in the blink of an eye. Alafair's discomfort at having her unbecoming curiosity unmasked made her contrary. "Why, Elizabeth, how could you be so flip about it? A man has died and his family is in pain. I feel bad since I was the one found him, and I want to express my condolence. That is all."

Elizabeth's conscience was not quite so tender, but she governed her expression of delight for Alafair's sake. "You're right, sister. I apologize for my callousness. I wish we had thought to bring something for the family, though. I hate to show up empty-handed."

"Oh, don't worry about that." Alafair retrieved her carpet-bag off the floorboard and drew out a square wicker basket containing Cindy Stewart's little white cake from the open house, so pretty that the guests had been loath to cut it.

"How thoughtful of you," Elizabeth said drily.

Guadalupe

The village of Guadalupe was less than six miles from downtown Tempe, but Elizabeth had never been there and was only reasonably sure of their route. She took the Hupmobile south down Mill Avenue out of town and across two tree-lined canals that cut through fields of newly planted cotton, all the way to its end at a wide dirt road called Baseline that stretched straight as a plumb line east and west. She turned west on the Baseline road and drove for about a mile out into the desert, past bean fields, a cow or two, and some fence, toward a long, treeless mountain that Elizabeth called South Mountain, since it was south of Phoenix.

Alafair was beginning to feel uncomfortable and glanced at Elizabeth, who was staring grimly down the road in front of her as she drove.

"Do you know where you're going?" Alafair asked.

Elizabeth's tone was untroubled. "It's around here somewhere. Look, there's a road!"

"More like a footpath," Alafair said.

Elizabeth downshifted and they rolled over the ruts slowly enough to be able to read the handmade sign stuck on a pole at the intersection. The paint had faded from black to a rusty brown, but they could make out the word "*basline*" over the horizontal east-west arrow, and "*ave de yaqui*" beside the vertical north-south arrow. "This must be it." Elizabeth sounded confident as she turned south toward the unknown, the long, bare South Mountain looming over them on their right.

They could see the settlement for ten minutes before they arrived, set as it was on a slight rise and shaded all around by palms and lacy desert mesquites. Guadalupe was a scrappy-looking place, but well-kept and homey. It even looked familiar, Alafair thought, since it was set up like a Cherokee village, with small thatched houses arranged in a rectangle around a large, open, packed-earth plaza. Only here the thatch was made of palm fronds instead of branches and cornstalks, and the walls were adobe brick instead of wattle-and-daub. The yards sported fences and shady ramadas fashioned from the tall ribs of ocotillo cactus. The air was perfumed with the aroma of parched corn, beans, and roasting meat. And unlike a Cherokee village, sitting side by side in the center the huge plaza were two beautiful mission-style church buildings instead of a council house. Both were painted dazzlingly white, and both sported three flower-draped crosses on the roof, one on each of the two bell towers that rose at either front corner, and one over the large central doorway.

The plaza was empty except for a pack of small brown boys playing ball. Elizabeth came to a stop in front of the larger of the churches, and the children quit their game and stood gaping at them as though they were some species of alien life.

Alafair and Elizabeth, feeling quite as alien as the boys suspected, gaped back.

"Do you suppose it would be all right if we went inside the church?" Alafair ventured at length.

She was speaking to Elizabeth, but the boys instantly took to their heels and disappeared around the church building toward a tiny house barely visible in the back.

Elizabeth swung one leg out of the car, but sat with her foot suspended over the ground. "I'm almost afraid to get out," she admitted. "I feel like an intruder."

A small black mongrel dog hoisted itself up from its resting place under one of the lacy trees and trotted up to sniff amiably at Elizabeth's boot. She drew her foot back into the vehicle, so the dog peed on one of the tires and returned to his roost.

The mob of chattering children reappeared from behind the church leading a man of close to Alafair's own age dressed in a long brown robe that was belted by a piece of rope with a long string of wooden beads suspended from it. The man was tall and thin and brown as a nut, but the eyes that gazed calmly at the two women were a clear light grey. He was clad in an outfit that Alafair could not explain at all, but his kind eyes instilled trust.

"Can I help you ladies?" He had a slight accent, but it did not sound to Alafair like Spanish. "I'm Father Lucius, the priest here."

Both women dismounted and shook his proffered hand. Elizabeth took it upon herself to speak first. "I'm Elizabeth Kemp from Tempe, and this is my sister, Alafair Tucker. We heard that Bernie Arruda's funeral was to be today. We were acquainted with him."

"Yes, it was. I'm sorry but you have missed it. The funeral Mass was at dawn this morning and Bernie has already been laid decently in his grave. How did you know Bernie?"

"For the past few years he has done odd jobs for my family. I liked him. And I am sorry to say that his body was found in the canal directly in front of my house."

Father Lucius looked startled at this pronouncement, so Alafair stepped in. "We wanted to express our condolences."

The priest turned his arresting gaze to her face and apparently liked what he saw, for he smiled. "Would you ladies like to speak to his family? They are all gathered at his mother's home after the funeral."

"We would hate to intrude," Elizabeth's lips said, though her eager expression said, *"more than anything."*

"I would be very glad to escort you. His mother's house is just a little way from the *playa* here. I am sure the family will be comforted to know that you held Bernie in enough regard to make the long trip all the way out here from Tempe."

"I do not wish to put you out, sir," Alafair said, and meant it.

"Not at all!" Father Lucius spread his arms and began herding the women and his flock of urchins toward the south side of the square. "Besides, you will be in need of a translator, since *Señora* Arruda is a Yaqui and speaks neither English or Spanish."

Alafair was glad he offered to come, though she knew from experience that at least one of *Señora* Arruda's surviving sons spoke English very well.

The Arrudas

Mrs. Arruda's house was more than just a little way from the *playa*. They set off on foot in the general direction of South Mountain, following a well-worn footpath that led between the houses lining the square, past a few truck gardens and a smattering of small adobe homesteads. Many families were outside on this pretty afternoon, adults sitting in kitchen chairs under the trees and children dashing hither and yon with dogs at their heels.

Their party gathered more than its share of stares, though none were unfriendly, due mostly, Alafair expected, to the presence of Father Lucius. He had a wave and a word for everyone he saw, and was always rewarded with smiles and a jovial word in return. He had not bothered to dismiss their accompanying hoard of juvenile ball players, who were still trotting along behind, beside, and before them, occasionally breaking off one member to dash into a yard in passing and chatter out an explanation to the curious family as to why the good father had a couple of strange white women in tow. These outliers more often than not returned with one or two barefoot additions to the parade, so that when they finally arrived at the forlorn group of adobe huts hunched together behind an ocotillo fence crowning the top of a small bare hill, Alafair figured that like the Pied Piper they had gathered up half the under-ten population of the town.

At a sharp word from Father Lucius the mob of ragamuffins halted at the front gate, which the priest opened before standing aside to allow his charges to pass through in front of him. The yard was already full of its own children, all of whom halted in mid-game, frozen by curiosity, as the visitors walked up the path. A large group of men of all ages, all dressed in their Sunday best, were gathered around the front door of the house, some standing, some sitting on benches and chairs. All rose when the priest approached.

Father Lucius explained his mission to the elders in a language the like of which Alafair had never heard. But even though she did not understand a word, she recognized it as an Indian tongue by its nasal tone and guttural accents. The elder nodded and the sea of men parted to make way for their visitors to go into the house.

She cast her eye quickly around the room. The lime-washed walls were covered with hand-loomed blankets, woven palm frond crosses, and sepia-tinted family photographs. A beehive fireplace had been built into one corner of the room, and a tall wooden cabinet, painted green with cheerful hand-painted decoration on the doors stood in another. Atop the cabinet sat a strange white cloth dome topped by the horned head of a small deer, its white-rimmed, black glass eyes gazing into the distance, preoccupied with the afterlife.

The scene in the tiny parlor was familiar to anyone who had attended as many funerals as Alafair had. Several women sat together in the corner, grouped around a worn armchair that practically swallowed up the tiny woman perched therein. They did not have to be told that this was the dead man's mother, surrounded by her daughters. The two or three young men who stood sentinel behind the armchair would be her sons, one of whom was gaping at them with even more astonishment than his brothers.

Alafair acknowledged Tony Arruda with a nod before Father Lucius drew her and Elizabeth forward and introduced them to the matriarch of the Arruda clan. She was incredibly small and brown, with sharp black eyes embedded in a mass of wrinkles. Even so, she was not so old as all that, Alafair reckoned. Not much older than herself. She did not appear to have been weeping. Resigned, more like. Alafair had seen that stoic expression on the faces of most of the country women she knew after they had endured a lifetime of what came with surviving on the frontier. For a moment Alafair forgot everything but her feeling for a woman who had just lost her son. Elizabeth blinked in surprise as Alafair handed her the carpetbag she was carrying, dropped to one knee and took the little woman's hand in her own.

"I will pray for your son," Alafair said, unconcerned that the lady could not understand her words, "and pray for your heart's ease."

Father Lucius translated and Mrs. Arruda's lips barely curved. No matter that they did not have the same language, she recognized a fellow traveller on this path of bereavement. Elizabeth offered her own sympathy, and the two women stood quietly as Father Lucius took a moment to explain their presence to the assembled group.

Mrs. Arruda spoke, but before the priest could translate, a young girl, twelve or thirteen years old, appeared from behind one of the men to stand beside the armchair. "My grandmother thanks you for coming." The girl's English was barely accented. Her wealth of blue-black hair hung over her shoulders in two plaits as thick as her wrists, and her eyes, so black that her irises and pupils were undifferentiated, seemed to take up half her face. She was clad in an understated gray dress with a white ruffled yoke and small white flowers embroidered around the neck. She gazed at the visitors, straightforward and innocently curious.

"This is Natividad Arruda." The priest's voice was warm as he made the introduction. "Bernie's daughter."

Alafair felt her eyebrows lift. Bernie's daughter was older than she would have expected. She had not pegged Bernie as being much over thirty.

"Grandmother would like to offer you some refreshment." The girl delivered the invitation solemnly.

Alafair and Elizabeth exchanged a lingering look. What were they doing here? What had they expected would happen? Did they really think they were going to be able to walk into a man's funeral gathering and casually question the grieving family about their loved-one's murder? Even if they had had the gall to try, many of the Arrudas could not even speak English, and the ones who could, like Tony, were gazing at them with expressions halfway between thunderstruck and affronted at the intrusion. All but Natividad, who was waiting for their answer as though she really hoped they would stay.

The sisters arrived at a silent agreement and Alafair addressed Mrs. Arruda directly. "Ma'am, I think we have imposed on you enough this sad day." She retrieved her carpetbag from Elizabeth and drew the cake out of its little basket. One of Mrs. Arruda's daughters stood and took it from her with a nod.

"We came only because we are very sorry about what happened," Elizabeth said, and as Father Lucius translated, the two women stepped back in anticipation of leaving.

"Would you like to see where Papa is buried?" Natividad asked.

One of her uncles—Jorge, Alafair thought—said something in a sharp tone, but Mrs. Arruda held up a hand and the murmuring stopped as she spoke two quiet words. Natividad smiled and took Alafair's hand in one of hers and Elizabeth's in the other.

A Nice Place to Rest

Many volunteers offered to come with them, but in the end Natividad had her way and led her unlikely callers to the graveyard on her own. The land rose gently but steadily as they walked away from the village and toward the mountain. The little family cemetery sat on the side of a small hill, encircled by a rough fence and shaded by half-a-dozen green-barked palo verde trees that were just beginning to show tiny, piercing yellow flowers at the ends of their branches.

Natividad led them to a flower-covered mound. "Oh, it has been filled up!" she said, matter-of-fact. "When we left this morning, the grave was still open. Papa was in such a nice coffin…look, here is the wreath I made for him!"

Elizabeth caught her bottom lip between her teeth and blinked at her unbidden tears as the girl talked, unsure of how to react.

Alafair was not so reticent. "Thank you for letting us see where your papa is. This is a very nice place to rest."

Natividad smiled. "Papa will like it here." She turned around and pointed into the distance. The land fell away into a long vista, over the rooftops of Guadalupe and the distant green expanse of trees that covered Tempe. "Papa and me used to come up here sometimes at night. You can see all the way to the lights twinkling in Phoenix when the weather is clear. I like to pretend that it is the light of heaven, and someday I will be able to go there."

"I'm sure you will."

Natividad slid Alafair a speculative look. "Did you know my papa well?"

It was Elizabeth who answered. "Not well, darling. He helped my family with things at our home many times over the past few years. He was a nice man, and we liked him. We felt very bad when he died."

Natividad's gaze wandered back to middle space. "No one tells me anything," she stated. "I know they want to protect me. They say it was an accident, but I know Papa was killed."

So this is why she wanted to talk to us on her own. She wants to find out if we know anything. Dangerous ground, though. Alafair figured it was not her place to gainsay the girl's family. "Why do you think that?"

Natividad's expression did not change, but a dark shadow passed over her eyes. "I hear things. Everyone in town is talking about it. Besides, that marshal came to our house twice. The second time he asked my uncles all kinds of questions about Papa, and if he was working for Pancho Villa and the revolution. Why would he ask about that?"

Alafair put a hand on Natividad's shoulder. "We don't know anything about that, honey, I'm so sorry."

"Padre Lucius said you found Papa's body that morning."

Alafair nodded. "That is one reason my sister and I feel bad and wanted to come by."

If the comment was meant to distract Natividad from this line of inquiry, she was not having it. "Was my father murdered?"

This time Alafair hesitated before she answered. The girl's determination touched her, and she was not inclined to lie to her. She did want to protect her feelings as best she could, however. "I don't know what happened, darlin', I really don't. The marshal thinks it looks suspicious, though. That is why he's asking so many questions."

Natividad considered this for a moment, and when she spoke again, she seemed to have made a decision. "I was only seven when we came here. I don't remember very much about our home in Mexico. Soldiers took my mama and some of my aunts and cousins away when I was very small and made them slaves. They would have taken me, too, but they tell me that Mama hid me in the hay rack, and Papa found me after the soldiers were gone. He and my uncles and grandfather joined up with Villa, then, and my grandmother and others of my kin who were left hid in the mountains for a long time. All I remember about that is that I was frightened and hungry all the time. Finally Papa and two of my uncles came back from the war and we all walked many many days to cross the border. He said he was tired of fighting, that all the generals and presidents were bad men. Then Papa and my uncles made a society that has helped many people, Indians and Mexican both, to get out of Mexico, to get away from the war. They ask people to give them money and then use it to sneak into this country those who are persecuted or have lost their homes and families. Papa said the Anglos in Arizona were good because they gave us land for this town. That is all I know."

The three dark-eyed women stood over Bernie Arruda's grave in silence for a long moment after Natividad finished her story.

"That is a lot to know," Alafair said at last.

"If you come to know something as well, *Señoras*, is it possible I too may learn of it?"

Alafair drew a breath to answer, but Elizabeth beat her to it. "I doubt if my sister and I will be able to learn anything that will help you. But if we do, I promise to tell you. You are a smart, brave girl, Natividad, and deserve the truth."

The Yaqui Railroad

Elizabeth and Alafair said little to one another on the drive back to Tempe. They had turned off the Baseline Road and were heading up Mill Avenue when Alafair finally broke the troubled silence.

"It's no wonder Bernie wanted to be in that motion picture. He and his family lived the story. To all intents, he *was* Tambor the Yaqui."

Elizabeth was shaken. "I had no idea. I'll tell you, sister, I think a heap better of Bernie than I did. I thought him no more than a flirt and a lightweight."

"I reckon that is just the kind of behavior that would keep you from suspecting he was a smuggler of human beings."

"A hero, more like." Elizabeth's tone was forceful. "I'm put in mind of the underground railroad—delivering folks from oppression, violence, and slavery."

"I told Shaw that I had a suspicion that it was Bernie who hid the money in the schoolhouse…"

Elizabeth took her eyes off the road long enough to give Alafair an incredulous glance. "It makes sense!" she interrupted. "He and his compatriots would have to raise money to bring people north."

"It makes more sense now that we know what Bernie was doing. Earlier on I just figured it was odd that Bernie was the one who chose the schoolhouse location for the flicker and then ended up dead just before money rained down from the sky. Made my thumbs prick. Too many peculiar happenings one upon the heels of another are like to be connected no matter how unrelated they seem at first blush."

"Why would he hide the money so far away from where he lived, and in a place he knew was going to be destroyed eventually?"

"Shaw asked me the same question. All I can figure is that he aimed to fetch it away before the explosion but never got the chance. Or it could be it wasn't Bernie who put it there. Maybe it was one of the brothers or someone else connected to Bernie who knew about the abandoned building but didn't know about the planned explosion."

"If that was money for the Yaqui railroad, like we suspicion, how do you think they came by it?"

"It was all sorts of money, American and Mexican, mostly small bills and change. I reckon they raised it slowly, maybe donations from working folks who sympathized with their cause." Alafair smiled. "We are making whole cloth out of a few scraps, here, Elizabeth."

That fact did not bother Elizabeth. "I know, but I like the look of it. I wish we could go back to Guadalupe and have a word with Tony."

"We'd be about as welcome as smallpox. You saw how he looked at us when we turned up so soon after his brother's funeral. The Arruda brothers are not going to be inclined to confide in the likes of us."

Elizabeth drove and pondered for a few minutes before she said, "You told me that Tony lit out from the restaurant after we told Matt about the money."

The Hupmobile shuddered over a bump and Alafair clapped her hand over the crown of her hat. "I did."

"Well, then, I expect we both know someone else who knew about this Yaqui railroad. Are you up for a little detour?"

The Cause

Alafair was surprised when Elizabeth drove past Eighth Street and turned left on Fifth toward Matt Carrizal's restaurant. "Won't Matt be busy with customers, Elizabeth?"

"It's nearly three o'clock in the afternoon, Alafair. Too late for dinner and too early for supper. He's more than likely working on the books or cleaning up for the supper crowd now, so he's bound to be there. All the better for us to talk to him in private."

She parked the Hupmobile on the street directly in front of the restaurant and the two women got out. They could see through the front window that no one was seated in the dining room.

"It looks empty." Alafair sounded doubtful.

"Come on." Elizabeth walked down the alley with Alfair on her heels and knocked briskly at the back door through which Tony Arruda had made his earlier escape. "Matt," she called, "open up! It's Elizabeth Kemp and Alafair Tucker. We want to talk to you for a minute."

The door opened to reveal a perplexed Matt Carrizal staring at them from behind the screen. "Ladies," he managed, not too surprised to be polite. "What on earth are you doing at the back door? May I show you to a table in front?"

"We just come back from paying our respects to Bernie Arruda's family in Guadalupe. Had a chat with Bernie's daughter, and she told us about her daddy's sideline as a rescuer of the oppressed. We were wondering if you and Bernie happened to maintain a few interests in common."

As Elizabeth spoke, Matt's expression changed from puzzled to guarded. He stood silent for an instant after she finished, considering. He pushed the screen open and stood aside. "Y'all better come in."

◇◇◇

"Yes, I am involved with a network of good people who conspire to bring those displaced by the war out of Mexico and help them get settled in the United States." Matt had led the women through the kitchen, past the dark-haired waitress they had seen the day before and a cook who was a stranger to them. The three of them were now arranged around a table in the middle of the empty dining room. The only illumination was coming through the big picture window, but it was a sunny day and weary sadness showed clear on his face as he spoke.

"Me, the Arruda brothers, and a very few other people are involved in helping those who have lost everything to the revolution get out of Mexico and make a new start in this country. We have help in all three communities, Yaqui, Mexican, and Anglo, though we have tried to keep the project as small and quiet as possible. Our operation is secret—or was, until y'all figured it out. We don't want anyone thinking we are raising money for Villa's army or any other faction."

"We have no intention of telling anyone," Elizabeth assured him, and he managed a grateful smile before he continued.

"I am in charge of logistics. We have a message system through which I connect those who provide supplies, services, help for the newcomers to get settled. I coordinate bribes. There are always bribes. Bernie sometimes carried messages for me, but more importantly he was the banker, you could say, in charge of keeping safe the money that we raised, then meting it out as we needed. One other person always knew where Bernie stashed the bank. He was very careful to choose unlikely hiding places and to change them frequently."

"Was the other person his brother Tony?" Alafair asked.

Matt hesitated, but it was too late to put that particular cat back in the bag. He shrugged and nodded. "Bernie must have moved the money just before he was killed, for when Tony went to look for it, it was not where it was supposed to be. We had no idea where Bernie had put it."

Elizabeth propped her chin on a hand. "Could it be that someone got the idea that Bernie had made away with the money?"

Matt laughed. "No one who was acquainted with Bernie would credit that notion. He was passionate for the cause, Bernie was. If you talked to his family then you may have some idea what they suffered in Mexico, before the revolution and during. No, I am sure Bernie simply never got the chance to tell anyone where it was. It makes sense that he would hide it there, at least temporarily. He was the caretaker at the old Rural School until it closed."

"It doesn't sound to me like y'all were doing anything illegal by collecting money to help refugees." Alafair observed. "Are you going to make a claim to the marshal to have your money returned?"

The very idea caused Matt to gape at her. "I think not, Miz Tucker! We are smuggling noncitizens into this country, which is hardly legal. Besides which, the law and the citizenry around here tend to get riled up if they suspect you're raising money for revolutionaries and terrorists, and after the raid on Columbus, things have gotten even worse. We are like to get clapped into jail, if not strung up, before we can do any explaining."

He sighed and slumped back into his chair. "And it's not like the Mexican government or the *Villistas* would have any sympathy for our endeavor, either. Villa was like a saviour to the Yaquis at first, and Bernie was a great loyalist to his cause. An officer in his army, in fact, and close to Villa personally. But he and all his kin had a belly full of Villa's depredations in the end and deserted. And Villa is harsh on people he considers traitors."

"Dillon seems to have suspicions that Bernie was a *Villista*," Elizabeth said. "But I guess he wasn't after all."

"No, not any more. In fact I reckon that if Villa knew where any of the Arrudas were, especially Bernie, he would send assassins across the border to do them in."

"Maybe that's just what happened." Alafair speculated.

Matt looked defeated. "That is what Tony suspects. He's casting a doubtful eye on everyone of Mexican blood, looking for *Villista* spies everywhere. I just don't know. It seems likely that the money is involved somehow. Elizabeth, do you know how much money they finally picked up after the explosion?"

"Last I heard, it was close to two hundred dollars U.S. Do you know how much there was in the first place, Matt?"

His answering smile was without humor. "More than that. Sounds like some of the folks the money fell on can afford to travel to the mountains this summer."

"How did you get mixed up in all this?" To Alafair, Matt Carrizal seemed far too open and straightforward to be involved in even such well-meaning intrigue.

"One step at a time, Miz Tucker," Matt told her. "When the Indians began to escape slavery and make their way into the Arizona Territory, there were a lot of people who wanted to help. My father was one of them. He was involved with helping Father Lucius acquire the land where the village of Guadalupe is now, so the Yaquis could have their own place to live together. I met the Arruda brothers through my father when I was only a youngster. Papa helped them find work and later they helped me start this restaurant. I have always sympathized with their plight and was more than happy to assist when they asked me."

"You said Tony has become suspicious of Mexican people. Do you think he suspects you of being a secret spy?" Elizabeth asked.

"I don't think so. I hope not. I am of Spanish descent, but I am an American and have lived in Arizona all my life. I have no sympathy for any warmonger. Tony knows that."

"You are the man in charge of communications between the Anglo and Mexican communities?"

"I am, Elizabeth, because I speak Spanish and English, and have many connections in both worlds."

"So you know the names of the other people involved in your society?"

The corner of Matt's mouth quirked. He knew Elizabeth was about to pump him for more information than he was willing to give. "Yes, I have said so."

"Anyone we know?"

"I would not say if I thought you did."

Elizabeth put on an innocent expression. "I would never betray your confidence."

"I will not betray my friends, Elizabeth. My contacts are right to keep in the background. Anglos especially must be careful how they go about helping colored people. No matter how sympathetic they are, you never know what whites will do if you…" He stopped abruptly.

He was looking at Alafair, but she did not think he was seeing her. Her first thought was that it had suddenly dawned on him that he was speaking to white women and he did not want to offend them. She started to reassure him that she and her sister were not as white as all that, but his expression forestalled her. Something had occurred to him that had nothing to do with them. She leaned forward. "What is it, Matt?"

He snapped back into the present. "I just had an idea, Miz Tucker." He stood up. "I am sorry, ladies, but if you will excuse me, there is something I must do."

The summary dismissal took them by surprise, and neither woman moved for a moment. "Does this have to do with Bernie's murder?" Elizabeth managed at last.

"Never mind, Elizabeth. I don't want to say anything until I have investigated, but it is probably nothing."

He herded them out the front door so quickly that they did not have time to do more than sputter in confusion. They found themselves standing in the street, staring at one another.

"What was that about?" Elizabeth asked.

Alafair cocked her head. "Looks like he's unwilling to share his idea with us until he gets a better handle on it. I reckon we have heard all we're going to hear from Matt Carrizal today."

The Sombrero

Blanche could not help but feel sorry for her cousin Chase. Neither of his parents seemed to pay much attention to him, even though he was an only child. Blanche thought this extremely odd, since she belonged to a virtual mob of siblings and her parents watched her every move like a couple of nosy hawks. She had always been especially irritated by her mother's unflagging surveillance, but all in all, she supposed she would rather be paid too much attention than none at all.

Even so, Blanche had to admit that most of the time Chase was quite an annoying little boy. Artie Carrizal had come to play after dinner and Blanche would have enjoyed being in his company a lot more if Chase did not keep getting in the way.

Artie was great, though, and did not seem at all put out by Chase's continual clamoring and interruptions. And Artie was not nearly as big a teaser as her brothers. He actually seemed to like being around her, talking about school and what they both liked to do. He would even play games with her without once tripping her, or pulling her hair, or pinching or punching when no one was looking. That fact alone was enough to make Blanche like him very much indeed. Not to mention his good looks.

The middle of the afternoon found them playing baseball in Aunt Elizabeth's back yard. Artie was pitching, Daddy was catching, and Blanche was at bat. Uncle Webster and Artie's big sister Elena were sitting together in chairs under the ramada, drinking ice tea and cheering them on. Chase was the outfielder for this round, though Blanche had her doubts about how long that was going to last.

Blanche had not been able to play baseball with the others on the night of the party, and if Mama had not been on a drive with Aunt Elizabeth, she was not sure she would have been allowed to play now. So she wanted to give a good account of herself while she had the opportunity.

Artie stood sidelong on the mound, holding the ball at the small of his back as he eyed her along his shoulder. He gave her a long, speculative once-over and she smiled. She knew he was trying to break her concentration. She had too much experience with tricky siblings to fall for that. She adjusted her stance and glared back at him.

Chase was dashing about the outfield, and behind her, her father was traitorously calling encouragement to the pitcher. Artie reared back, lifted a leg and let it fly. It was a rocket, but she had been watching his performance and was prepared. She stepped into it and connected, the crack of the bat reverberating like a gunshot. She headed for the rug fragment that served as first base amid whoops of approbation from Uncle Webster and Elena, from Daddy, and sweetest of all, from Artie himself.

"Chase! Chase!" Daddy yelled, "heads up, partner! Go get the ball, see it? There it goes yonder!"

Chase blinked as the ball went sailing over his head, straight over the tall oleander privacy hedge that lined the fence and into the Stewarts' back yard. Blanche rounded the rug and ran for the dishpan at second as Chase ran through the gate between the properties.

Blanche was rounding second when Chase reappeared at the gate empty-handed. "It rolled under the back porch!" he yelled, distressed.

"Well, shinny under there and fetch it out!" Shaw's voice shook with laughter. "Hurry up, Sport!"

The boy disappeared again, all knees and elbows as he dashed for the porch.

Blanche rounded third to cheers and whistles and ran down the home stretch. She jumped on the home plate feed sack with both feet and a cry of triumph, but Daddy was not there to tag her or say "good job".

All the grown-ups were heading for the Stewarts' fence. Blanche frowned at Artie, who was still standing on the mound, and he frowned back. "What is it?" she asked.

"I don't know, I didn't see. Your papa just took off to running toward Miz Stewart's house and Mr. Kemp and Elena went after."

The children trotted hand in hand toward the adults clustered at the gate. A self-satisfied Chase was standing in the midst, white with dust and cobwebs. The baseball in his hand and a fancy black *sombrero* with elaborate white embroidery around the brim was perched jauntily on his head.

The back door to the Stewart house creaked open and Cindy stepped out. Her eyebrows knit at the sight of her neighbors bunched together on her side of the gate. "Did you all...?" Those were the only words she got out before her eyes fell on Chase's newfound headwear. She froze in bug-eyed suspended animation, mouth open and one arm extended.

"Artie, go get Mama and Papa," Elena Carrizal called over her shoulder as she bounded up the steps to Cindy's aid.

Puzzle Pieces

Elizabeth and Alafair returned home full of news after their adventures only to walk into the middle of yet another drama in full swing.

Shaw, Web, and Mr. Carrizal were gathered under the ramada in the Kemp back yard, staring at the battered and filthy *sombrero* on the table before them and discussing their next move. Cindy had been led to the Carrizal's, unprotesting as a dumb beast, where she now languished under the tender care of Mrs. Carrizal and Elena. The children had been sent to play inside the Kemp house.

"What I want to know," Web said, after a quick summary of events for Alafair and Elizabeth, "is how Bernie's hat got under Geoff's back porch when Bernie his own self lay dead in the canal in front of my house."

There was no dearth of speculation. "Bernie must have been in the Stewarts' back yard just before he got killed," Shaw offered.

"I never saw him go over there," Elizabeth protested.

Shaw gestured toward the oleander hedge. "You can't see into the Stewart yard for all the tall bushes. A whole tribe of people could have gone over there that night and you'd not have known it."

Web's forehead wrinkled. "How'd he lose his hat? It looks like it's been tromped on, so maybe he was in a scuffle."

Alafair thought this unlikely. "I didn't see any any marks of a fight on him. The way he was stretched out on his back in the ditch I couldn't even see the head wound that killed him."

"We aren't going solve anything this way," Shaw said. "We need to call the law and let them figure it out."

An expression of distaste passed over Elizabeth's face. "I'd just as soon have Constable Nettles out here if we have to call someone. I don't favor that marshal."

"Has anybody talked to Cindy? Does she have any notion how that headgear got under her porch?" Alafair asked.

Shaw looked up at her, seeing her properly for the first time as she stood next to Elizabeth at the end of the table. His gaze sharpened, and Alafair knew very well what he was thinking. *What have you been up to all this time?* Time enough for that later. He answered her question. "She was about as much help as a stunned ox. We couldn't get any sense out of her, but from her blather I reckon she has no idea."

Elizabeth removed her hat and scrubbed her scalp with her fingers. "Web, go on inside and telephone the constable's office. Alafair and me will go over to Miz Carrizal's and see if we can get anything useful out of Cindy."

Elena led Elizabeth and Alafair into her mother's parlor, where they found Cindy seated cozily in an overstuffed armchair, taking advantage of a cup of calming tea and the tender ministrations of her hostess.

Mrs. Carrizal stood up from her chair and joined Alafair on the settee so Elizabeth could take her place at Cindy's side. Elizabeth's method of interrogation was not the most gentle, but her combination of compassion and exasperation seemed to be the best way to handle Cindy Stewart.

She did not beat around the bush. "Cindy, do you have any idea how Bernie's hat ended up under your back porch on the night he died?"

Cindy's wide blue eyes rolled upward as though she would faint, but Elizabeth was not going to allow any foolishness. She gave Cindy's arm a rough shake. "Cindy! Buck up, now, and answer my question."

Cindy bit her lip and gathered her wits as best she could. "No, Elizabeth, I swear it!"

"Where is Geoff?"

Cindy's eyes slid away. "He spent last night in town again. He's been so busy lately with that land transfer. Ask Web! Web will tell you!"

"We'll send Web to fetch him to you." Elizabeth began to turn in her chair, but Cindy quickly leaned forward.

"No, no, don't bother him, please!"

Elizabeth looked at her askance. "Cindy, he's going to have to know. Web is telephoning the constable right now."

Cindy turned white, but had nothing to say.

When Alafair spoke, her tone was kind. "Cindy, did you see Bernie at all that night after the party was over?"

"No, I promise I did not." Her voice caught, and a tear rolled down her cheek.

That was enough for Mrs. Carrizal. "She doesn't know anything, Elizabeth. Leave the child alone, now. Let her rest. There will be plenty of time for this later."

Elizabeth was reluctant, but she knew she was not going to get anything out of her friend right now. "All right. Don't worry, Cindy, we'll take care of everything this evening. In fact, I think it would be best if you were to spend the night at my house again. Alafair and I will fetch a few things for you from home so you don't have to go back there until tomorrow."

Mrs. Carrizal stood up. "Elizabeth, the least I can do is send something home with you for supper. I have just the thing ready right now, and I expect you will be busy enough this evening without having to cook."

Elizabeth opened her mouth to protest, but the look on Mrs. Carrizal's face gave her pause. "Well, if it's no trouble…" She rose to follow Mrs. Carrizal into the kitchen. "Alafair, come help us."

The relief on Cindy's face as they left the room was unmistakable.

Clandestine Activities

"I have a feeling she has an idea what Bernie was doing in her yard the night he was killed."

Mrs. Carrizal speculated as she packed crispy little fried pies into a basket for Elizabeth to take home.

"Did she say something to raise your suspicions?" Alafair asked.

Mrs. Carrizal hesitated. "No. But that is what seems odd. She is struck dumb."

"She's hiding something for sure." Elizabeth stated her opinion as truth.

"What makes you think so, Elizabeth?" Alafair asked. "I don't know Cindy near as well as you do, but even on short acquaintance she seems to me like the kind who falls apart with the smallest blow."

"That's true," Elizabeth admitted with a rueful shrug. "It's just that I'm beginning to form a notion of my own and I suppose I'm looking to make events fit in with it."

"What is it?" Alafair wondered.

"Never mind, now. I would rather have more proof than just a suspicion."

Mrs. Carrizal sighed. "Poor Cindy. Alejandro and I have known her since before she married Geoff, you know."

Elizabeth exchanged a glance with Alafair before she answered. "Yes, ma'am, I'd heard that she and Matt were classmates at the Normal School."

Mrs. Carrizal nodded. "They were good friends even then. Once or twice he brought her home to supper. She was the sweetest thing, laughing and bubbling as a mountain spring, not afraid and uncertain like she is now."

Elizabeth absently fingered the tail of her shawl. "I know Matt has feelings for her. Too bad she didn't return the sentiment. He would sure be better for her than Geoff."

Alafair was shocked that her sister would say such a thing to Matt's mother. "Elizabeth!"

But Mrs. Carrizal was not surprised. "He has never said so to me, but yes, I believe Matt had an eye for her once. But even if he did love her, he never approached her that way. It is just as well. You have met her father, so you know from what poisoned root she springs."

Elizabeth could not let this pass. "Mr. Gillander may be a bigot, but his evil ways haven't rubbed off on his children, to my observation. Rather made them both kinder, I'd say."

Mrs. Carrizal ceded Elizabeth's point with a smile. "I hope that is true. In any event, Cindy and Matt are still friends. I suppose she feels the need for all the friends she can get."

Moved Out

Alafair, Elizabeth, and Cindy exited the Carrizal house to be met by the two escape-artist goats, who appeared to have been waiting for them to come out onto the porch. Cindy shouldered the food basket and the other two women each grabbed a goat by the collar and hauled it back toward the goat pen, where they repenned the happy wanderers, and then crossed into Elizabeth's empty back yard.

"Do you expect Constable Nettles is here?" Alafair asked. The battered *sombrero* was no longer on the outdoor table.

Cindy stopped in her tracks. "Oh, I can't talk to the law right now. I can't bear to go over that night even one more time!"

"Cindy, you're going to have to tell whatever you know eventually."

"I don't know anything." Cindy sounded breathless again. "I have to talk to Geoff first."

"Well, then, let's hide out at your house for a spell," Elizabeth suggested. "I'll pack up an overnight bag for you."

Alafair's eyebrows drew together. "What about the constable?"

Elizabeth was intent on her task. "The fellows can take care of him." She led Alafair and Cindy straight across the yard to the gate between the Kemp and Stewart properties, and they entered Cindy's house through the back door.

The kitchen was dark, and not much neater than it had been the first time Alafair had seen it.

Elizabeth strode forward into the parlor with Cindy and Alafair on her heels. "Cindy, sit down." She turned up one of the gas lights and pointed to the sofa. Cindy flopped down with the basket in her lap, helpless in the face of Elizabeth's imperious certainty. "I'll fetch you a nightgown and a change of clothes. Come on, Alafair."

Alafair followed her sister through the parlor to the small foyer outside the bedrooms, but instead of turning right into the big bedroom at the back of the house, Elizabeth surprised her by turning left into Geoff's study. She halted in her tracks. "Elizabeth, what are you doing?"

Elizabeth stood in the center of the room with her hands on her hips and cast a careful look around. "Relax, sister, nobody is here to see us. You just keep watch in case Cindy takes a notion to see what we're up to." She nodded toward a corner, drawing Alafair's attention to a spot behind the big roll-top desk where a single bed stood.

"Elizabeth, come on, now!"

"Oh, all right." Elizabeth came, struggling not to smile at Alafair's delicacy, and went into the bedroom.

The room was completely feminine, no man's clothes in the clothes press or closet, no men's toiletries on the shaving stand.

It was Elizabeth's turn to looked shocked. Her volume dropped to a harsh whisper. "I declare! Looks like Geoff has moved out."

"Out of the bedroom, at least."

Elizabeth turned around and glared at Alafair as though she were the one who had been keeping things from her. "Why didn't she tell me? I didn't know things were that bad between them! No wonder she's been in such a mood lately."

Alafair shrugged. "Well, I can't say I'm surprised given the way he treats her."

Elizabeth sat down at Cindy's dressing table and opened a drawer. "Don't scold, Alafair," she said, forestalling any protest. "Cindy is my friend and I want to know what's going on."

Alafair kept quiet, but Elizabeth's snooping made her nervous. She stood close to the open bedroom door in order to distance herself from the deed as well as to keep an ear out for any movement coming from the parlor. She was not particularly loath to violate someone's privacy when a life was at stake. She had certainly done it before when her children were involved. She was not quite as sanguine about rifling through a stranger's belongings, however, especially when the stranger was sitting ten feet away. At least Elizabeth could claim that she was doing it out of concern for her friend rather than bald-faced nosiness. "Elizabeth!"

Elizabeth sighed and stood up. "Oh, all right." She found a little pasteboard grip in the top of the clothes press and neatly packed up Cindy's night things.

Hiding Places

They were so long about their business that Alafair fully expected a grilling from a suspicious Cindy when they finally went back into the parlor. Instead they discovered her slumped over on the sofa with her head on the armrest and the basket of food perched at a precarious forty-five degree angle on her lap.

Elizabeth carefully lifted the basket and placed it on a side table before draping a crocheted blanket from the back of a chair over her sleeping friend. She raised a finger to her lips and gestured for Alafair to follow her into the kitchen.

Alafair kept her voice low. "You reckon we should leave her where she is and go back to the house?"

"You go on if you want. But I'm going to stay here while Cindy rests for a spell. I'll telephone the house from here in a quarter hour or so, and if Nettles is gone I'll rouse her and we'll go on over."

Alafair nodded. "I'll stay with you." She looked around at the messy kitchen. "I might straighten up a bit. She'd more than likely appreciate it."

Elizabeth was amused. "With all the children you have I'd think you'd be used to a messy house."

Alafair began running water into the basin. "There's messes and then there's messes, Elizabeth."

Elizabeth chuckled and threw open a cabinet. At first Alafair thought her sister intended to help her clean, but it did not take long to realize that she was removing boxes and cans in order to see what was behind them.

"Elizabeth, you are hopeless! What do you think you're going to find?"

"I'm looking for anything that ain't supposed to be here. Geoff is gone, Bernie's dead and his hat is under the porch. Cindy is about to fall into little bitty pieces. Something is rotten for sure." Elizabeth closed the cabinet and stared into space, pondering. "Of course she could have got rid of it, whatever it is."

Her eyes lit with sudden insight. "And if she did hide it, I reckon I know where." She made a bee-line across the kitchen, talking over her shoulder to Alafair all the while. "Me and her talked once about places to hide things where our husbands would never look. Mostly a place to keep a little money of our own, don't you know."

She stopped in front of the flour bin, pulled it open, and plunged her hands in up to the wrists, raising a white cloud. She didn't have to dig around long. She made a triumphant noise and pulled out a flour-covered rectangular packet that was wrapped in cloth and tied with a piece of string. She carted it over to the basin and dusted it off enough to untie without getting flour all over the front of her blue dress. She put the cloth aside and placed a small pile of letters on the kitchen table. Half-a-dozen ivory-colored envelopes with no address on them at all. Hand-delivered.

Alafair drew a breath when Elizabeth slipped one of the notes out of its envelope. From where she stood across the table from Elizabeth, Alafair could see that the note consisted of half a page of text written in a bold hand.

While Elizabeth read the missive Alafair kept silent, unable to utter either "put that back" or "what does it say?"

Elizabeth turned on the stool to face her sister and waved the note at her. "Well, this explains a bunch." She began to read. "*Mi amor Cintia. I know you are suffering. How I long to take away your tears, to soothe your broken heart…*"

Alafair cut her off. Not that she was too shocked to hear more, but she could hardly stand the suspense. "Oh, my! Who's it from?"

Elizabeth looked up. "No signature. But I know who it's from."

"You're thinking Bernie Arruda wrote it. Is this what you suspicioned?"

"The notion had begun to eat at me," Elizabeth admitted. "Bernie was a scoundrel who liked to move from one lonely woman to the next."

"How do you know they're not from Geoff?"

Elizabeth snorted. "First of all, it's full of Spanish, which Geoff would never deign to speak a word of. Second, I know Geoff's handwriting and this ain't it." She opened another of the love notes and perused it. "Third of all, I have seen this hand before." She was unconsciously shaking her head as she read, an expression of sardonic disgust on her face.

Alafair cleared her throat. She was bursting with questions, but first things first. "Well, if Cindy was having to do with Bernie Arruda, that is a motive for Geoff to have killed him."

"Oh, Geoff had no idea. He couldn't have. He'd of never kept his mouth shut about it. He would have divorced her for adultery faster than you could spit, and probably got her thrown in jail for it, too, if he knew. "

"Elizabeth, are those notes dated?"

"No, not these two, anyway. Why?"

"Well, maybe she's had them a long time. Maybe he moved on to yet another lonely woman a while ago and left her grieving over him."

"Are you thinking Cindy might have discovered he had him a new lover and got jealous enough to swing a bat at him? She ain't got it in her, believe me."

"Stranger things have happened."

Elizabeth mulled the idea over, absently tapping the corner of one of the notes on the cabinet surface. "What do you think would be the best thing to do, sister? I don't want to turn these over to the law and ruin Cindy's good name, not without a real good reason. If everybody Bernie wooed was a suspect, half the ladies in town would be in jail. And their husbands, too." Her expression changed. "Maybe Geoff does aim to divorce Cindy and that's why he has cleared out. Maybe he has known about Cindy's indiscretion for some time and been fretting about it. What if he saw Bernie coming out of his house that night and gave him a clomp out of sheer wounded pride?" The idea seemed to appeal to her. "Why, that makes all kinds of sense! Maybe Geoff did do it after all!"

Alafair did not care for her sister's eagerness to embrace this theory. "Don't go jumping to conclusions just because you don't care for Geoff, now. Two hours ago we were convinced that Bernie was murdered because he smuggled displaced Mexicans into Arizona. I've found things are seldom as they seem to be, and besides you don't want to be tossing off accusations willy-nilly without a lick of proof. Have a private word with Cindy, Elizabeth. Give her a chance to explain. You're her friend. I'm guessing you'll be able to tell from her reaction whether we ought to take this any further."

Letters

Alafair left out the back door, sorry not to hear firsthand what Cindy would do when Elizabeth confronted her, but eager to find out what the constable had said to the men. As soon as she was gone, Elizabeth went back into the parlor and found Cindy still asleep on the sofa, lying on her back with the blanket drawn up to her chin.

Elizabeth stood over her for a moment, considering the peaceful expression on her face. "Cindy... "

The blue eyes opened slowly. Cindy looked puzzled as without a word Elizabeth tossed the slightly floury bundle of love notes onto her stomach.

Cindy gazed at them for a long moment, her brows knit, before comprehension hit her and the blood drained from her face.

"I found your letters," Elizabeth said. "Fool girl, what were you thinking to keep them? It's a miracle that the marshal's men didn't find them when they searched your house."

"My letters." Cindy's voice was a bare whisper.

Elizabeth plunked herself down in an armchair. "Well, at least you didn't faint away or bawl like an infant. That's something. I know who wrote them, Cindy. I recognize the hand."

Cindy sat up and lifted her hands in a gesture like surrender, unwilling to touch the offending documents in her lap. Her eyes were bulging with alarm. "Don't tell anyone, Elizabeth. Please, for the love of God!"

"I don't want to, but it depends, Cindy. Could these letters in any way help uncover who it was that murdered Bernie?"

"Oh, no, no, how could they? They have nothing to do with anything. Nothing ever happened between us, I swear on my life. He was just kind to me. He could see how sad I was and he just wanted to make me feel better."

"From the little bit I read, I reckon he did!"

The color rushed back into Cindy's cheeks, turning her face from ivory pale to feverish red. "You don't understand. I should have burned those, I know. But sometimes, when Geoff and I are…not close, I like to take one out and read it again. It makes me feel like someone still cares for me. I knew they looked suspicious. That's why I took them out of the bin after the marshall threatened to get a warrant and carried them on me until after the house was searched."

Elizabeth nodded. So that was why Cindy was moved to make cookies the day after the murder. "Tell me the truth now. What do you know about the hat under your porch?"

"I swear up and down that after I left the party I never saw Bernie again that night, Elizabeth! I have no idea how that hat got there."

"What do you reckon I should do with these *billets doux* now?"

Tears quivered on Cindy's lower lids. "Burn them, I guess, like I should have done in the first place. I'd never want them to come to light." She sounded regretful.

Elizabeth picked up the beribboned bundle and eyed it thoughtfully. She did not look at Cindy when she replied. "Well, don't worry about it right now. I'll take care of it."

Disaster for Somebody

Alafair found Web and Shaw in the parlor and the children already fed and in bed. The men were absorbed in their own activities. Web was at his desk in the back corner of the room, working over a law book by gaslight. Shaw was sitting in one of the armchairs in front of the stove in the fireplace nook, reading Dane Coolidge's book.

Constable Nettles had already come and gone, taking the *sombrero* with him, much to Chase's displeasure. Shaw told Alafair that after leaving the Kemp house, Nettles left to try and locate Geoff at the law office downtown.

Alafair gave Shaw and Webster a brief overview of her afternoon outing with Elizabeth without going into too much detail. She considered asking Web if he was aware that his law partner had left his wife, but changed her mind. Better to wait until she knew more about the situation.

Web returned to his work and Alafair sat down next to Shaw in the adjacent armchair. He scolded her gently for intruding on Bernie's family in their time of grief, and to please him Alafair expressed remorse, even though she was so perfunctory that Shaw bit his lip to keep from chuckling. Alafair did not notice. She was more interested in finding out what Shaw had discovered about the progress of the murder investigation.

Shaw told her that Nettles had complained that he was being sent hither and yon on fact, gathering errands, but he was not privy to inside information. The constable had sounded bitter when he speculated that if Dillon was telling anyone what he was thinking, it was Maricopa County Sheriff Adams and not the small-fry officialdom of the town of Tempe.

Shaw closed his book and lowered it into his lap before continuing the tale. "Nettles did say that the marshal found out Bernie was a captain in Villa's army back a few years ago, and now he spends a lot of time chewing on the fact. Dillon's gone out to talk to the other Arruda brothers a second time, and even hauled Tony in for questioning. Had no reason to keep him, though, and let him go after about an hour."

Alafair was surprised. "Dillon can't possibly think that Tony killed his own brother."

"I don't know what Dillon had on his mind, but Nettles reckons he's more interested in the idea that there may be a revolutionary spy cell here in the area than he is in finding out who killed Bernie. He's got an idea in his head that Bernie was into something nefarious, and he aims to find out who else was involved."

The Yaqui railroad. Alafair was struck with a pang of fear for Matt Carrizal. She leaned forward, ready to recap for Shaw everything she had learned about Matt's secret society, when she heard Elizabeth and Cindy come into the house and reconsidered. Best to hear what Elizabeth had discovered first.

After depositing Cindy in the upstairs guest bedroom, Elizabeth came down to the parlor and walked past Web without a glance. She greeted Shaw before leaning over and murmuring in Alafair's ear. "Come out into the kitchen with me, sister."

Shaw opened his book again and made no comment, but Alafair could feel the frisson of his curiosity in the air. She followed Elizabeth into the kitchen, and they sat down across from one another at the little table. It was an indication of Elizabeth's state of mind that she made no move to ply Alafair with food or drink.

Alafair propped her elbows on the table. "Well, what did she say about the letters?"

"She says that nothing ever happened between her and Bernie. He just sent her them letters to cheer her up because he could see how sad she is."

"Well, I never! You believe that?"

"Cindy is a bad liar, and if anybody is innocent enough to believe that lover-boy's intentions were honorable, it would be her."

"What is she going to do with the letters now that you've given them back to her?"

Elizabeth looked smug. "I didn't give them back to her. I told her I'd take care of them so nobody else could see them."

"Elizabeth! Do you think that's a good idea? I know you don't want to make Cindy an object of scorn, but those letters may end up being evidence."

"I know it. I figured I'd keep them hidden until we see how things fall out. Once we're sure that Cindy's little dalliance did not lead to murder, I'll burn them."

"What if Dillon comes back with another search warrant?"

"Oh, don't worry, sister." Elizabeth gave the air a breezy flick with her fingers. "I know a place where nobody'll ever look."

Alafair's expression was ironic. "Confident, ain't you? I hope you don't end up in jail for withholding evidence."

"I won't withhold the evidence if there's a need for it. Cindy told me that she hadn't gotten a note for a long time before Bernie met his end, so she doesn't think one has anything to do with the other. However, it could be that we're not the only ones who discovered those notes in her flour bin, you know." Elizabeth did not say Geoff Stewart's name, but the quirk of her mouth was suggestive.

"Maybe Bernie really did have feelings for the sad creature," Alafair speculated.

Elizabeth's expression indicated that she thought Alafair too generous. "Bernie had a nose for a vulnerable woman, is all. He'd of ended up breaking her heart."

◇◇◇

Alafair and Shaw were sitting side by side on the double bed in the veranda room as she gave him the details of everything that had happened to her during that eventful day. The room was dim, lit only by a small kerosene lamp on the bedside table, and they were speaking in quiet undertones to keep from disturbing Blanche in her little cot in the corner.

Alafair had begun her tale with the trip to Guadalupe and taken him through the visit with Matt Carrizal and the discovery of the stash of love notes in Cindy Stewart's flour bin. "I agree with Elizabeth when she says we oughtn't turn those letters of Cindy's over to the marshal just yet, though. They may cast suspicion on Geoff, but they'll surely ruin Cindy. Even if nothing actually happened between her and Bernie like she says, folks will believe that it did."

"Still, if Geoff did kill Bernie he can't be let off the hook just to spare Cindy's reputation."

Alafair looked unhappy. "I know it. I don't know if Bernie was murdered for being a debaucher of white women, a turncoat *Villista*, or a smuggler of escaped Mexicans, but when the answer comes to light, it looks like it's going to spell disaster for somebody."

"When you talked to Matt Carrizal, you think he had an idea about Bernie's murder?"

"I felt like he got an idea of somebody to talk to about it. When you told me that Nettles said the marshal is trying to root out Mexican spies, I got concerned that he's going to find out about Matt's Yaqui railroad and get the wrong idea. I swear, Shaw, that boy and his pals are just trying to help those poor folks who have nowhere else to go."

Shaw knew her too well. "What are you aiming to do about it?"

"I might run over there first thing in the morning and put a flea in Matt's ear. Maybe the Yaqui railroad would do well to shut down for a spell. Will you come with me? He'd be more like to listen to a man."

"You couldn't stop me from coming, sugar."

Something Ain't Right

The sun had not properly arisen when Shaw and Alafair set out to walk the six blocks from Elizabeth's house to Matt Carrizal's restaurant. Elizabeth and Webster were up and about, but Cindy and the children were still abed, so they had made the excuse that they just wanted a bit of a walk around before breakfast. Their plan was that they would be back at the Kemp house within half an hour. But fate has its own way with plans.

They walked in the pale, chilly light of morning past the campus of the Normal School. It was too early for classes, but the animals in the school's agricultural farm, the small herd of Holstein cows, the sheep and pigs, the doves and pigeons in their long rows of cages, were all stirring, creating a pleasant and familiar chorus they could hear from a block away. They walked through the athletic field on the northwest side of campus, where they saw Cap Irish drilling his newly-armed squad of the home guard and stopped for a moment to watch.

As they turned on Fifth Street and the restaurant came into view, they saw two men in business suits pause at the front door and then walk away.

"Guess they decided they didn't want breakfast after all," Alafair speculated.

When they reached the front door, Alafair and Shaw were surprised to see that the restaurant was still dark and the "closed" sign still in the window. Shaw put his hand on the knob and the door swung open at his touch.

"Well, somebody's here," he observed. He opened the screen and leaned in. "Anybody here?" he called, and was met by silence. He turned and gave Alafair a speculative look.

"Go on in," she urged.

Shaw pushed the door open and stepped into the darkened dining room with Alafair close behind. The restaurant should have been busy with breakfast customers at this time of day. Shaw put a restraining hand on Alafair's shoulder. "You stay here, honey. Something sure ain't right."

Her surprise at the turn of events made her uncharacteristically compliant. She stood where she was as Shaw crossed the dining room and went into the kitchen.

As his vision slowly adjusted to the dimness, Shaw surveyed the unlit kitchen by the light coming through the open back door. Everything was clean, neat, and undisturbed. Except for an odd blotch of something on the floor by the cutting table. He hesitated before stepping over to investigate. It looked like…

He bent down to get a better look, unable to credit his own eyes.

"Esta muerte!"

Shaw yelped in alarm as a dark shape popped up from behind the table like some sort of demon jack-in-the-box. *"Esta muerte!"* it repeated. The tone of horror was unmistakable.

Alafair appeared in the kitchen door, her eyes wide with alarm. "Shaw, what is it?" She halted in her tracks. "Tony! Whatever is going on?"

When Alafair said the name, the shadowy demon resolved itself into the shock-stiff form of Tony Arruda. Shaw blinked. "Great day in the morning, man! You like to scared the liver out of me. What are you doing?"

Even in the dim light, they could see that Tony's normally stolid expression had dissolved into a mask of alarm. He pointed, unable to speak, and Shaw squatted to get a better look at the grisly sight. When he stood to face Alafair, the color had drained out of his face.

"It's Matt, honey. Looks like he's dead." He stooped down behind the cutting table to examine the body, disappearing from sight.

Alafair's heart leaped into her throat, stopping her breath. She looked at Tony.

He answered the question in her eyes. "Stabbed. I came in only a few minutes ago and found him just as you see." He began to tremble as his recounting of events slid into Spanish, then Yaqui.

Alafair put out a hand to calm him. "Tony, I can't understand you. We have to get the marshal. Tony, Tony, you have to tell him what happened."

A change came over Tony's face. "No, I cannot talk to the marshal. I did not kill Matt. I did not do it."

Tony's panic forced Alafair to overcome her own distress. "Tony, no one thinks…"

She was cut off by Shaw's disembodied voice rising from behind the counter. "He's not dead! I don't know how but he ain't quite dead yet." His head materialized over the table top. "Alafair, hand me them towels, quick. Tony, run get Doc Moeur, run, run!"

This time Tony didn't argue.

A Particular Talent

Moeur came out of the kitchen and sat down next to the marshal, opposite Alafair and Shaw at one of the dining room tables. His pale eyes were as sharp as shards of ice. "Well, he's still alive. The boys are loading him into the ambulance now. I've done the best I can. Somebody slashed him across the neck with a butcher knife, which there are plenty to choose from around here. Looks like the blade nicked the jugular." He turned his disconcerting gaze on Alafair and Shaw. "He'd of died within minutes if you hadn't applied pressure when you did. I'm sorry to say that I think he will die yet. I've staunched the wound but he's lost so much blood that I don't see how he can survive. I think the best thing we can do for him now is to take him to his mother's house and leave him in the loving arms of his family to live or die as God sees fit." His tone was grim. "I'm going with him in the ambulance and will stay at the Carrizals' as long as I think I can do any good. Marshal, I'll talk to you later."

Moeur left Shaw and Alafair facing a speculative marshal across the table. There was a long moment of silence before Dillon leaned back in his chair. "How is it, Miz Tucker, that you've only been in town for a little more than a week and yet you're the one who keeps making these grisly discoveries?"

Shaw discreetly grasped Alafair's shaking hand under the table. "She's got a particular talent for it, Marshal."

"It does seem strange that y'all come to town and suddenly Mexicans start to getting killed left and right."

"Are you suggesting that we had something to do with the attacks on these poor fellows?" Shaw's tone was cool.

"No, I'm just saying it's strange, is all."

Alafair was not in the mood for conjecture. All she could think of was Mrs. Carrizal, who was shortly to learn that her beloved eldest son was soon to die, murdered. *That poor woman, that poor woman.*

Matt Carrizal was such a nice young man, so compassionate and concerned with the plight of the less fortunate. Who on earth would want to do him in? They had told the marshal about finding Tony Arruda at the scene, but Alafair did not believe that he would have cut the throat of his friend, co-conspirator, and employer. And yet, after he had summoned the doctor to Matt's aid, Tony Arruda had disappeared. "I can't figure it out," she said, more to herself than to Dillon.

"I know y'all have your doubts about the cook, but it looks pretty straightforward to me." Dillon said, as though he had heard her thoughts. "Tony fears that Matt will live to tell a tale that he don't want told. Maybe Carrizal found out something about the Arrudas' spy ring and Tony decided to shut him up. No matter why, it looks bad for Tony. I'll talk to the sheriff soon as we're done here and have a judge issue me a warrant for Tony's arrest."

"You can't think he killed Bernie as well," Shaw said.

Dillon shrugged. "Mexicans are easy to fly off the handle. They're always killing one another for some blame reason that makes no sense. Still, I doubt he murdered his own brother. Could be he figures Matt Carrizal did it and took his revenge. If that is so, I'd like to know what makes him think that Matt attacked Bernie. No matter the reason, once we bring Tony in he's likely to be able to untangle this skein for us."

Rage

The rest of the day was a blur. They finally returned home late in the morning to find Elizabeth pacing the floor with worry and Cindy in a state, bundled up in a quilt on one of the long couches in the parlor. Nettles had shown up at the Carrizal house an hour earlier to deliver the bad news, and Elizabeth had heard Elena's scream across the distance that separated their back doors. She had hollered at Blanche to watch Chase and ran across to learn the terrible news for herself. There was nothing she could do but weep along with Matt's parents and sisters.

"I offered to fetch Artie from school and keep him here a spell, but they said they're in no hurry to grieve him until they have to," she told Alafair.

Elizabeth and Alafair spent much of the afternoon cooking dishes to take to the soon-to-be-bereaved family. Cindy helped with the preparation, but when time came to carry the offerings to the Carrizals', she had demurred. Elizabeth did not argue with her. It was better for the Carrizals not to have to deal with Cindy's burdensome presence right now.

On the other hand, Blanche asked if she could come, and Alafair allowed it. Artie was her friend, and she had the right to offer her comfort and concern.

When they took the food over in the evening, they found the Carrizal house packed wall-to-wall with relatives and neighbors. Alafair had an eerie feeling of *déjà vu* when she approached Mr. Carrizal, sitting on the horsehair sofa in the parlor, next to his daughter Juana, receiving well-wishers, hollow-eyed but calm as he kept his death watch. Had it only been yesterday that she and Elizabeth had paid just such a condolence call on Bernie Arruda's mother? She wondered briefly if the two families knew each other at all. Probably not. The well-to-do descendants of the Spanish *conquistadors* and the refugee Yaqui Indians inhabited different worlds.

She extended a hand. "I'm so sorry," she said.

Mr. Carrizal's dark eyes regarded Alafair quietly before he replied. "Thank you, *hija*. Esmeralda and Elena are at Mateo's bedside. I know they would take comfort from your visit if you would like to look in for a moment. Juana, please take the ladies back."

Juana led them up the stairs to an airy bedroom at the back of the house, where they found Mrs. Carrizal and Elena seated in chairs on either side of a single bed. Elena looked stricken, her eyes red from weeping, but Mrs. Carrizal's eyes showed something that Alafair could not quite put her finger on.

The room was small, containing not much more than the narrow bed, the chairs, and a painted chifferobe, but pleasant nonetheless. The window was open, and occasionally the white lace curtains belled when they caught a puff of the scented breeze. A man's shaving cup and brush stood on top of the chest beside a framed picture of a sports team of some ilk. Alafair wondered if this had been Matt's boyhood room, still kept for his convenience whenever he decided to spend the night at his parents' house.

Matt was stretched out in the bed with the covers pulled up tight under his chin. His face was blank and bloodless and so still that Alafair's first thought was, *we're too late.*

Mrs. Carrizal looked up at the women and smiled. She looked pale and tired. "He lives still," she said, reading their thoughts. She gestured at Elena, who stood and offered her chair, but Elizabeth shook her head.

"Thank you, hon, but we won't stay long. We brought food and we want to express our love and prayers, but we'll not be intruding."

"I cannot tell you how much your prayers mean to us, Elizabeth."

"Is there any change?" Alafair asked.

Mrs. Carrizal shook her head tightly. "No, no better. But no worse. He walks in the valley of the shadow, and we must wait." She reached up and took Alafair's hand. "How is Blanche?"

Alfair blinked, not expecting the question but not surprised that Mrs. Carrizal could think of something besides her own worry and grief. Sometimes the reality of a tragic situation took a while to fully sink in. "Blanche is so near to well as to make no difference, ma'am. Thanks to you. God sent us to you. I don't know how I'll ever be able to thank you."

Mrs. Carrizal managed a wan smile. "She is such a lovely girl. I am so glad I could help her."

Alafair started to withdraw her hand, but Mrs. Carrizal drew her down close to whisper in her ear. "Tony Arruda never did this thing."

Alafair caught her breath before she pressed her cheek to the older woman's. "I don't think so, either. Do you know who did?"

"Not yet. But Tony will contact us eventually. He may know who Matt was meeting."

"Tony is in danger," Alafair whispered. "If he's smart he's already on the run."

"Matt told us you know about our enterprise." Mrs. Carrizal's voice was as low and soothing as one of the doves in her backyard cote.

Alafair murmured, "Yes, Elizabeth and I called it 'the Yaqui railroad.'"

"Our 'Yaqui railroad' runs both ways, dear one. We will save Tony Arruda and have justice for his brother and my son." Mrs. Carrizal placed her hand on the back of Alafair's neck and gave a squeeze. It was an affectionate move, but her hand was hot and alive with such rage that Alafair jerked as though she had been touched with an electric wire.

"If Elizabeth or I can do anything, let us know," she murmured. Mrs. Carrizal released her and she straightened up.

Mrs. Carrizal turned her attention back to the still figure on the bed. "Thank you for coming."

Speaking of Home

Alafair was surprised but glad that the activity and emotion of the day had not overtired Blanche or made her ill again. In fact, the girl had seemed energized by her determination to comfort her friend Artie. Perhaps Mrs. Carrizal had been right when she had told Alafair that folks can get into a habit of sickness.

Alafair had not realized how much she had missed Shaw's comforting presence next to her until they went to bed that night. Early in the winter, when Blanche first became so sick, Alafair had either spent her nights in a chair next to her daughter's bed when the illness was at its worst or curled up next to her when she was better. Since they had arrived in Tempe, as often as not Alafair had slept with Blanche and Shaw had taken the cot. No one had made any decisions about who was sleeping where. It just was as it was. But that night when his big frame sank the mattress next to her she nearly wept with gratitude that he was so near. The tickle of his mustache and the scratch of his unshaven cheek was as familiar as the touch of his hand on her body.

"What would I do in this strange place without you, honey?' she murmured.

"I'd hate to think." His voice held only a hint of irony.

"Blanche sounds a lot better." The child's even, unlabored breathing was like music to Alafair's ears in the quiet night.

"She does, thank Jesus," he murmured back.

"I want to go home, Shaw. I want to take my girl and go home. My sister has turned into someone I don't know at all. A murderer is on the loose and death is hovering close. Too many bad things are going on here, and I miss my children." Her voice caught. "I miss little Fronie. I miss my baby Grace."

"I know, honey." Shaw's tone was soothing. "We've been away long enough. I'll tell you what. Tomorrow I'll talk to Doctor Moeur and see if he thinks Blanche is healed enough to go back to Oklahoma without getting sick again. If he says yes—and you can see for yourself how much better she is—then we'll leave as soon as we can pack up and hope the rails are in better shape than they were when we came out."

"Oh, God willing," she breathed. "But what about the law? Will Dillon make us stay around until someone is arrested for these awful events?"

"I'd think he could take our depositions and let us go home. No one suspects we had any more to do with killing than just being in the neighborhood at the time."

Alafair was not as confident as he that all would go well. "I hope you're right."

Ritual

No matter how tired she was from the momentous events of the day, sleep eluded Alafair that night. She would drift off, then awake suddenly in the middle of some disturbing dream she could not remember.

Eventually she gave it up as a bad job and sat up on the edge of the bed. A sliver of the waxing moon and a diamond river of stars were bright in the cloudless sky, and the bucolic stretch of Elizabeth's back yard was clear enough through the long bank of windows. She sat with her feet dangling just off the floor for several minutes, staring into the night at the silent, peaceful forms of the trees and sharp, colorless outlines of outbuildings and fences.

Her mind was just beginning to settle when something caught her attention. A movement. Her forehead wrinkled, and she slipped out of bed and padded over to the window, where she absently pushed her long braid off her shoulder before leaning in toward the glass for a closer look.

Something white appeared in the distance, across the fence in the Carrizal's yard. It passed in front of Mrs. Carrizal's garden shed and disappeared from view behind a stand of citrus trees.

Alafair had not been able to see the moving object with any detail, but she knew without doubt that the White Lady was about in the night again. She took her shawl off the back of a chair and slipped her stocking feet into her shoes before stepping as quietly as possible out the door.

She did not go far into the yard, only enough to get a clear view of Mrs. Carrizal walking purposefully toward the goat pen. Her silver hair was loose about her shoulders, and she was clad in a light-colored dress covered by a white bib apron with several large, bulging pockets. She carried no light with her, so Alafair could not judge her expression, but she sensed that Mrs. Carrizal would not welcome an observer. Alafair looked back over her shoulder, seeking an escape route, but she had drawn too close to the Carrizal property to be able to get back into the house without being seen. Gently she stepped back behind a bush, out of Mrs. Carrizal's line of sight.

Mrs. Carrizal disappeared behind the chicken house for so long that Alafair wondered if she had gone back into the house by some unseen route. The night was dry, still, and cold, and Alafair's nose was getting numb. She shifted from one foot to another and made faces, trying to get the blood circulating. She was just about to give up the vigil when Mrs. Carrizal reappeared from behind the coop, carrying a large wooden box by a handle on its top in one hand and a small axe in the other. Chica and Nina, the two goats who had proven themselves more pets than working farm animals, were trotting at her heels.

Mrs. Carrizal stopped at the flattened stump of a tree next to the woodpile near the back fence, not six yards from where Alafair was standing behind the bush, and put the box on the ground. She drove the tip of the axe blade into the stump to hold it in place, then drew a couple of small objects out of her apron pockets—one small and square, one larger and rounded. It was too dark and too far for Alafair to determine by sight what the objects were. Mrs. Carrizal placed the round object onto the stump next to the axe and poured something powdery from the square item into it. *She is pouring something from a little bag into a bowl.* Alafair picked up the distinctive pungent aroma of thyme. The goats nosed the stump and the axe, but uncharacteristically left the bowl of powdered thyme alone.

Mrs. Carrizal bent down to open the box and withdrew a white dove, which she cupped in her two hands and brought close to her face. Alafair could hear her soft sing-song murmur as she spoke gently to the bird. When she finished whatever prayer or litany or words of comfort she intended, Mrs. Carrizal dislodged the axe, placed the dove on the stump, and whacked its head off in a businesslike manner.

Being as Alafair had beheaded many a bird in her time, it was not the act itself that caused her to gasp in shock, but the unexpectedness of it all. Mrs. Carrizal held the decapitated dove by the feet over the bowl and let its blood drip into the herbs for a minute or two before she swept the little severed head onto the ground with the edge of the axe and laid the body on the edge of the stump. She reached back into the box and withdrew a second dove.

Alafair stood watching the ritual in fascination and no little awe until six small headless bodies lay in a neat row on one end of the broad tree stump. Mrs. Carrizal calmly placed the dead doves back in the box before taking a candle out of her pocket and lighting it. After being so long in the dark, the flare of flame caused Alafair to blink. The candle glow illuminated eyes that were no more than dark hollows, but the shining track of tears shown on Mrs. Carrizal's cheeks. She tilted the candle over the bowl and uttered a few soft words as a drop of wax fell.

A small trowel appeared from those voluminous apron pockets, and Mrs. Carrizal knelt on the ground to dig a shallow hole beside the stump. She dumped in the grisly contents of the bowl, covered it over with dirt, then stood. She turned around, looked straight at Alafair's hiding place, then lifted the candle and blew it out.

By the time Alafair's eyes had readjusted to the sudden dark, Mrs. Carrizal and her goat companions were gone.

No Sleep Tonight

By the time Alafair returned to the veranda room and crawled back into bed next to Shaw, her fingers and feet were numb with cold. She pressed herself up next to his back and gratefully soaked up his solid warmth, fearful that the touch of her icy limbs would wake him. She need not have worried. No frozen wife was enough to disturb his easy sleep.

She wondered briefly what time it was. She could see through the window that the crescent moon was low on the horizon. It had moved perhaps two hand-spans since she had gone outside—an hour or so. She reckoned it was nearly one o'clock by now. Still time for three or four hours of sleep, but she knew very well that there would be no sleep for her tonight.

What had she just seen? Was it the conjuring of a curse? She could not be afraid of Mrs. Carrizal, not after what she had done for Blanche. Still, the woman was about to lose a beloved son to murder. Alafair could not forget the feel of hot rage in Mrs. Carrizal's hand when she touched her.

Alafair knew what she would be willing to do in the same circumstance. Even so, Mrs. Carrizal was nothing if not a gentle presence, so it was entirely likely she had been calling forth something benign; perhaps the uncovering of the assailant, or protection for her son on this side of the veil or the other.

Alafair had no intention of asking. And no matter how willing she usually was to share her fears and worries with Shaw, she knew she was not going to tell him, either. Men had a tendency to disapprove of such things, even a man who had been raised by as fey a woman as Shaw's mother. Alafair's Baptist preacher father would have thundered his disapproval at such goings-on, but Alafair was more inclined to take her own mother's attitude. *It is only natural for us earthly creatures to work with the tools God gave us—the winds, the seasons, the movements of the stars and planets. Let the men have their ways, and we will have ours.*

The Morning After

The dining hall bell at the Normal School rang every morning promptly at seven-thirty a.m. Its comforting toll served to mark the beginning of the work day for everyone within hearing distance, including the Kemps.

Elizabeth stood at her front door with Alafair at her shoulder and watched Webster walk purposefully across the yard toward the detached garage at the back corner of the house, clutching his briefcase in one hand, his breath making a light fog in the chilly air. Chase was dashing about in the yard and Blanche and Artie Carrizal were sitting in a huddle at one corner of the porch. Artie had appeared at Elizabeth's door as soon as light tipped the horizon, asking for Blanche, and the two of them had had their heads together in the parlor or on the front porch ever since.

Alafair had no objection. A stricken household often had no attention to spare for a shocked and devastated child, and Blanche was willing and happy to offer what little comfort she could to her new friend. Besides, it was good for her heart and health to be concerned for another.

"I should have wondered before now why Web has been going to work alone these past mornings," Elizabeth said. "I reckon I never pay enough attention when Web leaves the house to notice that Geoff hasn't been coming over to go into town with him."

"Do you expect we'll be getting another visit from Mr. Dillon today?"

Elizabeth shot her an ironic glance. "Oh, I expect." She turned away from the door. "After Bernie's *sombrero* turning up under Cindy's porch, followed close on by the attack on Matt, I wouldn't be surprised if he was be out here with a warrant as soon as he can roust the judge out of bed."

"Have you looked in on Cindy this morning?"

"I did. She's still asleep up there in the attic bedroom. Or shamming for my sake. In any event, I'll be surprised if she makes an appearance before noon."

Elizabeth seated herself on one of the cushioned benches in the parlor near the front door and Alafair sat down in the rocker opposite. "You know, Elizabeth, I was convinced for a spell that both these murders had something to do with the revolution in Mexico, but both those poor young men had some kind of connection to Cindy, whether she knew of it or approved."

"Don't think that hasn't occurred to me, Alafair. This is why my eye is on Geoffrey Stewart now."

Alafair shook her head. "I don't know. I might believe he killed Bernie in a fit of jealousy, but why try to kill Matt? Because Matt had tender feelings for his wife ten years ago? That connection is mighty thin."

"When you say it like that…" Elizabeth let the thought hang. "Just between you and me, I suppose I'd as soon it be him as any other candidate." She emitted an ironic laugh at her own uncharitable utterance. "Poor old Cindy is just such a mess because of him, and she didn't used to be. Why do folks love people who are bad for them, Alafair, and not love the ones who are good for them?"

"Oh, sugar, how should I know? When I think back on my own youthful folly, it takes my breath away. It was just ignorant fortune that I fell into a good marriage, because it sure was not due to any well-considered plan of mine."

They regarded one another for a moment before Elizabeth broke the silence. "I always thought you were a paragon, Alafair, who never put a foot wrong. Mama and Daddy, all the Tuckers, our sister and brothers, nobody ever had a bad word to say about you."

Alafair was stunned. "Good gracious, Elizabeth! You haven't conversed much with Shaw or talked to any of my children lately, have you?" The very idea elicited a laugh. "I think we are not much acquainted with each other anymore, honey. You were just a little gal when I left home. I'm surprised you remember anything about me at all."

"Well, truth is I don't much," Elizabeth admitted. "Just images like dreams."

Alafair smiled. "You don't remember me, but I remember you, honey. What a sweetie you were, just a'talking a mile a minute from when you were a little bitty thing. Law, you were smart! You used to love it when I'd read to you out of that book of Bible stories Daddy got us. You could listen to me read for hours, and the questions you asked! You always wanted to know the whys and wherefores of everything, and wouldn't take a flip answer, either. One time—you couldn't have been much more than three—I caught you with the book on your lap, pretending to read the story of Esther out loud to yourself. I hid myself and listened for quite a while, thinking how precious you were, and how well you had memorized that story, when it come to me that I never read it to you, 'cause Mama told me that wasn't a fit tale for a little baby like you.

"You were reading it for real. You had learned yourself to read by following along whilst me or Mama or one of the other kids read to you. Made my hair stand up on end when I realized. I run and told Mama, and she didn't hardly believe me at first. But then she give you a cattle sale broadside and asked you what it said and I'll be switched if you didn't tell her. I thought she ought to see that you went to a special school or had some extra teaching, but she told me that it would be better that nobody knew how smart you were, 'cause all them brains couldn't but cause trouble for a girl."

Alafair paused, remembering. "I look back now and wish I'd been smart enough myself to argue with her, but I reckon we just have to do the best we can with the mistakes we made in the past." She grinned at the dumbfounded look on Elizabeth's face. "Or the mistakes that got made on our behalf."

Elizabeth slumped back against the wainscoting. "Well! That explains a deal. Mama and Daddy, too, used to scold me for trying to act like I was better or smarter than anybody else. Said I shouldn't get above myself, for pride was a sin."

Alafair shrugged. "I always figured that a body oughtn't hide his light under a bushel. Of course, just because you're smarter than most folks don't mean you're a better person; or that Jesus loves you more if you're smart, or rich, or pretty."

The comment struck Elizabeth as funny, and she chuckled. "You reckon not? Too bad, 'cause Jesus sure would be partial to Blanche if that was true."

Alafair grimaced. "Mercy. When you say that, I almost understand why Mama did what she did. I'd just as soon Blanche not grow up to trade on her looks."

"I don't see how she's going to be able to help it. To my observation, most folks cater to good-looking people whether they mean to or not."

An Unwelcome Visitor

Alafair was considering Elizabeth's opinion and judging it to be sound when Blanche opened the front door and stuck her head inside far enough to catch her mother's attention. "Mama, Aunt Elizabeth, Miz Stewart's father is next door, come looking for her. Artie has gone to talk to him."

Elizabeth shot Alafair an inquisitive glance and stood up. "We're just coming, honey." She removed a couple of wraps from the coat tree beside the door and threw one to Alafair. "Now, what do you suppose is up?"

They went outside and followed Blanche over to the vine-covered picket fence that separated the Kemp and Stewart front yards. Artie Carrizal, his hands in his coat pockets, and Gillander Senior, arms folded across his chest, were facing one another across the fence. Artie's back was to them and Alafair could not see his face, but Mr. Gillander's expression was solemn as they spoke as man to man.

Gillander's obvious regard for the boy's feelings moderated Alafair's poor opinion of him. Even less than admirable people have some good qualities.

Gillander looked up as the women approached, and Artie glanced back over his shoulder. The boy stepped aside to allow the adults to speak. He looked pale and drawn, but his dark eyes were deep and resolute. Twelve-year-old boys could be brave even in the face of unfathomable loss. Alafair's heart went out to him as Blanche took his hand and led him back to the porch.

Elizabeth did not watch the children go. "Morning, Mr. Gillander," she said. "You looking for Cindy?"

But Gillander had been distracted from his purpose. "Yon boy tells me that some evil-doer tried to murder Matt Carrizal yesterday. I never heard such a thing! What happened?"

Elizabeth lifted a hand to shade her eyes from the glare of the newly risen sun. "You haven't heard? Yes, it's true, I'm sorry to say. Some varmint busted into the restaurant early yesterday or late the day before and cut Matt's throat with one of his own butcher knives. Doctor Moeur says he's not like to live."

"You don't say! The boy says his mother holds out hope." Gillander's eyes widened. "Do they know who done it?"

"Not as I've heard." She had no intention of telling the old man about Tony Arruda running from the scene.

"Robbery, do you figure?"

Elizabeth shook her head. "Not as far as I know. It was my sister here, and her husband, who found poor Matt lying in his own blood on his kitchen floor."

Alafair grimaced. She would have been content for Elizabeth to leave out that bit of information. Gillander's pale gaze clapped on her, and she said, "It didn't seem to us like anything had been disturbed. The marshal may have come to another conclusion after we left and he had the place searched."

"I will just be switched," Gillander said. "I don't know what this world is coming to. These Mexicans. If they ain't asleep they're drunk and if they ain't stealing something they're killing each other. I know that them Arrudas used to work for Pancho Villa ere they came to this country, so I figured that's why Bernie got killed. He ran afoul of the *Villistas*. Those Mexican factions are vicious, Miz Tucker. You don't know what they will do to each other. But Matt was one of the good ones, a good, clean, hard-worker."

Elizabeth let the remark pass, but when she replied her tone was brittle. "So I guess you've come looking for Cindy. Well, she's here. She was upset that our neighbor's son got done so cruelly, so she slept here at my house, since Geoff was not home again last night. Last I looked in on her, she was still abed."

"Glad to know you took her in. I heard from Constable Nettles that they found the dead Mexican's fancy hat under Geoff and Cindy's back porch. That's why I'm here. I come over to talk Geoff into letting me fetch Cindy back to our place for a spell. He's spending too dang much time at work lately and leaving her alone at night. What with all this devilry going on, I figured he might be relieved to have her out of harm's way until he's done with his case."

Elizabeth's frosty manner had not warmed when she answered. "If you want to talk to Geoff, you'll have to roust him out of the law office. But Cindy's right here and I reckon she can speak for herself if you want to have a word."

"Obliged." Gillander stepped over the low fence rather than walk around to the front gate, and Elizabeth ushered him to her front door.

A Pale Fantasy

"I'll have to ask Geoff before I can come out to stay with you and Mama, Father. I can't just up and leave him to fend for himself." Cindy had seated herself on one of the couches in the middle of Elizabeth's parlor, and Gillander was standing over her. Elizabeth had invited him to sit and have something to drink, but he had made it plain that this was not a social call.

Gillander nodded. It went without saying that his daughter would have to ask permission to be away from home. But he did intend to arm Cindy with an argument to present to her husband. "You tell him that I said he can come and carry you home after he finally gets all them papers filed. He shouldn't be spending most nights in town and eating boughten food, daughter. I admire that he's such a good provider, but it won't do for him to leave you on your own in that house at night while there's a killer on the loose. In fact, I intend to pick up more cotton seed at the gin since I'm in town, so I'll be passing right by his office on the way. I'll just stop and tell him myself. Then we can…"

Cindy cut him off. "Don't bother him, Father! I'd just as soon put it to him myself. You know he admires you and will do as you wish, but he will tell me if he really doesn't want me to go."

Gillander accepted her reasoning readily enough. "Well, tell him that if he would rather, I'll send Levi to stay with you over to your house for a spell."

Elizabeth had been leaning against the door frame with her arms folded, biting her lip at the father-daughter exchange until this opening arose. "She's welcome to traipse over here and spend the night any time she wants."

Cindy seized on Elizabeth's invitation. "Yes, it would be much handier to come over here on nights that Geoff is away. That way I would still be available to take care of him when he does manage to get home. Surely this won't last much longer, Father. Even his most difficult cases seldom go on more than a few weeks."

"You can't be imposing on your neighbors, Cynthia." His tone was stern, but not unkind.

"She is no imposition, Mr. Gillander," Elizabeth assured him. "We enjoy having her."

Gillander spared her a glance before returning to business. "You talk to Geoff, Cindy. Whatever he says is fine with me. I'll bid Levi look in on you this evening " He put his hat back on. "Well, Miz Kemp, I'm going now."

Elizabeth rounded on her friend as soon as the door shut behind the old man. "Why do you insist on sticking up for that snake of a husband of yours? You should tell your daddy that Geoff has moved out."

"He has not, Elizabeth! He'll be back. He always comes back."

Elizabeth found Cindy's heated response perversely gratifying. She sat down beside her friend. "Cindy, Web works on cases and briefs just as tough as Geoff does, and sometimes the same ones. Now, there has been the odd night before an early court appearance that Web has slept downtown, but he has never taken all his kit with him and camped out in his office for days on end."

Cindy flushed red and looked away, but said nothing.

"When did Geoff scamper off this time? Was it before Bernie died?"

"Oh, you can't think Geoff had anything to do with Bernie's death. No, he had *temporarily* moved his things out of the bedroom a couple of days before the open house. He came back that night just for my sake, Elizabeth. He didn't want me to show up to the party alone."

"I didn't notice that he spent much time at your elbow acting the attentive spouse."

"It was a big effort for him to take time to come at all, Elizabeth. You don't understand."

"Sugary shoot!" Elizabeth raised a finger to her lips to forestall any more shocking oaths. "I declare, Cindy, sometimes I want to shake you till your teeth rattle. Do you even know what Geoff is up to when he takes off like this? And here's what I want to know—has it for one minute occurred to you that Bernie may have taken advantage of his proximity to your house that night deliver another note, and that Geoff may have found it—or even come across Bernie while he was hiding it—and gone off like a firecracker?"

"It never happened." Cindy was resolute. "Geoff had to leave the party early and get back to his work. He was at the law office when Bernie died and when Matty was attacked, too. He told me so. Besides, Geoff hardly knew Matt. Why would he slash his neck?"

"Maybe the two attacks aren't connected. Maybe he only meant to kill one or the other of them. Or maybe Geoff had something in his head that we don't know about. Why do you swallow everything Geoff tells you whole hog?"

Cindy's newfound strength crumbled before her friend's eyes, and she sagged. "Because what else can I do, Elizabeth? I have to make my marriage work. What else is there for me?"

Elizabeth gripped her arm. "The truth, whatever that may be, and not this pale fantasy of a loving marriage which you have created out of nothing but wishes."

Pershing

Shaw and Webster came home for dinner, full of news as usual. The women did not need to tell them about Gillander's visit, for in spite of Cindy's request, he had stopped by the offices of Stewart and Kemp and spoken to Geoff himself.

Webster's tone was gentle when he related the tale, since Cindy was listening with her hands clinched in her lap and her lower lip aquiver.

"Geoff sends his love, Cindy. He told your daddy that he figured to make his deposition next week, and apologized for leaving you alone so long. In any event, I gather that your brother will come in from the ranch tonight and stay with you at your house for a couple of days. Geoff said he'd feel better with family looking out for you until he gets home."

Cindy managed a smile and nodded, which satisfied Webster enough that he moved on to other news.

"One thing about working across the hall from the newspaper is that I hear what's going on before everybody else," he said. "Mr. Miller showed us a wire story that came in this morning. Seems President Wilson has appointed a general from Fort Bliss by the name of Pershing to lead a punitive expedition into Mexico to capture Villa. The story said that Pershing's troops crossed the border into Mexico day before yesterday."

Alafair felt her eyebrows fly upward. "What does the Mexican president say about that?"

"I imagine he's none too happy," Shaw informed her, "but the article said he agreed to let the Americans into Mexico. Reluctantly."

"Where are Villa and his gang now, Shaw?" Elizabeth asked.

"Off in the Sierra Madres somewhere. Rumor is they're heading west."

Elizabeth pursed her lips. "I'll fall right over in a faint if they manage to find hide or hair of the brigands. It's rugged as the lip of perdition down there."

"Do you think Villa's bandits will make another raid into this country?" Cindy sounded anxious.

Web shrugged. "Rumors abound, Cindy. Some say he's making for California, determined to strike across into the U.S. as often as he can get away with it. But I don't credit that at all. The one time he did come across he took more losses than he inflicted. Besides, most of the border towns are ready for him now. There won't be any more surprise forays."

Cindy leaned forward. "Maybe they're waiting for a signal. Maybe there are spies all along the border states waiting to let Villa's army know which towns are watchful and which not, and where it's safe to cross and stage another invasion!"

The men fell silent, giving the idea due consideration, but Elizabeth was not persuaded. "Cindy, have you been listening to your father again?"

Before Cindy had time to take umbrage, the children dashed through the parlor from the kitchen, fortified with cookies and heading back outside to play. The sight of his daughter's hale and rosy form jogged Shaw's memory. "By the way, Alafair, I stopped by Doctor Moeur's office this morning and talked to his wife. The doc is making calls out south of town today, but Miz Moeur said when he gets in this afternoon she'll have him come by here and have a look at Blanche."

Elizabeth's brow knit. "Is she feeling poorly again, Alafair?"

"No, just the opposite. She's doing so well that Shaw and me were thinking of taking her home with us when we leave in a couple of days."

"So soon?" Elizabeth looked stricken. "We are just making one another's acquaintance!"

Shaw answered for Alafair. "We've been away a long while, Elizabeth. Time we got home to our young'uns." His smile forestalled her protest. "Now, did anything interesting happen here while me and Web were downtown?"

In for Some Grief

The mid-day meal was over, and the adults were taking coffee in the parlor by the time Dillon knocked on the front door. Elizabeth invited him in, though she did not look happy about it.

He stepped into the parlor and nodded at Cindy. "I thought you might be here when I couldn't rouse nobody next door, Miz Stewart." The marshal's eye lit upon Webster sitting on the sofa with a cookie in one hand. "Ah, Mr. Kemp." His relieved tone indicated he had had his fill of dealing with recalcitrant women. "I'm going to be needing to talk with your partner Geoff Stewart again as soon as may be. Did you leave him at your law office when you returned home for dinner?"

Webster's gaze slewed toward Cindy, opposite him in an armchair, before he hastily put his cookie down on a side table and stood up. "Let's you and me talk on the porch, Marshal."

They went back outside and stood on the corner of the porch, visible through the front window but far enough from the door not to be heard by those inside. Cindy made no move to follow, which Alafair thought odd. If a lawman had inquired after her husband in that tone, nothing would have kept her from demanding to hear what he had to say.

"What does he want with Geoff?" Cindy asked, as though those left in the room knew any more than she did. "Why did Web want to talk in private?"

"Web probably figures you've been upset enough," Shaw offered, "and reckoned to spare you the burden of dealing with the marshal any more today." It was a gallant attempt at kindness, and Cindy grasped at it.

"Yes, probably." She sounded relieved. "I do appreciate it."

Web came back inside with a thoughtful expression on his face. "Well, I reckon it's time for me to get back to the office. It's such a nice afternoon I think I'll leave the auto and walk. Shaw, you want to come with me? I expect Bill will have more news about Villa."

Shaw started to demur, but something in Web's tone made him reconsider. "Just let me grab my coat."

The men had only gone a few steps into the yard when Web said, "I didn't want to upset the womenfolks, but I'm afraid Geoff is in for some grief. I had to let Dillon know that Geoff is most likely not at the office right now. I sure didn't want to say so in front of Cindy, but Geoff has made himself an improper alliance with one of the actresses in the Yaqui movie, and he spends every minute he can over at the hotel with her. They think they are being discreet, but half the film crew knows about it. Her movie friends are protecting her. Seems Bosworth will have her kicked to the curb if he finds out."

Shaw gaped at him. "Well, knock me down and steal my teeth! I knew there was trouble in the Stewart union, but I'd not have guessed it was that far gone. Did you tell Dillon the whole story?"

"Yes, first time he came to the office, back on Monday. Well, I had to, didn't I? I don't want to be accused of withholding pertinent information. When Dillon had Geoff's house searched a couple of days ago he noticed the absence of a man's accoutrements right off. Then they found that burned stub-end of a bat in his incinerator. I had to tell Dillon where Geoff was when he came downtown to question him about it. After that, the marshal went over to the hotel and rousted Geoff out so he could finish his interrogation. Last I heard, he'd pretty much accepted that Geoff didn't know anything about the bat.

"But now there's this business with the *sombrero* under the porch. Dillon is getting the scent of something he doesn't like. He did tell me just now that he'd keep Geoff's indiscretion quiet if he can." Web paused. "I don't think Geoff means to hurt Cindy, if that makes any difference."

Shaw snorted. "To my observation he don't regard Cindy at all. Have you told Elizabeth about this dalliance of Geoff's?"

"I never have mentioned it to anybody, especially Elizabeth, but this is not the first time Geoff has done this. I disapprove highly, but he won't listen to me. You'd think he'd use a little sense, but this actress has him wrapped around her little finger."

Shaw gazed at his brother-in-law for a moment. "Web, it ain't my business to tell you how to talk to your wife, but you're kin, so I'm going to anyway. When Elizabeth finds out you've been keeping a secret that is going cause grief to her friend when it comes out—and it will come out, have no illusions on that score—she will not thank you for it."

Web's eyes widened. "Well, Shaw, I can't see as how it'll help anything to put the cat among the pigeons."

"I admire that you're trying to spare the ladies' feelings, but if Elizabeth is like Alafair, she won't see it that way. She'll feel like she's been played for the fool."

"But I'm her husband. It's my job to protect her tender sensibilities from ugliness."

Shaw almost laughed at that, but refrained when he realized that Web was sincere. He had said enough anyway. "Never mind then. It's Geoff Steward's head that's about to roll."

Levi

After dinner Web went back to work and Shaw went with him, too curious about Dillon's confrontation with Geoff to stay home. The children went out into the back yard to play as the women cleaned up in the kitchen. While Elizabeth and Cindy washed and dried, Alafair scraped the leftovers into a pail to scatter on the ground in Elizabeth's small chicken yard. She left a contented flock picking through the scraps and was just fastening the wire gate behind her when she caught sight of Levi Gillander standing in the street in front of his sister's house, gazing idly in her direction. When she called his name, Levi sauntered over to join her at the fence.

"Are you looking for Cindy, son?" she asked. "She's over here."

"I figured."

"Your father mentioned that you might come over to stay with Cindy at her house tonight."

One corner of Levi's mouth twitched up before he shrugged. "He twisted my arm, I reckon. I don't figure Cindy needs looking after, but there's no arguing with the old man."

Alafair was struck again by Levi's physical resemblance to his father; his small but sturdy frame and a complexion so pale that every passing flush of emotion showed on his face whether he willed it or not. Both had slightly protuberant, light blue eyes, but where the father's burned with a righteous fire behind the ice, the son's expression was guarded and wary. Having witnessed old Gillander in action, Alafair was hardly surprised that his children would go through life on edge. "Well, she'll be glad to see you, in any event," she assured him. "She's been lonesome since Geoff has been away from home. And these assaults and murders have upset her, too. I guess your daddy told you about poor Matt Carrizal."

When she mentioned Matt Carrizal, Levi's pale eyes narrowed. "Yes, Father said he was wounded near to death when you found him. Does he still live?"

"We've had no word for a few hours, but Dr. Moeur reckons it's just a matter of time."

Levi looked away, his fair skin mottled as he struggled with his emotions for some moments.

"Levi..." Alafair ventured.

His gaze slid in her direction. "Ma'am?" He removed his hat, a reflex move rather than any conscious recollection of proper manners.

"Are you all right?"

"Yes'm. Just that I'm riled that some wretch would do such a thing to Matt. Of course, if he still lives there is yet a chance he'll wake, God willing. At least long enough to tell who done this to him."

"Matt was your friend? I'm sorry. How did y'all know one another? From when your sister was at school with him?"

"That's when we first met, yes, ma'am. But later we got to be friends on our own. He was involved in a lot of charitable works helping poor Mexicans out. He approached me a few months ago about finding sympathetic folks in the Anglo community who might help with money, jobs, shelter, clothes, and the like. He figured that if anybody would know which white men would help and which would just as soon shoot coloreds, it would be me. I told him that I feel right sorry for the little brown folks. Even animals ought to have a place to be with their own kind and be left in peace."

"Ah," Alafair breathed, suddenly enlightened. "You were part of the Yaqui railroad."

His forehead crinkled. "Pardon?"

"Oh, that's what we've taken to calling Matt's project."

Levi looked baffled. "What project is that, Miz Tucker? What did Matt tell you?"

Alafair was surprised by his response. Had her instincts betrayed her? From the way he had spoken, she had assumed he knew all the details. "I'm sorry, I misprized the situation. When you said he had approached you about helping out with his charity, I figured you said yes."

"Well, I told him I was willing to do what little I could, but I'd have to be mighty careful that nobody find out."

"Especially your daddy?"

Levi's smile was without humor. "Who would suspect me of having any sympathy for Mexicans? My father is my best armor and hiding place. But Matt never said any more about it, so I never got a chance to help out. What was it he was doing, do you reckon?"

She hesitated before answering, unwilling to betray Matt's trust any more than she already had. "Matt told us that he raised some money to help the poor and hungry over in the barrio. I don't know, but I expect it was church work."

"He never mentioned the name of anybody else who was working with him?"

Something about the way he phrased the question gave her pause. "Son, do you have an idea who might have done these murders, or why? You should tell the marshal if you have suspicions."

"I don't. Just that if Matt was involved in any enterprise with that sassy Bernie Arruda then that's more than likely why someone tried to kill him too."

"Well, promise me that if you think of anything that would help catch a killer, you'll go to the law with it."

"I will. And will you promise me that you won't tell anyone that Matt wanted me to help with his Mexican charity? I'd just as soon my father not disown me."

There did not seem to be any more to say on the subject They fell silent for a moment as Alafair eyed the young man with sympathy. "Come on inside," she invited at length, "and have a bite."

"Thank you, ma'am, but I've et. If you'd kindly tell Cindy I'm here, I'd be obliged."

Lily-Livered Creature

"But why didn't Dillon arrest Geoff?"

"Well, what would be the motive, Elizabeth?" Web asked. "As far as Dillon knows, Geoff had no reason to kill Bernie nor Matt either, and he swears he was with his paramour when both attacks took place."

By the time Shaw and Webster got back to the law office earlier in the afternoon, the marshal had already rousted Geoff Stewart out of the hotel and was in the midst of conducting a blistering interrogation. On their way home that evening Shaw warned that their chances of being able to keep what they had overheard secret from their wives were just about zero. Web was finding out that his brother-in-law had keenly assessed the situation.

The women met them at the door. Neither Alafair nor Elizabeth felt the need to put up with any masculine reticence. Shaw and Web were not even allowed to remove their coats before their own interrogation began.

Shaw accepted the inevitable and did not keep anything back. "I gleaned from Dillon's questions that he thinks the hat under the porch and the stub end of a burned bat suggests somebody killed Bernie in the Stewart yard after the party was over. Then lugged him around to the front of your house, Elizabeth, and dumped him in the ditch. But it wasn't Geoff Stewart, if his alibi is to be believed. And aside from Matt's folks being neighbors to the Stewarts, there is absolutely no connection between Matt and Geoff that Dillon can find."

Except for Cindy. Alafair withheld her own questions long enough to allow everyone to sit down, side by side in a row on the long couch in the parlor, so they could mull over the possibilities in companionable solidarity.

As far as Alafair knew, only Elizabeth, Cindy, and Alafair herself were aware of Bernie's love notes, or of Matt Carrizal's unrequited feelings for Cindy. Alafair had no sympathy for Geoff, cheater that he was, and maybe murderer. She would advise Elizabeth to turn those letters over to the law in a flash—except for the fact that when the notes became public, Cindy's life would be ruined as surely as would her adulterous husband's.

"Dillon sure put the fear of God into Geoff, though." Shaw sounded amused at the memory. "When he threatened to arrest Geoff, Geoff turned white and went to quaking like a leaf. He spilled his guts, then, and swore up and down that he was just a deceiver and not a killer, and if she had to, his lover would stick up for him."

Elizabeth was incensed. "Did he name the hussy? Oh, I hope it isn't Miss Landowska. Or worse, young Dorothy!"

"He wouldn't name her in our hearing," Web said, "and Dillon didn't demand it of him right then, either. He told Geoff he'd talk to the woman in private later, so at least he's trying to spare the town a scandal on top of everything."

Alafair was more realistic. "Everything is going to come out eventually, you know that."

"It usually does." Shaw's quirky smile was more ironic than usual.

"Now that his ugly secret is out, why is Geoff still at the office?" Elizabeth insisted. "Why did he not come back to his wife and beg her forgiveness? Oh, don't tell me that he's still carrying on with that woman?"

Web shook his head. "No, Geoff told us that she was not pleased to have the law come rousting them out of their love nest in the middle of the day, so she has shown him the door. And as for Cindy, to tell the truth I think that since he can no longer keep his behavior a secret he's ashamed to face her."

Elizabeth flopped back against the couch. "I declare. Geoff Stewart ashamed of himself. Wouldn't that be something? I hope you at least tried to talk some sense into him, Web."

"How he conducts his personal life is none of my business, Elizabeth."

The look that she gave her husband after this answer told Web that Shaw had been right about Elizabeth's reaction, as well. Scorn, and something else. Something like bitter disappointment. His breath caught as it dawned on him that perhaps he did not know his wife as well as he thought.

After a few minutes had passed and no one offered a useful course of action, Elizabeth. said, "Well, supper is about ready if y'all want to wash up. Web, go call the children, would you?"

After the men left the room Elizabeth turned to Alafair. "If Geoff's indiscretion clears him of murder, then do we have to tell Dillon about the love notes? When it became generally known that Geoff was having an affair, Cindy will be horribly hurt and embarrassed, but if Bernie's notes to Cindy ever came to light, she would be shunned."

"I was thinking much the same thought," Alafair said. "Surely it would be better that Geoff take all the blame for adultery. There might be hope for the marriage that way."

Elizabeth snorted at the idea. "I hope she divorces the son-of-a-gun."

"You make it sound like that would solve her problems, Elizabeth. It wouldn't, you know."

Elizabeth lowered her gaze and gave a barely perceptible nod. "I know. Still." She looked up. "It's a good thing Cindy is such a lily-livered creature, Alafair. Otherwise somebody might suspect her of eliminating her unwelcome suitors herself."

Alafair's eyebrows shot up. She had never considered such a thing. "Elizabeth, you cannot believe it!"

"Fortunately, neither would Dillon. Now if it was me in Cindy's situation, he'd send me up the river the minute he found out I had a connection to the victims."

Much Improved

Dr. Moeur showed up to look in on Blanche as the family was finishing supper. His exam was short but thorough, and after pronouncing Blanche remarkably improved, he was plied with cake and effusive gratitude.

Afterwards, Alafair put the children to bed and Shaw once again took it upon himself to walk the doctor to his Franklin. "I don't think Elizabeth will be pleased to see us go, Doc. Having Alafair here has been a real treat for her, and they've been enjoying getting to know each other again after all these years."

"When do y'all expect to leave?"

"Alafair would have me buying tickets for home right this minute if it weren't for the attacks. We have yet to get Dillon's go-head before we can leave town."

"You've already given him your sworn statements, haven't you? I wouldn't think that would be any hindrance, then. But, like I told your wife, it would not hurt Blanche to to stay here in the dry climate for a few more weeks."

"But it wouldn't be bad for her to go home, would it?"

Moeur shrugged. "Not necessarily. Depends on what the weather is like back in Oklahoma. Even though I can't hear anything in Blanche's lungs any more, I think it would be a good idea if she wasn't in the rain and damp for a while."

Shaw brightened. "Well, that's all right, then. My daughter writes us regular, and she says that it's been sunny and mild for the past week."

"You know how Oklahoma is when it comes to the weather, though."

"Doc, I don't think I could talk Alafair into leaving Blanche here unless it'd kill her if she didn't."

"I got that impression." Moeur's tone was dry.

"I have no reason to ask but plain nosiness," Shaw continued, "but have you heard if the marshal is any closer to finding out who killed Arruda?"

"Dillon confiscated a passel of possible murder weapons during his house searches and gave them to me to check for blood, but I never found a trace on any of them. I expect the burned bat he found in the incinerator is what did the deed, but there is no way now to prove it. "

"How is Matt doing, Doc?"

"Still hanging on. He can't last much longer, I fear."

"So you hold out no hope?"

Moeur threw his bag into the passenger seat of his Franklin and together they circled around to the driver's side. "When I was there this morning, he was still alive. Breathing a little better, I think, though I don't know how. It's a wonder he has any blood left in his body after that slash to his neck. I didn't find any signs that he tried to defend himself, either. No bruised knuckles or fingers, or tissue under the nails. I reckon he got taken by surprise by someone he allowed to get close to him. Likely he knew his killer."

"Sometimes people decide they'd rather not die when you expect them to. Perhaps he has some unfinished business." Shaw had known such a thing to happen.

So had Moeur. "Perhaps."

"How are his folks?"

"I'm going over there again right now, so we'll see. Thus far they've been holding up good, considering. Mr. and Mrs. Carrizal are remarkable people of faith." Moeur grimaced. He had had enough of this depressing topic. "Well, let me ask you, Shaw, all this unpleasantness aside, what do you think of our rawboned little town, here?"

"Oh, it's mighty fine. Especially the winter weather! By gum, this climate would put anybody in a good mood."

Moeur laughed. "Our winter is the Lord's compensation to us for our summer."

"So I've been told. Even so, after the winter we've put up with back home, I'm soaking up all this sunshine like a lizard. If I didn't have a bunch of kids and a farm to run and a wife who's desperate to get home, I wouldn't mind staying here a spell."

Much to his own guilty surprise, even in the face of this double tragedy Shaw was enjoying his adventure. Until now he had never been further west than Oklahoma City to attend state Farmer's Union meetings, or east to Jonesboro to visit relatives. And he couldn't remember how long ago that was.

After Shaw waved Moeur on his way, he stood in the road for a while, enjoying the crisp, dry air. Maybe once the kids were grown, he and Alafair could do more traveling. He had always had an ambition to see some country. He had a great curiosity about the Gulf of Mexico.

He fell to figuring. He was forty-five years old and Alafair had just celebrated her forty-third birthday. Their youngest, Grace, was three and a half years old, which meant that if she stayed home until she was eighteen, they'd be free to travel in less than fifteen years. He'd only be sixty. *That's not so bad. My folks are well into their seventies and still blowing and going. If the farm keeps growing as fast as it has been of late, we ought to be able to afford it, too. After all, there will always be a big demand for horses and mules. Shoot, the way Oklahoma is booming, we'll have plenty to retire on in 1931.*

Eavesdropper

The Tuckers had already retired to their veranda bedroom when Blanche decided that her medicinal tea would go down much easier with a molasses cookie. Alafair wrapped her shawl around her flannel nightgown and picked up a kerosene lamp from the bedside table before making her way across the porch and through the back door into the kitchen. The kitchen was dark, but there was a light coming from the parlor that illuminated a square of the floor. Alafair was surprised. She had said good night to the Kemps half an hour earlier.

She had started toward the parlor, thinking that someone had neglected to turn off one of the gas lamps, when her ears picked up the faint murmur of voices. She could not tell whose, but she assumed Elizabeth and Web had come downstairs again. She stopped and returned to her quest, allowing the late-night talkers their privacy.

Now, where are the rest of those cookies? Oh, yes. She had seen Elizabeth put the few chewy delights which were left into a small crockery jar and take it into the pantry. Alafair walked into the curtained alcove close to the back door and began searching the shelves of cans, bottles, and boxes for the elusive little jar. She found it tucked up in a corner and had just removed a cookie when she realized that the murmuring voices had grown louder. She recognized Elizabeth's voice. And Cindy!

They were coming into the kitchen. Alafair turned around and saw the glow of lantern light through the pantry curtains as they entered the room, and she almost spoke in order to make her presence known.

"So has Dillon found Tony Arruda?" Elizabeth was asking.

Alafair wanted to hear the answer. She blew out the wick on her own lamp.

"No," Cindy said. "Levi told me that Tony has disappeared. I wouldn't be surprised if the marshal thinks Tony has run back to Villa's army. Levi tells me Dillon believes the Arrudas are part of a subversive organization. That's why a Federal marshal is involved in this murder investigation in the first place. But if Tony didn't try to kill Matty, why did he run away?"

Elizabeth's voice was icy with cynicism. "Do you think the marshal would believe for a minute that Tony only 'came upon the scene' so soon after Matt was attacked? Dillon doesn't know the Arrudas or the Carrizals either one, or what sort of relationship they had. No, Tony knew how Dillon would see it. He did right to run."

By now, Elizabeth was rattling around in the cabinets, her voice muffled. "I don't believe for a minute that Tony suspects Matt of killing his brother. Of all people, none of those Arrudas would ever hurt Matt Carrizal, not after all that him and his family have done for them. But the question is, if not Tony, who? Who would have a reason to hurt Matt? Bernie Arruda had a slew of enemies, but Matt had none that I ever heard of."

"Yet both were engaged in dangerous work." Cindy said. "I only have two thoughts about it. Either someone means to stop us from bringing refugees into the country, or the two incidents have nothing to do with one another and Matty's assault really was no more than a robbery gone wrong."

Alafair clapped her hand over her mouth to keep from gasping aloud. Was Cindy involved with the Yaqui railroad? She had never let on.

"Well, if it's to stop the Yaqui railroad, Cindy, then you'd better watch your back. It may be that everyone in the group is in danger. How many people are in your organization, anyway?"

Cindy's voice took on a bemused tone. "I don't know. We're like a chain, each only knowing a couple of links to the right or left. The only ones I knew of were Bernie and Matty and a woman in the barrio in north Tempe. My only job was to deliver messages or packages between her and Matty when I took clothing to the mission. I couldn't even read the messages because they were always in Spanish. Whenever I'd get one I'd slip it into a bundle of used clothing, take it down to the barrio and put it into my contact's hands. I don't even know the woman's name. She works for the mission. I kind of expect Matty was telling her how many refugees were coming across and when she should arrange overnight shelter or food or some such."

"How did Matt get these packages and letters to you?"

"Often he'd just give me an envelope over the fence while he was visiting his parents' house. Once in a while the lady in the barrio would give me something to bring back to Matty, as well. Most of the time he delivered his own messages to her. It all depended on if he had natural business in the barrio or in Guadalupe at the right time. He'd use Bernie as a go-between, too. Sometimes Bernie would leave a letter for the barrio under the flower pot, or sometimes one of the personal notes. I could tell if the note was for me personally, because he always tied those up with a ribbon."

"Have you told Levi about your clandestine activities?"

"No. Matt told me that secrecy is important no matter how sympathetic I think someone might be. But after what Levi told me tonight I think our enterprise is not such a secret after all."

"What about Geoff?"

Cindy sounded alarmed. "Mercy, no. Besides, after all that has happened, I think I'm finished with carrying notes. Dillon is bound and determined to find out who all is involved and clap us in jail."

"Well, I doubt if you have anything to worry about," Elizabeth assured her. "It will never cross Dillon's mind that you could have anything to do with it. And even if your group is shut down, it's likely there are a lot of people of good will around here who will continue to help those who need it, Cindy."

The two women took their snacks and their conversation back into the parlor, leaving their stunned eavesdropper staring into the darkness and trying to make sense of what she had just heard. This put a whole new twist on things. Never in a million years would she have suspected that woman was capable of intrigue. Then again… She found herself remembering the conversation she had had with Levi that afternoon. *Who would suspect me of helping Mexicans? My father is my best armor and hiding place*, he had said. Just so, who would suspect as vapid a creature as Cindy?

Alafair did not know how long she stood pondering, but she suddenly realized that the house was quiet. Cindy must have gone home. It occurred to her that Blanche had either gone to sleep by now or was impatiently awaiting her cookie. She looked down and was surprised to see that she was still clutching it in her hand. She picked up the snuffed lamp and stepped out from behind the curtains just as Elizabeth came back into the kitchen with two empty desert plates.

They both yelped, startled.

"Alafair! What in the cat hair are you doing up?"

Alafair was not in the mood to prevaricate. "I heard everything y'all said when you were here in the kitchen. Now fill me in on the rest."

A Different Cindy

Elizabeth was happy to tell her everything. "Cindy showed up at the door around nine. Seems Geoff telephoned her and confessed his little affair. The coward. Couldn't even do it face to face. And on top of everything, after Cindy hung up Levi told her he knew about Geoff's dalliances all along and suggested that if her husband was better satisfied, he would have stayed at home. She said she came over because she wanted a sympathetic ear, but I figured it was more like she was afraid she would smack Levi one if she didn't leave." Her mouth twisted in irony. "I told her it was Geoff she ought to smack. He swore to her he'll never do it again. No, never, never again. She told him he could just very well stay where he is tonight while she thinks over if she wants to forgive him."

Alafair was impatient. "That is all very fine and good, but did you know before this that Cindy was part of the Yaqui railroad?"

"No, I didn't. She sure played it close to the vest, didn't she?" Elizabeth sounded proud of her friend. "I reckon she's still got some of the old starch in her that she had when we first met."

"How did it come out?"

"She just told me, straight out. I guess Geoff's confession put her of a mind to quit keeping secrets."

"Did she say anything about her own dalliance?"

"I tried to bring it up, but she wasn't inclined to discuss it. She still maintains she did nothing wrong, apart from not putting a stop to his blandishments. I told her that in view of how Geoff treated her, I wouldn't blame her no matter what she did."

"Elizabeth, when Cindy said something about her secret organization not being such a secret any more, it gave me a notion. Do you suppose that Cindy's daddy got wind of what she was doing?"

Elizabeth's eyebrows flew upward. "Mr. Gillander? For Cindy's sake, I'd hate to think so! But he was there at the party, and you did see that there was tension between Gillander and Bernie. He could have found out about Bernie's indiscreet notes to his daughter as easily as anybody else. But if I remember right, he left the party early."

"So did Bernie. But as it turns out he was just next door being murdered."

"Well, if the murderer has got to be someone who was at my house that night, I'm partial to the idea that it could be old Gillander. A more unpleasant and tendentious person I never did meet. I could believe that he just might have killed Bernie, sister. But why try to kill Matt?"

"I don't know. And the old man did act surprised when Artie told him that someone has as much as murdered Matt." Alafair fell silent for a moment, thinking. "Do you remember when we stopped in to the restaurant after the trip to Guadalupe? Matt got some kind of idea after we had talked for a spell and hustled us out of there right smartly."

"That's true, I had forgot! He said that you never know what white folks will do."

"He also said he didn't want to tell us anything until after he had talked it over with someone."

"So you reckon Matt figured out Gillander may have done it and confronted him, and then the old man tried to kill him in order to shut him up?"

"I don't know, Elizabeth. It makes as much sense as anything else."

"Or maybe Cindy has it right when she says that Bernie's murder had nothing to do with the attack on Matt."

They reached the end of their train of logic and stood gazing at one another in the dim light. Finally Alafair broke the silence. "Now what do we do?"

Cutting Down

Alafair walked out to call the children for breakfast and was taken aback to realize that for the first time since she had been here, she could see directly into the Stewart's back yard. The overgrown hedges that separated the Stewart and Kemp properties had been trimmed down far enough to see over. Cindy was on her porch, talking to Levi who was standing on the ground below her, clutching a rake handle in one hand. Though it was a cool morning, his face was rosy from exertion and his fair hair was plastered to his forehead with sweat.

Levi had more than enough help with his yard maintenance chores. Chase and Blanche were busily underfoot, raking the trimmings onto a large tarp for disposal. Cindy caught sight of Alafair standing by the gate and waved her over.

"Morning, Miz Tucker." Levi tipped his straw hat to her and she nodded at him.

"Oh, Alafair!" Cindy was aglow with happiness. "Wonderful news. Elena was over here just a minute ago to tell us that Matty's doing better. In fact, he's taken such a turn for the better that Doctor Moeur thinks there's a chance he'll live yet. Elena says the doctor is amazed."

An amazing turn, or something else? Alafair immediately conjured the image of Mrs. Carrizal chopping the heads off of six little doves in the dead of night. "That is wonderful news! Elizabeth will be so glad to hear it."

"I told Elena I'd go over for a visit later, though she said he's not waked up yet."

Levi was more cautious. "Don't get too hopeful yet, Cindy. She also said he ain't out of the woods yet."

Cindy threw her brother an annoyed glance. "Well, I'd rather have some hope than none at all."

Alafair decided to change the subject. "Ya'll have got the yard looking nice. When I came outside it give me a start to be able to see right over the hedge."

"It's about time we had that hedge cut down," Cindy said. "The place has just about gone to rack and ruin without a man around."

"I imagine Levi is glad to earn his keep." Alafair smiled at Levi, though she thought, *about time indeed.* If the bushes had not obstructed the view on the night of the party, someone might have seen whoever followed Bernie Arruda into the yard with murder in mind.

Cindy bubbled on, still in a happy mood. "The leaf litter under the bushes has not been raked for a long time. Since last fall probably, so Levi and the kids got quite a pile. They raked the chicken yard, too, and under the porch here. Who knows how long it's been since that was done?"

Propriety satisfied, Levi plopped his hat back on and turned to go back to his task. He had only taken a few steps when he halted in his tracks. His lips thinned and his cheeks flushed even redder. Alafair understood his sudden pique when a familiar figure in a business suit rounded the corner from the front of the house.

Cindy stiffened. "Geoff!"

Alafair took a step back into the shadow of the porch overhang, willing herself invisible.

Geoff stopped walking when Cindy said his name. He snatched his fedora off his head, and for a long, uncomfortable minute, nobody moved or spoke.

Alafair studied the prodigal husband with interest. She had only seen the man once, at the open house, and it had been evening then. She was struck by his superficial resemblance to Levi Gillander. Both men were blond-haired and blue-eyed, with complexions that flushed at the slightest provocation. Geoff was a much more substantial figure, though, sleek and well-fed. He didn't look quite as self-satisfied as the last time she had seen him. He looked much chastened, in fact, like he wished he could sink into the ground rather than bear Cindy's withering regard.

"Cindy…" The name came out in a croak. Geoff cleared his throat and tried again. "Cindy, I'm sorry. That woman never meant anything to me. You're the only one I care for. I never meant to hurt you. I did my best to be discreet. I always tried to be considerate. It doesn't mean anything."

"Considerate!" Cindy's tone was incredulous.

"Please, Cindy. I never wanted to hurt you. Haven't I always given you everything you wanted? Don't you think we could start afresh? I'll do whatever you say."

A change came over Cindy's girlish face, aging her a decade in an instant. She walked down the steps and brushed past her husband without looking at him.

"Where are you going?" He sounded surprised.

Cindy continued walking. "I'm going to ask Mrs. Carrizal if I can sit with Matty for a while."

"I'll wait for you."

"I don't care what you do, Geoff." She never looked back.

"I'll help with the tree trimming, shall I?" Geoff called to her retreating figure. When Cindy did not reply, he stood and watched her until she disappeared through the hedge gate into the Carrizal back yard. He glanced up at Alafair with an absent expression before he sighed, picked up an armload of sticks and twigs, and carried them away. Blanche and Chase were standing by the hedge with their rakes in hand, observing the confrontation with wide eyes and mouths agape. Levi was nowhere to be seen.

A Turn for the Better

Cindy walked into the Carrizal house through the back door to find Mrs. Carrizal sitting alone at the kitchen table. Most of the Carrizal relatives had finally gone home to sleep, wash, change clothes before resuming their vigil. The older woman and the younger gazed at one another for a long moment, saying nothing.

Cindy finally broke the silence. "I am so sorry I haven't been to see you before now. When it seemed so sure that he would die, I just didn't have the heart to come. But this morning Elena told me that he has taken a turn for the better. Is it true?"

One of Mrs. Carrizal's shoulders lifted. *Maybe,* the gesture said. "He is better. He is not out of danger yet."

"Miz Carrizal, may I see him? Matty has never been anything but kind and solicitous to me, and I fear I have only given him cause for grief."

"Matt loves you, I think."

Cindy's face reddened and she looked away. "Yes, I know he does."

When no further comment was forthcoming, Mrs. Carrizal took the initiative. "Sweetheart, do you have feelings for my son?"

"I am a married woman, Mrs. Carrizal."

She smiled. "That is not what I asked, Cindy."

Cindy puffed out an embarrassed laugh. "Of course I have feelings for Matty. He is a wonderful man. But I have no right. When I was first married to Geoff, Matty was my friend as

t he kept a respectful distance. But in the past year
as been importune, or so I thought. I couldn't figure
ddenly felt free to court me in such a forthright way,
though he never went so far as to make me uncomfortable."
She paused to study her hands. "I think now that he was aware
of Geoff's unsavory womanizing. I told myself I didn't encour-
age his familiarity, but the truth is I did not try very hard to
discourage him. I liked his attention." She felt tears prickle her
eyelids. "When he asked me to help the refugees, I said yes not
so much because I cared about the poor displaced wanderers. I
wanted to be around Matty. He made me feel special in a way
Geoff never did." She looked up.

Mrs. Carrizal said nothing, so Cindy continued. "Seems
everyone knew of Geoff's affairs but me. Matty, Web Kemp, my
brother, my father. Even Bernie Arruda, it seems. I feel like a
fool, a figure of fun. Geoff tried to make me feel like our troubles
were all my fault. And he succeeded, too."

"Sometimes if man feels guilty for something he's done, he
will turn the blame onto the very one he has wronged." Mrs.
Carrizal sounded sympathetic.

The smile Cindy gave her held no humor. "You may be right,
ma'am, but I can't say that makes me feel a whole lot better."

"So what do you intend to do?"

"I don't know. There is no good solution, I fear. I feel such
anger. How can I ever let Geoff touch me again? And I can
hardly look at my brother, or Web."

"Or Matt?"

"I know he was trying to spare my feelings, but I wish he had
told me," she admitted.

"Shall you leave Geoff?"

Cindy made a sound that resembled a laugh. "Elizabeth
thinks I should, that's for sure."

Mrs. Carrizal raised her eyebrows, awaiting a more satisfac-
tory response.

Cindy's gaze wandered off into space. "I would leave if I had
somewhere to go, even if it meant being a divorced woman."

She straightened in her chair, tired of the subject. "I apologize, Miz Cee. I surely did not come over here to burden you with my small troubles when you have such big ones of your own. I came to see Matty, to sit for a while at his bedside and pray, if you will permit it."

◇◇◇

Mrs. Carrizal led Cindy through the house to the airy little bedroom tucked into an upstairs corner. The door was open and the bed was surrounded by chairs, but at the moment no one was holding vigil but a small statue of the Virgin of Guadalupe on the bedside table, smiling her blessing on the still figure in the bed. Matt lay on his back under a quilt that rose and fell with his quiet breathing. His complexion was so washed out that at first Cindy did not notice that his neck was completely wrapped in a clean white bandage.

She went to her knees beside the bed. "Oh, Miz Carrizal, he is so pale!"

Mrs. Carrizal put her hand on the younger woman's shoulder. "You did not see him before, *querida*. The tide has turned, I think."

"May I sit with him for a spell?"

"Of course. Your prayers will do him much good. I will return in a little while."

Mrs. Carrizal turned to leave the room but pulled up short at the sight of a figure standing pressed against the wall next to the bedroom door. "Levi!"

Cindy swiveled on her knees at Mrs. Carrizal's exclamation. Levi was leaning back on his hands, watching them with a troubled look on his face. "Levi, what are you doing skulking there? You gave us a start!"

Levi pushed off the wall and took a step into the room. "I'm sorry, Miz Carrizal. I didn't aim to hide from you. I heard Cindy say she was coming over and I reckoned to join her and pay my respects. I called when I came in the front door, but when nobody answered I come looking for Matt's room. I figured you'd all be in here. I just stepped in a minute before you…"

Mrs. Carrizal nodded. "If you would like to stay with Cindy it's all right, son. Take a chair."

After Mrs. Carrizal left them, brother and sister regarded the invalid in contemplative silence for some minutes.

"He looks peaceful, don't he?" Levi leaned forward and studied Matt's wan face. "You expect he knows we're here?"

"I hope he does."

Levi did not lift his eyes. "I knew you were friends with Matt, Cindy, but you weren't keen on visiting before." His statement held a question. "I'm surprised you came over without your friends. I was beginning to think you never took a step without Elizabeth said to."

"Elizabeth has been over already. Besides, I thought before that Matty was dying."

"But now you heard he may live, so you decided to pay a visit?"

She gave him an odd look. "That's right. My prayers may do some good, now."

Levi crossed his arms and nodded. "Maybe they will. I'll sit with you until you're ready to go home and face Geoff."

Sad to Leave a Friend

Blanche walked outside by herself after breakfast was over and sat down on the innertube swing that hung from a branch of the big eucalyptus tree in the middle of her aunt's back yard. All the citrus trees were in full bloom now, and the perfumed air was dizzying. She swung back and forth for a time, glad that Chase was occupied elsewhere and she could enjoy her own thoughts. She caught sight of something white in the grass at her feet and leaned over to pick it up. A baseball, probably overlooked after their game the other day. She turned it over in her hand and saw a large "A" inked into the white leather. This was Artie's ball, which made her smile.

She wished that Artie could come over. She could not remember when she had had such a nice friend all of her own, a playmate who was not a relative or schoolmate whom she had to get along with whether she wanted to or not.

Blanche was aware of the adult turmoil going on around her, but it did not concern her overmuch. In her experience, grown-up people died all the time, and there was no use to dwell on it. You could get tetched in the head that way. She was sorry about what happened to Matt Carrizal, though, because Artie was so sad that he might lose his brother. They had talked about it a lot since it happened. Two of Blanche's own brothers had died when they were little, but Blanche did not remember either one. She just knew that her parents still grieved over them all these years later.

Artie had been oddly comforted to hear that. He did not like to think there would come a day he would not remember how much he loved Matt.

Blanche was still gazing into the distance when she noticed that one of Mrs. Carrizal's goats was out again and had somehow made its way through the back gate and into Aunt Elizabeth's yard. It had knocked over Aunt Elizabeth's leaf barrel and was nibbling through the avalanche of spilled trash and greenery. Blanche laughed and stopped swinging. She admired those two naughty little creatures who refused to stay put, but Aunt Elizabeth would be upset if one of them ate the bark off one of her hydrangea bushes and killed it.

She slipped Artie's ball into her skirt pocket before she stood up and walked over to the goat, who was already trotting over to meet her, shameless.

"Which one are you, now?" Blanche wondered. "And where is your sister, you bad girl?"

The goat bleated a reply that Blanche could make nothing of. She seized the goat's collar with the intent of leading it back to its pen when she noticed something long, shiny, and pink hanging out of its mouth. She leaned down for a look and saw that it was a piece of sateen ribbon, perhaps six inches long.

She was unsurprised. There was nothing a goat would not eat. "Where did you get this, Nina or Chica, whichever one you are? Did you pluck this out of Aunt Elizabeth's trash or are you dining on one of Juana's hair fancies?" The goat gagged a little but otherwise had no objection when Blanche pulled at the half-eaten ribbon and drew forth a piece of wet and half-chewed paper still knotted into one end. Blanche made a disgusted sound before dropping the whole mess onto the grass and proceeding to lead the goat back to its own side of the fence.

She had been so occupied that she had not noticed her mother and Aunt Elizabeth standing near the swing, watching her.

Alafair smiled when Blanche started. "I'm sorry, honey, we didn't mean to sneak up on you. I declare, them goats are a caution, aren't they? What is that she was eating on?"

Blanche's lip curled. "It's just a hank of ribbon tied around a disgusting chewed up piece of paper. At least that's what I think it is, being as it's already mostly digested. Look yonder, she knocked over your leaf barrel, Aunt Elizabeth, and went to snacking. She probably was tempted by all the fresh greenery that Chase and me hauled over from Miz Stewart's house after her barrels got too full."

"What a mess! I hope she confined herself to the mulberry leaves and left the oleander alone lest she poison herself!" Elizabeth did not really sound disturbed about the prospect. "I'll commence to righting the barrel if you two will get this Houdini of a goat back into her pen."

Mother and daughter were happy enough to leave the clean-up to Elizabeth. They chatted pleasantly about inconsequential things as they returned the prodigal goat to the other side of the gate, and were making their way back toward Elizabeth's house when Alafair told Blanche about their plans to start for home within the next day or two.

Blanche stopped walking and looked up at Alafair, stricken. "Oh, Ma, do we have to go so soon?"

Her reaction surprised Alafair. "Aren't you homesick, honey? Don't you miss Sophronia and Grace? Don't you miss all your little friends at school and your teacher?"

Blanche thought about this. She had been too intrigued by her adventure to think about what she was missing. "I reckon I do." She sounded reluctant. "But I like it here, Ma. It's nice. It smells nice and it's not cold, and it hasn't rained once since we been here. And I like being with you and Daddy and just me all by myself."

Alafair smiled. What must it be like to be lost in the middle of a crowd of children vying for your parents' attention? "I know, baby girl. But you are all better now, and Doctor Moeur says it will be all right for you to go back home. Besides, me and Daddy have to go back right quick, and we don't want to leave you. You know, your birthday is coming up and I have to make your cake for you, and I can't do that if you're here and I'm in Oklahoma. And you sure don't want to miss Mary's wedding."

Blanche considered for a moment, torn. "I don't want that," she admitted.

"But you'll miss Artie."

Over the years, Blanche had had plenty of evidence of her mother's mind-reading abilities, so she was not surprised at the statement. She gave a brief nod.

Alafair put her arm around the girl's shoulders. "It's sad to part from a friend," she acknowledged. "But if you want to see him again some day, there ain't no law that says you can't. Once you save up the money, you can come visit him. Or maybe he can come out to Oklahoma to see you."

The thought seemed to cheer Blanche, however unlikely it was that she would be able to save enough to buy a train ticket to Arizona in the foreseeable future.

Alafair was comforted to see Blanche's expression lighten. "Now, go on inside, sugar. It's time for your medicine. I'll be in directly as I pick up that hunk of goat cud and help your aunt clean up the trash pile."

Blanche ran toward the back door as Alafair went back to pick up the mess her daughter had left on the lawn.

The Wayward Note

Alafair stood for a moment looking down at the cream-colored wad of paper attached to the pink ribbon, her hand extended in the act of reaching. Why had it not occurred to her the instant she saw it that Cindy's love letters had been tied up in pink ribbon? Was this one of those?

If so, how on earth would the goat have gotten hold of it?

She tried to remember the last time she saw the letters. It was at Cindy's house, after Elizabeth had fished them out of the flour bin. Alafair did not actually know where they were now. Elizabeth had told Cindy that she had put them in a safe place.

There was only one way to find out. She picked up the un-slimy end of the ribbon and lifted the paper off the grass. The goat had been thorough. The paper was reduced to a well-masticated, cream-colored ball. Alafair could see some dark smears where the ink had been, but there was no way she was going to be able to read whatever had been written on the paper.

Alafair had mucked sties and stalls, slaughtered and gutted animals for dinner, cleaned up after many a sick child, adult, dog, and cat, and changed thousands of diapers in her time, so a little goat saliva did not faze her. She began to peel the wet ball apart with her bare hands.

Nothing. Nothing legible, nothing even recognizable. Until she reached the very center of the ball, where the middle half of one crumpled page of dry paper lurked. She teased it apart and

saw two and a half sentences clearly written in the same hand
that had written the love notes to Cindy Stewart.

...meet me there if you can, amada. *I have something to tell
you that may change your mind. Your faith and trust have been
betrayed...*

◇◇◇

"Elizabeth, what did you do with Cindy's love letters? You told
her that you would hide them in a place where no one would
find them. Are they still there?"

Unlike Alafair, Elizabeth had retrieved a pair of gloves and
a shovel from the garden shed before she began scooping trash
and yard waste off the lawn. She straightened from her task and
gave Alafair a puzzled look. "I did hide them where no one will
seek." She patted the bosom of her dress with a gloved hand. "I
took a lesson from Cindy and keep them on my person all the
time. Why do you ask, sister?"

Alafair held up the piece of pink ribbon. "The goat was eating
on this hank of ribbon and the paper it was tied around. I figure
it must have been in the leaf barrel."

Elizabeth's eyes widened. "Well, shoot fire! How'd it get in
there? I never threw any of the notes away. Besides, I saw with
my own eyes that Dillon's men raked out this barrel and went
through the mess when they were here with their search warrant. And I burned everything that was in here after they were
done. Every bit of this rubbish was put in the barrel after that,
and most of it this morning by Levi and the kids."

"And Geoff."

Elizabeth was taken aback. "Geoff? What was he doing here?"

"He came to beg Cindy to take him back. Her and me was
standing on her porch at the time, and Levi and the kids were
raking up the leaf litter. She gave him short shrift, though, and
went off after Levi to look in on Matt."

"Well, I'm glad to hear that, at least. You suppose Geoff is
still over there?"

"I don't think so," Alafair said. "After Cindy flounced off,
Geoff puttered around for a while hauling limbs over here and

dumping them. Trying to look useful, I reckon. But by the time I got Blanche and Chase into the house for breakfast, I expect he had got tired of waiting for Cindy to come back, because I saw him walking off down Willow."

They gazed at one another for a moment, trying to fathom what it could mean. "Maybe this ribbon and paper are something entirely different than the love notes, and we're making assumptions." Elizabeth ventured. "After all, the goat did a fine job on it and we can't really tell much about it."

Alafair shook her head and held out the scrap in her hand. "Afraid not. I did find one smidgen of writing that I can still read, right in the center of the chawed-up wad. Look, it's the same handwriting. He was trying to get her to meet up with him. It looks to me like he was going to tell her about Geoff's fancy lady."

Elizabeth's curiosity overcame her distaste for the masticated paper and she leaned in to have a look.

"*Change your mind…*" Elizabeth repeated the words thoughtfully. "About what? Running off with him? That's Bernie's hand, all right. I recognize the fancy 'm'. One thing for sure, it wasn't him who put that note into this barrel. It had to have been Geoff, surely. The timing is too perfect."

"Now, I know you want to blame him, but don't go to making a whole cloth out of two threads. The note could have just as easily got raked up from under some bush along with the clippings. Even if it was Geoff disposed of it, he might never have known it was there in an armload of yard waste."

Elizabeth did not like this reasoning, but she had to admit it had merit. "Heavens, Alafair. Last night you asked what we ought to do next, and we never could come up with a good plan. I think Cindy Stewart has not told us everything and it's time she spilled the beans."

The Wrong Idea

They went into Cindy's house through the front door and found her in the parlor, standing in front of a mirror and putting on a hat.

Her blue eyes widened and she half turned when they walked in, one hand poised above her head, ready to plunge a lethal-looking pin through the crown of her hat.

"Cindy," Elizabeth opened, "we have to talk to you."

Cindy placed the hat pin on a side table and raised her finger to her lips to shush them. "Levi went to lie down with a bad headache directly we got back from Miz Carrizal's this morning. I was on my way to take some old clothes to the bBarrio, but there's no hurry." She kept her voice low. "Let's go talk on the porch."

She led them through the house and onto the raised back porch which ran completely across the rear of the house. Cindy had arranged a nice sitting area with cushioned wicker chairs, a table, a large rag rug, and potted plants.

The women arranged themselves comfortably around the table before Cindy asked, "Has something happened?"

Elizabeth held out the scrap of paper without a word. Cindy's eyebrows drew together as she took it from Elizabeth's hand and looked down at it. She paled as she read it. "Where did you get this?"

"It was stuck down into my leaf barrel under the trash from your yard, wrapped in a pink ribbon and all. One of the Carrizals' goats knocked over the barrel and made a good job of eating on it before Blanche managed to retrieve it. This little scrap is all we could decipher. It looks like one of your love letters, Cindy, but I promise you I still have all the ones I got out of your flour bin. Did you keep some of them back?"

"No, I didn't. You have them all. I've never seen this one."

"You didn't put this in Elizabeth's leaf barrel?" Alafair asked. "Elizabeth burned off the barrel since Bernie died, so someone put this note in there within the past few days."

"Well, it wasn't me! Gracious, it does look like one of his love notes. Whenever he left a personal note for me he used always this ivory-colored paper and a ribbon and wrote by hand. The messages for my contact in the barrio were always in a brown envelope and written on a typing machine."

Elizabeth opened her mouth to speak but the question died on her lips. Something about Cindy's statement gave her pause. She glanced at Alafair for illumination, unable to put her finger on it, but Alafair was staring at Cindy with a puzzled expression.

Cindy did not notice. "Oh, mercy, he must have sent Bernie to put another note under my flower pot that night. Perhaps someone killed Bernie while he was in my yard on that errand! What if his killer took this and just recently tried to dispose of it? '*Meet me,*' it says." She was suddenly on the verge of tears. "He never suggested an assignation before. What could he have had in mind? I may never know."

Elizabeth's eyes were wide with surprise. "Sent Bernie? Bernie didn't write this?"

"Bernie? No, he just delivered messages, and rarely, at that. Bernie was mighty smart with numbers, but he couldn't hardly read, much less write such a fine hand." Cindy hesitated as the implications of Elizabeth's question dawned on her. "Oh, surely you haven't been thinking all this time that Bernie wrote those love notes to me. How could you get that idea? I never said so, did I?"

Elizabeth was blinking rapidly in astonishment, trying hard to remember exactly what Cindy had said to her about the love notes but unable to process the information she needed. "But Bernie was a flirt and a seducer!"

"A flirt, yes," Cindy agreed. "But I made it clear from the beginning that he should keep his place. Besides, he knew Matty had feelings for me. He respected Matty."

Alafair slowly sat back in her chair, enlightened. "Matt…"

Elizabeth was stunned into silence for a long moment. Her expression slowly changed from amazement to realization to bitter understanding. At last she smiled. "Well, don't I feel foolish?"

Good Figurers

Since Levi had trimmed the hedge down to waist height, Blanche had no problem seeing that Alafair and Elizabeth were next door, sitting with Mrs. Stewart at the table on her back porch. She skipped through the gate and up the porch steps and flopped herself down in the unoccupied chair between her mother and aunt.

She was supposed to have taken her medicine by now. But Alafair never did come in the house to give it to her, so Shaw had sent her to fetch her mama home. But the women were talking about something interesting, Blanche could tell. They all smiled and greeted her absently before continuing their discussion as though she weren't there. She decided the message could wait a few minutes. Blanche took Artie's baseball out of her pocket and began spinning it around on the table, apparently paying no attention to her elders' conversation. All the better to absorb every word.

Alafair was still concerned with the paper remnant and did not note either Elizabeth's consternation or Blanche's feigned disinterest. "Well, it's pretty clear that somebody found your stash of letters, Cindy, and kept one until after Bernie's death. Then he decided he'd better get rid of it. But why now?"

"It looks to me like it had to have been Geoff," Elizabeth declared. "He'd be the most likely one to come across Cindy's letter-hiding place in the flour bin. I can see him carrying one around with him and stewing on it. And if he was just here…"

"But why toss it now?" Alafair repeated.

"Because he decided it looks suspicious, him toting around it around, so he decided he'd better get shet of it before the marshal finds it on him and decides it's a motive for murder!" Elizabeth looked proud of her reasoning.

Cindy shook her head. "But like I said, this is not from my collection of love notes. I've never seen this one before!"

The women paused to consider for a moment. Elizabeth was the first to come up with a theory. "It's more likely that Bernie's attacker found this note after he killed him. Either on Bernie's body or under the pot. And he's been carrying it around ever since. But who? It had to have been tossed into the leaf barrel by someone we wouldn't raise an eyebrow to see around our houses, someone who is here regular."

Alafair's gaze wandered off into space. She was visualizing Geoff Stewart with his arms full of hedge trimmings, heading toward Elizabeth's yard, as well as Chase and Blanche laughing as they sledded the tarp and its mound of leaves and branches through the Stewarts' gate. She remembered Cindy telling her, "*The leaf litter under the bushes has not been raked for a long time. They raked the chicken yard, too, and under the porch here.*"

"Tossed into the leaf barrel perhaps this very morning," she ventured. "I was saying earlier that it could be Levi raked up the note when he cleaned out the rubbish under the porch. That's where Bernie's hat was found, after all."

Cindy thought about this. "Maybe, maybe not. If the killer could sneak around here on the night of the murder, he could just as well sneak back here in the dead of some other night and dispose of that note. Then the trash got dumped on top of it later. Who would notice a scrap of paper at the bottom of that deep barrel?"

"Or maybe it wasn't the killer who did any of them things."

The women started at the unexpected sound of a man's voice. They all twisted around in their chairs to see Levi Gillander standing in the back door. He stepped out onto the porch and lifted a hand to shade his eyes from the late morning sun.

"Levi, how long have you been standing there!" Cindy exclaimed.

"I've been standing here for a good while. Sounds like you girls are pretty good figurers. But I think it's more likely that somebody found the letter and tossed it out without knowing what it was. Or it may be that somebody aimed to get rid of that letter because he's trying to protect someone else."

Cindy's eyebrows knit. "Protect someone? You mean whoever put the letter in the barrel has kept it hidden in order to protect a killer?"

Alafair was tiring of this game. "Levi, was it you who put the letter in the barrel? Where did you find it?"

Levi blinked, but did not avoid the question. "Under the flower pot."

Cindy gasped, but Alafair continued, "Do you know who wrote the note?"

Now that his secret was out, Levi was eager to tell it all. "Matt Carrizal, who else? Yes, it was me put that letter in the leaf barrel this morning, before I went to the Carrizals', Cindy. I been carrying it around for a week trying to decide whether to give it to the marshal. I didn't want to incriminate you, but it was attempted murder, for the love of Jesus. But then this morning Elena told us that Matt may live, and if he wakes up and tells who slit his throat, then the jig is up. But if he don't, well, that letter was the best evidence against you, and if it hadn't been for the damn goat nobody would have been the wiser."

Cindy was agog. "You think it was me who cut Matty's throat? Why in the name of sweet Jesus would I hurt Matt Carrizal!"

"Ah, yes, our dear friend Matt." Levi's voice was charged with sarcasm. "I wondered why you didn't want to pay your respects to Matt's family before now. Until you found out Matt is like to live and tell on you, that is. Who'd be suspicious if you asked to sit with him alone for a spell? Just five minutes and a pillow and you'd be in the clear. Even you could do that. It's a good thing I got there before you had the chance."

"Do you really believe Cindy attacked Matt at the restaurant?" Elizabeth's tone was incredulous.

Levi's answer was directed at his sister. "How easy it would have been for you! He'd never suspect ill of you. You could have got right up to him and one quick slash is all it'd take."

"But why? How could you think I would do such a thing?"

Levi looked at her as though she was being deliberately obtuse. "Because he knew that it had to have been you who murdered Bernie Arruda."

Speculation

Levi explained his thinking to his stunned audience. "Listening to y'all has give me an idea of how it happened. See what you think of this. The party is just about over and a bunch of folks volunteer to help clean up—stack chairs and tables, pick up trash, gather bats and balls, that sort of thing. Then some innocent citizen walks back here into the yard intending to return something of yours, Cindy, and lo and behold he's just in time to see two people here on the porch. But before the hapless bystander can decide whether to spit or say howdy, one of them bashes the other in the back of the head a couple of times with a bat. It's getting dark, but the witness can see well enough to know that the head-basher is someone he would not care to see get hanged for murder. It's somebody he knows well. Somebody he cares about."

"Are you telling us that is what happened? That you saw what happened?" Elizabeth's voice was shaky. "Why on earth haven't you told the marshal?"

Levi lowered the hand shading his eyes and squinted at her. "I didn't say that. I said that listening to y'all speculate gave me the idea."

Alafair was not having it. "Quit playing with us. What did you see?"

Levi smiled a twisted smile, caught. "All right, yes, I did see the whole thing. Arruda putting the letter under that pot right there…" He pointed to a large clay flower pot rife with cheery red petunias. "I couldn't tell who it was. Just a Mexican in a big hat. When he got hit I was so flabbergasted that I stood there like a fool when Cindy threw down the bat and ran off. But when I finally got my wits about me, I rolled Arruda's carcass under the porch, along with the murder weapon. Then come midnight I snuck back here, pulled the body out and lugged it to the ditch. I threw the bat in the incinerator and set it alight. I fetched the note and read it, Cindy. Him saying he loved you and wanted you to leave Geoff for him. I couldn't believe my eyes."

Elizabeth was aghast. "Why did you dump him over in front of my house?"

"It didn't even cross my mind that it was your house. I was just trying to get him away from my sister's yard."

Alafair was suddenly very aware of the young girl sitting on the other side of the table, gazing up at her with wide eyes. "Blanche, go fetch Daddy." Her voice was strained.

Blanche had sunk down in her chair, making herself as inconspicuous as possible to the agitated man behind her. But when she made a move to stand, Levi put his hand on Blanche's shoulder and pushed her back down. "No, let her hear this." He leaned forward until he was practically nose to nose with Cindy. "I was trying to protect you, Cindy. You made me into a liar. It was you killed him. You killed him and near to killed Matt, too, you whore."

Still as a fawn in the forest, Blanche gazed up at her mother white-faced, awaiting instructions. All three women were on their feet.

Alafair's tone was soothing. "You're telling us that you saw Cindy hit Bernie with a bat that night?"

"I did." Levi's face was red.

Cindy's eyes darted left and right as she sought a quick exit, but Elizabeth stepped in front of her, cutting off her escape.

"Cindy, is any of this true?"

Cindy blinked at her, befuddled. "Of course not…"

"Then stand up for yourself and don't let him say so."

Elizabeth's imperious tone stiffened Cindy's spine. Her cheeks flushed and she turned to her brother. "Levi, what are you doing?"

"If you really suspect that it was your sister who tried to kill Matt, I can set your mind at ease, Levi," Elizabeth said. "She spent that night at my house, and was still here when my sister found Matt at the restaurant. There are a bunch of witnesses who can attest to that."

Levi blinked at her, taken aback. He stuttered when he finally managed to respond. "I didn't know that. Still, she might have sneaked out and back in without any of you hearing her."

The full import of her brother's accusation was just sinking in and Cindy's voice was filled with hurt mixed with incandescent anger. "You know I didn't hurt Matt, nor Bernie, either. How could you sell me up the river? Who did kill Bernie? Was it Geoff? Was it Matt? It was Father, wasn't it? He's the only one I can think you'd sacrifice me for."

There was an instant of silence as the women awaited Levi's response. His expression had changed. He was reconsidering his story.

Alafair tried to keep her eyes on Levi's face and off of his hand resting on Blanche's shoulder. "Whoever it was, you don't need to be protecting them anymore, Levi. You said it yourself. When Matt wakes up he'll tell who tried to cut his throat. And that person either murdered Bernie too, or knows who did."

Levi's gaze skittered off to the left. "It doesn't matter who it was," he said. "If that letter had come to light, Cindy's reputation would be ruined forever. Our family's reputation. She'd have never been able to show her face in polite society again."

Alafair knew that he spoke the truth about that, at least. If the contents of the letter became public, Cindy would become an outcast whether she had actually done anything wrong or not. She would suffer more than the killer, in all probability. He had killed a Yaqui man who he thought was making improper advances to a white woman. Alafair had no illusions. In this year of our Lord nineteen and sixteen, no jury of white men in

America would hang him for that, or maybe not even send him to jail. But then there was the matter of the attempted murder of Matt Carrizal. Carrizal was a Spanish name, but compared to Bernie Arruda, Matt was another order of being as far as the law was concerned.

Alafair looked Levi directly in the eyes, intent on keeping his attention off of Blanche. "Did Matt confront Bernie's murderer or just confide in someone who was bent on protecting the killer? But Matt didn't die, and now he's like to wake up and tell what he knows. You were right when you said that a pillow over his face would have taken care of that. But if I remember right, you didn't follow Cindy to the Carrizals' house this morning. You were already gone before Cindy decided she was going to go over there. It wasn't her who aimed to silence Matt once and for all, was it? It was you."

Cindy staggered as though she had been struck. "Brother, you went over there this morning to finish off Matt?"

He shook his head, but no one took the gesture as a denial. "If I'd had the grit to smother him when I had the chance, what he knows would have died with him and we wouldn't be standing here talking like this. But I couldn't do it. Not so cold-blooded as that, with him unconscious and helpless."

Alafair was acutely aware of her daughter scrunching further and further down in her chair. Blanche was planning to make a break for it. "Matt will live to tell the tale because you're no natural killer, Levi. But he will tell, so you might as well come clean. You didn't set out to kill Bernie, did you, son?"

I Hope You Die

An instant of weary defeat flashed over Levi's features and was gone, but Alafair saw it and knew that she was right. The realization gave her no pleasure.

Levi sighed. "I didn't even know who he was at first. I was aiming to take Geoff's bat back into the house. It was dark by then and I only saw a shadow of somebody in a big Mexican hat rummaging around on the porch. I seen him fool around with something under the flower pot. I figured he was robbing the house. I had the bat in my hand and knocked him cold. I meant to fetch the law to arrest him, but I got curious about what he was doing with that pot. So I found the letter and read it. I thought it was him trying to seduce my sister."

Suddenly he was purple with rage. "It's your fault, Cindy! Greasers! How could you? Father will disown you. You're ruined. You've ruined both of us. I hope you die!"

Alafair reached out to calm him. "Levi…"

"I put the letter in my pocket." He was barely understandable. "He started moving around, moaning. I went down off the porch and picked up the bat again and let him have it. I meant him to die that time. I dragged him under the porch. Went home then and came back here after midnight to get rid of the evidence."

"Your sister wasn't having an affair with Bernie Arruda or anybody else. You know that." Elizabeth sounded stern. "Bernie didn't know what was in that note because he couldn't even read.

It was Matt who desired a liaison with Cindy. Is that why you swung a knife at him?"

The rage had burned out as suddenly as it flared. "I didn't go to the restaurant of a purpose to kill him. He asked me to meet with him. He told me that on the night of the party, he saw me come over here with the bat in my hand not long after he sent Bernie to hide the note on Cindy's porch. He called me a murderer, and so I was. But what was done couldn't be undone. The look on his face…I could not stand his judgment. That big knife was just lying there on the counter and I grabbed it up." He paused, and when he spoke again his voice was clear and full of wonder. "I never knew killing was so easy."

"What do you aim to do now, Levi?" Alafair could not help but glance at Blanche, whose head was now scarcely visible above the table. Levi's fingertips were dangling over the back of the chair, barely in contact with Blanche's shoulder.

"You have to turn yourself in," Cindy insisted.

Levi's lips parted, but before he could answer his gaze shifted and he paled. Alafair turned to see what had distracted him.

Shaw was standing at the gate, watching them with a puzzled expression.

Blanche chose her moment. "Daddy!" she cried, and dove for freedom. But Levi was too quick. His hand darted out and grabbed the back of her dress, jerking her back against his chest. Shaw had taken two or three alarmed strides toward them when his daughter called for him, but froze motionless at the bottom of the steps when Levi folded his arms around Blanche.

"Don't come no closer!" Levi warned. Blanche stood still, a compliant captive.

Cindy made a squeaky noise, but Elizabeth gave her friend a tight shake of the head. Alafair mustered all her will to remain silent and not inflame Levi further.

Levi took a step back toward the kitchen door, drawing Blanche with him. "I don't want to hurt this child," he warned, "but I will if I have to. Her and me are leaving, now. I'm taking

Geoff's auto, Cindy. Don't y'all try to follow us. I'll let her out in a safe place once I'm away…"

But Blanche had no intention of letting herself be taken hostage. She clamped her teeth onto Levi's arm and bit down hard. He squealed and pushed her to the floor, and the instant she was clear of him it was as if a storm broke. Shaw ran up the steps as Levi made for the back door that led into Cindy's kitchen, the only escape route open to him. He was far enough away from Shaw that he could have made it, had Alafair not grabbed the first thing she could get her hands on—Artie's baseball, still lying on the table—and hurled it at Levi's head, striking him squarely on the temple. He sat down hard on the porch, stunned. He recovered instantly and scrambled to his hands and knees, but the fall caused all the delay that Shaw needed to reach him. He stomped on Levi's back with a booted foot, knocking the breath out of him and sending him sprawling. Shaw straddled his captive and twisted Levi's arm up between his shoulder blades.

"Call the marshal," he ordered. Cindy raced to comply. Shaw seized Levi's hair with his free hand and ground his face into the floor. "And you don't move."

During the long stunned silence that followed, Shaw gave Alafair and Blanche a speculative once over. Mother and daughter were entwined in each others' arms, red-cheeked and heaving. Once he had assured himself that they were none the worse for wear, one corner of his mouth twitched up in an ironic smile. Alafair caught his expression and her eyebrows raised.

He broke into a grin. "They call that a *beanball*, honey,"

The Sonora Gang

Mr. Dillon stood in the middle of the Stewart parlor eyeing the unhappy occupants for a long time before he spoke. "Well, well, well."

Alafair and Shaw were wedged together in one of Cindy's big padded armchairs, and Elizabeth, Web, and Cindy were arrayed across the sofa, along with a much chastened Geoff Stewart, summoned home by the marshal despite Cindy's objections.

"So all of this mayhem and murder is just the result of a tragic series of misunderstandings over some love notes?" Dillon's question was heavy with sarcasm.

"Killings have been done for even less reason," Shaw pointed out.

"Don't I know it," Dillon agreed, "but it is a mighty odd coincidence that Arruda and Carrizal were both part of a smuggling gang out of Sonora, ain't it? What did your brother-in-law know about that, Mr. Stewart?"

Geoff started when Dillon spoke to him. He was slumped in the corner of the couch, next to Web, with his hands clasped between his knees, trying to remain as inconspicuous as possible. His eyebrows drew together, as confused as if Dillon had spoken to him in Sanskrit. "Gang? I don't know anything about a gang, Marshal, or smuggling, or anything about that."

Elizabeth snorted. "He's been too involved in other matters to know what has been happening around here, Marshal."

Geoff reddened, but otherwise ignored the remark. "The only thing I knew about Bernie Arruda was that he was a jack-of-all-trades around the neighborhood and that he played Mexican music with his brothers. As for Matt Carrizal, he is my neighbors' son, and I ate luncheon in his restaurant sometimes."

Dillon regarded Geoff with narrow eyes for a moment. His gaze moved across Elizabeth and Web and came to rest on Cindy. "I have evidence that Matt Carrizal participated in the Arrudas' smuggling ring, and I strongly suspect that your brother may have been involved as well."

Cindy gazed back at Dillon, her blue eyes awash with help-less loss, looking shrunken and confused and utterly unlike the Cindy who had confronted her brother an hour earlier. "Mr. Dillon, Matt Carrizal told me that he was involved in charity work with the Yaqui Indians who lost their land to the Mexi-can government years ago. Sometimes he helped refugees from the revolution. He provided food and clothing and shelter and jobs. All I know about my friend is that he is a kind man who respected the law, sir. As for Levi, you'll have to ask him about that. If he helped Matt and the Arrudas with their work, I'm proud to hear it, but he never told me about it."

Dillon crossed his arms over a broad chest. "Well, if Carrizal thought his work with the Arrudas was strictly for charity, he was sadly duped. The Sonora Gang is heavily engaged in human smuggling, and not only of ill-used refugees, but of spies and criminals of the worst ilk."

"I don't believe it." Elizabeth was aghast. "Matt would never have anything to do with that."

"I hope that's true, and it may well be he didn't know the extent of Arruda's vile enterprise. For in the course of my inves-tigation I've discovered that Arruda was a manipulator of the first water. The money he hid in the Rural School building, the quarters and dimes and pesetas that he collected from well-intentioned folks that could ill afford it, was not used only to bring people into this country and secure their comfort, but to buy and send guns to Villa on the other side of the border."

Alafair was shocked. "But we heard that the Arrudas had deserted Villa and went in fear of him!"

Dillon huffed. "Yes, good story, Miz Tucker. Who'd have thought? Bernie Arruda was a captain in Villa's army and one of his most trusted cohorts till the day he died. In fact, he supplied the guns that massacred some of those who so kindly helped your ailing daughter in Columbus, New Mexico. Believe me, ladies and gentlemen, for the past ten years you good people of Tempe have sheltered a viper in your bosom. But you will be glad to know that it's not just Tony Arruda who has taken a powder. The whole pack of them have up and disappeared. That shack of theirs in Guadalupe is empty. I reckon they've took themselves off home to Mexico." He turned back to Cindy. "If Carrizal and your brother didn't know what they were involved with, take comfort in knowing that they weren't the only ones who Arruda used. But if Carrizal was aware of what the Arrudas were really up to, I am sorry to tell you but he was a murderer as sure as Levi Gillander and will have to answer for it."

Natividad is gone! That was Alafair's first thought. She would never have the chance to tell that sweet girl what happened to her father. She felt bereft.

Cindy, sitting on the opposite end of the couch as far from Geoff as she could get, spoke up. "Marshal, I'm confident you will discover how innocent of intrigue Matt Carrizal was. No human being is kinder, unless it is his parents yonder. As for my brother..." She hesitated, searching for the right words. "You've spoken to my father, so you know what he's like. You have talked to others who know him and who know my family. They'll say that my father hates all colored people, but that Levi is sympathetic to the plight of the displaced down in Mexico. But take it from me, you cannot be raised by such a man as Father and not be tainted by his beliefs. Levi has the same kind of compassion for the Mexicans and the Indians that he does for a good mule. No use to be cruel to the pathetic creatures, you know. He wouldn't shoot it, but he wouldn't want it moving in next door, either. This is why I believe that Levi would never have been involved in any secret plan to help Mexicans or Indians."

Alafair felt her cheeks burning. Things that Levi had said to her suddenly took on new significance in the light of Cindy's comments. *I feel right sorry for the little brown folks. Even animals ought to have a place to be with their own kind and be left in peace.* It said much about the world she lived in that she had hardly noticed the casual racism of his statement. But Matt would have noticed. Levi had told her that Matt had approached him about helping with the Yaqui railroad, but nothing had come of it. A few minutes of conversation would have shown Matt that Levi Gillander's sympathies were only skin deep.

Dillon's skeptical expression did not change. Well, it was his job to be skeptical, Alafair thought. But he had not even suggested that Cindy herself was involved in Matt's enterprise, or indeed that any woman might be engaged in such illicit activities. Alafair was amused to realize that Dillon was blinded by prejudices of his own.

Except for the Stewarts, Dillon dismissed them all with a warning that he was not finished with this investigation by a long shot. As Alafair followed Shaw and the others out the back door, she could hear the interrogation resume. Cindy's prodigal husband was going to have to work to convince the marshal that his sins were strictly of the sordid type and he had been totally unaware of the drama happening all around him. Alafair felt a perverse satisfaction that Geoff was going to sweat for a while.

She wondered if the Carrizals knew where the Arruda family had gone. She said a little prayer for dear, innocent Natividad.

Not This

"I kind of liked Levi, too," Elizabeth said. "At least I thought he was more reasonable than his old man."

Elizabeth and Alafair were sitting alone together in the parlor, each dressed in nightclothes and curled up in one of the large armchairs in front of the fireplace. The only light in the room was from the glowing embers behind the grate in the iron stove. The husbands and children were in bed.

Alafair drew her shawl closer around her shoulders. "What Cindy said about Levi put me in mind of something I heard a fellow say back in Oklahoma last year, after Congress passed the law forbidding folks from marrying outside their race. He said it was a good law and people ought to stick to their own. That colored people are all right in their place, but he wouldn't want one to marry his sister."

Elizabeth chuckled, but there was no humor in it. "Well, the whole business is too wretched to contemplate. For a little while, when I thought Bernie and Matt were engaged in a noble undertaking, I held out hope for the nature of man. But as it turns out, Matt was probably being used by Bernie, who was as big a deceiver and manipulator as I believed him to be in the first place. They were both set upon by a disgusting little toad who couldn't stand the thought that a brown man had touched his sister." She heaved a sigh. "I despair."

"Elizabeth, I have something to ask you. A few days ago when you dug Cindy's love letters out of her flour bin, and later when we found the last note in your leaf barrel, you said you recognized the hand. That Bernie wrote them. Yet they weren't written by Bernie at all, but by Matt. Maybe I mistook your meaning… " Alafair let the question hang in the air.

Elizabeth let it dangle for a few moments. "That is what I meant," she acknowledged. "I did think Bernie wrote them." An ironic smile formed on her lips. "That scoundrel gave me a couple of letters just like them, same paper, same hand, same kind and tender sympathy. It never crossed my mind that it wasn't Bernie who wrote them. The notes were neither addressed nor signed. Cindy said he couldn't read, but he had to have known what was in the letters that Matt had given him to put under her flower pot. He either got somebody to read them to him or he wasn't as ignorant as he pretended. In any event he had a nose for a sad and willing woman, so I suppose he purloined a few of Matt's notes to Cindy and used them to woo me. And I fell for it."

Alafair blinked, but did not respond. Odd. Her sister's unexpected revelation did not particularly surprise her.

Elizabeth looked up at her from under her eyebrows, awaiting Alafair's reaction. When none was forthcoming, she continued. "It didn't last but a week or so. Then I quit him and he was off looking for another conquest." She sighed. "Every time I saw him after that, I pretended like it never happened, and so did he. This is why I was dumbfounded to think Bernie was part of a noble endeavor, but I wanted badly for it to be so. Isn't it funny how a man can be a hero and a blackguard at the same time, I thought? Turns out he can't. When I found Cindy's cache, I just wished she had let me in on it. I thought to tell her a few things about all those sweet words. I figured he would break her heart."

"Like he did you?"

Elizabeth turned her head to gaze at Alafair across the dim space between their chairs. She had been expecting to have to explain herself, so when she answered, her tone was calm. "He didn't break my heart, Alafair. I was glad to get shet of him in the end. He was a diversion, but the whole thing was too tawdry for me, and I didn't care for the idea of getting caught and run out of town on a rail."

Alafair felt unexpected tears prickle her eyelids. "When did you get to be so hard, Elizabeth?"

"Am I hard? If it looks that way, it's just because all my life I have done what everybody told me was the right thing, even when in my heart I knew it was not right for me. And all it's got me is misery and disappointment. Web may be a good provider, but he's dull and pompous and not very kind to folks he considers his inferiors, which is anybody not richer or more powerful than he is."

"You don't love him anymore?"

Elizabeth thought about it for a moment, then shrugged. "I don't know that I ever did. When we were first married, I was all excited that we were going to come out here where you made your own destiny whether you were a man or woman. Me and Web were going to civilize the West together. He disappointed me, if the truth be known. At least Bernie was bright and attentive, and acted like he was interested in me for more than… you know." She looked away. "That's why I kind of understand why Cindy kept Matt's letters."

Alafair's eyes crinkled. She understood longing and desire better than Elizabeth thought. "How did you manage to carry on with this fellow and not get caught?"

"It wasn't easy. Once he came here to the house when Chase was away, and a couple of times I met him over to the room behind the restaurant where he stayed sometimes."

"Oh, honey." To hear the details described made the affair sound more pathetic than titillating.

Elizabeth's voice took on a wistful quality. "Do you despise me, now?"

Alafair studied Elizabeth's face for a moment before she ventured a response. "You're my darlin' little sister, Elizabeth. Nothing you do will ever change that. Besides, I ain't like Mama and Daddy in that I think folks ought to stay married even if they make each other miserable. But if you're bored and lonely, it seems to me like there are a lot more honorable ways to fill your time than cheat on your husband."

Elizabeth's expression conveyed her opinion that Alafair was not qualified to judge her situation. For an instant, she looked so much like Blanche at her sulkiest that Alafair could not help but smile. "At least you ought to have the manners to leave Webster before you go to canoodling with somebody else."

Elizabeth looked away. "I reckon that wasn't my best decision, and I wish I hadn't done it. But at the time... Well, no matter what, I appreciate that you didn't drop dead with shock or tell me I'm going straight to hell or that you don't ever want to see me again."

"All are weak and fallen short, Elizabeth. I'm just glad you've repented of it."

"Now you sound like Daddy."

"Thank you," Alafair said, though she knew Elizabeth did not mean it as a complement.

"I am sorry you're so unhappy. Why don't you find something to do? Both my older girls have jobs, and Martha intends to work after she marries."

Elizabeth laughed. "What? You think Webster Kemp, Esquire, would allow his wife to have a proper job of work? If Web would let me work for money that would help a lot. I liked it when I was clerking for Web at his law firm before Chase was born. He said I was smart and would make a good lawyer myself. But after the baby come, Web partnered up with Geoff Stewart and hired a clerk and that was that."

"Well, there's plenty of charitable causes. Church work..." Elizabeth made a rude noise, which Alafair ignored. "...civic work. Red Cross, or votes for women."

"I did work for suffrage before statehood, and women do have the vote here in Arizona. What, didn't you know that? Don't look so surprised. I got disenchanted with politics, though. Too much corruption. And no good ever comes of trying to help people. Look what happened to Matt."

"Well, what do you want?" There was an edge of exasperation in Alafair's voice.

Elizabeth hesitated, thinking, before she answered. "Not this."

Goodbyes

Shaw had already stacked the luggage beside the front door by the time Blanche and Alafair emerged from the bedroom before breakfast, dressed for travel in their utilitarian dresses and sturdy shoes. Alafair sent Blanche into the kitchen before walking into the parlor to gaze at the pile of carpetbags, burlap sacks, and cardboard boxes and wonder how it was that they were going home with so much more than they had started out with.

"Y'all about ready to go?"

Alafair turned at the sound of Elizabeth's voice behind her. "Just about. I reckon we'll take a turn or two around the bedroom later and make sure we haven't missed anything." She smiled. "If you find anything after we're gone, you can just keep it. Little enough reward for your hospitality."

Elizabeth's answering smile was wan. "I kindly wish you weren't going, Sister. I have taken a shine to having you around."

Alafair felt tears well on her lower lids. "Well, now we must take to writing even more often than we did. And for goodness sake, since you and Webster manage to get back to Arkansas to see Mama and Daddy every other year or so, next time take a little detour on the way back and stop off in Boynton! Let Chase get to know his kinfolks."

For an instant, Elizabeth looked as though she would cry. "That would be the best thing in the world for him, I do declare." She reached out and enfolded Alafair in an impulsive hug tight enough to squeeze the breath out of her.

Alafair was surprised and touched. Elizabeth had never been particularly sentimental. After a few breathless seconds, Alafair gently pried herself out of her sister's loving grip.

"It's all right, honey. It ain't like we'll never see one another again."

The tears that had been threatening finally spilled down Elizabeth's cheeks. "I hope you're right, Alafair, I surely do." She gave her eyes a brisk dab with her handkerchief and straightened, shaking off her melancholy mood with a will. "Listen, sister, y'all's train doesn't leave till noon, so you've still got some time. The motion picture troupe is packing up and leaving town on the nine o'clock to Los Angeles and me and Cindy are going to head up town to see them off. Why don't you and Blanche come along? It should be great fun."

"Oh, I don't think so, but thank you. We have a long trip ahead of us, and I'd just as soon take things easy this morning."

Elizabeth gazed at her in silence for a moment before she nodded. "I figured you'd say that. Well, I expect that's for the best. Me and Cindy will be heading off after breakfast. Would you be so good as to take care of Chase?"

"Surely. We'll have time for a nice talk when y'all get back."

"Why aren't they back yet, Shaw?" Time had come for the Tuckers to leave for the train station and Elizabeth and Cindy had not yet returned to the house. Alafair knew the California train had come and gone, for she had heard the whistle when it departed at close to ten o'clock.

Shaw was loading valises into the back of Webster's Hupmobile when he answered. "The movie train pulled out near to an hour late, so I expect the girls decided to just stay downtown and meet us on the platform. Don't worry about it, honey. We'll have plenty of time to say our goodbyes before we have to board."

He and Blanche walked back toward the house with Chase hopping and skipping, benignly ignored, in their wake. Alafair was standing by the auto, fretting in spite of his assurances, when Mrs. Carrizal joined her.

She placed the large basket she was carrying on the ground and gave Alafair a hug. "I could not let you go without saying goodbye. Of course Artie wants to take his leave of Blanche. I sent him up to the house to find her. My husband wanted to come but he is off about his business. Much has been neglected of late. The girls are with Matt."

"How is he this morning?"

The smile that lit Mrs. Carrizal's face made her look twenty years younger. "He is stronger every day. He cannot speak yet, but he manages to make his wishes known. He wanted to wish you a safe journey, and to let you know how much he appreciated your visit yesterday."

"I'm just glad to see him looking so much better. Has Dillon been by to question him yet?"

"Yes, but just long enough to get Matt to write the name of his attacker on a piece of paper. The marshal told us that Levi will be bound over for trial and transfered to the jail in Phoenix tomorrow. I expect Mr. Dillon will be back to get a full statement from Matt later about his involvement with the refugees and how much he knew about the Arrudas and their gun running. Which is nothing. That won't be until Doctor Moeur says he's strong enough, though."

"I'm sure everything will work out. I'm so glad to get a chance to see you again before we go. Shaw and Web are fetching the luggage, and Elizabeth and Cindy are already at the train station. Seems the acting troupe left town this morning and they wanted to see them off."

"Then I will keep you company until you leave."

Shaw and Web and the children moved back and forth between the house and the car, leaving Alafair and Mrs. Carrizal to sit beneath the ramada and talk of homely things. How Alafair would miss the gorgeous winter days here in Tempe, with its perfumed air and the sound of bells marking the hours. How she would miss her lovely new friends. The route that Shaw had chosen for their return trip to Oklahoma was through the mountains to the north, for the ticket agent had assured them that the tracks outside of Flagstaff had been repaired.

Mrs. Carrizal told Alfair that they were about to see some spectacular scenery, much more felicitous than the endless stretch through the southern desert they had crossed on the way out; and considering what had happened at Columbus, a lot safer, too.

Alafair said that was nice, but after all their adventures, she only wanted to get home where she belonged and plant herself like an old tree, never to roam again.

For a long time they avoided talking about murder and bloodshed, but it was inevitable that the topic would arise. It was Mrs. Carrizal who finally broached the subject.

"I want to tell you, Alafair, how much I appreciate what Blanche has done for my Arturo. She has been a true friend during a very hard time. What happened to his brother has been devastating for him, and I fear that his father and I have not been of much help."

Alafair shook her head. "It is so difficult for a family when evil befalls one of their number, and all those who are left must deal with their own fear and grief as well as the pain of the others. I'm pleased that Blanche's presence soothed Artie a little. She's very fond of him, and declares she will write him every day until the end of time. Besides, we will never be able to repay you for what you did for Blanche. You're a truly gifted healer and without you I don't know what would have become of her."

Mrs. Carrizal looked uncomfortable with such effusive praise. "I am but an instrument, *hija.*" She reached down and hefted the large wicker basket at her feet, forestalling any more compliments. "I know that Elizabeth sends you home well provisioned, but I have made up a few things for you to take on the train." She handed the giant basket to Alafair.

"It's not much," she apologized, which caused Alafair to smile. "It is only that we have been given so much food over the past two days. We will never be able to eat it all before it spoils. There is some cake and a few *buñuelos*. I know you liked them. I wrapped up half-a-dozen tamales and some corn tortillas. I also put in a bowl of dove with beans. It is Matteo's favorite dish. I made it for him, though he is not quite ready to eat it yet. I cooked it very slowly in a clay *olla* in the oven. I hope you like it."

Alafair looked down at the basket in her lap. Dove with beans? She gave a quick glance over her shoulder to make sure the men were out of earshot. "Mrs. Carrizal," she blurted, "did you call your son back from the brink of the grave?"

A long silence ensued as Mrs. Carrizal gazed at her, her dark eyes unrevealing, but apparently not shocked to be asked such a thing. Alafair could feel her cheeks burning and expected that her face was tomato red. But she did not retract the question.

For a moment, Alafair wondered at Mrs. Carrizal's lack of surprise. Until the obvious answer dawned on her. "You saw me watching you the other night when you killed the doves?"

The corners of Mrs. Carrizal's mouth turned up. "Not at first. But yes, eventually I knew you were there."

"Why didn't you say anything?"

"Why didn't you?"

Alafair considered her answer before shaking her head. "I don't know. Killing the doves was a violent act, but I felt no evil purpose in you. I knew your gentle heart. And then against all odds, Matt turned from the face of death."

"I am no *bruja*, Alafair. No witch. I sought only to invoke the saints and spirits, and how they choose to answer me or deny me is their business."

The Wrong Hill to Die On

Blanche was not willing to take her leave of Artie, so in the end he and his mother crammed into the Hupmobile with Web and Chase and the Tuckers and rode with them to the train station.

They unloaded and checked their larger baggage inside the station house before going out onto the platform. Much to Alafair's surprise, Elizabeth and Cindy were not there.

"Where do you suppose they went?" Alafair demanded of Web.

Webster was not concerned. "I know those gals." His tone was confident. "They went to eat a bite of cake at the restaurant in the Casa Loma, and got to talking and have lost track of the time."

Shaw pulled out his pocket watch and checked it. "Our train will be here directly, Web. Alafair will be heartbroke if she misses saying goodbye to Elizabeth. Would you kindly run over there and see if you can roust them out before we have to board?"

Web hurried to his task, leaving them all on the platform. The children were playing on the stack of cargo boxes waiting to be loaded. The adults were chatting about anything but what was on their minds. Where were those two? Alafair had a bad feeling.

The northbound train was just pulling into the station when Web came out of the station house. Alafair caught her breath at the look on his face.

Shaw took a step forward. "I declare, Web, you're as white as a sheet! What has happened?"

"Elizabeth's gone. Cindy too."

Mrs. Carrizal sat Web down on one of the cargo boxes. "Gone? What do you mean?"

"When the waiter at the restaurant said they hadn't been there, I got fretted and came back here to ask the station master if he'd seen them. He did! He said they went out to the platform to hail the movie folks off, and when the train pulled out he saw Elizabeth and Cindy jump on! He said that the actress who dallied with Geoff held out a hand and hauled Cindy on, then Elizabeth jumped on after her!"

Web's pitch rose a level as he continued. "I can't believe it! By gum, Mr. Wills told me that the two of them had sure enough jumped on without tickets, but they could buy tickets on the train so we wasn't to worry!" His wild-eyed gaze switched from Alafair's face to Mrs. Carrizal's. "She didn't take a thing but what she stood up in. If they hadn't been seen, we wouldn't know they were gone for hours yet. What are they thinking? What am I going to tell Geoff? Did they think about their husbands?" Web straightened and slapped a hand to his cheek. "What about Chase?"

Alafair was stiff with shock and unable to say a word of comfort to Web as she awkwardly patted his shoulder. She was remembering the encounter with Elizabeth that morning by the front door. If she had agreed to go with Elizabeth and Cindy to the train station, would this have happened?

She realized that even if her presence had stopped their getting on that train today, it would only have been a matter of time until Elizabeth made her escape. Alafair had known in her heart for some time how her sister's story was going to turn out. *But what about Chase?* If it had not been for Chase, Alafair could have had some sympathy for Elizabeth's action.

Mrs. Carrizal was hunkered down in front of Web so she could look him in the eye. "I am so sorry, Webster," she was saying. "But be calm, now. They have only been gone a couple of hours, and Elizabeth and Cindy may think better of what they have done by the time they reach Phoenix. You must wait and see what happens."

Web's expression eased. He pulled a big white handkerchief out of his pocket and blew his nose on it. "Well, Shaw, I know y'all have to board now, but I reckon I better go tell Geoff that his wife is gone. Cindy has kin in California. Maybe Geoff can shoot off some wires so they can hunt for them." Web made a fist and gave it a feeble shake. "I'll get her back! I'll get myself on the very next train west and find Elizabeth. I'll beg her to come back to me if I have to."

"I know you will." Alafair's tone was soothing. She and Shaw locked eyes for an instant, and he gave her his quirky smile, full of irony and bemusement at the folly of humanity. Together they seized Web by the arms and hauled him to his feet. "Go on and find Geoff, now," Shaw urged. "Don't worry about us. We'll get off just fine."

"You send us a telegram as soon as you find out anything," Alafair urged, anxious.

"What about Chase," Mrs. Carrizal asked. "Shall I take him home with me?"

Web blinked at her. *Oh, yes, Chase.* "But you have your hands full what with nursing Matt and all," he mused. His lips thinned and he turned to peer at the oblivious little boy who was still playing with his cousin. "Shaw, a word before I leave." The two men drew aside for a private conversation.

Alafair intended only to collect her things and begin boarding, but Mrs. Carrizal was watching her with sympathetic anticipation. Alafair could not help herself. Her shock and indignation at the havoc her sister caused burst forth. "Miz Carrizal, I don't blame Cindy a bit for what she did. But Elizabeth! I could choke that foolish girl! What was she thinking indeed? I mean, I knew she was unhappy with her life and with Web, and I felt sorry for her. But to haul off and leave your six-year-old child! I swear, if she wants sympathy from me, she picked the wrong hill to die on. I could never conscience what she just did."

To Alafair's surprise, Mrs. Carrizal smiled. "That is a funny saying, *the wrong hill to die on*. I have never heard it before. What does it mean?"

Alafair blinked, momentarily taken out of her pique. "Well, ma'am, it's just something my mama used to say whenever we got to whining about something and making excuses. 'If you want sympathy from me,' she'd say, 'you picked the wrong hill to die on, young'un.' That's when we knew we'd come to the wrong place for comfort and we'd better quit bellyaching and do as we were told."

Mrs. Carrizal considered this. "Perhaps this is just what Elizabeth thought. Do not be too angry with her, Alafair. You are right when you say Elizabeth is unhappy. She covered it well, but I have seen that she has been unhappy for many years. Life is short, as you and I well know, and it could be that Elizabeth finally decided that she did not want to pick the wrong hill to die on, indeed."

Mrs. Carrizal went to round up the children just as Shaw came up to Alafair's side. She could not read his expression.

"Has Webster gone?" she asked.

"He's gone back into the station to buy a ticket on the first train headed toward California."

"What did he want from you?"

He looked at her sidelong. "Well, it seems he has a plan to get Elizabeth back…"

Something Out of Nothing

Matt was awake when Mrs. Carrizal and Artie returned home from seeing the Tuckers off at the station. He was propped up on fat pillows in a half-reclining position, eyes closed, listening to his father read to him from a chair at the bedside, when his mother and brother came into the room.

"Is he asleep?" Mrs. Carrizal whispered, but Matt opened his eyes and smiled at them.

Artie leaned across his father and took Matt's hand, eager to relate their adventure. "Matt, you'll never believe what happened at the station. Before we even took Blanche and her folks to to catch their train home, Miz Stewart and Miz Kemp went to say goodbye to the movie people going back to California, and when they got there they took a notion to go with them! They've both skedaddled!"

Matt's eyes widened and he looked at his mother for confirmation.

"Is it so?" Mr. Carrizal asked for both of them.

Mrs. Carrizal nodded. "Looks like it is. The station master told Webster that Elizabeth and Cindy jumped on the train with the troupe just as it was pulling out of the station. I don't know if they had planned it beforehand or not, but it seems they have both decided to leave their husbands and become actresses."

One of Mr. Carrizal's white eyebrows arched. "This does not surprise me overmuch, except for the timing. What will the marshal have to say about Cindy leaving town in such an unexpected hurry?"

Mrs. Carrizal sat down in the chair next to her husband. "Oh, he will not care. He has no idea that Cindy had anything to do with helping Matt and the refugees, and I for one do not intend to tell him. I'm sure he will decide Cindy is leaving town to get away from her cheating husband and her murdering brother, which she probably is. Elizabeth is no suspect, but I am surprised that she went as well. I told her sister that Elizabeth may think better of her action and turn back up after awhile."

Matt began making scribbling gestures, and his father laid a pencil and pad from the bedside table on the mattress beside him. Matt picked up the pencil and scrawled on the pad in large block letters, *CINDY DIVORCE?*

His parents glanced at one another before his mother answered. "I expect she will. Matteo, I know how you feel, but now is not the time to think of that. Even if she does divorce Geoff, it will be many months, maybe years, before she is free. And Mr. Dillon is not through with you, not by a long shot. You may be entangled with the law for a long time. Not to mention that it will be months before you are strong enough to do more than walk around the block."

Matt's eyes narrowed and he wrote, *"Fl better daily. E & J restrnt. Dillon got nthing."*

A worried look passed over Mrs. Carrizal's face, but her husband's expression looked more like admiration. He bit his lip to head off an impolitic smile. "You are certainly determined, son, I admit it. I know you feel better, and I know that your sisters are running your restaurant just as well as you can. But better is not well, and Dillon may not have anything on you, but that doesn't mean he will not make something out of nothing."

Mrs. Carrizal put her hand on Matt's arm. "Son, you must not concern yourself with anything but your recovery right now."

Matt gave his mother a reassuring smile and scribbled, *Dnt worry ma. Not going anywhr now.*

Artie read between the lines. "When you go to California, can I go with you?"

Matt croaked out a chuckle and gave his brother a wink.

Second Chances

Web was sitting at a table in the hotel dining room, absently fingering the delicate china cup full of tea, when he caught sight of her coming down the staircase. He stood and waved to catch her eye, and she paused before walking toward him across the lobby. Web held her chair for her before he sat back down. They regarded one another for a long moment.

Elizabeth was beautiful, Web acknowledged to himself for the hundredth time. Such lively dark eyes. What was that expression he was seeing in those eyes as she looked at him? Was it anger? Desperation? No, it was disappointment. His heart sank. He considered his words carefully before he breached the silence. They were standing on a razor's edge now, and he knew it.

"Elizabeth, I'm sorry." He paused, leaving room for a response, but none was forthcoming. "I'm sorry I covered up for Geoff. I'm sorry that I've been so wrapped in my own affairs, building the practice and all, that I never noticed how unhappy you've become. I never wanted that, believe me."

"I know that." There was no emotion behind the words, Web noted. He could have done with a little emotion.

The waiter approached and Elizabeth ordered her own cup of tea, giving Web a few moments to consider his strategy. Odd. He had been rehearsing arguments over the past several days, ever since he had boarded the train in Tempe to come to Los Angeles, trying to think any combination of words that might persuade her to come home with him. He opened with his high card. "Chase misses you."

A thin smile appeared. "I doubt that."

Her response took him aback, though upon consideration it shouldn't have. Web didn't really know if Chase missed his mother or not. He approached from another angle. "Don't you miss your boy, Elizabeth? He needs his mama."

Elizabeth took a sip of her tea, then carefully set the cup down. "I love Chase. Of course I do. But I never have been as good a mother to him as he deserves. I don't have the knack. I fear his childish antics don't fill me with glee like they would a natural mother. I crave the stimulation of adult matters. Besides, no child thrives with unhappy parents. Do the boy a favor, Web. Let Mr. and Miz Carrizal raise him. They'll make a fine man of him."

"Catholics?" Web blurted, before he could catch himself.

Elizabeth's lips narrowed and he knew he had made a mistake. He recovered the best he could. "No, you're right. There are no finer people than the Carrizals. But it don't matter what the reason, a child should know his own parents love him."

She sighed. "Web, I'm tired of it. I'm tired of trying to fit myself into a life that don't suit me, of pretending to be somebody I'm not. I've told you a hundred times and you've never heard me. I'm done. Cindy and me have got ourselves jobs with Mr. Bosworth's company at Paramount Pictures. I'm a production assistant on his next flick and Cindy has an acting part. Once I'm settled proper we can discuss Chase's future."

Web suddenly felt cold. "What about our future?"

Elizabeth seemed amused. "What future is that, Web?"

"Surely you don't aim to go through life as a divorced woman? You are too high-class a lady for that."

"Cindy is divorcing Geoff, and nobody here in California has batted an eye over it. I don't expect to ever want to marry again, but you may want a proper wife someday. I'd think you'd be glad to get shet of me. If you knew me better, some of the things I've thought or done...I know you would."

"Oh, Elizabeth. Geoff did Cindy very ill, and she's well rid of him. But I don't want any other wife but you. I've never looked at another woman, I swear it."

"I know you never did."

Web leaned forward and took her hand across the table, earnest. "We had our happy times, didn't we, Elizabeth? You remember when we first set out for the Arizona Territory? We were going to be pioneers. We were going to bring law and civilization to the untamed West, and were pretty surprised to see that the West was already fairly tamed. But we built that house. We built that law practice together. Why, you were my first law clerk, and I swear I never have had a better one since."

The memory made Elizabeth smile. "That was my happiest time," she admitted. "I loved researching your cases with you. Then you partnered up with Geoff and the practice grew like Topsy. I was even pondering studying for the bar myself, till I got in the family way. And that was that."

"But you'd always said you wanted a passel of youngsters, like your sister."

She shook her head at her own youthful folly. "I did. But I found out that I'm not cut from the same bolt as Alafair."

"Please, Elizabeth, please consider coming back to us. I've broke off with Geoff. His wife leaving him over his bad behavior has caused a scandal and he's leaving town, as well. We'll start a new law firm, you and me. You can be the law clerk again. I'll help you study for the bar, if that's what you want. Why, you know enough law that you could likely pass the bar right now. In fact, there's that new law college down in Tucson. If you want the law degree, it wouldn't take you but a couple of years."

Elizabeth gave him a sad smile, as though she pitied his hopeless perseverance. But there was a speculative light in her eye that encouraged him.

"May I stay a while, Elizabeth?" he ventured. "I know you're committed to Mr. Bosworth's picture for the duration, but I'd enjoy to see a bit of California and watch some movie-making.

Perhaps we can keep company, go to dinner every once in a while. I won't press you any further, I promise."

She flashed a smile. "You're determined to lose all your clients, aren't you, Web?"

"Bother my clients. I don't care about clients. I'll get new ones. I care about you, Elizabeth."

His impassioned pronouncement surprised her so much that her mouth fell open. Web couldn't help but laugh at her stunned expression. "Don't look at me like I grew two heads all of a sudden. If you don't know how much I care for you then I've failed you even more miserably than I thought."

Elizabeth chewed her lip for a moment. "What about Chase? We can't just dump him on poor Miz Carrizal if you stay here in California for months. Or if I was to travel down to Tucson to study for a year or two…"

It was all Web could do to tamp down the fire of hope flaring in his breast. "I thought of that before I come, honey. Chase is in a real good situation."

Home

Alafair could not keep from weeping when the train pulled into the station at Boynton. They had wired their itinerary from Amarillo, so the children knew that they would be coming on the train from Oklahoma City at three in the afternoon. As soon as the train left Sapulpa and entered familiar terrain, Shaw, Alafair, and Blanche made the rest of the trip with their noses pressed up again the windows, excitedly pointing out recognized landmarks. The train came into Boynton from the north, rounding a long curve, which made it possible for them to see the station several minutes before they reached it. It looked as though every relative they had was crowded onto the platform.

They were sitting toward the back of the car and had already gathered their belongings from the overhead rack when the train came to a stop, so they were the first to disembark. They found themselves immediately engulfed in a sea of whooping, crying, shrieking relations. The tide was so inexorable that it effectively dammed up the exit and trapped all the other occupants of the car behind them. Finally the station master had to fight his way through the crowd and bellow loud enough to be heard over the din that they had to disperse.

Three-year-old Grace had ripped herself out of Martha's grip and climbed her mother like a tree, where she now hung suspended in Alafair's arms, pressed so closely cheek-to-cheek that Alafair found it hard to speak. Not that she would have had it any other way.

Once they had made their way off the platform where the group could spread out and breathe a little, their third daughter, tall, blond Alice, heavily pregnant but aglow like the full moon, took her turn at hugging her mother, Grace and all. As Alice drew back, a movement below her sight line caught her eye and she looked down. A cute, funny-faced boy with buck teeth and knobby limbs, long-legged and skinny, was dashing about between his elders' legs and brushing by their skirts, apparently having a high time.

"Well, Mama," Alice said in that dry fashion of hers, "another youngster. Just what you need."

Alafair followed Alice's gaze and her lips curled when she realized who her daughter was looking at. "That's your cousin Chase. He'll be staying with us for a spell. It's a long story."

Alice looked up, an impish twinkle in her pale blue eyes. "I know. Martha got a telegram from Uncle Web this morning. Seems Aunt Elizabeth is going to be a lawyer."

Alafair's Recipes, Southwestern Style

Any woman who provides three hearty meals a day to a large family and anyone else who shows up is always on the lookout for new recipes. Alafair's trip to Tempe, Arizona, provided her with the perfect opportunity to expand her cooking repertoire. From the spring of 1916 on, the Tuckers family's regular menu included several items of native Arizona cuisine which had been passed through an Arkansas-Oklahoma Scotch-Irish/Cherokee prism to create a unique culinary rainbow. Beans and fatback could now be refried and served on tortillas (which the children called "flapjacks"). *Buñuelos* were simply an adjustment to Alafair's already-beloved doughnut recipe. Slow cooked dove and bean stew evolved over the years into any-available-game-bird and bean stew. Some of the foods Alafair enjoyed in Arizona were not readily available to her in Oklahoma, such as *nopales*. So she adapted the recipe to use with okra, which has a similar flavor and consistency. Every family that ever lived has its own personal take on daily diet, and the Tuckers were particularly blessed in their talented mistress of the kitchen. Her creations live on to this day on the dinner tables of her descendants.

Buñuelos

2 cups flour
¼ cup sugar
4 eggs
1 tsp melted butter
2 tsp baking powder
1 tsp salt
Oil for deep frying (Alafair would have used lard)
1 cup sugar mixed with 2 tsp cinnamon

Beat the eggs and ¼ cup of sugar until thick and lemon-colored. Add the 1 tsp of melted butter. In a separate bowl, combine 1 ½ cups of flour, 2 tsp baking powder, and salt. Slowly add the flour mixture to the egg mixture and beat well. Turn the dough out onto a floured surface and knead until smooth and elastic. Keep flouring the board and your hands as needed to keep the dough from sticking. Shape the dough into about a dozen-and-a-half balls and flatten each ball with the palm of your hand until it is four or five inches in diameter and about 1/2 inch thick. Fry in hot oil until golden. They will rise while cooking. Drain on a towel. While still warm, roll each *buñuelo* in cinnamon sugar until well coated.

Tortillas (Flapjacks)

3 cups white flour
2 tsp. baking powder
1 tsp salt
4-6 tbsp shortening or lard
about 1 ¼ cups warm water

Mix flour, baking powder, and salt together in a large bowl. Cut in the lard with a fork or mix in with your hands until mixture resembles coarse crumbs. Add warm water a little at a time until you have a soft dough, pliable but not sticky. Knead the dough for a few minutes until smooth. Let it rest in the bowl for ten or fifteen minutes. While the dough is resting, heat a large cast iron skillet over medium to medium-high heat.

Pull the dough apart into 10 or 12 balls and on a floured surface roll each ball into a flat, round disc about an eighth of an inch thick.*

Lay the tortilla in the hot, dry, skillet and cook until it is covered with brown speckles. This takes just a few seconds if the skillet is hot enough. Turn the tortilla over and brown the other side. Pile the finished tortillas one on top of the other on a plate and keep warm with a towel. Eat plain, fresh, and hot. Or smear with refried beans or fill with meat or cheese or what you will. Nothing like it.

* Alafair could roll her 'flapjacks' into a perfectly circular shape with three or four swipes of an entirely unremarkable kitchen rolling pin. No one knows how she managed to do this, since after four passes with the rolling pin ordinary mortals will end up with a tortilla that looks like an amoeba. She could also do this with pie crust. She was a rolling pin savant.

Refried Beans

Refried beans are not really refried. They are simply squashed. There are many fabulous ways to cook and season *refritos* from scratch, but Alafair simply took the leftovers from the big pot of beans and fatback which she always cooked on wash day, reheated them in a skillet, then mashed them with a potato masher or the back of a big wooden spoon. You can press the beans through a sieve if you want to get rid of the skins, but if you cook your beans without salt in the water in the first place, the skins will be tender.

Dove with Beans

8 cups cooked or 3 lb uncooked pinto beans
4 cups home-canned stewed tomatoes with juice
1 large onion, chopped
diced hot peppers to taste
1 lb dove meat, chopped into bite-sized pieces
salt to taste

If the beans are precooked, put all ingredients into a large stew pot and simmer together on low heat for at least an hour. If the beans are uncooked, the all ingredients except the dove may be simmered in a very slow oven in a clay pot eight hours or overnight. Add the dove meat during the last 45 minutes of cooking.

Nopales

Nopales or *nopalitos* are made from the pads of the *nopal*, or prickly pear, cactus. *Nopal* fruit, stems and pads are all edible and have been used as food and as medicine in the Americas since long before the Europeans came. There are literally hundreds of ways to cook *nopales*. Since *nopal* is a cactus, it does have spines, of course, which have to be removed before preparing. Only the tender young pads are used in cooking. The spines are cut out or peeled off with a knife, or scrubbed off with a stiff brush. The pads may then be boiled, stewed, fried, or grilled. Boiled *nopales* tastes rather like green beans. Like okra, *nopal* has a sticky, mucilaginous juice that some people find off-putting. Rinsing will get rid of most of this as will cooking them with tomatoes. Cut the pads into strips, dip them in batter and roll them in cornmeal and fry them up for a real treat.

Here is the recipe for the dish that Elizabeth served Alafair. Alafair liked it a lot, but getting her hands on *nopal* pads was not that easy for her in 1916, so she usually used okra in place of *nopales*. The taste is somewhat different, but the consistency is quite similar.

1 lb chopped *nopalitos*
½ large onion, chopped
1 large jalapeno pepper, stem and seeds removed, chopped
1 large tomato, chopped.
1 tbsp oil or lard for frying

In a large cast-iron skillet, saute onion and pepper in hot oil for one minute. Add the chopped *nopales* and cook for ten more minutes, stirring occasionally. Add tomato and cook until heated through. Salt to taste and serve hot. Serves 4.

Historical Notes

Tempe, Arizona

Charles Trumbull Hayden, owner of a mercantile and freighting business in Tucson, homesteaded the town first known as Hayden's Ferry in 1870. In 1872, several Hispanic families from southern Arizona founded a town called San Pablo just to the east of Hayden's Ferry, but by the time of our story in 1916, both settlements had grown together and formed one community. The town was named Tempe in 1879 by "Lord" Darrell Duppa, the Englishman (and something of a scoundrel) who helped establish Phoenix. He said that the sight of the butte, the wide river, and the green fields reminded him of the Vale of Tempe in ancient Greece. After the towns combined, the former San Pablo was simply called the barrio.

In 1885, the Arizona legislature selected Tempe as the site for the Territorial Normal School to train teachers. By 1916, the school was called Tempe Normal School of Arizona and had an enrollment of around 300. In 1958, after several name changes, the Tempe Normal School became Arizona State University. As of 2011, ASU's enrollment at all campuses is around 72,000.

Guadalupe

The village of Guadalupe, located southwest of Tempe, was named after the patron saint of Mexico, the Virgin of Guadalupe. It was founded by Yaqui Indians around the turn of the twentieth century when they fled their traditional homeland along the Yaqui river in Sonora, Mexico, to avoid enslavement by the Mexican government under President Porfirio Diaz. In 1916 Guadalupe was a purely Yaqui town, but over the years, it became become a stopping point for Mexican immigrant workers. The population make-up of the present day town of Guadalupe is about 50 percent Hispanic and 50 percent Yaqui.

Raid on Columbus, N.M.

During the early years of the Mexican Revolution (1910–1920) Pancho Villa was portrayed in the U.S. media as a populist hero and was supplied arms and aid by the U.S. Government. After years of public support for Villa, Washington decided that Villa's rival Venustiano Carranza was in a better position to bring the revolution to an end, so President Wilson bowed to the inevitable, recognized the Carranza government as legitimate, and stopped all aid to Villa's army.

Villa was outraged and swore revenge for what he considered Wilson's betrayal, and began launching raids along the U.S. border and murdering and kidnapping U.S. citizens living in Mexico. Because of Villa's depredations, there was a great deal of pressure on Washington to intervene in Mexican affairs. But for many months Wilson stood firm and refused to send troops into a sovereign country. However, Villa's activities so close to U.S. territory frightened the American government enough that President Wilson ordered General John J. Pershing to deploy troops across the border region from Texas to Arizona.

Early on the morning of March 9, 1916, Villa and about five hundred *pistoleros* crossed into the U.S. near Columbus, New Mexico, and attacked Camp Furlong, the outpost of the Thirteenth U.S. Cavalry. The cavalry was caught completely by surprise, but after several hours of fighting managed to repel the invaders. As the *Villistas* retreated back toward Mexico, they looted and burned the civilian town of Columbus. Fourteen U.S. soldiers and ten American civilians were killed and Villa lost around eighty men.

This time, the Cavalry did not wait for orders from Washington to respond. Col. Frank Thompkins and thirty-two cavalrymen from the Thirteenth took off after the fleeing raiders and chased them into Mexico, killing many before the *Villistas* managed to escape into the rugged Sierra Madre mountains.

President Carranza was incensed by the intrusion, but the U.S. populace was not going to be appeased without payback for the killing of Americans on American soil. Under intense pressure from Wilson, Carranza grudgingly allowed Gen. Pershing to enter Mexico and pursue Villa's army across Sonora and Chihuahua for nine months. In January 1917, World War I intervened and Pershing was called back to take command of the newly formed U.S. Expeditionary Forces. Villa was never apprehended. He retired in 1920, but in 1923, after deciding to become involved in Mexican politics once again, he was assassinated by persons unknown.

The Yaqui, the Motion Picture

For three weeks in December of 1915, a major Hollywood motion picture entitled *The Yaqui* was shot in Tempe, thanks to the influence of its lead actor, Hobart Bosworth. A former stage actor, Bosworth had lived in Tempe in 1906–1907, working as an artist and painter before leaving for California, where he went into the movie business, eventually making feature pictures for release to the Universal Film Company out of Universal City, California. Bosworth chose to shoot his movie in Tempe both for the scenery and the availability of Mexican and Indian extras. Close to two hundred locals were hired to act as crowds and armies in the picture.

The story of *The Yaqui* was taken from the book *The Land of the Broken Promise,* by Dane Coolidge, an acquaintance of Bosworth's who had also lived in Tempe.

Twenty people came to Tempe from California for the filming, including the director Lloyd Carleton, Hobart Bosworth as Tambor the Yaqui, Goldie Caldwell as his wife Modesta, and Dorothy Clark as his daughter Lucia. Yona Landowska played a sympathetic ranch owner's wife. The teenaged Dorothy was accompanied on the shoot by her mother, Ethel. Several years after she appeared in *The Yaqui,* Dorothy was involved in a Hollywood scandal with a married man.

For the purposes of this story I moved the timing of the shoot forward three months to March of 1916. Otherwise, the cast and crew did in fact come to Tempe by train, bringing with them 700 pounds of TNT, and blew up the abandoned Rural School building for a scene in the movie. Though there were plenty of splinters and shards there is no report that money rained down on the crew or the townspeople who were there to observe.

While the movie was being shot, Bosworth treated the town to a showing of his first movie, *Fatherhood,* and the cast and the townspeople did pose for a group photograph in front of the Goodwin Opera House. If a print of either the photo or of *The Yaqui* movie still exists, I am not aware of it.

Curandera

A *curandera* (female) or *curandero* (male) is a traditional Spanish-American healer. There are many different kinds of *curanderas,* including massage therapists, psychic healers, and midwives. Mrs. Carrizal was a *yerbera,* a specialist in herbal remedies. *Curanderas* are known to use their talent only for good and usually do not charge for their services, whereas *brujas* (witches) will use their knowledge for evil, to cast spells and hexes. A curandera's power to cure is considered a gift from God that is acquired early in life, sometimes through a sacred vision or experience.

The Real People

Hobart Bosworth
Hobart Bosworth may not be a household name today, but he was a major figure in the motion picture industry at the turn of the twentieth century. He started his professional life as a Broadway actor in the late 1800s, but after he lost his voice and could no longer project to an audience, he moved to Arizona to work as an artist for a couple of years before going back East to enter the silent movie business in 1908.

The West apparently made a lasting impression on him, because he came to Los Angeles in 1909 and starred in what is thought to be the first film to be shot on the West Coast, *In the Sultan's Power*. Bosworth founded his own company in 1913 and shot several pictures before joining with Paramount in 1916. After talkies came along in the late 1920s Bosworth had a long career as a character actor, mostly in B movies, working until shortly before his death in 1943.

Marshal Joe Dillon
Joseph P. Dillon was the U.S. Marshal for the District of Arizona during the period our story is set. I used his name, but the character of Marshal Dillon in this tale is my own creation.

Fred "Cap" Irish
Fred "Cap" Irish was one of Tempe Normal School's most popular and influential instructors. Irish was the school's first athletic

director, coaching football and men's and women's basketball. In 1916, he oversaw enrollment, taught chemistry, and was in charge of the local militia. Irish Hall, built in 1940 and named for Fred Irish, is in use at Arizona State University to this day.

Dr. Benjamen B. Moeur

In 1916, Benjamin B. Moeur was a fixture in Tempe, Arizona. He had immigrated to Arizona from Texas with his family, eventually ending up in Tempe 1896 and quickly becoming the busiest and most popular physician in town. He was a well-known philanthropist who never charged a widow, a preacher, or the family of a serviceman for medical services.

Besides his medical practice, Moeur was a successful businessman, served on the Tempe School Board and on the Board of Education at the Tempe Normal School. He also started a scholarship program that gave loans to schoolteachers. He was a delegate to the Arizona Constitutional Convention in 1910 and was responsible for drafting the state constitution's educational provisions.

Moeur became the Democratic governor of Arizona in 1932, at the height of the Great Depression. The state was deep in debt and unemployment was rampant, but he was able to reduce government expenses, institute a personal income tax, sales tax, and luxury taxes while reducing property taxes. He instituted relief programs for the unemployed and brought millions of dollars in federal aid programs to the state. By the end of his first term, the state was solvent again.

Moeur's most notorious act during his governorship was to call out the Arizona National Guard in 1934 to stop construction of Parker Dam on the Colorado River. The purpose of the dam was to divert water from the river and send it to Southern California, but according to the Arizona attorney general, the Los Angeles Metropolitan Water District had no right to build on Arizona's territory without permission, much less steal its water. Moeur declared martial law and sent two patrol boats (converted riverboats), forty riflemen, and twenty machine gunners to stop construction on the Arizona side of the Colorado River. Unfortunately, the boats ran afoul of some cable and had to be towed free by the Californians. The sortie of the Arizona Navy was the last time one state took up arms against another.

Moeur died in Tempe in 1937, less than four months after leaving office.

Fr. Lucius Zittier

In 1914 a missionary Franciscan Friar by the name of Lucius Zittier petitioned Congress for forty acres of land so the Yaquis could permanently settle on the site of the present-day town of Guadalupe. The Fr. Lucius whom Alafair and Elizabeth met when they drove to Guadalupe to pay their respects to the Arrudas is my own creation.

To receive a free catalog of Poisoned Pen Press titles, please contact us in one of the following ways:

Phone: 1-800-421-3976
Facsimile: 1-480-949-1707
Email: info@poisonedpenpress.com
Website: www.poisonedpenpress.com

Poisoned Pen Press
6962 E. First Ave. Ste 103
Scottsdale, AZ 85251